THE CRASH COURSE

ELVIE EVERLY

CONTENTS

For Mr. Everly,
Thank you for your support and your huge love of cars.

CONTENT WARNING

Please be aware that this book contains discussion or references to: toxic childhood environment, neglectful and toxic parents, death of a parent, PTSD, and physical violence (on-page, multiple scenes, and not between the main characters).

1

REESE

It's ten minutes past closing time, and I'm waiting for the group of obnoxious teenagers to leave so The Little Roast can finally close up for the night.

They've been here for hours, coasting on a five-dollar coffee purchase that they consumed and discarded long ago, using the Wi-Fi to look at God knows what.

The impatient side of me wants to clear my throat loudly and shoo them out with the crappy broom Mr. Auster has left in the supply closet. However, Rational Reese knows that it's best to ask them politely to leave, *again*, for the twenty-third time tonight.

Mainly because Mr. Auster has a *customer is always right* policy. Any negative review will give that man an ulcer and have him unleash hell on the few employees masochistic enough to willingly stick around. Work is already unbearable enough as it is.

Thankfully, I'm on the way out myself. My two weeks' notice has already been turned in. I need the paycheck, but life's too short for me to subject myself to more verbal abuse from him.

I can work anywhere else. There are plenty of jobs on campus. I don't have to put up with this. Especially not after he ignored my one request to not have me work the closing shift all by myself.

Still, I need Mr. Auster to give me a glowing recommendation for any future employment opportunities that I'm going to keep sweet for whatever time I have left here. Therefore, I stand there behind the counter and wait impatiently, dreading every minute that passes by as I mentally do the math and wonder if it's still even possible to catch the bus back to my apartment.

Verdict: *it is not.*

I need them to leave, so I can count the register, clean up the cafe, and take out the trash—within the next ten minutes if I don't want to miss the last bus. There's a higher chance of Caleb Marsden barging through the door and confessing his unyielding love for me than me catching the bus tonight.

For a brief moment, I entertain the idea of Caleb, with his dreamy smile, telling me he thinks I'm swell. My brain is apparently on a thirties kick tonight, purposely obtuse to the fact that a cute frat guy like him would ever notice a girl like me.

A loud honk pulls me out of my daydream, my shoulders tensing at the sudden sound. The teenagers buzz with loud chatter as they all rush to collect their things, leaving behind a copious number of balled-up napkins and spitballs for me to clean up.

I quietly groan to myself as I lock the front door and double-check the padlock twice, then once more for good measure. I tug on the door from the inside, satisfied that it can't be opened, and then get to work.

As I'm wiping down the tables, something rumbles in the distance and sets off a cascade of dog howls. The sound of squealing tires immediately follows. Loud. Deafening. Much closer than I expected, and I freeze in place like a spooked cat.

Vaguely registering the headlights shining brightly through the windows, the car guns past the cafe just then, going at least ten over the speed limit, rattling the glass, and launching my heart into the stratosphere.

It doesn't matter how many times I've reminded myself the area is the safest place I've ever set foot in; my heart is still easily spooked.

With a slow and steady intake of breath, I do a cursory glance. Everything looks just clean enough that it might pass Mr. Auster's ridiculous standards. Not wanting to stick around, I grab the bulky bag full of trash and dart to the back of the store.

Barely exiting the back door, my body staggers backward in surprise when I'm instantly met with blinding LED lights that would be fatal to vampires.

The trash bag slips out of my grasp. My hand flies to my mace clipped to the belt loop of my jeans. There's a black car parked in the alleyway behind the store, its bright headlights aimed directly at me.

I'm beyond terrified. So afraid for my own life that it takes a long, long moment to register what's happening just a few yards away from me. Beside the commercial dumpster, two men are kicking the crap out of the third one on the ground. His body is curled, his arms flanked above his head to shield himself from the ongoing onslaught.

My breath drags raggedly through my chest, panic seizing me the moment I see something glint in the dim streetlight.

"Stop it," I choke out, the tremble in my words only outmatched by the tremor in my hands. "*Stop it.*" My words are louder this time. Firmer. "*Please. Stop. Stop hurting him! I'm calling 911!*"

Time expands before me as the crowbar clanks loudly against the asphalt, echoing through the alleyway. My throat constricts, a frisson of anxiety racing down my spine as my brain entertains the idea of what could have happened—of what was just averted.

I barely tear my gaze away from the metal bar, scuttling backward as the car bulldozes past me, whipping my hair violently across my face.

The heat of the vehicle is still warm on my skin as I let out a shaky exhale, spitting the strands of hair out of my mouth. A split second later, my hands land on my knees as I bend over, trying to get ahold of myself to no avail.

That could have been bad. So, so bad. My stomach churns, more tears filling my eyes when I tense at a sudden noise—*a sluggish groan*. One that sends my heart plummeting like an anchor in the fathomless sea. Renewed terror and adrenaline course through my veins as I lift my head and look over. My knees almost give out on me when I see him still curled up on the ground.

Making haste, I skirt around the bag of spilled trash and nearly trip over what appears to be a bashed-in helmet, sprinting toward the dumpster while fishing my phone out of my pocket.

"Are you all right?" *Such a dumb question to ask.* I toggle my phone's flashlight on, and my grip slackens when the light illuminates his face.

Blood. So much blood. So many bruises. Oh God.

Acid burns in my throat. My vision blurs at the edges, more dread creeping up my spine as my gaze cuts to his eyes. "Let me call 91—"

"No," he wheezes before he turns over and coughs, spraying droplets of blood across the black concrete.

Oh God, oh God, oh God.

More panic catches hold of my breath as images of that one terrifying night flicker into my head. My eyes screw shut as I remind myself to focus. To stay in the present. To stop panicking. *To fucking get it together and fucking help him out.*

"I'm fine," he spits out.

I blanch as he wipes his bloodied lip with the pad of his thumb, and I swallow hard. "You're hurt."

"Just a scratch," he grunts. His movement is painstakingly sluggish as he pushes himself up. His hand smacks against the dumpster for purchase while he slowly rises to his feet. "See?"

Just a scratch? *Just a scratch?*

I'm barely keeping it together as I stare at him incredulously, taking inventory of what I can make out in the near dark that's *not* just a scratch. His torn white shirt. His blue jeans grimy with dirt. The dark bruises peeking through the ripped fabric when my phone's flashlight shines over his torso.

A cold sense of dismay washes over me when the beam of light lands on the stained collar of his shirt.

"I'm fine," he repeats, but I almost don't hear him. All I see for a moment is an unshakable image of him lying flat on his back, blood gurgling out of his mouth, clutching desperately at his bleeding neck.

The sound of shattered glass repeats in my ears like a broken record.

It takes all my conscious effort to remind myself that we're in the alleyway. *There's no shattered glass in sight. He's not bleeding to death. He wasn't choking on his blood. What I'm imagining isn't real. Everything will be okay.*

It does little to halt the ball of distress forming deep in my chest, especially when I see blood seeping through his tattered shirt. My fingers tighten around my phone as an icy shiver races down my spine.

Silently urging myself to remain calm now and panic the fuck out later when I'm in the safety of my apartment, I shudder out a quiet breath. "I have first aid."

Or rather, the cafe does, but I don't think now is the appropriate time to bring up semantics. I half expect him to decline, to play it off, if anything, so I'm surprised when he nods.

"Don't call 911," he wheezes.

"Okay," I whisper back. Gesturing ahead, I take one careful step, keeping an eye on him to see if he'll follow. If he can follow.

His hand moves from the dumpster, and in a heartbeat, his body nearly crumples to the ground. Within seconds, I'm at his side, tucking myself under his arm and supporting his weight the best I can.

The guy is so much taller than my five-one frame that I'm struggling to keep him upright. A foot taller, at least. Every muscle in my body burns in protest as I shoulder his weight. There's a tightness to my jaw as I grit my teeth and focus on bringing him inside without the both of us falling and face-planting.

Somehow, we manage to cross the threshold. It's nothing short of a miracle. He untangles himself from me and staggers against the wall, panting heavily as he clutches his side and leans his head back.

I flick all the lights on, lock the back door, triple-check it in case his friends decide to come back for him—check once more for good measure—and frantically sprint toward the supply closet.

Then I rush back, spilling an armful of clean towels and first aid onto a nearby counter.

"This is going to sting," I warn, running a clean towel under cold water. I turn to face him, and I'm stock-still as the gravity of this situation hits me all at once.

Get it together now, freak the fuck out later.

"Can't be worse than this." His words are a harsh, gritty whisper as his eyes fall shut.

Steeling myself, I press the wet towel to a bloody laceration on his face, trepidation filling my every vein when he expels a low hiss. Besides a few groans here and there, he's silent while his body shakes before me.

There's a burning ache in my calves as I remain on my tiptoes, tending to every wound on his face I come across. *God. There are so many.*

"You go to Belford?" he mumbles, his breathing still ragged. Heavy.

I lift my head to see his pale blue eyes looking at my baseball cap. There's a limp strand of hair in his right eye, and my fingers are twice as gentle when I brush it to the side.

"Yes," I respond, swallowing the bile creeping up my throat when my line of sight catches the faint smudge of crimson on the corner of his lips.

I avert my gaze and try to focus on something more positive —anything to keep me distracted from the recurring imagery of shattered glass playing in my head.

Replacing the bloodied towel with a fresh one, I wait until my hands stop trembling to face him again. "Now, take off your shirt."

He huffs a low, gritty scoff. "Without buying me dinner first?"

Maybe he's trying to be cheeky, but his attempt is thwarted when he staggers before me. A humorless chuckle rumbles from his chest as he struggles to tear his shirt off—his arms too stiff, his movements too awkward.

Once rid of his shirt, he leans back, his face marred with overexertion, and clenches his jaw tight.

He doesn't make another cheeky comment, just a rough exhale as I clean up every inch of dried blood I catch sight of. It requires every ounce of sheer willpower to keep my hands from shaking with each wound I find.

"Do you go to Belford?" Small talk isn't my thing, but we could both use a distraction.

He lets out a snort.

"No?" I guess, pulling my head back to peer at his face. The limp strand of hair is back in his eyes.

He hitches a shoulder, a look of regret crossing his profile a split second later. His hand lifts to the junction of his neck and shoulder as an inaudible hiss expels between his busted lips. "Yes."

"Have you heard about the car wash?" I whisper, returning my attention to the array of bruises alongside his ribs.

Plenty of cuts—both fresh and old ones, by the looks of it— pepper his lower torso. My throat goes painfully dry. There's only so much I can do.

"Maybe we should report this—"

"No," he cuts in bluntly.

"—to the campus police," I finish, furrowing my brows.

"No," he repeats, gritting his teeth again when I dress one of his cuts. "No fucking way. Does it. Look like. We're. On campus?" he bites out. "*Fuck!*"

I finally remove the damp cloth and force my eyes to meet his, hoping that my face is calmer externally than I am internally. "You should go to the hospital."

"I'll be fine," he insists, breathing hard through his nose.

"No insurance?" I guess.

He grumbles something too low for me to hear. I'm going to assume yes. I know how expensive medical bills are, so I can't fault him for wanting to avoid being saddled with debt.

"How far do you live from here?" When I see the distrust glinting in his eyes, I quickly tack on, "I don't want you bleeding out in the middle of the street before you get there."

He says nothing. Awkward silence swells in the small space between us.

I know I should finish patching him up the best I can. Get home and barricade myself in my apartment. Instead, my gaze continues to hold his as my concern, genuine and palpable, grows exponentially with each waking second.

His eyes shut, the lines of his face twisting into something solemn. A weary sigh sounds deep from his chest. "Antarctica."

Disbelief spears me as I splutter. "Please just tell me."

I don't think I'll be able to sleep if I know you're not going to be okay. The words linger on my tongue as I stare pleadingly into his eyes.

"I'm not telling you jack sh—" An abrupt hiss escapes him, and he extends his elbow toward me as if he's trying to ward me off. "I can manage."

It takes a moment for me to realize I've inched closer. Blinking, I take a step back. "You can't even stand properly."

"I'll be fine," he says, but the rough-hewn notes of his voice betray him. "Just need a minute."

"Maybe we should call an Uber."

"I have my bike," he protests.

"I don't think it's wise to pedal that far—"

"A motorbike," he clarifies with an agonized chuckle. *"Motorcycle."*

"Oh." My cheeks scald with embarrassment. "But still. I don't think it's safe to operate a *vehicle* when you're seconds away from death."

"Seconds away from death?" He scoffs. "What do you suggest I should do with the last few seconds left of my life, oh wise one? Walk my ass home?"

There's a sharp sting to my eyes that I blink away.

He almost got beaten to death with a crowbar, I remind myself. *Of course, he's not going to be in a friendly sort of mood.*

Swallowing hard, I plaster an easygoing smile across my lips. "Uber home—"

"Don't think any driver would let me in their car with this going on." His hand gestures to his face in a slow, circular motion.

"Call a friend to pick you up?"

"He's not back until tomorrow."

"Do you know anyone nearby—"

"Here?" Even in his battered state, he manages to sound appalled. "Fuck no."

"This area isn't bad," I quietly protest. "My place is nice."

He makes a disbelieving noise. "Are you suggesting that I crash at your place?"

"What?" Now I sound appalled. The idea of letting a strange guy—fellow Belford student or not—crash at my apartment is possibly the most reckless and dumbest thing to do.

The rational side of me knows that.

However, the bleeding-heart side of me is already rationalizing that he can take the futon, and I can take his keys as insurance he won't do anything risky in his current state. Or try anything.

Damn my soft heart. It's going to lead me into a whole lot of trouble.

"That's not a no," he says, and, again, damn my soft heart. It ignores every sound reason in my head, folding so easily like a flimsy house of cards.

"*If*," I say slowly, holding his gaze, "you give me your bike's keys."

"Deal," he replies, lifting a finger a split second later. His upper body twists as he coughs into his forearm. When he looks my way again, his chest hitches, a heavy weariness already settling across his features.

"I don't live that far from here. It's a ten, maybe fifteen-minute walk." It's a much faster and safer bus ride, but I know that ship has sailed. "You can lock your bike in the storage area."

The commercial dumpster is usually locked in a fenced-off area to keep random people from throwing away bulky trash. It's probably for the best to leave the motorcycle here rather than try to bring it back to my place when he can barely stand without finding himself on the brink of collapsing every few minutes.

His mouth curves into something harsh. I brace myself when he shuts his eyes. "I'll leave my bike."

I blink, momentarily stunned. "Okay. Let me close up the cafe." I nearly groan when I remember the trash I've dropped outside, my reluctance to step out in that alleyway twofold. My two weeks' notice couldn't have come sooner enough. "And deal with the trash. Then you can crash at my place."

"Sounds good," he says. I glance in his direction once more, take in the sight of him wheezing into the crook of his arm, and hope that I'm not about to make the gravest mistake of my life.

2

___

DANE

Every inch of my body is aching with pain. I twist on the futon, trying to get comfortable, but there's this one damn spring that's jabbing one of my cuts no matter how I contort myself. It's irritating the shit out of me to the point where I almost consider sleeping on the cold, hard floor.

I carefully maneuver onto my side, my bruises protesting in sheer agony, fully aware that I've bled onto the two fleece throw blankets my savior provided me.

Last night was bad. *Really bad.* I should thank my luck that I didn't meet my maker, but my mind's preoccupied, replaying the events of last night in my head and scrutinizing every little detail.

I'm minding my own fucking business, as one does, cruising down the street on my bike.

Two dickheads I don't know tailgating me and riding my ass.

Trying to lose them to no avail and stupidly turning into an alleyway where I careen into a pile of pallets and crates like a rookie.

My ass getting swarmed and curb-stomped by Tweedle Dee and Tweedle Dum, with no sign of stopping.

I ache for another painkiller. Instead, I lie there shivering under two small blankets in a small apartment on a small-as-fuck futon. Small appears to be the theme of this place.

Sleep evades me. Shutting my eyes, I only see the crowbar swinging up over and over and over. Staying awake, a dull pain throbs across my body. After another excruciating hour has passed, I weasel my phone out of my pocket, my lips curling at the bent and cracked glass.

Dane: come get me
Dane: and bring your truck
Marco: Man wya?

That's the million-dollar question.

Dane: I'll drop a pin

I drop my location just in the nick of time. The screen freezes momentarily before it goes black. Cursing under my breath, I toss the broken thing onto the coffee table.

It's still a quarter to five. I listen to the clock tick every agonizing second as I remain awake.

Not wanting to lie on the futon and have my spine become extremely familiarized with that fucking spring any second longer, I sit up slowly, ignore the screeching protest from every joint and muscle, and push to my feet. Clenching my jaw hard, I pocket my phone and examine the small apartment I'm in.

There are two barstools lined against the kitchen counter. A shoe rack by the futon where every pair of shoes is sorted by color in order of the rainbow.

On the fridge door, there's a whiteboard calendar listing shifts, paydays, exams, birthdays, and tutoring sessions. A hexagon corkboard hangs on the side of the fridge, pinned with Polaroid pictures and fake flowers.

A round tray filled with spice jars sits on the corner of the kitchen counter, and a candle is placed beside it. I spot a short charging cable near an outlet and immediately plug my phone in.

The screen flashes when it comes to life, displaying a text message sent from Marco twenty minutes ago telling me he'll be there soon.

I know Marco. The guy will drive ninety miles per hour at minimum. If he's not outside already, he will be soon.

The sound of running water brings my attention to the kitchen wall. I'm guessing there's a bathroom on the other side.

Marco: Yo I'm here
Dane: be out soon

Of course, my little savior is taking a shower right when I need my keys. I don't want to wait any longer—I want to go home and take my very own shower—so I erase one of the flower doodles on the bottom right corner of her whiteboard and scrawl out a message.

Went home. I owe you one. Will get my keys later. D.

I don't like owing favors, but I figure I owe the chick something for letting me crash here and for cleaning me up the best she could. That and she didn't call the cops, which means Daniel Kingsley won't know a single thing that transpired last night, and I plan to keep it that way.

I hobble out of the apartment, my lips forming a hard, grim line at how run-down the building is. The floor I'm on is tilted. The outdoor pool on the bottom floor is murky brown with leaves and bulky junk floating inside. A couple can be heard screaming at each other while dogs howl in the distance.

It's not The Westbrook Resort, that's for sure. I can't blame the girl when my eyes snare on the rusting security bar bolted to her apartment window.

It's a miracle the elevator here is functioning. More importantly, it's empty when I limp in. I exit on the ground floor, my joints aching every step of the way, taking immediate notice that none of the gates are closed. The parking gate is wide open, and the smaller one for the courtyard is propped ajar with a trash can.

"Holy fucking shit."

I glance over to see Marco sticking his head out of his truck, his long brown hair swaying with the wind. It's been a few weeks since I've last seen his mug. He's been out of town, and I haven't been bothered to ask what he's up to. Especially when the answer's always *chasing the surf.*

"What happened to you?" he calls out.

"Don't want to talk about it," I grunt. "Help me find my bike."

I pull out my spare set of keys while he hops out of his vehicle. As we look for my bike in the building's parking lot, I suddenly remember leaving it behind some dumpster. He doesn't get on my ass about it as we make our way back to his truck.

It's a short drive over to the alleyway. Not only is my bike still there, but the dumpster enclosure is already opened, allowing me the opportunity to retrieve it.

After the disc brake alarm has been unlocked and unlatched from the rear wheel before it can go off, I check to make sure nothing's been tampered with. Once that's squared away, I tip my head to the side, and Marco gives me a nod.

Considering how loud and chatty Marco generally is, I savor the rare moment of silence lapsing over us. He doesn't utter a word, remaining quiet as we load the motorcycle onto the back of his truck.

"Giancarlo?" Marco guesses.

"Maybe." It's the only thing I can think of to explain what happened last night. "Or maybe it's road rage gone wrong," I mutter when we observe a giant SUV cutting off another car.

"Yikes." Thankfully, Marco doesn't press on the subject. The only things he cares about are catching waves, playing blackjack, and smashing chicks—all in that order.

Marco likes being one with the fucking wave or something, and I like racing cars and bikes. Different things, but the same underlying theme. We like thrills. Get that hit of dopamine that can only come from all of that pure adrenaline. Chase that next high.

"Want me to take you to the h—"

"No hospital," I bite out, cutting him off. The last thing I need is for any word to get back to Daniel Kingsley.

"All right, man." He turns the radio on, switches to an alt-rock station, and fiddles with the volume. Without warning, he stomps his foot on the gas, causing me to launch backward and ram a bare, bruised shoulder into the leather seat. My set of keys flies out of my hand.

"Jesus!" I seethe through clenched teeth, and I reach down blindly to grab for it, fingers brushing against all sorts of random shit he's shoved underneath the seat. There's so much crap under here. I wouldn't be surprised if there's an empty jar of surfboard wax from five years ago with how he treats the passenger side as some sort of honorary junk drawer.

"I can be gentle for you, baby," Marco cackles.

My fingers wrap around my keys, and I snatch them. "Fuck off."

He only chuckles even harder. If he were anybody else, I wouldn't have let that shit slide. But Marco and I go way back.

Way, way back to when we used to go by the devil and the king. Back when we thought we were hot shit. Untouchable. Invincible. Destined to be Gods, brothers in arms: Divenanzio and Kingsley.

The point is, we've been there for each other through thick and thin. He's got my back for the longest time, and I've got his.

Unlike most of the people at Belford U, we are the only two who don't give a shit about Greek life, athletics, or academics. Doesn't mean we're dumbass losers; it just means we don't give a shit about something as meaningless as throwing a ball or wearing tacky polo shirts while spitting shit game at incoming freshman chicks.

Suddenly, the truck hits a fucking pothole, and the belt locks against me. A hiss escapes between my gritted teeth as I tug the seatbelt away from my injured shoulder.

This area isn't bad, my ass.

I throw my forearm over my eyes to block the morning sun, hoping that the ride will be smooth sailing from here.

GIVEN THE FACT THAT MY APARTMENT'S ON THE TOP FLOOR, I'M genuinely fucking grateful elevators exist for the second time today. I hobble inside the moment the door barely swings ajar, ignoring the gasp from the cleaning lady as I head to my room and straight for the bathroom.

The lights flick on, and my eyes cut to the mirror. Well. It's not as terrible as I had expected, and I was expecting the worst, given how badly the chick from last night was reacting to my injuries.

*Over*reacting, if I'm being honest. Sure, my face isn't pretty to look at, but I'm still alive. That's got to count for something.

The entire right side of my chest is covered in a cluster of bruises. There's a tiny pink bandage along my jawline—straight from my savior's own personal stash of first aid—as if it's supposed to help with everything going on with my face. I rip it off and cuss loudly when it yanks a few strands of hair with it.

Without standing around any longer, I crank on the shower, kick off my jeans and boxers, and wait for the telltale signs of my mirrors fogging up before I slide the shower door open and climb inside.

Scorching hot water pelts me. I nearly groan in bliss from the soothing relief my aching muscles are receiving—enough to ignore the sharp stings of my cuts getting soaked.

My hand braces against the shower wall as I let the heat seep through my skin to my bones. I stay there until the hot water finally runs out, and I continue to stand under the showerhead as cold water takes its place.

I only get out when Marco shouts about the fucking drought. Dragging my wet, dripping, butt-ass naked body out of the bathroom, I face-plant on the bed and welcome the sleep that finally comes to me.

3

———————

REESE

"WHAT THE HELL WERE YOU THINKING?" LILIAN SCREECHES, HER eyes flashing with renewed horror. I instinctively look down like I always do whenever I get yelled at.

My sister is only a year older than me, but in many ways, she's always been a maternal figure to me. Probably because she was practically the only one who raised me my entire life. Our dad wasn't in the picture, and our mom's a piece of work.

"I wasn't thinking," I admit with a cringe. "But, Lili, he looked awful—"

"He could have been a criminal!" she booms, her voice sharp as a blade, and I almost flinch.

My mouth curves into something reassuring before I return my attention to the breakfast sandwich I'm making. "He wasn't. He goes to Belford—"

"Ah, yes," she says dryly, "because criminals would *never* lie about their lives."

"Lili." I set the sandwich down and push the plate toward her.

Her gaze remains on me, a troubled expression crossing her face. "You could have gotten hurt," she hisses, stressing out every syllable as the amount of focus in her eyes doubles.

"I wasn't," I murmur, but I know she has a point. Taking a stranger back to my place was not a good call.

"You should have called me," she adds, and the note of hurt in her angry tone sends a wave of regret through my heart. "I could have helped you."

Ducking my head, I turn my back to her so that I'm facing my kitchen stove, no longer hungry as guilt assails me. My stomach twists into a complicated knot. "I didn't want to bother you," I whisper lamely, admitting the truth.

Lilian has done so much for me.

Almost two years ago, my sister and her sorority hosted a bunch of fundraisers to help pay for my medical bills.

Last year, she'd been my emotional rock, always consistently by my side, so I'd never felt alone. It took a lot of swaying from me to convince her to live at her sorority house again this year—that I'll be fine living by myself, and we can save a lot of money by not renting an on-campus apartment together again, especially when campus housing is absurdly expensive.

But beyond that, she's *always* been there for me through everything, and I feel like a never-ending source of responsibility to her. I don't want to be her responsibility. I just want to be her sister again.

"You don't bother me," she snaps. "This bothers me."

"What happened happened," I whisper, feigning nonchalance. I quickly fix my own egg sandwich, eagerly seeking any distraction I can afford. "And he didn't steal anything."

I don't point out that I have nothing to steal. Besides my expensive laptop, which is immediately locked away in my desk's drawer the moment I come home from school or work.

"I wouldn't have minded him taking the blankets," I add, swallowing hard. The bloodied throw blankets were what alerted Lilian to what had happened in the first place.

Her protective mama bear instincts came in first; then her overprotective sister mode kicked in seconds later when she found out the days-old bloodstains weren't from me.

I can understand why she freaked out, though. I couldn't stomach looking at the throws when I tossed them into the washer downstairs, either.

With my sandwich made, I slide into the seat beside her, waiting for her to chew me out some more. The atmosphere is taut with silence; the tension hangs palpably in the air.

"I'm glad you're safe," she reluctantly admits, her voice softening.

Wordlessly, I peek over at her in surprise. A flicker of skepticism sparks inside me. I love my sister, but she can be headstrong and bullheaded on certain things the moment her mind's made up, and that's me being polite with my choice of words.

She sighs loudly, pressing her thumb against her brow bone. "It was nice of you to offer him a place to stay, but he could have bled to death on your futon."

My chest tightens. Her face falters.

"Sorry. Poor choice of words. What I mean is that he's not your responsibility," she explains. "You should have called the police."

"I know." Truthfully, I don't think it'll do me any good to argue with her that the guy was the one who wouldn't stop insisting on no cops. I finally look up again to meet her moody gaze. "How are the girls?"

"Fine." Lilian sniffs, blessedly going along with the shift in conversation. She's usually not the type to let the topic derail from what she wants to talk about. "Lauren's throwing something next week if you want to come."

The idea of going to a sorority party is as appealing as getting a root canal. I don't say that out loud, of course. I just let my grimace speak for me.

My sister's been trying to get me out of my shell. That's been her game plan since the moment I stepped foot on Belford U's campus, and she's doubled down on it in the year since. She thinks it'll do me some good and help me get my mind off of things. More importantly, it'll help me with my healing process or whatever it was she said at the beginning of the semester.

It won't, but I'm not telling her that. I don't want to set off her alarm bells. As long as she thinks I'm better than ever, she'll cut me some slack. And I'd much rather my sister not worry herself sick over me.

Besides, I *am* doing better. I'm not in as bad a place as I was two years ago or even last year. There's been some improvement. I'm just moving at my own pace.

"Everyone is going to be there," Lilian adds before I can say anything. It's probably the understatement of the year. They throw the biggest ragers at their off-campus house, and anyone who's someone always shows up. "Like Caleb."

Heat blooms on my cheeks. My shoulders hunch while I stare at my egg sandwich like it's the most fascinating thing in the world. "*Shh.*"

"It's not like he's here." She makes a circular motion with her hand, gesturing to my bedroom door. "Unless he's hiding in there while we're having breakfast."

My sister and I usually have breakfast together on the weekends, even though I know it means she bailed on her sorority brunches. Usually, I enjoy spending time with her, but lately, we haven't gone one day without her bringing up my crush.

"Just ask him out," she tells me, like it's not hard. Maybe for her, it isn't.

"No way." I shake my head. "He doesn't know who I am."

"Yes, he does," she insists, and I stifle a groan.

I know she means well, but I wish she'd take a step back and let me breathe a little. I've been working up the courage to ask Caleb out myself, and her pushiness has only set me back, if anything.

"He knows who you are."

"Yeah, as *Lili Vann's younger sister.*"

She allows herself a weary sigh. "Maybe you can point me out to him there."

Shooting her a sidelong glance, I furrow a brow. "Caleb?"

"The guy you saved," my sister clarifies.

"Oh." I shrug a shoulder. "Yeah, maybe."

My sister loves parties, but I'm not keen on them.

There are just too many people. Too many strangers. Too much noise. It's overwhelming, and I get overstimulated fast. I feel even crappier when Lilian sticks to me like a second shadow, so I don't feel alone or out of my element.

As much as I appreciate the gesture, it makes me feel guilty that I'm keeping her from enjoying her sorority's parties because she's too busy practically babysitting me.

I decide not to point out that I *have* been keeping an eye out for him for a couple of days now. It's not like he'd be hard to miss with how bad his face looked. But I can't blame him for missing classes if he's trying to rest and recuperate.

Unless he bled to death…

Oh God, Reese. What if he's like a cat? The ones that'll let their natural instincts kick in and isolate themselves to die alone? You should have forced him to go to the hospital.

Yeah, how would you manage that? He's twice your size and could probably overpower you even when he's injured.

That's not a comforting thought at all. My stomach churns, and I set my sandwich down.

"So, you'll be there?" my sister asks, breaking my train of thought.

"I guess," I hedge, picking up my mug. "If I don't have work that night."

"Great!" Lilian beams, ever the optimist.

I take a huge mouthful of coffee and swallow it down so that I don't have to say anything else.

"ARE YOU SURE YOU'RE GONNA BE FINE HERE?" MY SISTER'S standing in the doorway, reluctance ringing in her deep voice.

"You're going to be downstairs," I remind her. With my body curled under her violet-colored comforter, I'm practically tucked away in the room she shares with her roommate, Karla. "Go have fun."

I'm just thankful they're letting me hang out here instead of forcing me to mingle with people downstairs. This seems to be the silent compromise Lili and I have agreed upon. At least they're respecting my boundaries.

She heaves out a sigh, streaking her fingers through her glossy blonde hair. Trepidation shines across her heart-shaped face. "Text me if you need anything." With a rare warm smile I haven't seen in a long while, she shuts the door behind her.

Readjusting myself so that my back's pressed against the corner and I get a good view of the door, I spend the next two hours combing through on-campus job listings to see what else is out there.

Art pop plays softly through my trusty pair of headphones. I can hear EDM blaring downstairs and vibrating through the floor, but I mostly ignore it.

Browsing the list, a part-time gig at an ice cream shop snares my attention. I click on the link, ready to send in a copy of my resume when I hear the creaky sound of a door opening.

I look up and scoot backward, elbow immediately connecting with the headboard of Lilian's bed. Terror seizes every muscle in my body, and I'm rendered frozen. Stock-still. Nausea creeps up my throat just as the guy pulls his hoodie down and steps into the room.

"Whoa, I didn't realize anyone was up here."

"Caleb?" My heart goes from thumping wildly out of sheer fear to thumping wildly out of panic as my stupid crush returns in full force.

He flashes his dreamy smile, and my pulse flatlines. "Mind if I use the bathroom?" He gestures to the door near the foot of Karla's bed.

"Go ahead," I tell him, a blush creeping up my neck at how squeaky my voice is.

It's just Caleb, I remind myself, wringing the fabric of Lili's comforter. *You know he's a nice guy. An absolute sweetheart.*

The first time I saw him was at a sorority party Lilian dragged me to last year. I was overwhelmed, not having a good time, and doing my best not to freak out in front of Lili, so I snuck to the kitchen for a breather. That's when I saw him. He was in the middle of rescuing a spider from its shoe-stomping doom and setting it free outside in the backyard. Since then, I've been carrying a silly crush on him.

Another smile is sent my way, one that makes his green eyes crease and my heart stutter, before he ducks into the bathroom.

I exhale deeply when the bathroom door shuts, counting to ten repeatedly. My fingers rake my hair, and I'm suddenly aware of how messy it is—and that my sweater is off, exposing my collarbones with the thin tank top I'm wearing.

I'm quick to grab one of Lili's blankets and wrap it around myself, bundling up as if it's not a hot September evening.

He emerges from the bathroom a minute later, and my mouth twists into something awkward, tight-lipped out of sheer nervousness. And so I can refrain from the horrifying idea of stammering at him.

"So," he prompts, glancing my way. "Why are you hiding up here?"

"Me? Hiding?" I cough awkwardly. He's not wrong. I am hiding, but that sounds lame to say out loud. I rack my brain for a legitimate excuse. "I'm not in the partying mood."

"Me neither," he admits, sparing a soft chuckle as his eyes scan the room. They land on a picture on Lilian's desk. It's a framed picture of us two when we were kids, looking out of place with how dramatically dark her side of the room is. Her half is decorated in shades of black, violet, and lavender. "Not really feeling it, either."

"Then why are you here?" I blurt, then wince at my outburst.

"My friends dragged me here." He blows out a breath. "If I had my way, I'd be at home right now, reading."

He reads for fun? Oh God, my silly crush on him grows even bigger.

"What are you reading?" I ask, curious. It doesn't escape me that this is probably the longest conversation we've ever had, and it's taking all of my willpower to stay calm and not freak out.

He bashfully runs his hand through his curly brown hair, hesitating for a moment. "It's this book that takes place on a spaceship. The engine stops running, the hatch to the shuttle bay is faulty, and people start to turn on each other—"

"Wait. Is this the one where they have to vote who they're going to send outside to fix the engine and pretty much sacrifice themselves?" I ask, my heart drumming against my breastbone in a steady thrum. When he nods, I sit up straight, excitement buzzing across my entire body. "Oh my God, I've been reading that book."

"Really?"

"*Yes.*" I grin at him. "I haven't had a chance to finish it, though."

"I'm not done with it either," he says. "Maybe we can be reading buddies?"

The corners of my lips hitch upward into something bright and untamable. "Really?" I say, nodding enthusiastically. "Okay. Sure."

I can't tell if it's because I like the idea of having someone to be reading buddies with, or if I'm enthusiastic about getting to do something with Caleb Marsden. Both, obviously.

"Cool." His tongue clicks a beat. "We should exchange numbers."

"Of course." I unplug my phone from a charger on Lilian's nightstand and hand it to him, watching him punch a string of digits.

"I'm Caleb, by the way."

I know. I don't point out that we've interacted a few times last year. Or that Lilian's sorority sisters would gently tease me and try to no avail to get me to ask him out. Instead, something shy graces my lips. "Reese."

His mouth curves. God, it's such a nice smile. "Nice to meet you, Reese."

My heartbeat begins to race. He called me Reese. Not Lili Vann's younger sister. *Reese.*

4

DANE

For a long, lingering moment, I check out her rear, nearly whistling a sound of appreciation as I ogle her backside shamelessly. "How much?"

"Thirty k."

"Twenty. Cash." I steal another look. "Final offer. Take it or leave it."

Sergei's jaw sets. He doesn't like that I'm shorting him, but this is clean money. He'll never have to check to see if I'm scamming him with counterfeits.

Finally, after an eternity has passed, his chin hikes with a gruff mumble. "Twenty cash it is."

He drops the set of keys into one hand while I pass him the wad of hundreds with the other. He doesn't count the stack. We've done this dance enough times for him to know I'm good.

Instead, his gaze lands on my face for a taut, awkward, and extremely drawn-out beat of silence. We aren't ones for words.

"Pleasure doing business with you, kid."

My chin lifts as I stalk over to the driver's side of the car, and a low whistle escapes me. Goddamn, do I love the body style of muscle cars from the sixties. The long hood, the short deck, the power it yields—*Goddamn*.

The fucking cherry on top of this sweet-ass sundae?

The sweet girl's a manual.

She's stunning, even though she's not in her prime state. Her blue paint is peeling. Rusting. One of her side-view mirrors is missing. The cracked windshield needs to be replaced right away unless I want to chance it shattering on me while driving.

I can't tell what I love more: the sheer beauty of a sixties muscle car or taking on project cars and restoring them to their former glory.

Holding back a grin, I slide into the driver's seat and start the ignition, the V8 engine roaring loudly within the following seconds. It's music to my ears. After all this time, it never gets old.

Then I hit the gas, keeping an ear out for any rattling noise or anything out of the ordinary as I head toward the outskirts of town.

Too many neighbors back in Las Marinas have whined about my cars waking them up in the early morning. In an effort to get them to stop filing complaints against me, I've resorted to renting out a garage in a nearby city.

I know I'm no longer in the heart of the city when the smooth paved roads become riddled with potholes and cracked asphalt. Graffiti bombs every exterior inch of run-down buildings as far as the eye can see. Bus stops are littered with trash. Overgrown weeds peek through the crumbling sidewalks.

A flare of ease fills my chest, my restlessness growing dull. I haven't been to my garage in weeks, cooped up at my apartment on a bunch of painkillers, living off of takeout and whatever food Marco would bring back after he's been out surfing all day. The itch to do something with my fingers will soon be scratched.

Pulling up to my garage, I reach for my set of keys, only to frown a split second later. "What the?"

I shake the set, squinting hard as I look for a specific key. Suddenly, I remember handing over my main set of keys to the brunette chick over two weeks ago.

"Fucking shit."

I slam my fist on the steering wheel in frustration, and the horn blares. *Pitifully*, because it needs to be fixed as well. Right now, it's the least of my concerns.

My main set is the only one with the key to my garage. I don't have a backup. I lost the spare ages ago and have been meaning to replace the lock but haven't gotten around to it.

Considering my luck of having things bite me in the ass? I should have dealt with it the moment it went missing.

Backing up quickly, I look up the location pin I sent Marco two weeks prior, speeding down the winding roads until I pull into an empty parking space on the street.

Working my jaw, I glance at the run-down building before the realization hits me, and a groan breaks free while a frown forms between my eyebrows.

Shit. I have no fucking idea which apartment she's in. My memory's usually not this bad, but the days following the incident have been a foggy blur. And excuse me if I want to avoid acting like a creep scoping for a chick's apartment for hours until I run into her again. It's basically a one-way trip to the police station.

Peeling away from the curb, I visit the coffee shop next only to see that it's closed early tonight, along with a HELP WANTED sign hanging in the window.

Agitated, I drive back to my apartment and park the car in the building's underground parking garage—neighbors be damned. If I want to get my main set of keys back, I need to find her. *Fast.*

"WHAT DO YOU MEAN, SHE NO LONGER WORKS HERE?"

"She no longer works here," he repeats, stretching out the vowels of every word. That explains the sign in the window.

That doesn't help me one bit, though. And that's the only thing I give a shit about.

Resisting the urge to grind my molars into dust, I fold my arms. "Any chance you know where she went?"

"No." He gives me a saccharine smile that's met with a hardened glare. "Now, what can I get you?"

My fucking keys back.

"Nothing," I grumble as I exit the line.

My only lead is dead.

Wait, that's not exactly true. I know she goes to Belford, but thousands of students go there. What exactly am I supposed to do with that information, though? Check out every classroom on campus in hopes of finding her? Nah, fuck that noise.

My grimace deepens as I step out of the coffee shop. I refuse to entertain the idea of sitting in my car, lurking outside her apartment building until she returns home. I've already wasted one day trying to find her, and I can't afford another. Not with the passive-aggressive comments from my neighbors about how loud my engine is.

Along the way back to my car, my eyes inadvertently cut toward the building adjacent to the coffee shop. It's some random learning center that sets off a light bulb above my head. I recall seeing TUTORING in loopy handwriting on the whiteboard calendar.

If my memory serves me correctly, she has a tutoring session today. Belford U has a tutoring center. The dots easily connect themselves as I haul ass to my vehicle and gun it to campus.

Belford's tutoring center is located next to the language lab. I've only been there once by accident freshman year when I was trying to find the language lab to take my Spanish final, so I know where I need to go.

The moment I reach the second floor of the Hepner Building, life decides to be kind to me for fucking once and put an end to my wild goose chase when my gaze lands upon waist-length hair.

It's the first thing I remember noticing when my little savior screamed she was going to call the cops. Her long, thick, cascading brown locks underneath her Belford U cap.

"Hey! You!"

It's not my most eloquent moment or words by far, but it captures her attention immediately… as well as everybody else seated on the hallway floor or in the lounge chairs placed against the walls.

She waves her fingers at me, and the instant I take a step closer to her, the guy she's talking to appears in my line of sight.

He squints his green eyes at me.

Two can play this game, amigo. I narrow my eyes back at him.

There's something about him that's familiar, but I don't know where I recognize him from. And to be honest, my ass can't be bothered to fraternize with the guy to figure it out.

"I need my keys," I say when my little savior walks up to me, softening my tone to make up for my bluntness earlier.

"I was waiting for you to ask for them back," she says softly, retrieving a huge set of keys from her coat pocket.

"You kept mine on you?" I ask incredulously, watching her unhook my set from hers.

"Didn't know where I was going to run into you." Her face splotches pink as she passes mine over.

"Thanks. I'll let you get back to your boyfriend—"

"He's not my boyfriend."

Yet.

I can hear it in her tone. And see it from the way her face has turned scarlet red, along with her neck and ears. I wonder if she's the type to flush red everywhere.

She tugs on the collar of her tight sweater, and that's when I spot it. A harsh, terribly healed scar slashed diagonally just below her slender neck, between her clavicles, marring the pale skin.

"Who did this to you?" I demand. I don't remember seeing it before. Then again, that night's been a hectic blur.

Her hand flies to her neck, and her dark brown eyes go wide, her face stricken with a deer-in-the-headlights expression.

"Who did this to you?" I repeat, softer. "Did *he*—"

"Caleb? No," she whispers, her voice a mere tremble. She lets loose a shaky breath, her eyes misty with tears. "I was... *attacked*."

"On campus?" I heard about the crime sprees popping up last semester while I was on my so-called *leave of absence*. Received plenty of emails about it from campus police every time a robbery occurred.

"N-no," she stammers, readjusting the neck of her sweater. Her distress is so palpable that my chest tightens. "It happened w-when I w-was in high school."

My hands ball into fists. What kind of asshole would do that to her? "Are you all right?"

"They said I was lucky," she croaks. "Any few inches higher and... I might have lost my voice or..." My blood runs cold as she trails off, her gaze suddenly far away. "I'm fine," she whispers, forcing a smile a little too bright onto her slender face. "Really. I'm fine."

I don't think it's me she's trying to convince.

"I'm going to find the bastard who did this to you—"

"That's okay—"

"—and kick his ass."

Her eyes widen. "You don't have to."

"But I owe you one."

"I'm fine," she squeaks, "but thank you for the offer."

"What else can I do?"

"What do you mean?"

"You helped me out," I remind her. "Now, I want to return the favor."

"I don't... It's fine." The kind smile that appears this time is genuine, lighting up her entire face. "I'm not the kind of person who expects something in return just because I did you a solid."

"It's not how I roll," I say flatly. "You helped me out; now I help you out. That's what I wrote on the board. You can try to talk your way out of this, but I'm not budging."

She tilts her head back to gawk at me, the barest hint of confusion bringing her brows together, like she can't believe a word I just said. "You're not going to give up?"

"I'm not the type to give up on anything."

She swallows, expelling a shaky breath. "Okay then." She looks down the hallway where the guy is still standing, worrying her bottom lip between her teeth. I'm not sure what's taking her so long or if I should be wary of what she's about to say. *If* she's going to say anything. Before I can prompt her to give me something to work with, she blurts out, "*HowdoItellaboy-Ilikehim?*"

I stare at her, gobsmacked. *There's no fucking way those words truly just came out of her mouth.* "What did you say?"

Her face mottles a bright shade of scarlet. Even the tips of her ears aren't spared. "How do I tell a boy I—"

"I heard you the first time. You want to use your favor for *dating* advice?"

Somehow, her face turns even redder. "He's really cute. And nice. And we like the same books and music and TV shows—"

Christ. My eyes nearly glaze over from her ramblings. "You want *dating* advice?"

"Yes."

"Why?" I scan her up and down.

She's not bad to look at. Wide brown eyes framed with spiky lashes, a faint amount of freckles sprinkled across her upturned nose, and soft-looking lips in a dusky shade of pink. She's a little on the shorter side, but her tight sweater leaves nothing to the imagination as it clings to her generous rack.

She starts stammering, and it finally dawns on me. I manage to catch my grin just in the nick of time.

"You've never had a boyfriend?"

"*Shh.*" She smooths the fabric of her white pants, bashfully ducking her head to look at the ground. "Not that it's any of your business, but no. I've… never had a boyfriend."

"It's easy. Just go over there and tell him you like him."

"You make it sound simple."

"Because it is."

"It's not."

"How is it not? It's three fucking words." She visibly cringes, so I soften my tone as I say, "Try it on me."

"Wait, what?" Her eyes burn with confusion.

"Tell me you like me," I prompt, my gaze never leaving her face.

When she realizes I'm not playing around, she lets out a blustery exhale and sweeps her hair out of her dark eyes. It takes a sheer amount of willpower to refrain from saying *any day now*.

She reluctantly steels her shoulders, biting her bottom lip again as she refuses to make eye contact with me. Lord, don't make me coach her word-for-word.

"I like you," she gasps, her voice so damn hoarse and raspy that I genuinely deserve a medal for not bursting out laughing. I'm a dickhead, but I'm trying my fucking best not to be a dickhead to her. It's the least I can do for the one person who helped me out of a really rough spot.

"Christ, you sound like someone put a gun to your head and forced you to say those words." All right, maybe I don't deserve a medal after all.

"You're a jerk," she gasps. "Do you know that?"

"That ain't the worst thing said about me. Being called a jerk? It's a compliment at this point."

"I like you," she repeats, and I'm somehow impressed and appalled that she manages to butcher these three words even more the second time around.

When I tell her that, she scowls.

"If *you're* such an expert, why don't *you* tell him you like him?" she asks hotly.

I nearly hoot with laughter. "You need to relax. Whatever

hang-up you have? It won't be solved this afternoon. *And* I still owe you one."

"What?" Her brows scrunch together in bewilderment. "Why?"

"The favor you want is asking for the impossible to happen." I let out a snort when she spares another scowl in my direction. "Reach out to me," I say as I start heading for the stairs, "when you have a favor that's actually achievable."

"How am I supposed to do that?" she asks.

Right. My feet skid to a halt. "Got your phone on you?"

She retrieves a pink phone from her back pocket, passing it to me after she unlocks it. I text my number and then hand it back to her.

"If you still need dating advice," I say hesitantly, knowing fully well that I'm going to regret the words coming out of my mouth next, "then... you can ask me for dating advice. But, please, for the love of God, ask for something else. I'm no Cupid. If you have car troubles—"

"I don't have a car."

"*Anything*. Seriously. Anything else. Anything but dating advice."

"Okay." She nods woodenly. "Sure."

"Great." My tongue clicks two beats. "Thanks for the keys."

"You're welcome," she mumbles, not meeting my eyes.

"Good luck with everything," I say, my gaze flicking to the guy who's still standing there. "You got this."

Then I hightail it out of there before she can ask me for more help with getting the guy.

5

REESE

"WHAT DID DANE WANT?" CALEB ASKS AS I MAKE MY WAY BACK to him.

"Dane?" My cheeks are still burning with embarrassment.

Why did I ask him to give me advice on how to ask Caleb out? That is so unlike me. I usually keep my mouth shut about my crushes, so nobody can tease me about it. I don't even want help from Lilian, so why would I want help from a complete stranger?

"Dane Kingsley," Caleb clarifies. Am I supposed to recognize that name? Go *oh my God, that's Dane Kingsley*? The only thing I recognize is that I finally have the name of the guy I helped out.

"His keys," I explain. "He wanted his keys back." Which I'm super thankful about. For a while, I was dreading the idea of accidentally losing his keys before he came back for them.

Caleb cocks a brow. "Why do you have them?"

"It's a long story." I don't want to see if he'd react similarly to my sister over letting Dane crash at my place, so I tactically ask, "How far have you gotten with the book?"

He winces, letting out a slow exhale. "I've been slammed with homework and practice."

"Oof." My eyes crease with sympathy. I know he's not exaggerating. If anything, he's definitely understating it.

Caleb's majoring in music, and I know it's time-consuming. He will most likely spend at least five years here at Belford just to complete his degree.

"And you?" he asks. "How far did you get?"

"I haven't gotten far, either," I admit as I head toward the tutoring center.

I've done two interviews today instead of reading the book during my free time. The sorority girls have been blowing up my phone all morning, wishing me luck.

"Hey, listen," he says, falling into step beside me. My pulse quickens again, just like it did earlier when he asked if he could walk me here on his way to French. "Do you want to do something this weekend?"

Like a date? I want to ask.

Instead, I just stare at him with wide eyes, my heart thumping sporadically. I can't tell if asking that is going to make me sound awkward or clueless, or perhaps even both.

"Okay," I squeak out. Inwardly, I wince. Outwardly, I bite my lip to stop myself from physically wincing.

"Great."

Easy for him to say. *Great* is not how I'd describe it. *The end is nigh. Doom is upon us.* Clearly, there are better phrases for him to choose from. I'll even settle for *mayday, mayday.*

Since I don't want to freak him out, I force myself to chuckle and put on the *biggest* smile I can muster. My brain doesn't stop screaming the entire time.

"He asked you out?" Lilian stops her skincare routine to slide a curious glance at me.

"Well," I hedge, "I don't know if he technically did, so let's not jump that far ahead of ourselves."

She rolls her eyes and cocks her hips. "Is it just the two of you?"

"Well, yes—"

"*Date.*" She returns her attention to her mud mask. "How exciting."

"It's not exciting," I stammer, picking at a loose thread on the sleeve of my sweater. "I'm freaking out."

She lets out an exasperated groan. "Reese." I can feel her gaze boring a hole through the side of my head. "Just be yourself."

Be myself? I can already imagine myself freezing like I've got a bad case of stage fright and making a fool of myself that I'm mentally preparing for how self-conscious I'm going to be.

Unlike Lilian, who's ready to take on the world and tackle whatever challenges come her way, I've always been the one who second-guesses everything and freaks out accordingly. And then there's the whole scar issue I don't even want to address.

"You'll be fine," she insists.

Ha. Doubt it.

The date isn't happening for a few more days, yet my nerves are shot already. If I'm this nervous now, how bad will I be the day of? My face scrunches at the thought.

Trying to distract myself by any means necessary, I tidy up the toiletries on the edge of my bathtub. "Oh. Before I forget. I know who I helped that night at The Little Roast. This guy named Dane Kingsley—"

"*Ow!*"

My breath catches in my chest at her sudden outburst, and I look up to see my sister quickly splashing her left eye.

"Shit, that burns," Lilian swears. It takes a minute before she finally stops, and then she spins around after she turns the faucet off. "*Who* did you help that night?"

"Dane Kingsley?" I repeat slowly.

"Reese." She gapes at me like I just announced I'm about to join a pyramid scheme and want her to sign up with me. "*No.* Tell me you didn't."

My body goes stock-still from the level of focus in her gaze, from the terror trembling in her voice. I swallow roughly as she barrels on.

"Reese, he's *dangerous*. Unhinged. He's involved in a lot of shady things."

"*What*?" I gasp. That does explain why I witnessed two men beating him up that night.

Kind of. Not really.

He was more their punching bag than punching them, I think. And that doesn't scream dangerous. That just screams victim.

"He's not a good guy," my sister adds. "He beat the crap out of Travis Walker—"

"Who?"

"This frat guy I know," she clarifies, waving her hand dismissively before she sternly points her index finger at me. "Dane beat the hell out of him my freshman year, and everyone thought he got expelled. He got away with it because of who his mom is and because his family paid Travis off."

"I…" I exhale slowly, bewildered. I'm having trouble wrapping my head around this. All I can picture is him lying on the ground, face bloodied, body bruised. Something acidic rises in my throat. My pulse ratchets up a notch.

"You don't want to get dragged into his business. He gets away with everything because of his family's connections," my sister adds, genuine worry tightening her eyebrows. "He's a total skeeze. He fucks anything in a skirt. He drinks a lot. *Smokes* a lot. Gambles. And he has a really bad temper."

Oh my God. I don't have any regrets about helping him out, but I don't see myself jumping at the chance to interact with him any further after today.

Lilian and I grew up in a nightmare household. Our family's trailer always reeked of stale beer and cigarettes, no matter how hard my sister and I tried to get rid of it in any way we could.

Mom's on-and-off boyfriend gambled away every paycheck

he managed to scrounge, and then he'd blame it on us. He always blamed everything on us.

Mom was no better. Her favorite pastime was taking out her resentment on us—physically, emotionally, mentally—whenever she was home. *If* she was ever home.

Sometimes, I wonder how Lilian and I made it out of there alive. I'm so thankful we both escaped that suffocating trailer, leaving behind the white trash moniker that seemed destined to follow us around the rest of our lives.

"You don't have to worry," I tell my sister, flashing her a reassuring smile. "I'm never going to see him again, anyway."

"Good," she says, a sudden tide of relief washing across her features. She parks her hip against the bathroom counter, planting her hand on the other. "I don't want you to end up hurt because of him."

"Me neither," I reply without missing a beat. "Or for you to get hurt as well."

We smile at each other for a drawn-out moment before she returns her attention to my bathroom mirror and resumes her skincare routine.

"Any idea what you're going to do on your date with Caleb?" she asks, and while I appreciate the tactical shift in conversation, I don't like the current topic, either.

"I think we're going to see a movie," I say, pulling out my phone for confirmation. I spot my second most recent text conversation and blanch when I remember I have Dane's number. More importantly, he has mine.

Swiping my finger over his message, I delete it and quietly hope we never run into each other ever again.

6

______

DANE

Already a few weeks back at Belford U and I wish my ass had gotten expelled after all.

Saving face is doing me no favors. It's doing *nobody* any favors. Belford should have just quietly given me the boot, so I can be free to go back to working on my cars like I've been itching to do all week.

"Yo, Dane!" Marco's voice carries over the campus quad, and I glance to my left to see him trekking over at a koala's pace. "Figured that was your sunshine ass glaring at everybody."

I roll my eyes as we head to the Business Building, listening to him ramble on about the surf today. I haven't been here since the first day of the semester to sign my name on the sign-in sheet just so I'm not dropped from the class, but there's a quiz today. One that's worth ten percent of my grade.

We part ways as I head into the large lecture room and he goes to the stairwell. The moment I step foot inside, the unease in the air is both instant and palpable. Guess that's what happens when you're forced to take a leave of absence while the school does a shit job of figuring out who's at fault for what happened during freshman year.

I should be a junior right now, but it took good ol' Belford U over a year to realize I wasn't at fault for what happened despite the general consensus.

I bet that if the chancellor and my father weren't golfing buddies, if he didn't have an arsenal of the best defense attorneys he could ring up at a moment's notice, or if I were a poor street urchin like the Walker family made me out to be, I would have been expelled immediately that March. No hesitation. No holds barred.

Belford U doesn't take kindly to any scandals within its poorly maintained, run-down walls.

Life was much sweeter last year when I was still in limbo. My father was riding my ass about everything, but that's nothing new. I had so much free time on my hand that I was able to do whatever the fuck I wanted, since it wasn't as if he had the time to babysit me.

Now that graduating from BU is an option for me again, he's been on my neck about passing my classes and not taking for granted how lucky I was that I wasn't expelled.

My phone buzzes with texts from Marco as I grab a seat in the back corner and stare blankly ahead at the front of the room, waiting for the quiz to be dealt with, so I can go back to my regularly scheduled program of being left alone.

And as I glance around at the sea of undistinguishable, unfamiliar, and unremarkable faces stealing peeks or outright gawking at me with apprehension—in a finance class I'm retaking since all of my spring semester classes were marked as incomplete, no less—I *definitely* feel like the luckiest son of a bitch in a world.

"What are you looking at?" I bark at the guy in front of me.

He abruptly winces and whips his head around, sinking in his seat as if he's trying to get out of my direct line of sight. Grabbing my phone to distract myself, I catch a glimpse of my still-healing but still-injured face on the cracked black screen. I finally have an actual reminder of the one thing I should feel lucky about.

I should feel lucky my ass didn't get curb-stomped to death behind some fucking coffee shop in some dingy neighborhood that reeked of stale piss and cheap detergent.

I HIT UP A SORORITY HOUSE LATER THIS WEEKEND WITH MARCO FOR the first time in years. As it turns out, having a face that's still fucked up *just* enough brings out plenty of sympathy and attention from girls.

The music playing through heavy bass speakers is awful. The alcohol is abysmal. I want to leave, even more so when this angry blonde chick won't stop glaring daggers at me and running her mouth about Walker's arm to everyone within earshot.

A weak-ass punk would go scampering out the door with his tail tucked between his legs. I'm no weak-ass punk, so I sit there and *enjoy* the fuck out of the alcohol provided, even though it's practically fruity beer-flavored water.

I toss a wink at the curvy blonde when she brings up Walker's arm again, which seems to be her snapping point. She breaks away from her small group of sorority sisters, storms over to me, and throws her finger in my face.

"Careful, blondie," I warn, and she leans forward. A sharp pulse of agitation flares through me from how her fingertip is so damn close to poking my eye out. It takes everything I've got to keep my teeth from gritting.

"What are you going to do?" she taunts with a sneer, crossing her arms. "Break my arm, too?"

Even though she's standing, I stare her down from where I'm lounging on the sofa. I don't miss the hushed murmurs. The pointed stares. Something bitter crashes over me as time drags on for a never-ending minute.

"Maybe I'll finish what I started," I say finally, allowing

myself a sly smirk, just to piss her off. "What's Walker been up to lately?"

She visibly snarls, and I have to fight my scoff. "Your ass should have been expelled," she hisses at me, her jaw clenching tight. "I don't know why your sorry ass even bothered to come back here, but you better stay away from my sister. If you know what's best for you, Kingsley, *stay the fuck away.*"

Is this chick for real? What can she even do? Stab me with the pointy end of her heel? Get her sorority sisters to give me the cold shoulder?

"Like I'm interested in any of them," I grunt, glancing around the sorority house, bored out of my mind. I drain the rest of the fruity concoction in the red plastic cup in irritable silence.

This is why I knew returning to Belford U was a bad idea. There are idiots like this chick who think they know what happened that night since Walker was able to run his big fucking mouth and push his narrative out first.

I don't give a rat's ass about defending myself from people who can't do anything but jump to fucking conclusions based on flimsy fucking lies.

Besides, I don't even want to bother. I know the truth—I remember what went down that night. Every nitty-gritty detail has been committed to memory and seared into my brain.

Even if I didn't, I've got the fucking scar to show for it.

7

REESE

It's funny how the universe works. I've spent weeks trying to return his keys to him and never ran into him once. And yet the second I don't want to interact with him any longer, I see him everywhere on campus.

It's super apparent Lilian isn't the only one aware of his reputation. People scramble out of Dane's way when it's clear their trajectories are about to cross. It's as if nobody wants to be within a ten-foot radius of him.

I see the stares and hear the whispers, and it's enough for me to know that he's on my list of people to keep at arm's length. The only other people on that list are my mom and her boyfriend. And there, it's easy to steer clear of them when there's a healthy distance of nine hundred miles between us. It's harder to avoid *him* when Belford's a small campus.

"How was the date?" Lilian asks, pulling my attention away from Dane.

She doesn't see him; she's just being nosy. She's *always* been nosy about my life.

"It was not a date," I say because it wasn't.

Caleb and I sat there and watched an action flick. I didn't care for it as much because the plot had no substance, the lead actor was as wooden as an oak tree, and the fight scenes left a lot to be desired, but Caleb was invested in it. *Really* invested in it. Maybe it's just my imagination, but it felt like he was more into it than he was into me.

He never once kissed me, flirted with me, or said anything that would imply it was a date. And it was an empty theater. That screams *primo make-out spot* to me.

"It was just two friends hanging out," I say, forcing a carefree smile onto my face. Something that says I'm unbothered and couldn't care less that nothing happened between me and Caleb.

Lilian's brows furrow in concentration. I can see the gears running in her head as she tries to figure out a way to frame this non-date as an actual date.

I know my sister's nosy, but I'm not. I'm a private type—reserved to my very core. I don't kiss and tell. I also don't *not* kiss and tell, apparently. "Are you ready for the car wash?"

My sister's sorority is doing some charity wash with Caleb's fraternity taking part. Half the proceeds are going to the local children's hospital, and there's been a friendly rivalry brewing between the two Greek chapters as this Friday inches closer.

I've volunteered to keep track of the money and update the scoreboards, super thankful that it's my only involvement in this. Lili's sorority sisters have spent the entire week talking about bikinis they're going to wear to draw in the crowd.

Me? Bikini? Risking a sunburn I'm definitely going to get? No thanks.

"I'm so ready," Lilian says as we set out a picnic blanket by the campus duck pond.

On warmer days, my sister and I will try to have a picnic. Lili will sunbathe, and I will read a book and feed the ducklings with the frozen peas I've packed. This had been the first tradition we made here after it took a couple of months for my brain to latch onto the fact that the campus is safe.

The area is breathtakingly gorgeous. Jacaranda trees with pockets of flowers in a lovely shade of purple surround us. An ornate-looking footbridge arches over the pond in a vibrant shade of red. Ducks and koi fish splash among the lily pads, and bees buzz in the air. My phone has taken so many pictures of this spot.

"Chrissy, Jenna, and I are going to wear matching suits."

"How fun," I tell her. My attention immediately cuts to a man dressed in baggy clothing swaggering over to Dane. He sticks out like a sore thumb. They both do.

I'm not sure what I'm witnessing, but I watch them discreetly exchange hands right there on the campus quad. A knot of dismay cinches tight in the pit of my stomach, and dread sinks into my bones.

Lilian did say he was seedy, my brain whispers. My heart gives a sharp twist.

"You could match with us," Lilian offers, drawing my attention back to her.

"Huh?" It takes a second for me to realize what she's talking about. I barely catch myself before my mouth twists into a deep grimace, sparing her a soft smile a beat later. "I'm okay."

"Caleb won't be able to take his eyes off of you."

My skin flushes with heat. I haven't told my sister the truth— that I'm afraid to show off the scar below my neck.

I don't like the attention that comes with it. It never healed properly. I'm not good with makeup, so covering it up isn't an option. And it's so *noticeably* big that everyone always stares at it —or makes a face—which makes it harder for me to want to do anything other than hide.

Then there are also all the well-intentioned questions I get, and I know some people are genuinely concerned when they ask what happened, but they dig up old memories, and I end up having panic attacks. I want to move on from that awful day, but it's difficult to do so when people inadvertently make it hard for me to do so.

"I'll wear something cute," I tell her, "but I draw the line at a bikini."

And before Lilian can try to goad me into doing something I don't want to do, I cram one of the sandwiches I've made into my mouth and focus my attention on the ducks.

"SHE'S HER SISTER. SHE'S GOING TO HELP THEM WIN."

"Reese isn't like that," Caleb says, coming to my defense. I smile weakly at him, feeling shy when he glances my way and juts his chin.

"And we don't need to cheat to win," Lauren chimes in sweetly, her lips twisted into a carnivorous smirk. "We're going to kick your asses fair and square."

"Yeah?" A cool look flashes over Nico's face. "I'd like to see it happen."

"Can I go now?" I ask, looking at both presidents.

As thrilling as it is to watch them hate-flirt with each other, I'm starting to burn from standing under the blazing sun, and I can see a line of cars beginning to form that I should deal with before it backs up onto the street.

"Fine," Nico says stiffly. "But I'm keeping an eye on you."

"If that floats your boat," I tell him, beelining straight to the shady tree by the entrance of the parking lot.

"Thirty of that is ours," one of the frat brothers tells me, as Lilian's sorority sister hands me a couple of bills that have been collected so far.

"Noted." I move to stand in the shade. They both watch me intently as I split the cash, scribbling *30* on one side of the whiteboard and *25* on the other.

"Thanks, Little Vann," Stacy shouts, flashing me a thumbs-up.

"No problem," I shout back, watching her brazenly push her boobs together as another car rolls up. She tosses me a saucy wink, and I smother my laughter with a shake of my head.

It's like this for the rest of the afternoon. Both chapters flirt shamelessly with everyone who shows up with their cars and spray their own bodies with water when they're not trying to sabotage one another with chucked sponges and tossed rags.

Despite the water bottles Lilian keeps supplying me with, it's still ridiculously hot. I'm sweating from the heat, the cable-knit sweater I'm wearing, and running around collecting money after Stacy and Todd have been called in to help wash the growing number of vehicles.

Unlike the sorority girls and the fraternity brothers, I'm not flirting with anyone. I just ask *the girls or the guys?* point-blank, and that system hasn't failed me yet.

I grab another bottle, barely draining half of it, when a vintage-looking muscle car rumbles loudly into the parking lot, drawing everybody's attention.

I know very little about automobiles, but it's definitely one of the nicest cars I've ever laid my eyes on. It looks like something out of the movies. Sleek, shiny, and cherry red. I can already imagine it racing down a busy street with crazy accuracy and speed.

Setting the bottle on the ground, I make my way over as the window rolls down slowly. "The girls or the—*Dane*?"

His dark eyebrow slowly inches up. "I'm the other choice?"

Flustered, I sweep my sweaty hair out of my face. "I meant, do you want to go with the girls or the guys?"

Wordlessly, he spares me a pointed look.

"Right. The girls," I say. Because *duh*. "That will be five dollars."

"I don't have change."

"I do." My words come out tight and clipped, and I wring my fingers as I watch him reach for his wallet.

Suddenly, I wonder where he got his money from when he pulls out a thick wad of cash. Before I can even speculate, he hands me a hundred-dollar bill.

"You don't have anything smaller?" I squeak, only to be met with an arched brow from him.

Ugh. I'm going to have to break this, and I don't know if there are enough tens and twenties from the sorority's profit to do so. I shuffle through the stack of cash, counting and sorting out the ones and fives as he waits. His car idly thrums in the meantime, barely outmatched by the heavy thump of my heartbeat in my ears.

I swear, I usually don't take this long to count, but my breathing has gone ragged as I force myself to comb through the cash faster.

His hand drums an unfamiliar beat on the door of his car. "Have you decided on your favor yet?"

"What?" My fingers slip, and I lose my count. Dammit. I start over. "It's okay. I don't need anything from *you*."

My tone comes out way colder than intended, and I cringe when he narrows his eyes. *Smooth move, Reese. Piss off the one guy with the worst reputation on campus.*

"You've already helped with the advice you gave me," I remind him, wishing my smile wasn't so nervous. I let out a nervous giggle. "We're squared."

His expression is inscrutable. The blues of his irises are unnervingly frosty. I feel inexplicably trapped under his piercing gaze, and I force my mouth to curve into another nervous smile.

"Are you two together now?"

"What?" My whole body erupts into flames while I motion for him to keep it down, offering him a shake of my head as I cling to the hope that Caleb wasn't in earshot to hear any of that. "No."

"Then we're not squared," he says, casually shrugging a shoulder.

"What do you mean, we're not squared?" I choke out. "Do you think I have to land the guy for us to be squared?"

"Yes," is his blunt response. "If you're not gonna use your favor for anything else."

"Then we're never going to be squared," I say, a wave of frustration crashing over me. I lose my count again and have to start over for a third time.

"Here's what you need to do," he says, and my attention lifts from the cash to him. There's a tightness to the line of his jaw as he furrows his brows in deep concentration. "Come closer."

"*What*?" I gasp. "Why?"

"He's the jealous type," Dane says, and I have to laugh. Caleb is not like that at all. "What? I'm serious. Should have seen how he glared at me while you were talking to me that day."

My breath catches, and my heart begins to pound like a kick drum. The urge to sneak a peek in Caleb's direction is strong, but my eyes remain focused on Dane instead.

"You want him to notice you, right? Make him notice you." He props his arm on his rolled-down window and leans slightly out of his car. "If you want to get the guy, make him realize you're not gonna be around forever waiting for him. Now come closer."

"Closer?" I repeat, bending down slightly, so that we're at least eye level. There's still a foot of space between me and his car door, but it does little to settle my stumbling heartbeat.

His blue eyes gleam with amusement. "Closer. I don't bite."

I move just a fraction closer. An inch, at most.

"Now touch your hair."

My head pulls back as I blink. "What?"

"I'm serious. Touch your hair," he demands, the amount of focus in his gaze steadfast and unwavering. "You need to sell this—"

"This seems a bit much," I tell him, my mind barely adjusting to the fact that we are having this type of conversation. I almost pinch myself just to make sure this isn't some weird dream. "And someone is waiting in line behind you."

I glimpse over to see a tan sedan idling behind his car.

"Who gives a shit?" is his resounding response.

"I don't like to keep people waiting—"

"Then hurry the fuck up," he says impatiently. "Come closer, touch your hair, and laugh like I said something funny."

"This seems really excessive, though," I reiterate with a slight frown, folding my arms across my chest.

He lifts a brow, his mouth twisting into a wild smirk. There's a fresh cut alongside the bottom of his lip. I don't even want to ask where it's from.

"But it's working," he declares, his tone dripping with amusement. "Your boy is murdering me with his eyes as we speak."

"What?" I finally peek over my shoulder to see Caleb staring at us. He's not the only one looking. Half of Lilian's sorority and a couple of frat guys are, too. Even Lilian.

"You're welcome," Dane says smugly, his car rumbling forward as he steps on the gas.

"Wait," I call out, and his vehicle abruptly halts. The sedan behind him honks. Whoops. "What about your change?"

"Don't need it. Keep it. Donate it to the kids. Whatever. I don't care what you do with the money."

He waves me off before he drives his car toward the group of girls, leaving me standing there, gawking at his taillights. Swallowing hard, I glance at the hundred-dollar bill still in my hand. With haste, I neatly stack it with the sorority pile and turn my attention to the sedan that pulls up.

"What did he want?"

I freeze at the loud voice behind me. My heart seizes in my chest. Bile lurches up my throat. The palms of my hands turn clammy as my mind flashes back to that awful night. I almost touch my scar, swallowing a lungful of air instead.

Caleb appears in my periphery, but he's not looking at me. He's got a curious expression aimed at Dane's car. With a too-bright grin, I wait until my nerves subside to answer. The few seconds feel endlessly long.

"We were just talking," I explain, then hesitate. It quickly occurs to me that I can't exactly tell him what Dane and I were truly up to. Then I realize how absurd it is that Dane, *the* Dane Kingsley my sister warned me about, has just tried to help me get with Caleb. Even though his suggestions were a tad bit ridiculous.

Would a bad guy try to help someone like me land Caleb? I know he said he owed me one, but this seems like the last thing a guy with his reputation would do.

Maybe he's not that bad, a voice in the back of my head whispers. I should know better than to take rumors at face value.

Back home, guys thought I was easy and girls thought I was slutty trash because I'm one of the Vann girls from the trailer park. I developed early, and it only brought me attention of the unwanted kind. Really, I should be the last person to believe whatever rumors I stumble across.

"What were you talking about?" Caleb asks, planting his hands on his hips.

"The charity," I lie. *Technically, he did tell me to donate his change to the kids.*

"Huh." He sounds surprised. I'm not sure what else to say, so I'm glad he's the one who's keeping the conversation flowing. "So, listen, do you want to go on a date with me tomorrow?"

"A date?"

"That's what I said, right?" A teasing smile pulls at his lips.

My pulse flutters with excitement. My brain's already running through various scenarios of what our date can entail when I suddenly remember that I'm busy. I swear, I can feel my heart deflating in my chest like a popped balloon. "I can't. I mean, I want to, but I have work tomorrow."

I scored a job at the on-campus bookstore. I'm supposed to shadow Mandy tomorrow to learn how to ring up certain items before I start on Monday. The pay is minimum wage, but the hours are flexible and work with my class schedule. And it'll be nice not having to worry about catching the bus to get to work on time.

"I can pick you up after?" he suggests and then pauses. "If that's what you want."

Excitement threads through my veins as I find his gaze. "You'd wait for me?"

He shrugs a shoulder, raking his fingers through his curly hair. "Why not?"

"Okay," I stammer. "Sure. That sounds great."

"Looking forward to it."

"Me too." I cast a glance at the vintage cherry-red car, and my cheeks singe with mortification when I realize that Dane's watching us. Just him, by the looks of it. At least I didn't make a complete fool of myself for everyone else to witness.

He mouths *well?* to me.

As discreetly as possible, I flash him a subtle thumbs-up.

And as indiscreetly as possible, he throws two thumbs-up gestures in response. With both hands out the window.

What the hell is he doing? My face burns with even more mortification. I widen my eyes at him, hoping he'll take the hint to stop. Only, he does it again. This time, pumping his hands twice. Oh my God.

"So," Caleb says, "your place or mine?"

"What?" My attention darts back to him to see him smiling softly at me.

"Where do you want me to pick you up?"

"Oh. Hmm." I mull it over, waiting for my cheeks to stop burning from Dane's antics before I give him an answer. "Can you pick me up at the sorority house?"

Caleb grins. "You got it."

8

DANE

It's hot as balls in my garage. Perspiration beads down my forehead while I look over the carburetor of my latest project. Grease coats my fingers down to every last crevice that I know better than to swipe the trickle of sweat away from my eyes.

I dab my face with the short sleeve of my shirt and then inspect the accelerator pump diaphragm, trying to determine why it's still leaking on me.

The only thing I love more than driving cars? Tearing them apart and fixing what needs to be fixed. It's nirvana to me. Heaven. Pure ecstasy.

I only stop working when the rock song playing on the shitty stereo system cuts out with an incoming call.

"Are you going to send your goons after me again?" I answer, wedging the phone between my shoulder and ear.

Giancarlo chuckles. "No idea what you're talking about, Kingsley."

Grinding my molars, I want to call bullshit, but he's not one to lie. Something a lot like frustration works through me. As twisted as it sounds, some part of me wishes it had been him. Then the case would be closed, and I could move on without wondering if I pissed the wrong person off to be ambushed like that.

Now I've got no idea who could've been behind my attack. I don't have any enemies. And I haven't gotten myself in any trouble since the Walker incident. Besides going over the speed limit, I've been a law-abiding citizen.

"I have a business proposition for you."

My gaze goes to the middle ground. "Pass."

"Are you sure?" he asks, his voice light. "You might want to hear me out."

I white-knuckle my fucked-up phone. I know me. I live off of thrills and chases, and racing is one of my vices. A vice I'm trying to break because I need to lie low this year and the next if I want Daniel fucking Kingsley to leave me the fuck alone. "I'm sure."

"What if I told you *he's* in trouble?" he continues.

My body goes still. My eyes narrow at the ceiling. I don't need specifics. I know who he's talking about. There's only one person who introduced me to Giancarlo, one mutual link between us.

"All you have to do is win one race. Win one fucking race, and I'll let him off the hook." He hangs up on me before I can tell him to take his offer and shove it up his fucking ass.

I nearly chuck my phone against the wall. Instead, I stand there, clench it in a tight grip, and breathe until I'm no longer radiating with anger.

Putting a halt on my latest project, I make my way over to Ol' Reliable, a sleek black sports car I've modified to hell and back over the last three years. Custom carbon fiber body kit and all—everything handpicked and carefully considered by yours truly.

Rock music resumes on the shitty stereo as I pop the engine and get to work on making sure everything is good to go by tonight, gritting my teeth the entire fucking time.

What the fuck did you do, Marco?

THE CAR MEET HAPPENS AT SUNDOWN, IN A BUSINESS DISTRICT NOT too far from the waste treatment center. Numerous cars are already parked under the overpass when I arrive. There's rarely any civilian activity in these parts once it hits six p.m., which makes it an optimal location for this kind of endeavor.

Around me, hoods are popped open and on display. License plates are practically nonexistent as far as the eye can see. Rap music blares from various tinny speakers; it's all an overlapping, jangled mess of nonsensical lyrics. Raucous chatter fills the air as the evening wears on.

"*Dane, Dane, Dane.* It's been a while. Did Giancarlo do this to you?" Shyla slinks up to me, brushing her fried blonde hair over her ear. She's wearing a checkered tube top that generously shows off her tits and the eagle tattoo sprawling over her chest. When I don't respond, her mouth draws into a pouting sneer. "I heard your ass got beat."

She touches my lip before I can pull away.

"Nah." I paid Sergei's nephew a visit to see if *he* was the one behind my ass getting kicked in the coffee shop alleyway. He wasn't. He made that point very clear. "This isn't from him."

"Aww," she coos, and I duck away before she can touch me any further. A phony pout forms on her lips as she assesses me from the healthy amount of space I've created. "I can make you feel better."

"I'm good." Already, I'm backing up some more. "I don't want any part of your game with Eddie."

Marco hooked up with Shyla once—on the night I beat all odds and won my first race—and Eddie was a fucking nightmare about it when he found out. At sixteen, we were a pair of egotistical dumbasses and thought we could get away with anything. At twenty, we should know better.

As it is, I wouldn't be surprised if Eddie's still pissed about it to this very day. I know no love will be lost if Giancarlo does anything to him.

I cast a glance over at Eddie, catching the look on his face that makes it as obvious as two plus two she's trying to use me to piss him off. I've been around them long enough to know this is part of their twisted foreplay, and I don't want to get dragged into it.

Crossing my arms, I observe the crowd once more. "Where's Marco?"

Shyla chuckles, shaking her head. "If he's smart, Mexico."

My eyes narrow as I follow her line of sight. Just a few cars down, I see Wally making an ass of himself as he shows off his shiny green coupe with its tacky green rims and flames being shot out of the exhaust. After all this time, he's still sporting the most boot-ass haircut I've ever seen. A high and tight crew cut, so you can see the W he tatted behind his ear himself.

"Are you gonna come back?" Shyla finally asks, popping her gum. "You should. It hasn't been the same since you left."

Clenching my jaw, I shake my head no. "Ain't about this life anymore."

She rolls her eyes and readjusts her tube top. "The offer still stands, Pretty Boy." She caresses my cheek before I can react, skipping off to flirt with the next unsuspecting sap.

Releasing an irritable sigh, I stand there, stewing in annoyance and anticipation and waiting for the show to get on the road. I want to be anywhere but here. I want to be back in my garage, working on my latest project car. It's the only thing on my mind. The only thing I'm looking forward to.

I'm already behind the wheel when it's time. Usually, I go first. I don't stick around for the entire event because I don't like my time being wasted. Right now, I just want this over with, so Giancarlo can leave Marco and me the fuck alone.

"Pretty girl," Wally shouts as his vehicle pulls up beside mine, a maniacal smirk stealing across his face. "A shame it's gonna get destroyed."

"What kind of shitty trash talk is that?" I ask with a shit-eating grin. "Your mom has a better mouth than you."

He glowers. "Shut up about my mom."

I know better than to resort to a bunch of *your mama* insults. "Don't shove your head so far up your ass. Wouldn't want you to look like a rolled-up pair of socks before we even start."

His face contorts with sheer confusion at the English accent I heavily lean into. I roll up my window before he can get another word in.

Giancarlo moves to the front of the crowd, his two body-guards idling nearby. My focus goes to Marco, who stands beside him, and anger spikes in my bloodstream at what I'm able to discern. Busted lip, black eye—his face looks half as bad as mine did a few weeks back.

You better win, Giancarlo mouths, his gaze directly aimed at me.

No fucking shit. *What other alternative is there*? Clenching my steering wheel, I wait for Shyla to drop the flags after securing my helmet.

Up ahead, Shyla swings her hips slowly and seductively as she sashays to the starting line, dragging this out for no other reason than to drag this out.

When the checkered flags finally swing through the air, I hit the clutch, shift to first gear, and accelerate forward.

I'm in the lead. Ol' Reliable is roaring loudly as the car thunders down the endless winding streets surrounding the business district, her wheels screeching as I turn around the first bend I reach with ease.

I've got an easy advantage. I've driven this course multiple times; I know every curve, every bend, and every intersection of the street like it's the back of my hand.

Headlights flash into my rearview mirror, a lime-green abomination keeping pace with only a few yards separating us.

Wally's a fucking tool and a menace on the road, but he's got some talent. Not that I'll admit it to his face. His inflated head will pop if his ego expands any further.

My car moves along the charted course that'll circle back to the starting point. Take a left, watch out for the hairpin turn, go straight down the stretch of road alongside the waste treatment center, and take another left. It's a three-mile route with only two intersections to keep an eye out for. Luckily, the lights are always green at this time of night.

Anticipation builds as I gun past the first intersection, eyes focused on the green lights of the next one ahead.

That's when I see it.

Pale headlights on a barely visible vehicle running its red lights and barreling straight into the intersection.

"*Fuck!*" Ol' Reliable jerks into the opposing lane, narrowly avoiding a T-bone collision. A blur of lime green flashes by me on the right.

My high beams illuminate the sedan in front of me, and my grip on the wheel tightens when I see some punk sticking his tongue out and flipping me off.

I've been played.

Pissed, I veer around the sedan, rubber burning against asphalt, until I'm right on Wally's bumpers. He shows me his middle finger. His car swerves in the process.

Suddenly, the idea of pulling the pit maneuver on him flickers in my head. The temptation is high, barely edged out by my desire to win. For Marco's sake, I need to focus on winning.

On his tail, I cut into the passing lane, and the car skids as I make the last turn. His coupe swerves toward me, inching closer and closer until our vehicles are dangerously a centimeter apart—until he comes close to clipping me—but I'm not rattled.

I stare ahead in sheer determination as Ol' Reliable skirts into the opposing lane—just in the nick of time, barely crossing the crudely spray-painted line across the black asphalt.

As he skids to a stop beside me, I climb out of my vehicle and chuck my helmet to the ground. Yanking his car door open, I grab him by the shoulders and toss him onto the concrete.

"You fucking moron." My fist barrels into his face. Blood spurts out of his nose as he grins maniacally up at me. Someone grabs onto me from behind before I can land another punch, giving the fucker a chance to sneak a stinging right hook at my eye. "I'm gonna fucking kill you, you fucking dumbass!"

"Try me, bitch!" Wally spits out.

Well, if the fucker insists. I lunge forward, only to be yanked back. My limbs swing at him in vain; my body is still restrained.

"Easy!" Eddie sputters into my ear, the crook of his arm tightening around my neck. "*Easy, Kingsley.*"

"Enough!" Giancarlo's voice, gravely low and resolute, silences the crowd. "What's the meaning of this?"

"Old News," Wally gripes with a smarmy grin, "can't handle an obstacle course."

Eddie pulls me back before his face receives a reunion with my fist.

"We don't play dirty," I growl. "And *I* don't need to cheat to win."

"It's not cheating." The blood from his nose streams down the lower half of his face, staining his teeth red. "A car could always drive by at this time."

He's lucky Eddie has tightened his grip on me once more, or else I would have pummeled his ugly mug in. Not only was it dirty, but it was a fucking dangerous move. Nobody in their right mind would ever pull a stunt like that.

"He's right." Giancarlo's mouth pulls into a taunting smirk. "A car *could* happen along these streets at any time."

Brutal fury spears through me, bringing a tightness to my shoulders. Apparently, there's no such thing as honor. Fucking whatever. I will not stand here to pitch a fit like a whiny baby. Not when it's obvious I'd have an easier time winning a debate with a statue.

"Is he good?" I growl.

He regards me coolly for a never-ending minute. "Consider his debt paid for."

Eddie has the smarts to let me go before I wrestle myself out of his headlock. I look at Marco, who refuses to meet my eyes. My attention drifts to Giancarlo, who's studying me with sharp, hawklike interest.

"I fucking won," I declare, staring him down, "and I'm done."

"For now."

He doesn't have to say the next line that already auto-fills in my head. *You'll be back.*

I stalk off to my car, steaming in silence. My jaw locks tight when I can sense everybody in the close vicinity watching me as I go. I need to get out of here before my smart mouth gets me into more trouble. I'm barely behind the wheel when Marco limps over to my door.

"Thanks," he mumbles weakly, holding my discarded helmet up.

My line of sight slides up to his features as I snatch it and chuck it into the passenger seat. It takes all of my energy to unclench my jaw. "What the fuck did you do?"

He lets out a dry laugh and then a painful cough. "Got in way over my head with GC." He's quiet for a moment. I don't have the patience to sit here and try to coax it out of him. I just want to get out of here. Leave this place a distant memory. "Never thought we'd end up here again, huh?"

I don't crack a grin at his wry, self-deprecating comment. Between the both of us, Marco's supposed to be the one who got his shit together. I'm the one who'd get into trouble with Giancarlo and the likes. But we had an unspoken agreement to avoid anything GC-related since the Walker incident, silently pledging to stay out of any trouble. Neither of us should be here tonight.

"I got caught counting cards," Marco mutters, lacing his hands behind his head. He looks skyward, the tilt of his head allowing me to get a better glimpse of a dark bruise forming below his jaw.

"Need me to give you a ride—"

"Nah, man," he says, jerking his thumb over his shoulder. I spot his truck just then, and it's hard to tell if its headlights have been bashed in or not from this far away. "I'm good. Thanks for—"

"Don't thank me. You know why I did it," I cut in, and he reluctantly spares me a nod. No doubt his pride is wounded.

"I owe ya one." He pats the roof of my car before he steps back. "See ya later, man."

He knows me well. We both know I don't want to be around here any longer. There's no point in standing around, shooting the breeze.

With a terse nod, I slam the door shut and take off. People have the good sense to scramble out of my way, so that I can peel down the street and put this fucking night behind me.

I don't like to go home when I'm in a foul mood. Usually, I prefer driving, cruising down the empty highways and their winding paths, and letting the scenery unravel my brain until the tension is gone from my body.

Tonight, I'm too raw with anger. Not about Giancarlo. I'm pissed over the stupid stunt Wally and his idiot friends pulled. Nobody in their right mind would ever do something that fucking risky. It ain't fucking worth it.

Not when death is always in the cards. Death is final. Undiscriminating. You can't walk away from it. We're lucky tonight didn't end with our cars crumpled like soda cans and our bodies crammed in body bags.

A harsh exhalation breaks free, and I glare ahead. Sticking to the side streets, I drive until I hit this shitty hole-in-the-wall venue where the bar doesn't even check for IDs. There's a tight spot by the front, one I skillfully swing into in an impressive few seconds.

"What?" I gripe irritably when it occurs to me I've got an

audience. Pedestrians on the sidewalk continue to gawk at me while I climb out of my vehicle. "You've never seen someone parallel park before? Ain't that fucking hard."

Since the ticket booth is closed for the night, I toss a hundred-dollar bill at the bouncer, storm inside the venue, and regret my decision to come here immediately.

It ain't aggressive rock tonight. Whatever is assaulting my ears sounds pitifully indie as the lead singer crows into the mic with a whiny, nasally voice.

It's not the music I want to get hammered to, but I'm too heated to care.

I snake through the crowd formed at the bar, slamming another hundred-dollar bill down on the counter to catch the bartender's attention.

"*Dane*?" comes a soft whisper.

Instinctively, my spine goes ramrod straight. Muscles tense, I turn my head to my right and find myself looking into a pair of dark brown eyes.

My little savior. What are the odds?

"What happened to your eye?" she gasps, her hand flying to her chest, the abrupt movement drawing my attention to her nice rack.

"Got into an altercation," I say, carefully choosing my words. My father would be proud of me for that.

She flags the bartender. "Can we get some ice?"

"I don't need—"

A plastic cup of ice slides our way.

"Beer," I demand, pushing the bill toward him. "Keep it coming."

From the corner of my good eye, I see her reaching for the cup of ice.

"What are you doing?" I ask when I see her dump trail mix out of some Ziploc she takes out of her purse.

"You need to ice it," she whispers, pouring the ice cubes into the plastic bag and zipping it up.

"I don't—" She doesn't give me a chance to finish my sentence, already rising on her toes to press the bag against my cheek. "I can do it," I say irritably, taking it from her hand.

"Okay." Thankfully, she lets go, scooping the mess of trail mix off of the counter. She rushes over to the nearby trash bin and returns with that look of worry I've seen before on her face.

Exhaling deeply, I readjust the ice, pressing it firmly against my eye. "What are you doing here?"

"I'm on a date with Caleb."

That explains the tight white sweater and the pale blue miniskirt she's wearing. Even her long hair has a curl to it. She's practically beaming as she rocks on her feet, radiating pure sunshine in this dark venue. That is until her gaze goes to my eye again, and her smile falters.

Since she's the one person I don't want to tell off for looking at me, I decide to make nice. "Where's your date?"

She lets out a soft exhale. "He went to the restroom, so it's just me by myself right now."

"You like this kind of music?" I ask incredulously, and the singer's voice cracks just then. He can't sing for shit, but he's got impeccable timing, I'll give him that.

She makes a face, twirling a strand of her hair around her finger. "Well, um, no. Caleb likes them, so I thought I'd give them a shot."

"Damn, you must truly like him if you're willing to torture yourself with this." I point at her. "Or you're secretly a masochist."

"I'm not a masochist," she huffs, her attention going to the counter when the bartender slides a couple bottles of beer my way.

"You want one?" I put the bag of ice down.

Her nose crinkles. "No."

"Get the lady whatever she wants, then," I say, slapping another bill onto the counter.

"I'm fine." With a painted-blue fingernail, she slides it back toward me, and I can see the bartender's gaze wistfully following the hundred. She pulls out her credit card instead, and there's a hint of honey in her voice as she asks, "Can I get a root beer soda?"

"Goody two-shoes," I tease.

She shakes her head but doesn't respond. When I glance over, I catch her peering directly at my eye, a small crease forming between her eyebrows.

"It's rude to stare," I grumble. "You know that, right?"

"What happened?" she asks, ignoring my comment.

"Some fucker punched me."

She winces. "I see."

"He didn't get away unscathed," I add, before I take a huge swig of beer. Then another.

"You shouldn't drink on an empty stomach," she says softly.

"You are *obsessed* with my well-being," I snark.

She visibly stiffens, a wounded look flashing in her eyes.

"I'm sorry," I mutter, feeling shittier than usual. I guess my gut has decided it doesn't like it when I hurt her feelings. "I'll get some appetizers if that will make your highness feel better."

She rolls her eyes at me and sighs, reluctantly nodding a beat later. I order a side of chili fries at her behest and let the bartender keep the change.

With an arched brow, I dryly ask, "Happy?"

I'm met with a closed-lip hint of a smile. It's barely noticeable, but it's there. Faintly curling the corners of her lips. I'll take that over the wounded puppy-dog look any day.

"Much." She grabs her soda and peeks over her shoulder, perking up immediately. "Oh, I see him."

"Have fun on your date," I tell her, grimacing when the lead singer's voice cracks again. "Don't buy a CD tonight."

"Um, sure," she whispers back to me. "Don't drive home drunk."

"I'll call an Uber this time," I promise her, and a ripple of surprise surges through me when her shoulders sag with relief. "Aw, you care about me."

"I don't want to find out later that you died," she says.

I scoff. "I know better than that."

The expression flickering across her face lets me know she doesn't believe me. I don't know why that gets to me, but it does.

"Bye, Dane," she whispers.

"Bye—" Huh. I only now realize I have no clue what her name is. I have her saved as *Little Savior* on my phone, which I need to rectify. "What's your name again?"

She hesitates for a brief moment, and I swear, I see genuine reservation gather behind her eyes. It's not as if I asked her for her social security number and bank information. "Reese," she tells me. "Reese Vann."

"Reese," I repeat. "Fun Sized Re—"

"*No.*" She levels me with a murderous glare. I almost crack a grin. It's probably for the best that I didn't. My face stings like a motherfucker. There's no reason to hurt it even more. "I know what my favor is. Don't call me that. *Never* call me that."

"What about Reese's Pieces?"

"Or that."

"Mini Reese's?"

"I think they're called Reese's Minis? Still." She points at me with a stern frown. "*No.*"

"Goodbye—" I fish my phone out of my pocket and unlock it.

"Bye," she replies curtly.

"—Reese's Big Cups." I look up from the search results on my screen, blinking innocently.

Her face is beet red; her neck is twice as flushed. "I will steal your keys and run you over with your very own car if you ever call me any of these nicknames again," Reese threatens me. She's adorable. "*Especially that one.*"

I cackle loudly, despite my busted face aching and all. This is the same girl having trouble telling that guy she likes him? Truly adorable. "Have fun on your date."

She squints her eyes, clearly bracing for what I have to say next.

"*Reese.*" I flash a half-smirk at her.

She stares at me for one quick beat before she flounces back to her date with shit taste in music.

I wait until she's halfway through the crowd before I send her a text. She halts, checks her phone, and spins around to glare at me.

I don't even have to be close to her to know she's definitely red all over.

Reese: Stop it

I send the same text again because I'm having too much fun at her expense.

Dane: Reese's stuffed with Caleb's pieces
Reese: I'm blocking your number
Dane: I'll shout it from here
Reese: Please don't
Dane: fine
Dane: have fun
Dane: being stuffed
Reese: Shut up

I watch her hastily shove her phone into her purse, sparing me one final glare before she returns to her date.

I know when to rein it in. The girl should be able to enjoy her date, shitty music and all. I return my attention to the chili fries set in front of me, snickering to myself as I dig into the greasy food.

9

———

REESE

Dane: have you been thoroughly stuffed?

I NEARLY DROP MY PHONE IN UTTER HORROR, TURNING IT OFF WHEN Lilian emerges from my bedroom with her laptop in her hands.

"Which one should I get for Jenna?" She opens her laptop to let me see two expensive rave suits—happy faces patterned on a very strappy piece and wavy tie-dye on the other.

"Um, the second one?" I point to the latter. Both aren't my style, but I'm relieved we're talking about something other than Caleb for once.

"Thanks. I need to get my Secret Santa gift dealt with."

My eyes widen in alarm. I've been so distracted with finding a new job and staying on top of my classes that I haven't been paying attention to anything else. I glance at my calendar, feeling slightly relieved that we're only two weeks into October before my gut pinches at the idea of Christmas looming around the corner.

I usually plan ahead when it comes to Lili's present because she always gives me an extravagant gift and I want to be equally thoughtful, but now I wonder if I need to worry about getting Caleb something as well. Money is already tight as it is. All of

69

my scholarships and financial aid have covered tuition, with most of my paychecks going to my rent. Whatever's left is spent on bills and groceries.

My sister knocks her ankle against mine. "How was your date last night?"

"The music was awful," I admit. I don't hide things from my sister. Then I trail off, dropping the subject since I don't want to expand any further on how awkward it was after he brought me home.

There was no stuffing to be had—*ugh*. I mentally curse Dane Kingsley for putting that euphemism out there in the universe.

I wanted him to come in and see where the night could lead, but my nerves got the better of me and I didn't even kiss him goodnight. We just talked about our sisters as he walked me up to the door. Then it was just one awkward wave followed by me slamming the door shut in his face. Loud enough that I'm sure anyone could hear it from Pluto.

He hasn't texted me since dropping me off. Whatever interest he had in me probably died a swift, yet painful death.

"And?" Lilian reaches for a mini bag of potato chips I've swiped from the employee lounge and tears it open.

"And?" I repeat nonchalantly.

"What happened next?" she prompts.

"He asked for my hand in marriage," I deadpan, "and he's now waiting for a dowry of ten sheep and two goats."

"Wow." Her expression turns solemn as she claps her hand on my shoulder. "The best I can do is one goat and two ducks wrangled from the campus pond."

I crack a smile. "Gee, thanks."

"I'm guessing nothing happened?" She frowns when I shake my head in agreement. "Really? But aren't you guys vibing?"

"If we're vibing, it didn't happen last night," I say. "I think he was more into the music than me."

"He *is* a music major."

"True." I gnaw on my lower lip. "I didn't have much fun last night. I think I had more fun…"

My sentence dwindles as the actualization dawns on me. I don't want to tell Lilian I ran into Dane. She already went into another *Dane Kingsley is dangerous* spiel after the car wash the other day.

I don't need her to tell me that again. The nasty shiner I saw forming last night was more than enough to warn me to be cautious around him. To stay on high alert.

Racking my brain for something to say, I ask, "What if Caleb isn't into me?"

"He's into you," she says firmly, out of sisterly obligation, I bet. It's not like she'll tell me he's not into me.

"And what if he's no longer into me because…" I hesitate.

"Because what?"

"I'm not good at this stuff," I whisper, my voice flat.

"Dating?"

"Yeah… and…"

Her amber eyes sparkle with clarity. "Sex? You've never had sex? *Never*?"

"The door is right there if you feel the need to announce that to the rest of my neighbors," I say dryly. "I don't think the family down the hall heard you."

"I'm sorry," she says quickly, offering me an apologetic expression. "But how?"

"I only had my first kiss last year," I remind her, embarrassment flaring through me. This conversation is excruciatingly painful.

It's kind of hard to be kissed back home when everybody thinks of you as trailer trash. Even more so with what happened during my senior year of high school. My hand almost goes to my neck, but I catch myself just in time, pressing it flat against my knee instead.

"Are you asexual?" my sister asks. There's no judgment in her tone. Only curiosity.

I shake my head. *Definitely not asexual.* Not with the kind of thoughts I have from time to time.

Surprise slackens her features. "Aromantic?"

My head shakes no again. This is one of the most awkward conversations I've ever endured, more excruciating than the first kiss I had with a random frat guy—one that was super clumsy and had too much tongue. Maybe it would have been less painful if I liked him. Or if I wasn't trying to prove to myself and everyone else I'm capable of living my life.

Releasing a sigh, I streak my fingers through my hair and fight my groan. I love my sister, but there are some things I don't want to talk about with her. I'd much rather walk downstairs and fling myself into the nasty pool than talk about my nonexistent love life.

"I don't know how to deal with the nerves," I explain.

"Just ignore it," she says as if it's that easy. For her, it probably is.

However, my brain doesn't work that way. It doesn't ignore things. It goes from zero to sixty quickly and overanalyzes everything.

"You just need to relax and be comfortable," she adds.

I realize we're veering straight into a conversation I'm not enthused to have with my sister. If Lili starts giving me sex tips, I'm flinging myself into the outdoor pool from this floor.

"Go with the flow and—"

"What do you think I should get Caleb for Christmas?" I hop onto the barstool beside her. "I should start planning now, so I know how much I need to set aside."

She narrows her eyes, pinning me with a sharp, scrutinizing gaze. I silently barter with the universe to help me out here. *Give me the strength to handle her nosy wrath.*

"Maybe get him something from the band you guys saw?"

"Ooh. Great idea." I jot down a list of memorabilia I can look for later. From another artist, of course. He's mentioned plenty to me in passing, and one of them has to be better than the act he tried to introduce to me last night. I know Caleb's really into obscure music, and I want to express interest in what he likes, but I don't think avant-garde experimental screaming is my kind of scene.

"I'll be right back," she tells me, setting her laptop down. "I need to pee."

I nod, prying my phone out of my pocket to search for gift ideas, only to be reminded of Dane's text message when I see the notification on my lock screen.

Against my better judgment, I respond.

Reese: Nope

I've barely opened my web browser when I get a response.

Dane: let me guess, you're a three dates kind of girl
Reese: No
Dane: damn. FOUR dates? he really likes you if he's willing to endure all that blue balling
Reese: You think so?
Dane: no shit. I would have bailed after the first one
Reese: Wow. Classy
Dane: don't waste my time ya know?
Reese: But how can you tell if you've connected based on just one date?
Dane: oh we'll connect in other ways

I blink, blushing immediately.

Reese: Wow
Dane: let me pour one out for blue balls
Reese: OMG. Don't call him that
Dane: apologies, Reese's Pieces
Reese: And don't call me that
Dane: bossy

**Dane: let me know when the poor guy's blue balls are
no more
Reese: I will not because this is none of your business
Dane: I think it became my business when you asked me for
help to get the guy
Reese: I asked for DATING advice
Dane: isn't sex part of dating?
Reese: You tell me!**

Oh crap. I regret those three words the second my finger hits send. Then I shriek in surprise when my phone starts ringing in my hand.

I hit ignore. My phone rings again. I grit my teeth and decline it again. My phone starts buzzing instead.

**Dane: WHAT?
Dane: tell me you're joking
Dane: you're not going to put the guy out of his misery?
Reese: He's not going to die**

My phone rings for the third time. I answer it with a heated, "What do you want?"

He's howling with laughter on the other end; I have half an inclination to hang up on him. "You're telling me you're not going to sleep with him?"

"This is none of your business," I tell him flatly. I can hear my toilet being flushed, so I know I need to keep this short.

"Oh, Reese's Pieces—"

"Don't call me that," I grumble.

"—you're torturing the guy," he finishes.

"You think I'm doing this on purpose?" I ask hotly.

"You… not?"

"No," I confirm stonily, wrinkling my nose.

"Then sleep with him."

"I…" My voice dies, catching in my throat.

His end of the call becomes unnervingly silent. "Wait. Are you putting this off—"

"Good—"

"—because you're a virgin?"

"—bye." I hang up on him, my face burning with unadulterated mortification. Then I groan when I feel yet another buzz in the palm of my hand. A series of them, actually.

Dane: nothing wrong with being a virgin
Dane: everyone is born one
Dane: some people even die as one

Like me, because this virgin is going to die of pure embarrassment right here, right now.

Reese: I'm blocking you

And since I'm a woman of my word, I do so. But not before he manages to send another text to me.

Dane: I can help you out like last time

Even though the rational part of my brain is telling me to delete his number, my curiosity gets the better of me. Scrambling to unblock him, I craft a quick response.

Reese: … How?
Dane: thought you blocked me, Reese's Pieces
Reese: Don't call me that
Dane: I'll give you pointers
Dane: help you seduce blue balls
Dane: then we're finally even

I think about it. Every sensible, *logical* fiber of my being knows this is a disaster waiting to happen. Catastrophe is stamped all over it. Alarm bells are going off. Heck, even Lili's word of advice to steer clear of him rings loudly in my head.

But the curious part of me is interested in what advice he has to offer. Technically, his antics at the car wash helped me land a date with Caleb.

Maybe he can help me *land* Caleb in general. He's a guy. Caleb's a guy. Perhaps he'll have insight that's more useful than what Lili has given me so far.

Why not? my brain whispers. *It can't hurt to take him up on his offer.* I hesitate for a millisecond before I text him my response.

1 0

DANE

"WHERE ARE WE?" REESE ASKS, HUGGING HER ARMS TO HER CHEST. She's wearing a light blue sweater made of what appears to be a thick material. Some part of me feels kind of guilty given how fucking hot and dry it can get here due to lack of ventilation.

"My garage," I deadpan, and I'm met with a leveled stare that's bordering on withering.

"I see," she grumbles.

"Hey, you said you wanted to meet somewhere that wasn't on campus." I cock my head her way. "Did you really take the bus here?"

As her gaze goes to the building next door, she nods.

I think of all the trash at the nearby stop and frown. "I could have picked you up."

"It's fine." She wrings her hands together as I remove the padlock. I can sense her unease radiating off of her in waves.

"Want to do the honors?" I offer, gesturing to the garage door. This time, I'm met with a pointed look from her, and I'm quickly reminded of the fact that she's more than a foot shorter than me. I quietly chuckle. "Right."

Then I hoist the garage door up with one hand, my attention

solely focused on her face, taking in the transformation that occurs before me.

"Whoa." Her lips part around her gasp. I don't even fight my grin as she whirls around, momentarily speechless. There's a hint of awe behind her eyes. "That's a lot of cars. Are these all yours?"

"Yup." I flick the light on and pull out the chair from my workbench.

"Do you work on cars for a living?"

"Yes and no. Work on cars. Not for a living."

Her eyebrows pull together in confusion.

"I take junked cars and fix them up in my spare time. Some I keep, like this beauty over here." I put my hand on the first car I ever purchased with my own hard-earned cash.

It's a '68 Mustang Coupe, one I hitchhiked all the way to Arizona to buy in rough condition after two and a half years working at Sal's Auto.

"Bought it just a week after my eighteenth birthday." After I slap my Mustang on the roof, I point to Ol' Reliable next. "Then there's this beauty."

It's my Subaru WRX that's won me many races. It's also the only ride of mine that's not from the sixties. The air intake is fucking spectacular.

"What about that one?" Reese gestures at the only vehicle of mine hidden underneath a cover. A '64 Pontiac GTO. It was Sal's pride and joy before he gifted it to me for graduating high school.

"Something from an old friend," I say gruffly. "These stay with me forever. The rest come and go."

She looks around my garage, poring over every detail with her dark brown eyes. It's a long minute where she takes everything in before she finally asks, "How junked? The cars you fix, I mean."

"Well, I can't do much if it's totaled and fucked up beyond repairs. But I know a few things here and there. And I like a good challenge," I say, hitching my shoulder. "If you ever need a kill switch installed, I'm your guy. Every car should have one."

She continues to scan the garage with wide-eyed curiosity. While she squints at a personalized license plate, I retrieve a bottle from the mini-fridge by my workbench. Then she peeks at me when I twist the lid off and take a huge gulp of water.

"Warning," I say, tipping the bottle at her. "It gets really hot in here."

Her nose wrinkles as she declines it. "We're not staying here long," she asks, "are we?"

"Depends on how terrible your game is," I say dryly.

The edges of her lips twist into the barest hint of a scowl, but she stays firmly rooted by the entrance.

"Come on, Reese," I coax. "I won't hurt you."

"I think I'll stay here," she murmurs, sneaking a couple of glances to the street behind her.

"If that suits you," I say with a shrug. "But if this is how you are with him, I'm now starting to see why you're getting nowhere with the guy. Here's a helpful hint: it'll improve your game tremendously if you're in the same room with him."

She expels a soft sigh and stomps inside, crossing her arms as she comes to a stop a few feet away from me. Her gaze turns to the opened garage door, and trepidation forms across her thin face.

My tongue clicks a beat. "Show me what we're working with."

"What do you mean?" Her brows knit together.

"Pretend I'm the guy."

She purses her lips while she shoots me a quick appraising glance. Her apprehensiveness gives way to reservation as the seconds extend into what feels like an eternity. I'm about to get the ball rolling when she allows herself a stifled sigh. "Caleb, how did you get the black eye when you're a huge pacifist?"

My gaze connects with hers. I adopt the most solemn expression I can muster, slowly placing a hand over my heart. "I, Caleb

Whatever, whacked myself in the eye while furiously jacking off to deal with a bad case of blue balls—"

"Oh my God." Reese drags both her hands down her face, and I snicker. "Why are you like this? Caleb is not like this at all."

"That you know of," I say, keeping my voice as grave and sincere as possible. "Maybe he's furiously jerking off right now."

Pink colors her cheeks. "Is this how we're going to spend the afternoon?"

"Good point." I'm gracious enough to drop this, putting my water bottle down on the counter. "Let's go back to the beginning. I'm Caleb, some bland frat guy who wears too many snapbacks and polo shirts."

"Says the guy who wears too many basic white tees."

My lips tilt into a smirk. "Reese's Pieces got a little bite to her."

She rolls her eyes and shifts her weight onto one foot. "Okay. I'm ready. Hi, Caleb."

"Hi, Reese's Pieces."

"He wouldn't call me that."

"Why not?" I ask. "It's the perfect nickname for you, Reese's Pieces."

"Reese *is* my nickname."

"No shit? Really?" I take in her expression. She's got the most earnest face I've ever seen, so unless she's a good actress, she's telling the truth. "Short for Charisse? Therese? Theresa? Teresa with no H?"

"Nope," she responds brightly, popping the P.

"Charisma?" I throw out my next guess, and she blinks in surprise. "You've got plenty of it."

She huffs out a groan, her expression downright unamused. "You're not going to get it."

I ignore her comment. I'm not done. "Were you addicted to Reese's growing up?"

"No." She shakes her head.

Well, there goes that theory. "Huh."

"We're getting off-topic," she says, holding her hands up. "We say *hi*. Caleb will call me *Reese*. We are on a date."

Nodding, I fold my arms. "All right. What's the setting of this date?"

"I don't know," she mumbles, furrowing her brows. "The museum?"

"The *museum*?" I almost snort. "Is this a date or a punishment?"

"I like museums," she says, her tone stiff and flat as a board.

I give her an incredulous stare. Good God, is this girl serious? "Museums aren't sexy."

"Tell me, then," she grumbles, "what you think is sexy."

"Confidence," I say simply.

Her frown deepens. "I meant a *place* that's sexy."

"Any place can be sexy." I shrug. "Besides the fucking museum."

"Even this garage?" She grimaces at a pan collecting fuel leaking from the carburetor of my latest project.

"It's about the moment," I explain. When she opens her mouth, I barrel on. "Roll with me here, Reese's Pieces. You and I are Caleb and Clarissa—"

"That's not my name," she chimes in.

"—and we are feeling super horny for each other at the moment."

"In this garage?" Reese asks incredulously, a splotchy pink hue dusting her face at the words *super horny*.

"Anywhere. But for the sake of this scenario, Caleb and Marissa—"

"Not my name."

"—are feeling *super horny* in this garage."

She tips her head sideways, a sincere expression of disbelief etching across her features. "Are you seriously telling me I'm going to feel hot and heavy with whatever this is?" She taps her foot against the oil drip pan, making a face when the liquid content ripples from the sudden movement.

"Come on. Roll with me here. Carissa is so fucking turned on by the pan."

"Of course," she deadpans, exhaling a deep, blustery sound. She scrubs her hands down her face before she relents, nodding for me to continue. "Then what?"

"You guys go for it."

Her disbelief doubles. "How?"

"Do you need me to show you a step-by-step?" I ask dryly. "Map out a game plan for you?"

"I'm super fuzzy on the details," Reese answers with a sheepish expression.

"Fine." I motion for her to come closer with my index finger. "Come here."

Thankfully, she doesn't object. She moves in closer until we're standing a few inches apart, facing one another. I'm looking down, and she's got her head tilted far back enough that I hope she's not getting a crick in her neck.

"Now what?" she asks.

"This." I keep our gazes locked as I saunter toward her, matching her pace while she scuttles backward until her back hits the front of my Mustang. She's pressed up against my car's hood with my legs in between hers and my hands firmly on her thighs.

"One problem with this," she whispers, our faces a mere few centimeters apart. My head is craned down tremendously. Maybe *I* should be the one worried about getting a crick in my neck.

The garage feels hotter than usual with each second that ticks by, and I hope she's not burning up in here like I am. Especially in that thick sweater she's wearing.

"Caleb isn't the type to make the first move," she explains, blinking up at me through her spiky lashes.

I peer into her eyes, noticing for the first time the tiny flecks of gold in them before her words register in my brain.

"Then you make the first move," I whisper back, my palms instinctively sliding up her thighs an inch when I realize what I'm doing and keep them still.

"Okay," she says, gently prying herself out from the sandwich she's found herself in. She smooths out a strand of flyaway hair, smiling softly as I turn around to face her.

Leaning my back against the front of my car, I prop my elbows on the steel panel of the hood, watching her intently as she takes her time. She draws in a deep, calming breath, swiveling toward me with a determined nod, her expression resolute. My lips twitch when she rolls her shoulders. Then she strides forward until she's wedged between my legs, her fingers gripping the material of my shirt.

A giggle bursts free as the corners of her mouth slant upward. "I'm a little too short to be able to pull this off," Reese says, pure amusement lighting up her eyes.

"Then straddle me."

"Huh?" Her smile drops as her eyes squint with confusion.

"Hoist yourself up and straddle me." I don't give her the chance to get another word in, wrapping my hands around her waist and pulling her up until she's situated on top of me.

Straddling me.

Her legs are splayed out over my lap with her bent knees flanking both sides of my thighs.

Those dark brown eyes are the widest I've ever seen as she looks down at the lack of space between us. Breathlessly, she brushes the loose strands of hair out of her face, and I get a whiff of her faint and fruity shampoo as a silky lock tickles the side of my jaw. Coconuts. Her hair smells like coconuts.

Something bashful forms on her soft-looking lips, and my attention fixates on the shape of her Cupid's bow. "Do you honestly think this is going to work on Caleb?"

My focus slowly pivots from her mouth to her hopeful gaze.

"Yes," I strangle out in a voice that doesn't sound like my own, my throat feeling painstakingly dry all of a sudden. "The guy has to be a fucking idiot if this doesn't work."

"Thanks," she says shyly. "But what if we're at his fraternity?"

"Do you really," I nearly scoff, "want to lose your virginity at a frat house?" *Or to a dumbass frat bro?*

Her face tints a bright red shade. "You have a point." She slides off of me, taking the heady warmth of her body with her. "I think I got it. I got this." She rubs her hands against her thighs, and that's when I notice for the first time a can of mace hanging on the belt loop of her white pants. Huh. "*I got this.* Thanks, Dane."

"You're welcome," I say gruffly, before throwing out my next guess. "Riza?"

Faintly, her lips sneak up at the corner. "Not even close."

11

REESE

According to Dane, the moment is never going to happen at the art gallery near campus, so I turned down Caleb's suggestion to check out an exhibit there. But it didn't happen at a used bookstore Caleb took me to after I got off of work, either.

The only thing that happened there? We recommended books to each other. At this point, I think *the moment* is hogwash.

"So," Caleb says.

"So," I say back to him, my voice trailing off as we exchange glances. Why. Is. It. So. Awkward?

There's always this lull toward the end of our date. Like we're uncertain of what to say or how to end the night. Or what to do with ourselves.

I know I'm partially to blame for how uncomfortable it is, my mind scrambling to figure out what to say to kill the silence, but I wish Caleb was more of a conversationalist, so I'm not the one leading most of our small conversations that meander and end just as quickly as they begin.

We exchange another glance before I look elsewhere as we walk, wondering what else we can discuss that wasn't already covered during our date earlier.

I don't think we can keep talking about his sisters' gymnastics recital or my sister's upcoming presentation for her business major. There are only so many times we can agree Lili's going to crush it regardless of how good her group partner is. My sister has always been the type to take charge and bulldoze everything until she gets her way, which we're both apparently aware of.

Abruptly, he steps to the side, allowing a mother to push her stroller past us. Gosh, he's so sweet. But it's not like I need the reminder when he's carrying my bulky bag filled to the brim with used books I've purchased and escorting me back to my apartment.

Caleb's eyes flicker to the busted gate, and a wary expression flits across his features. "Have you ever considered moving someplace else?"

"The rent here is super cheap."

Mostly because the building is in dire need of renovations, but also because I'm willing to pay in cash. And I won't sugar-coat it—my apartment is ridiculously small. My theory is that it was a storage room at one point. Lilian believes it was a custo-dial closet.

"And that's why you aren't living with your sister?"

"She's staying at the sorority house?" I remind him. "And I'm not in a sorority?"

"Right." He winces. This is a *very* titillating conversation. A pulse of heavy silence falls over us. "Do you want to join one?"

"*No,*" I blurt, then release a shaky laugh. "No offense."

"None taken," he says with a gentle grin.

"But it's not for me," I stammer and spare him another shaky laugh. I don't want to offend him, seeing as how he actually likes his fraternity. "I can't afford it. I don't think it's beneath me, because—"

"It's okay." Caleb flashes me a reassuring smile. I decide to keep my mouth shut before I say anything else that makes me seem extremely inept.

We trek up the exterior stairs until we're finally on my floor. The silence isn't as unbearable. It's kind of peaceful. Nice. But doubt fills me at the moment because I'm not sure if silence, even though it's comfortable, is supposed to be a good thing or not.

I know I'm not an extrovert by any means, but I always figured that the perfect guy for me would be someone I could easily talk to. Where the conversation doesn't have any interruptions or pauses. Where the conversation just *flows*.

Before I can internally agonize over this some more and wonder if I'm overthinking this, someone walks by us right then. Dark jacket. Hoodie up.

My hands instantly go clammy as I reach for my mace. I hate that it's a gut reaction; that I'm easily rattled. I don't know if I'll ever be able to shake it for the life of me. It's an unsettling thought.

Exhaling deeply, I run through a bunch of mental exercises, reminding myself that I'm okay and trying to unlock my door with shaky fingers all at once.

If Caleb notices me silently freaking out, he doesn't say a word about it. "You know," he finally comments, nodding his chin at my apartment window. "Those bars are dangerous."

"Oh." I swallow thickly. "Well. They kind of make me feel better."

"They can be a fire hazard," he explains, shifting closer to examine the security bars.

"Oh," I repeat, releasing a humorless chuckle. Is this really going to be the conversation we end the date with? "Well, let's just hope the door's still operable if this place were to burn down."

Smiling weakly once I've keyed us in, I flick the light on as we step inside my tiny apartment.

"You live here by yourself?"

"Yeah. Sometimes, Lili crashes with me," I confirm, "but, usually, it's just me."

"You're really close to her," he observes.

"I mean, we are sisters," I joke, trying to alleviate the tension.

He cracks a grin. "Obviously, we'd be close. I mean, you're close with your sisters."

I shut the door behind him, my frayed nerves calming down just a smidge after I triple-check the locks, only for my heart rate to go up again for a different reason when it occurs to me we're both alone in my apartment. I smile nervously as he sets my bag on one of my kitchen barstools. Anticipation flares within me, along with a crapload of jitters.

I know I need to take initiative, so I mentally prepare myself to cross the floor, hook my arms around his neck, and pull him in for a scorching kiss of a lifetime. One that would end up with me yanking him to the bedroom where we do more than just make out.

Instead, I chicken out and ask the one thing that feels safe to bring up. "Water?"

"Sure."

I reach for my filtered pitcher in the fridge and grab two mismatched glasses, filling them halfway before handing him the taller one. Taut silence ensues.

Come on! My brain is both encouraging me and discouraging me. *Make the move!*

Don't embarrass yourself!

Kiss him already!

Ugh. I twist my hair, count to three, and then count to three again. Maybe I'll kiss him on the next count of three. Or maybe I should wait until he's finished with his water to make a move.

"I should get going," Caleb announces after a couple of moments have passed, setting his glass down on the kitchen counter. "I don't want to be out too late."

"Oh." Something inside me wilts as he starts heading toward the door. "Are you sure?"

"That I don't want to be out too late?" He gives me a teasing smile. "I'm pretty sure. I need to pick my sisters up from practice, anyway."

As if I need another reminder of what a kindhearted guy he

is. Ever since his dad got injured at work, Caleb's been stepping up to help his family out. It's another reason why scheduling dates has been tricky for us. He's constantly busy.

"Let me walk you to the door," I suggest, moving from the kitchen to the door in literally seven steps with my short legs. This apartment is ridiculously small.

He turns around the moment he's standing under the door-frame. "I'll see you later?" His curly hair falls over his eyes as he looks at me.

A beat passes. His gaze lingers. My face goes warm. Crap, is *this* supposed to be *the moment*?

It's now or never, my brain urges me. So I take the initiative, my heart pounding out of sheer nervousness.

I rock forward on my toes just as he says, "You have some-thing on your nose."

"Huh—*Ow!*"

"Oh fuck—"

"I'm okay!" I wheeze, clutching my cheek as my face flares with mortification. I walked right into his hand.

"Do you need—"

"I'm fine!" I back away from him before I can somehow injure myself again. "I'll see you later!"

"I'm sorry—"

"It's all good. Don't leave your sisters waiting for you." I shoo him out the door, twist both sets of deadbolts, and triple-check them before I rush to my freezer to grab the frozen peas. Pressing the cold bag against my eye, I let out the weariest sigh I've ever mustered.

"What happened to your eye?" Peyton gasps, nearly dropping her grocery bags. She rushes over to me, her face flooded with genuine worry.

I cringe. Lilian's sorority sisters have been asking me that all day long. After being stopped six times while heading to my morning class alone, I haven't been keeping count since.

"I'll take you up on your offer after all," I tell Lili's room-mate, Karla. She beams in response.

"Great! I'll be right back, Little Vann." She darts upstairs, leaving me alone with Peyton and a couple of their other sorority sisters. I'm a little fuzzy on their names, and I don't have their composite portrait right in front of me to know who's who.

"Jesus." Peyton drops into the seat beside me, leaning in close to examine the bruise. "Who did this?"

"Caleb," I explain, wincing yet again when she gasps. "But it was an accident." Something skeptical tightens the lines of Peyton's face, and I hold back a sigh, launching into a quick recount of what happened the night before. "So you see, it was a total mess."

"Huh," she says, frowning.

"I don't know why it's so hard with him," I admit glumly. Truthfully, if I hadn't nearly blinded myself walking into his finger, I would have written the night off as another uneventful and super awkward date. Even snails move faster than this.

Oddly enough, it honestly felt easier with Dane. But then again, that was all acting. Roleplay. Maybe things aren't supposed to be that easy when it's real.

"Ta-da!" Karla returns, dropping the biggest makeup bag I've ever seen on the coffee table. I swear, every knickknack in the room rattles from the heavy thud. "It's time for me to work my magic."

I SHOULD'VE KNOWN SOMETHING WAS SUSPECT THE MOMENT Karla's makeup brush veered to the other side of my face. She said it was to balance things out. *Ha*.

I still feel like a clown as I hop off the bus and head right, trudging past a bunch of repair shops and mechanics until I find myself standing in front of a nondescript garage.

A sudden knot of uncertainty forms in my stomach as I take in the fact that the door is down. He's… not here. My cheeks blaze as the reality of the situation hits me.

Oh God. I came here for no reason. I should have done what everyone my age does and texted him to save myself all the trouble. *Why did I come here?*

Retrieving my phone, I barely unlock it, when loud clunking noises startle me.

Like a deer in the headlights, I freeze. I barely grasp the fact that the door is rolling up. Or that he's right there, standing just a few yards away. His hair looks extremely tousled, as if the gel has worn off. His white shirt is filthy and stained with grease. His biceps strain against the tight, short sleeves while he wipes the lengths of his fingers with a yellow cloth.

He doesn't notice me gawping at him like a fish. He's too preoccupied with the phone nestled between the side of his head and shoulder.

"Not happening." He glances over at that very moment, and a stunned expression overtakes his face at the sight of me. Without saying goodbye, he shoves his cell into the front pocket of his denim jeans. "What are you doing here?"

Good question. "Your advice," I grind out, "was *awful*."

"Did you just come from your date to tell me this?" He squints at me as he sets the dirty rag down.

"No. I came straight from the sorority house… to tell you this." I self-consciously touch my hair out of habit, then shift my weight onto one leg. "My date was last night."

"I see." He steps around a car I haven't seen before and moves toward me.

"It didn't go well," I tack on wryly.

"*Awful* tends to imply that."

"I didn't know you were a smartass, too."

"Too?" His lips give a sudden twitch. "What else do you know about me?"

"You're tall."

"*Wow.*" He props his elbow on the top of the vehicle and rests his chin against his palm, motioning for me to continue with his other hand. "Go on."

"If you're trying to fish for compliments—"

"*You're tall* is a compliment?" he cuts me off, smirking.

I bristle. "I meant in the sense that I'm not going to give you any compliments, so please don't expect any from me."

His grin only deepens as he tosses a wink. "What else do you know about me?"

"You're kind of crass."

"Kind of?"

"*Very,*" I correct, folding my arms over my chest. "Very blunt. Somewhat abrasive. A bit rough around the edges."

"Yeah, these aren't compliments," he says out loud with an exasperated, yet teasing shake of his head.

"Well, I did warn you," I tell him. "But they're a lot nicer than what I've heard about you."

"That is?"

Shoot. I don't think there's a polite way to tell someone people think they're seedy. *Dangerous.*

"Is this one new?" I gesture to the car he's leaning against.

"Don't change the subject, Reese's Pieces. What have people been saying about me?"

"I mean, does it truly matter in the grand scheme of life what strangers think of you?" I ask, feigning nonchalance.

"Just let me hear it." His playful smile is gone. The atmosphere becomes unnervingly quiet as he straightens his stance.

I feel inexplicably cornered, like a small animal snared in a trap with no way out, under his hardened gaze. My heart beats in my throat. Unease stabs into my chest.

With a hoarse inhalation, I rush out, "They say you're

dangerous; that you fight people for fun. You drink and smoke and gamble and sleep around…"

Dane blinks, and the muscle of his jaw flexes tight. "You don't honestly believe any of that, do you?"

My lack of an immediate response darkens his frown before a perceptible shift occurs in his features. He looks so genuinely… hurt that my guilt feels insurmountable. Regret grabs at my heart. *I never should have brought this up.*

"Why the fuck would I fight people for fun?" He shoots me an incredulous look. "Do you think I had fun getting my ass handed to me that night?"

Okay, he has a point there. "What about the black eye?"

"Some punk tried to screw me over." He exhales sharply, a crease forming between his brows. "I nearly got into an accident because he had his stupid friend try to cut me off while I was driving," he clarifies when something guarded steals my expression. "Look. I won't lie to you. I do get into fights, but it's not for fun. And I do drink every now and then. But I don't gamble and I don't smoke. These aren't my vices."

"Okay." I swallow roughly as I digest his words. "What are your vices?"

"I like to *drive.*"

"Clearly," I say dryly, looking around the garage.

"I like to *race.*"

That *definitely* explains all the sports cars around us.

"I like to *win.*"

"Got it," I say, registering the fact that Dane Kingsley is, to no one's surprise, a huge car buff.

"And…"

"And?"

What else is there to say about cars? That he likes to fill up their tanks, too? Top off their wiper fluid? Change a tire?

"I like to fuck," he says out of nowhere. Shamelessly, too.

My neck catches fire. As does the rest of my body. I stare at him, stunned, unable to process the words that just came out of his mouth.

A slow-breaking smirk materializes across his face. *Oh.* He's messing with me. Unfortunately, I can't think of a response, and my cheeks scorch even hotter underneath his amused attention, my neck feverish when he chuckles.

Rubbing my hands down the material of my sweater, I force myself to meet his eyes. "And where do you race?" I ask, trying but failing to keep my voice even.

"There's this scenic route I take to clear my head," Dane says, and I can't help but notice him dodging my question. "I try to drive it once a week. Leads straight to the beach. You've ever been?"

"There are *many* beaches around here," I remind him, and he husks out a dry laugh.

"I can show you." He lovingly runs his hand over the top of another car. "Need to see if this beauty runs smoothly, anyway."

"Sure," I say with a shrug. It's not like I have any other plans for today.

"Hop in, then." He opens the passenger door for me, which causes the corner of my mouth to sneak up.

He's dangerous, Lilian's voice screams in my head.

And yet it's not the familiar sense of trepidation surging through me. There's a startling, wild thump to my heart as I climb into the passenger side of the coupe.

Immediately, I glance around and take in every little detail that catches my eye.

There's no stereo. A few wires are poking out in the most random spots along the dashboard. The passenger door is missing the lever to crank the window down. The interior reeks of gasoline, so rich and strong that I wonder if I'll get high off of it—if that's even possible.

Before long, he slides into the driver's seat. I peek over to watch him turn the ignition on. Abruptly, the entire vehicle rumbles beneath me as it comes to life, barely outmatched by the rush of adrenaline coursing through my every vein.

"Ready?"

"Yeah," I mumble, checking once again to make sure my seatbelt is secured. It's only a lap belt. Some part of me is concerned about what would happen if we were to get into an accident, but otherwise, I'm not nervous at all.

Planting his hand on the back of my seat, he expertly throws the car in reverse and backs out onto the driveway. For a moment, I'm breathless as unexpected, *unanticipated* excitement sparks inside me like a lit flare. It takes me several seconds to tear my gaze away from him and his calm and casual posture.

"I'll be right back." Leaving me alone in his idling muscle car, he goes to deal with locking his garage up. I observe the dashboard out of curiosity, instantaneously distracted when I see him extend his arm up in my periphery. His triceps dimple his back while he pulls the garage door down.

Inexplicably, my neck burns.

The moment he returns, he gives me a look as if he's waiting for me to change my mind. When I don't say anything, he shifts a lever into first gear. "Ready to see the scenic route?"

Wordlessly, I nod. It's all I can manage. I'm just too excited. Too buzzy with anticipation over what awaits us.

The edges of his lips pull up into something playful. "I can show you where I go to fuck, too—"

"Oh my God," I hiss out, mortification crashing over me like ocean waves. "Just drive."

12

DANE

From the periphery of my vision, I can see brown hair billowing wildly as the car accelerates faster while we coast down the winding street.

In the distance, a golden sunset unfurls across an orange sky. Blue ocean waves break against the sparkling sand. Palm trees sway along the road. Goddamn, it's beautiful. Heaven. It's the most scenic route I've ever driven across.

Reese clearly thinks so, too. She's spent the last few minutes recording the coastline with her phone.

"What are you doing?" I ask when I realize she's aimed her camera at me.

"It's the golden hour," she explains, tapping on her screen to take a selfie. "Everyone always looks good during the golden hour."

I want to scoff at the ludicrous statement, but the hazy golden sunlight bouncing off her skin makes her look softer. *Warmer*.

"Even with your messy hair?" I tease.

"Especially with my messy hair," she replies without missing a beat.

A rare, gentle smile touches her lips as she leans over and

holds her cell up. Then she crosses her eyes while she prepares for another selfie—with me in the background. My mouth slants into a grimace right as the photo is captured.

She barely conceals her laugh. "It won't hurt to smile."

Disgruntled, I mutter, "Do you take pictures of everything you do?"

That gentle smile makes a reappearance. This time, lasting twice as long. "Just the things I want to remember."

I sigh before mustering up something half-hearted, and Reese snorts.

"Never mind," she murmurs. "It *does* hurt you to smile."

My smile drops. "I don't like having my picture taken."

"Then I won't—"

"But for you," I begin and immediately pause, frowning. Then, after a hasty moment of silent deliberation, I grumble, "I won't mind. Just don't post it online."

"Not even on my Finsta?"

"What the fuck is a Finsta?"

"Instagram. Well, *fake* Instagram," she rambles. "It's reserved for your close friends. My sister and her sorority sisters all have one. Mine's mostly pictures of onion rings."

My brow rises. "Onion rings?"

"Yeah, onion rings. And memes. *And* this one alleycat I see when I take the trash out at my apartment, but that's because he is the chunkiest cat I've ever seen—"

"You're losing me, Reese's Pieces," I cut in. "Why don't you just post 'em on your real one?"

"The aesthetics." Am I supposed to understand what she means by that? I don't even use social media. "And because people I'm not close to follow me on that one."

"Why? What's the point? Just stop letting them follow you."

"They're following me for school stuff, usually," she explains. "And some of the people I work with will reach out to me there when they need someone to cover their shifts."

"People don't know how to text anymore?" I ask dryly. "What do you post on your real one?"

"Books. Trees. Low-angled shots of buildings. I was really into cameras when I was in high school, but they're expensive. And don't get me started on the lenses."

Now it's starting to make a lot of sense why she keeps taking pictures. "Are you a photography major?"

"Nope. I'm going into civil engineering." I almost turn to look at her in surprise. "You?"

I rake my hand through my hair, then drum my fingers along the top of the steering wheel. "Finance."

"*Finance*?" She drops her phone into her lap and swivels in her seat to face me. "Really?"

Guess surprising each other is the theme today. "You don't see someone like me with a knack for numbers?"

"That's not what I meant," she stammers. "I would have assumed you were studying mechanical engineering."

"Because of the cars?"

"Well, *yeah*." She ducks her head and picks up her phone.

A low chuckle escapes me. "Sorry to disappoint you, then."

"I can't picture you in a finance class."

"Neither can I." My words are punctuated with a loud snort that draws her attention.

"You don't show up to class?" Reese gasps, scandalized like the good girl I bet—*know*—she is.

"I'll show up for midterms and finals," I explain, "but otherwise, I don't give a shit."

I don't have to glance her way to know she's frowning, clearly bothered.

"Tuition is expensive."

My shoulder hitches. "I'm not the one getting billed for it."

She's silent for a moment. Her voice is gentler when she asks, "If college isn't for you, then why don't you drop out?"

"It gets my dad off my back and me out of the picture." I lift a hand in a casual shrug. And because I'm not in the mood to be all touchy-feely with my feelings, I hike my chin toward a food truck parked nearby. "They might have some onion rings for your fiesta."

"Finsta."

"*THIS* IS WHAT YOU NORMALLY DO?" REESE ASKS AS SHE FALLS INTO step beside me, enjoying her sprinkled cone. Behind her, the sun dips toward the horizon, streaking the sky in various shades of red, orange, and pink. It's no golden hour, but it looks like something out of a movie.

"I usually don't make any stops," I tell her.

"Shame." She spreads her arms out and tilts her head back. "Ice cream on the beach is a nice way to end the day."

"We're in the last week of October."

"So?" She gives me a tiny shrug. "You're missing out, Dane."

"All right then," I reply, arching a brow. "Give me a lick."

"What?" She slides away from me. "Go back and get your own."

"Let me see what I'm missing out on."

"Again, buy your own cone."

"I only want a lick," I point out. "Not the entire damn thing."

She squints at me for a beat before she slowly drags her tongue across the side of her ice cream scoop.

I gawk at her, halting mid-stride. It's an innocent gesture on her end. My mind refuses to see it that way. I force myself to think about cars and the set of custom rims I've ordered coming in the mail.

"No," Reese says, sticking her tongue out at me before she takes another languid lick of her cone. The set of rims is nonexistent in my head. Then, without warning, she darts off, kicking sand in the process.

I'm still staring at her, bewildered, as I shake myself out of my stupor.

My heart is thumping like it does when my bike accelerates across an empty stretch of road and makes me feel like I'm flying.

I'm just fucking horny, I tell myself. *I need to get laid.*

I need to get laid before I think of all the things sweet little Reese's Pieces can do to me with that tongue of hers.

Too fucking late.

I'm already picturing those wide eyes looking up at me as her lips wrap around my cock and suck me off. My blood rushes south. My dick seems to enjoy the idea a little too much that I have to grit my teeth and wait for my fucking erection to go the fuck away.

"I thought you liked to race!" Reese shouts from where she stands farther down the beach. "And I thought you liked to win!"

Fucking hell, I'm more turned on than ever as she sticks her tongue out at me again.

"I'm giving you three seconds."

"Three seconds for what?"

"For a head start before I'm coming for you."

She tilts her head.

"One."

She turns around and breaks off into a sprint.

"Two."

"Suck it!" she cackles with glee.

"Three."

Then I haul ass as I take off sprinting, my longer legs allowing me to close the distance between us so quickly that she's squealing with laughter when I hook my arm around her waist and lift her into the air.

"All right, all right! Here!"

I don't see it coming until she smushes sprinkled vanilla into my face. I stare at her in bewilderment yet again while she hoots with unbridled glee. There's a low, husky note to her laughter. Not the kind of laugh I'd expect from her.

"Happy?" she giggles, pulling the cone away from me.

I slowly lick the melted ice cream off of my mouth as she wriggles in my embrace, causing my dick to stir again.

"Pretty good," I drawl.

"Want another taste?" She threatens me with her cone.

"I think *you* should have it." Before she can make do with her promises, I rub my sticky ice-cream-coated jaw against her cheek and venture south. A shriek rips up her throat. "Payback's a bitch, huh?"

The urge to drag the flat of my tongue against her neck is so damn strong as I nose my way down the collar of her sweater, smearing the sticky ice cream from my face onto her soft skin, that I deserve a medal for my willpower to fucking behave right now.

"W-wait!" Her body goes rigid in my arms as her cone slips from her hand, and she elbows me roughly to pull herself out of my grasp. She lands unceremoniously on her feet, almost toppling over from the graceless drop. Her fingers clutch the space just below her neck.

"Reese—"

"C-Can you take me home?" Her eyes grow wide with panic. "*P-Please?*"

13

REESE

THE DRIVE BACK TO MY APARTMENT IS AWKWARD AND TENSE. I almost want to duck and roll out of the muscle car and walk home on foot, but one glance at the complicated door handle lets me know I'm going to have trouble trying to open it again.

Instead, I settle for gnawing on my bottom lip. I don't know what's worse. The fact that I had a mini panic attack, the fact that I'm genuinely embarrassed about my scar being seen in broad daylight, or the fact that Dane Kingsley was there to witness it.

"This never happened," I say, my words a scratch above a whisper.

I know it's not healthy to live in denial, but it's free. Not only that, it's been the best coping mechanism for me. Pretending nothing's wrong has been the best course of action because I don't have to think about it, and more importantly, it gets people off my back.

To them, you're either one hundred percent better or you're not. And when they think I'm not fine, they believe I'm broken. I'm not in a bad place as I was two years ago. I'm a good seventy or eighty percent most of the time these days. It hasn't dipped under sixty since I left the state of New Mexico behind me.

When people want me to talk about the night I was attacked,

it truly digs up old wounds and ruins the semblance of a new normal I've created for myself. I appreciate the concern, but I can't move on with my life if people keep expecting me to revisit the past.

"What never happened?" Dane asks after a beat, voice casual.

The tension seeps out of my shoulders. I sigh with relief. Some part of me expected him not to let this go, given how stubborn he's proven to be.

"Reese's Pieces," he says, and I'm still too embarrassed to look at him. I keep my attention elsewhere, peering intently at the side-view mirror beside me. "There's nothing wrong with scars."

"Dane."

"I got plenty."

That gets me to glance his way. Genuine worry knits my brow together and sends my heart to a skidding halt. "That doesn't make me feel better. It only makes me more concerned."

Without taking his eyes off the road, he snickers. "Are you worried about me, Reese?"

"I am," I answer truthfully.

"If it makes you feel better, it's only when some fucker takes me by surprise—"

"That does *not* make me feel better," I gasp hotly.

"—or when they gang up on me."

I drag in a deep breath as I gape at him. "That," I strangle out, "does not make me feel better at all."

He chuckles. "I'm just saying, I got plenty of them."

"Yeah, but…"

"But what?"

Giving him a slow perusal, I don't see any scars on his body —on any inch of his exposed skin—at the very moment. There's nothing I can make out besides how toned and muscular his arms are underneath the dim streetlight. My neck prickles with sudden heat.

"I'm going to have to take my shirt off—"

"Excuse me?" I gasp, and my neck heats even more.

"—if you want to see my scars."

"Oh." My face is scorching hot with so much embarrassment that I almost duck my head to avert my gaze. I clear my throat. A flutter of nerves remains low in my belly. "I'm fine. You don't have to take off your shirt. And I've already seen your scars… kind of."

"When?"

"The night I helped you."

"You still owe me dinner for that," Dane says, his expression serious. "Can't believe you made me take my shirt off without buying me dinner first."

Bewildered, I gawp at him again, watching a wolfish grin tug at the edges of his lips. "You want me to take you out to dinner?"

"What? Are you afraid to be seen out in public with me?"

"I was literally just at the beach with you," I remind him.

"It's all right, Reese." He shakes his head, clutching his chest as if he's been wounded. "If you're afraid to be seen out in public with me—"

"I'm not afraid to be seen out in public with you," I protest, and his smirk widens.

"Then you plan on taking me out to dinner tomorrow?"

I stare at him, blinking slowly. *Did he just hoodwink me?* Against my better judgment, I say, "I'm free next Saturday if you want to get sushi."

"When you say sushi," Dane cuts in, "do you mean high-grade sushi or mediocre sushi?"

"Reasonably priced sushi."

He expels a snort. "What is reasonably priced sushi to you? Because I'm not risking food poisoning from gas station sushi."

I make an offended noise. Is he for real? "Who would eat gas station sushi? *I* would not subject us to that."

"Wouldn't you?"

I glare as he rumbles with laughter, a sound so warm and rich that it's downright lethal. I'm so genuinely floored by the heady notes and the way his mouth tips up at the corners that my heart gives a soft flutter.

"Okay," he says. "I'll pick you up next Saturday, and you can point out which gas station—"

I reach over to poke him in the ribs.

"Point out which *restaurant,*" he amends, "you want to go to. And"—he pulls up to the curb beside my building and kills the engine—"put on something you want to wear. You don't have to hide your scar around me."

With that, he looks directly at me, and the sincerity in his gaze causes my chest to squeeze tight in a wordless answer.

"I…" I bite my bottom lip as I struggle to open the passenger door. *The damn pesky handle.* "Thank you for driving me home."

"I mean it, Reese. You don't have to hide yourself from me."

My cheeks go warm while I step out into the chilly autumn night, and I offer him a reluctant nod. "Bye, Dane. Thanks for everything." Then I frown when I realize he's getting out as well. "Where are you going?"

"I'm going to walk you back to your apartment."

"Really? Why?"

"What do you mean why?" A small divot forms between his brows. "Have you seen the area you live in?"

Despite my gratefulness for his offer, I huff out a scoff as I start walking toward my place. Is there a sign on my back telling people to give me crap about where I'm living?

"Well, where do you live that's so fancy?" I ask him. "Antarctica?"

His lips quirk into a thoroughly amused smirk. "Las Marinas."

Oh God, that's fancy. No, that's *beyond* fancy. Las Marinas is a wealthy, affluent beach town, one I've only taken the bus to once with Lili during the summer before my freshman year started. I know how expensive that place is. Coffee in that city is in the double digits.

"It's not as nice as Las Marinas," I hedge, "but it's not that bad here. But, um, thanks for the concern."

"No problem, Reese."

As we climb up the stairs, I find myself really, really, *really* hyperaware of him and the proximity of his body to mine. The sway of his arm. The flex of his biceps. The gentle rise and fall of his strong chest with his every breath.

Peeking up, I lock eyes with him, instantaneously aware of the fact he caught me stealing glances. For some reason, I can't look away. A lump begins to take shape in my throat with each second that passes while I hold his gaze.

"Thanks again," I whisper. "For everything today."

"It's no problem." His mouth slants up at the corner. "I mean it, Reese. You don't have to hide yourself from me."

I break eye contact and glance at my shoes, stiffly bobbing my head as I reach for my keys. "I got it."

"I mean it."

"I know." With a weak smile, I enter my apartment and quickly turn to face him. He remains standing on the other side of the doorway, and my pulse rushes in my ears when it occurs to me that I don't want to stop hanging out with him. Not yet. Besides my freakout... *today's been one of the nicest days I've had in, well, forever.*

Before I can say anything, Dane hikes his chin. "I'll see you Saturday for gas station sushi."

"Uh-huh." Rolling my eyes ever so slowly, I bite back my amusement when I catch him smirking. "Can't wait for all the gas station sushi we'll be having."

His grin widens. My breath is momentarily arrested. "See ya then, Reese." With a final nod, he shoves his hands into his pockets and makes his departure.

Watching him go, I wait for him to disappear down the stairs before I shut the door and try to make sense of my wildly beating heart.

DANE

"Tsk, tsk, tsk, tsk, tsk." I pause for dramatic effect. "*Tsk*."

Reese lifts her head to glare witheringly at me. "It's *cold*, Kingsley. It's the perfect weather for a sweater."

I don't say a word as she slides into my Mustang's passenger seat; not until she's buckled up, at least. "If you're that cold, pants would be more suitable. Wouldn't you agree?"

Her attention drops to her plaid skirt, which shows off her bare legs. Before her head even whips toward her apartment, my car pulls away from the curb.

My mouth slips into a smirk as she settles in. "So, where are we getting gas station sushi?"

She makes a show of rolling her eyes. "There's a revolving sushi place about thirty minutes from here. I already put us on the waiting list." She shakes her phone. "When we get there, we don't have to wait too long to be seated."

"You're very efficient."

"Thanks?" Reese laughs.

"It's either that or you're trying to end this as quickly as possible. Either way, my ego's hurt, Reese's Pieces."

"It is?" she stammers, sounding so damn worried it's cute.

"And here I was," I drawl, "looking forward to spending

hours in line with you for gas station quality sushi. Isn't that supposed to be part of the experience? You're depriving us of the experience."

Her head falls into her hands as she groans. "Do you really think I'd risk the both of us getting food poisoning?"

I crack a grin.

"Have you ever had gas station sushi?" she asks me. "Because you are very fixated on it."

"I've tried gas station cheese sticks—"

"Cheese sticks?" she echoes. "Do you mean mozzarella sticks?"

"That."

Disbelief tightens her features. "How do you not know what they are?"

"Considering that was the first and last time I've ever tried *mozzarella* sticks," I begin, voice deadpan, "can you blame me?"

She barely manages to stifle her snort. "I'm blaming you for getting them at a gas station."

"Hey, when you're starving and it's late as hell, those greasy little cheese sticks look mighty damn delicious."

"I'm assuming appearances were deceiving here," Reese mutters, resting her hands on her lap, "considering that was the only time you've had it. How bad was it?"

"To tell you the truth," I say slowly, "it was pretty good. I knew I had to quit while I was ahead before I became addicted. Gotta think about my arteries, you know?"

Reese quirks a brow. "Now the actual truth."

A beat passes. I lift a shoulder in an easygoing shrug. "My dumbass puked it all up into a bush."

She lets out a soft moan, squeezing her eyes shut in horror. "Oh my God, don't mention puke before we eat."

A slight smirk comes to my mouth. "Hey, you asked me for the truth." I pause. "Now that I think about it, it does look like the plate of matcha they give us."

"Matcha?"

"That green paste?" I say with a straight face.

"Wasabi?" Reese clarifies with a gasp. "Don't tell me you actually believe it's—Oh. Ha, ha," she deadpans. "You're just messing with me."

"Guilty as charged."

She pokes my shoulder, instinctively holding her hands up to defend herself.

I pretend to reach over to get her back—moving my arm so exasperatingly slowly that she braces for impact—only to mess with my stereo system instead, cranking up the volume.

She waits. I'm the picture of innocence as I keep my attention trained on the road ahead. As much as I'd like to mess around, I want to get to the restaurant in one piece. And it's fun making her squirm a little.

Soon, after she knows I won't try anything, she's nosying her way through all the items stored in the glove compartment and center console.

"If you're going to rob me," I tease, "start with the twenty dollars I stashed in one of the CD cases."

"Your car is surprisingly clean," she observes as she flips through the manual book for my car.

"Surprisingly?" I feign offense. Unlike Marco, I actually stay on top of keeping my vehicles clean. I don't want to risk anything jamming the brakes.

"I've seen some rooms at a frat house," she explains, and my grip immediately tightens around the steering wheel, my stomach souring at the idea of sweet Reese having her first time at a fucking frat house with fucking Blue Balls.

It's the least classy place for a girl like Reese.

"You have?" I clip out. Jesus fucking Christ, my chest winds up as a lump lodges in my throat. I release a sharp exhalation and force my shoulders to casually relax.

"Y-yeah. My sister dragged me to one of their parties last year..." Her expression becomes weary and guarded in the corner of my eye. "I'm not really the partying type."

"Got it," I say, and the genuine relief I'm feeling right now has me uncertain if I'm happy she hasn't slept with fucking Blue Balls at his frat house or if she hasn't slept with him, period.

I choose not to answer that.

When we get to the sushi place, there's a sizable crowd waiting outside the door. The lot's full, so I end up leaving my car in the parking structure a block away. Then I wave Reese off when she tries to go halfsies on the all-day pass.

"Don't worry about it. You'll be paying for all the grocery store sushi, anyway."

She shoots me a withering look as we head to the restaurant on foot. "Actually—"

"No." I gape at her. "Don't tell me you've—"

"Hear me out—"

"Good Lord, Reese's Pieces," I gasp theatrically. "Am I about to find out this place gets its fish from a pet store?"

"Just—A pet store?" she splutters, a look of horror flashing across her slender face.

"Am I about to eat someone's pet fishy?"

"Just hear me out," she protests with a pointed stare. "I've had grocery store sushi before—"

"And yet you judge me for my gas station cheese sticks."

"—from a Japanese market," she finishes. "They make it fresh every morning."

"Or so they say."

"They do," she protests, folding her arms across her chest. "They even include a timestamp on the label with the time they were made—"

"Or so they say," I repeat with a sly grin.

"*Dane*," she grunts, her dark eyes narrowed. "It was surprisingly good."

"The fact that you chose to mention *surprisingly*—"

"It was good," she clarifies with a grumpy expression, cutting me off. "Really good for the price I paid."

She squarely meets my gaze, silently challenging me to

respond. A smug smile tugs at my lips, which makes her eyes narrow.

"I'll take your word for it."

With a sigh, she thumbs the high neckline of her sweater. Surprise registers across her face when I reach for the door and open it for her.

"What? I can be chivalrous."

"Thank you." She beams up at me, and I find myself staring at the dip of her Cupid's bow for a beat too long.

Abruptly, I force myself to think about anything else but her while she checks in with the hostess. I manage to go five seconds before she looks my way, and when I'm hit with the sweet impact of her smile, the world quiets. The restaurant fades.

It's just her.

My throat works with a rough swallow, and I'm granted a short reprieve when the hostess steps around the podium and shows us to our booth.

Before long, we're seated across from each other. I don't miss the fact that she sneaks a picture of me, even though I'm not cheesing for the camera.

Gesturing to the conveyor belt, I mutter, "I think I saw that one at a pet store last week."

Her nose wrinkles as she sets her phone face down. "At least this beats gas station sushi."

I chuckle under my breath. "So, how did you find this place?"

Suspicion gathers behind her dark eyes. "If this is your attempt to segue into another joke about a pet store—"

"Not at all." I make an X motion near my heart.

"Oh. Well," she begins, "my sister likes to go out."

"And you don't?" I guess. It's not hard to imagine that she's more of the homebody type. Everything about her screams introvert.

She grabs a plate and hesitates for a contemplative moment. "Not as often as she does."

"No shame in that," I say with a shrug.

"Really?"

"You think my ass enjoys being around people?"

Chewing on her bottom lip, she doesn't say anything for several seconds. "Do you find them exhausting, too?"

"*You* find people exhausting?" I grab the first plate of eel rolls I see and make a silent prayer to my maker that I won't die from this. "I thought nice girls like everybody."

"You can be nice and still find people... intimidating." She flushes. "I was never really a social butterfly like Lili."

"Lili's your sister?"

"Mmhmm. Sometimes, I wish I was more like her. She just... *flourishes* in any situation she finds herself in. Meanwhile, I..." Lost in thought, she tugs on the front of her tight sweater absentmindedly.

"Reese."

Her eyes sharpen with focus. Her cheeks blossom pink. Her fingers go to the purple star-shaped clip keeping her chestnut hair out of her face.

"You don't have to—"

"Hide..." She trails off, wetting her bottom lip with her tongue, and I catch myself staring again.

Jesus fucking Christ, is now really the time to check her out while she's clearly under duress?

"I mean it," I say gruffly, forcing myself to look directly into her eyes while I mentally kick myself in the ass. "I never want you to feel like you'd have to hide yourself from me. I want you to feel..." *Safe with me.*

"To feel?" she prompts, blinking her spiky lashes.

"To feel like you can be yourself without ever worrying that I'd judge you," I tell her. "Because I'm the last person on this planet who would ever give you shit about a scar when I've"—I tap at a spot near my ear—"got a million of them."

Her gaze goes to my finger, and the genuine concern registering across her face has my chest coiling tight. "It doesn't make me feel better—"

"You don't find them charming?" I ask with a wink.

"Almost every night since we've met, I go to bed worried about you," she admits, her voice so faint that I almost don't hear her over what sounds like K-pop playing overhead.

There she goes again, telling me she worries about me. The pressure settling in my chest feels even tighter.

"You don't have to worry a thing about me, Fun Sized," I respond.

"Why wouldn't I?" she whispers, gazing up at me through her lashes. "I care about you."

Fucking hell. Her sincerity is insurmountable. Overwhelming. All too much. My throat becomes stuck; unable to sound a single word.

"Please don't tell me that the big bad car guy is too good for that," she says softly, her lips curved slightly in a teasing smile. I can't stop staring at her as my heart thumps—a little too hard for my fucking taste.

Too good for you, too good for you, too good for you. The words flicker over her head like a broken stoplight. Not that I need the damn reminder. Everything about her practically screams she can do better than the likes of me.

"Do I have something on my face?" she asks, reaching for a napkin.

"You," I say, and my voice sounds a bit too rough for my liking, "don't have to worry a thing about me. Really. It's almost insulting."

"Insulting?" she echoes.

"I can handle myself just fine, Reese's Pieces," I say, picking up my drink. "I've made it this far in life, haven't I?" Her brows crash together in what appears to be an earnest protest, so I quickly tip my head toward the conveyor belt. "Does that look like a pet goldfish to you?"

She's quiet again. She keeps her focus on me for a drawn-out beat, and I start to feel itchy while I remain trapped underneath her keen, observant gaze.

"You have nothing to be concerned over," I reiterate. "I'm a big boy. I can handle fucking anything."

"Anything?" she echoes.

"Anything." For emphasis, I shoot her an easygoing grin while I lean back in my seat.

"Anything except having someone care about you," she says, and I'm momentarily blindsided. I don't know how to respond to her comment. Or the adorable little smirk she flashes back at me.

With a rough cough, I point to a sushi plate on the conveyor belt. "You think they get them from the pet store while they're still alive or do they go for the cheaper ones that have already croaked?"

She sighs, shaking her head in exasperation. Then she spares me a tiny smile. "Well, obviously the croaked ones. Think about the profit margins."

"Gotta offset the cost of avocados, right?"

Her lips shape into a bigger grin. "Totally."

15

REESE

After sushi, we're roaming around the city aimlessly. There's no destination in mind. It's as if neither of us wants the day to end yet. Well, I don't. It's oddly nice walking around with him. I haven't felt this comfortable around people—sans Lilian—in ages.

The sun is setting; the sky is lit in a gorgeous rosy hue I want to take a picture of. Or maybe even capture the cityscape surrounding us, a mismatch of architecture from sleek skyscrapers to mid-century buildings. In the distance, I can make out the pockets of Spanish mission revival homes sprinkled across the hills.

I'm about to reach for my phone when Dane breaks the pleasant silence between us. "Hey, look, it's the least sexy place on the planet."

Following his line of sight, my gaze lands on an art museum, and I smother my snort. "Oh. I've been there before."

"Of course," he deadpans, his words heavy with a tease.

"I think they have a new exhibit," I add, turning to face him. I don't miss the half-smile at the corner of his lips. Or the amused gleam materializing behind his eyes.

"You think?" He lifts a brow. "You didn't go there with Blue Balls?"

"I haven't been there since my first semester," I explain, "when I was taking art."

"You took art?"

"Emphasis on took."

"Why'd you stop?" There's a hint of curiosity threaded in his voice.

Hesitation courses through my bloodstream. I can only speak for myself when I say that there are elements of shame you carry with you when you grow up in poverty, something I'm ashamed I still carry with me. You don't want to talk about being poor. You don't want to address it at all.

"It's so expensive," I admit, swallowing nervously. "All the materials you need to buy. And this was for an intro class, mind you. I only took it when I was still considering a minor in the art field, but that's because photography is only offered through the art program."

I sheepishly rub my hands against my skirt. Dane doesn't want to hear this. He's probably thinking about the extremely loud muscle car that just gunned past us and its many shiny parts, so my words dwindle as I trail off and glance elsewhere.

"You're one of those artsy shy girls?" Dane asks, and my focus pivots back to him. He's so much taller that he always has to look down while talking to me. I regret not wearing heels. *Or being capable of walking in them without looking like a newborn baby deer trying to cross frozen water.*

"Um, I'm no artist," I admit with a soft laugh. "Not in the traditional sense. If our lives depend on me painting the next Mona Lisa, we're so screwed."

"What about finger painting?" he teases.

I fight my laugh. "*Beyond* screwed."

"At least tell me you can mix colors."

"Oh, I got an A on that," I say, beaming.

"Shit, really?" He folds his arms. "You got graded on *mixing* colors?"

"Color theory," I explain. "It's an intro class."

"In college?"

"In college," I confirm.

"At Belford?" he asks, surprised.

"Yes, Dane," I say with a half-smile. "At Belford."

"Shit. For real?" Disbelief furrows his eyebrows. "Are you telling me I've been taking hard-ass classes for economics and information systems when I could have been finger painting colors like a preschooler for an easy A?"

I roll my eyes. "That class was actually a lot harder than I thought it would be."

"How do you screw up mixing colors?" he asks. "Are you colorblind?"

"No, I'm not colorblind. It's... You have to present your work." I blow out a breath, feeling my cheeks bloom with heat. "All of them. In front of the class. For critique and peer review from your classmates."

Dane frowns. "All right, whose ass do I have to kick for you? Point them all out to me on Monday—"

"Okay, cool your jets," I say, suppressing the twitch to the edge of my lips. "Nobody was tearing me down for my work, even though I wouldn't blame them if they did—"

"I would," he cuts in, his expression oddly fierce and protective.

"Constructive criticism is a good thing," I say softly. "It's always good to know what your strengths and weaknesses are, so you can work on them."

"Sometimes, things are perfect the way they are," he replies immediately, his gaze landing on my face. "And you shouldn't mess with perfection."

My heart pounds with each waking second that follows, and my breath collects in my lungs when he shifts imperceptibly closer.

"Come on." He tips his head. "Let's go check out the unsexiest place on the planet."

And because I don't want to stop hanging out with him, I agree.

The instant we're inside, I'm easily distracted by the interior design of the building. The lobby, as far as the eye can see, is a subtle balance of glitzy and sleek, with bold geometric shapes, sharp lines, and vibrant colors.

Right as I'm about to snap a photo, Dane sidles over with admission tickets in his hands. My mouth parts in protest.

"You paid for dinner," he says, and then he waltzes off before I can object and remind him he's the one who left a huge whopping tip on the table that will *definitely* make our waiter's day.

With a muted sigh, I quickly trail after him.

Apparently, we missed the last tour for the day by twelve minutes, which Dane doesn't seem bothered about. But we're given free rein to check out the exhibits before the museum closes in an hour, which I don't mind since I always like to examine pieces at my own pace.

I take the NO PHOTOGRAPHY signs seriously or else I would have captured a picture of Dane, with his plain white tee, dark jeans, scuffed black boots, and gelled-back hair, looking extremely out of place in the room we're in right now. Paintings from the Baroque period hang on every wall, shrouding us in muted shades of green and pink, so it's no surprise he stands out.

"All right, I take it back," Dane says, his attention going over my shoulder. I whip around and spot a nude oil painting of a woman spread demurely across a chaise baroque lounge chair. "Forgot museums can have artsy-fartsy porn in them."

"*Porn*?" I splutter, offering him a disbelieving stare.

"You don't think people back then looked at this and went, *oh yeah, that's the stuff,* while cranking one out?" Dane arches a brow, and bewilderment scorches a path across my cheeks and leaves me stunned. "Come on, Snack Size. This has to be from the time when *ankles* were scandalous. Or before that? And it's not like they had the internet at their fingertips." He shrugs. "Somewhere out there are a bunch of buried skeletons that have, once upon a time, seen this painting and were like—"

"Is sex always on your mind?" I blurt.

"Look at her face," he wheedles, ignoring the words that just rolled off of my tongue. I should probably be grateful for that. I don't think I could handle hearing what he has to say. Not without inventing a new hue of red to blush with. "Are those *do me eyes* or what?"

"Do me *what*?"

He puts his hands on my shoulders and spins me toward the painting, and my body goes heavy like a stone when he leans in to whisper into my ear, "Look at those eyes."

I would if I weren't trembling right now, my whole frame seized with panic. The muscles of his chest go taut against my spine. Within a heartbeat, he whirls me around so that we're facing each other. Concern laces his features while his frost-colored eyes scan me from head to toe, and his grip gentles.

"Reese?" he murmurs.

The back of my throat prickles with hot tears as I struggle for breath and gasp, "Sorry, sorry, I'm—"

"Was that how he did it?" The humor in his voice is long gone. It's startlingly eerie. An even calm I'd hyper-fixate over on any other occasion. Just not while I'm struggling to remain poised; desperate to regain a normal heart rate. "The guy who attacked you?"

"What about her eyes?" I choke out, slightly flinching when I see a swift movement from the edge of my periphery, only to freeze again for an entirely different reason. Some part of me barely registers the fact that his bruised knuckle is carefully brushing against my cheekbone, moving so painstakingly slowly as he wipes away a tear tracking down my cheek.

For a moment, I almost lean into his hand. I stop myself just in time, my eyelashes fluttering as I try to gather my wits.

"Oh, Reese," he breathes, a deep juxtaposition to the raw anger I can feel vibrating off of him. His touch remains so faint, so *featherlight*, that it's surreal. This is the bad guy my sister warned me to stay away from?

"It's okay," I whisper back, sniffling hard as I pull away from him, hugging my arms tightly to my chest.

"This fuckhead is number one on my list of people to beat up."

"It concerns me you have a list of people to beat up," I reply crisply, furrowing my brows.

"Be a little less concerned," he tells me. "I only made it up just now, and there are only two people on it."

"Two people?" I peer at him through my wet lashes, and confusion streams through my chest. "Who's the second person?"

"Whoever dissed your work in your fucking intro art class," he responds without missing a beat.

I snort before I can help myself, my shoulders shaking as I try to stifle my laughter. "Nobody dissed my artwork. I'm not a fan of public speaking. I… freeze easily when all eyes are on me. I don't like attention. And it's really hard to avoid it when… you know."

His gaze flicks to my neck for a split second before it pivots back to my face. "Point me out to everybody who makes you feel uncomfortable—"

"We are *not* adding to the list." I pause, considering. "The list shouldn't even exist."

An exasperated groan breaks free from him. "I hate the fucker who did this to you," he says, furrowing his dark brows. "The fucker's lucky I didn't know you then—"

"Or else you'd be hurt, too?" I try to joke, but my voice comes out flat.

"I hate the fucker who did this to you," he repeats, and

there's a visible tightness to his jaw as he levels a glare over my head.

"So does my sister," I say lightly, trying my best to liven the mood.

"Good," Dane grunts. "As she should. I would have spent my free time hunting him down. And believe me, I had plenty of it."

I suddenly remember what Lilian had said about Dane nearly being kicked out of school. "Free time?"

"Leave of absence," he clarifies, after a moment's hesitation.

I'm worried I might be intruding, and I know that it's not my place to ask, but my curiosity gets the better of me. "What did you do during that time?" My voice is gentle as I dry my cheek with the heel of my palm.

His focus remains on my hand, and visible concern creases his forehead. "I worked on cars. What else?"

A muted snort escapes me. "And go to concerts, right?"

"With musicians who can carry a tune," he deadpans.

My lips twist. "That's not a nice thing to say."

"Reese, if you want me to buy you VIP tickets to their next show here—"

"*No!*"

He cracks a grin. "That's not a nice thing to say," he mimics. "Here I am, being thoughtful by getting you some tickets to a band you apparently like—"

"Oh, hush," I say.

He winks. "Look at us, finally having something in common," Dane teases, and I squint at him. "Neither of us wants front-row tickets to see that band again."

"This is such a weird thing to bond over," I admit with a quiet laugh. Then I pause as I consider his words. "We don't have much in common."

"You don't think I also *love* wearing sweaters while it's sweltering hot outside?" Dane asks innocently, his mouth twitching with a hint of a smile. I have to admit, I like it when he smiles. It softens his face tremendously. Even though it's barely there, something that's gone in the blink of an eye.

"Do you think we would have been aware of each other's existence under any other circumstances?" I ask because I don't want to phrase it as: *Would you have even talked to me otherwise if I never helped you in the alleyway of The Little Roast?*

His Adam's apple bobs reflexively. His gaze locks with mine and holds strong. "I'm glad you crashed into my life, Reese's Snack Mix—"

"Did you memorize the complete list of Reese's products out there?"

"And what about it?" he replies instantly, a lazy smirk curling the edge of his lips. It takes everything I've got to refrain from dissolving into giggles.

"And I think you crashed into mine," I reply. "If we're going to be technical here."

"Well, I'm glad we met because I... I don't know. For someone I haven't known for that long..." He lets his sentence taper off, a thoughtful quality to his expression, as he contemplates. "You're already someone special to me."

My brain latches onto those words, repeating them over and over to the beat of my heart.

We just stand there, rooted in place, staring at each other for a lingering moment. Soft music plays faintly in the background. A quiet hum of chatter flows in from nearby rooms.

Is he waiting for me to respond? I worry my lower lip between my teeth. "You're the first real friend I made here at Belford."

"I am?" His eyes go wide with surprise, and embarrassment scalds my face.

"Yeah." Awkward laughter bubbles out of me. "And I'm also super grateful you haven't been giving me that much grief over Caleb." It's as if I said the magic word because something in the air changes—the soft music even halts; the idle conversations nearby cease.

His lips form a hard line, and the toe of his boot scuffs against the floor. "Don't you mean Blue Balls?" he grunts. He hikes his chin toward the canvas and folds his arms. "Old art porn or not, museums still aren't sexy."

"Got it. Don't take *Caleb* here if I plan on seducing him," I deadpan, rearing my head back when I think I hear him mutter under his breath, *Don't take him anywhere.* "Did you just say—"

"Let's go look at the rest of the shit here before the place closes," he interjects, and already, he's striding toward the other side of the room.

I amble after him and sneak a peek at my watch. "Oh, good idea. It's going to close soon."

"Then let's go, Reese." He nods at a different painting and folds his arms tightly across his chest. "Don't you think that one looks like Blue Balls?"

"What?" I sputter, twisting on my feet to stare at him in disbelief. The man in the painting is bald, for starters. "That looks nothing like him?"

"Really? They both have that sinister quality to them—"

"Sinister?" I shoot him a bewildered look.

"Look at those dead eyes—"

"Caleb does *not* have dead eyes," I gasp. "He has the dreamiest smile—"

"So does everybody else who shells out thousands for dental procedures."

"Do you not like Caleb?" I cut in, my mouth dropping open in surprise.

"Me?" He lifts a shoulder and drops it. "I barely know the guy."

"And yet you're helping me get with him anyway," I point out teasingly, and his features harden with a stormy scowl. "Dane, do you not like him?"

"What do you even like about him?" he asks. I blink, taken aback. "Because we both know he's got shit taste in music."

"*Dane,*" I admonish, even though I do agree. Kind of.

Besides avant-garde experimental screaming, Caleb's really into musicians who sing in a nasally, slow, and monotone register. It's not my cup of tea at all. And I say this as someone who does like indie music.

"He's nice."

He gives me an expectant look. "And?"

"And?" I echo. "I don't know. He… sees me for me? He doesn't see me as Lilian's little sister."

"I see you as Reese's Pieces," he reminds me.

"And that's why you're the first real friend I made here," I say, rolling my eyes good-naturedly. I won't admit it, but the nickname has grown on me. "Even though we don't have much in common."

Dane continues to stare with a gaze so piercing and intense that it feels like he can see right through me. "Is he nice to you?"

"I said he was nice."

"He's never done anything to hurt you?"

"No." I shake my head vehemently. "Not at all."

He's eerily quiet. There's some part of me that wants to reach out, hold his arms, and swear to him up and down that Caleb isn't going to hurt me—to reassure him that I'll be okay—just to smooth away the grumpy expression that's taken over his face.

"Okay." He lets loose a rough exhale, nodding a split second later. "Good. Because I'd hate to bump your art critic to number three when Blue Balls gets added to my list—"

"Oh my God," I say, shaking my head in disbelief. "That list shouldn't exist."

"The moment I find out Blue Balls hurt you—"

"He's not going to hurt me," I say, voice firm.

Dane peers into my eyes, almost as if he's trying to search for another answer, and the chords of his neck go tense when I give him a reassuring beam. "You like him, huh?"

"I should or else all of your efforts to help me with him would go to waste," I joke, shifting my weight from one foot to another.

He doesn't even laugh, and my smile falters. A muscle twitches in his throat; then he sighs. "I personally don't understand what's so great about Blue Balls. I think you could do much better—"

"I—"

"You could do so much fucking better than him," he grunts. "You really could. You really, really could—"

"Dane."

He straightens his stance and holds his hands up defensively. "Just saying."

"He's not that bad," I say. "He's sweet, and we like the same books—"

"And movies and TV shows," he mutters. "Yeah, I remember. That's what you said that one day."

I blink, a little thrown off by the tension in his voice I can't place.

"What kind of movies do you two even bond over?"

I shrug. "I don't know. The arthouse ones—"

"Of course, Blue Balls *would* like that."

"I like them, too?" A quiet exhalation escapes me. "I know it's not everybody's cup of tea, but I do like arthouse and indie movies." My words dry up in my throat, and heat rises in my cheeks. "Like, there's this one I've been meaning to see about the coming-of-age experience—I just like them. A lot."

He winces. "Shit. Reese, I wasn't... I didn't mean to offend you."

"It's... I've never really met anybody with the same interests as me," I whisper lamely. "It just feels very... meant to be, you know? To find someone who likes the same thing you like?"

He pins me with another searching stare. "And that's why you like him? Because you have a lot in common with him?"

"I... I guess? When you put it that way..." I release a laugh, something equal parts awkward and stiff. "Can we look at the rest of the art here before the place closes?"

His attention is rapt. Unreadable, even. I start to feel fidgety under his concentrated, heart-stopping gaze. Uncertainty builds inside me. I don't know what else to say when he finally juts his chin.

"Lead the way, Reese's Pieces."

So I do. Thankfully, he doesn't bring up Caleb again the rest of the time we're at the art museum.

DANE

I'M NOT ASHAMED TO ADMIT I JACKED OFF TWICE THIS MORNING, AS well as every other morning for the past week. I'm so keyed up that I take my frustration out on my latest project car, probably— no, *definitely*—doing more damage to it than fixing it at this point.

So when I get a coded text about a meet happening soon, I'm already deciphering it within a heartbeat.

Before I even think about it, I gear up for my next street race. There's a small voice in the back of my head telling me to stop. That I know better. That I should do everything I can to lie low and avoid any possibility of my father finding out I'm slipping back into my old habits.

But then my attention snags on an admission ticket left on my workbench. Whatever reservation I have ceases to exist as a taut ball of tension grows in my stomach. As my mind wanders to the one person I know I should stop thinking about.

Frustration boils over, and I storm to the other side of the garage, pop Ol' Reliable's hood, and make sure everything is good to go. Anything to keep my thoughts off of her.

A short drive later, I find myself pulling up to the location

I've decoded. It's this stretch of road no one ever takes. The freeway running flush to it is much more convenient.

There's a sizable crowd—mostly familiar faces in attendance tonight. I clock Giancarlo first and clench my jaw at the smug, knowing look plastered across his face. I then spot Wally, who won't shut the fuck up with the Old News comments in the hour we wait for other racers to arrive.

Some part of me is almost bummed when I'm not selected to go against him. With the bald tires his vehicle's sporting, it would be an easy win for me. It won't be much of a challenge, but nothing would be sweeter than to witness him throwing an inevitable little hissy fit.

Thankfully, there's one person I don't see anywhere. I even check in with Shyla and Eddie for confirmation that Marco's nowhere near here. One of us needs to keep his head out of trouble, and I'd be fucking pissed if it's not him. Especially after his last run-in with Giancarlo. The only thing he should be focusing on is the morning surf. Besides, what would his mom think if she were still here?

With the first race about to start, I return to my car. Just as I'm about to put my helmet on, my phone buzzes. I catch a glimpse of the text the moment I fish it out of my pocket.

**Reese's Pieces: I took your advice about making the
first move**

The shattered screen digs into the flesh of my palm.

Dane: and?
Dane: has Reese finally been stuffed?

How my phone's not breaking in my viselike grip right now is a testimony to the material it's made of.

Reese's Pieces: OMG stop it

Reese's Pieces: I asked if he wanted to go see this movie that's still screening at the theater near campus
Reese's Pieces: But he's busy with music homework :(

His fucking loss. My fingers are moving at a rapid speed as I send her my response.

Dane: want me to take you?
Reese's Pieces: You don't like indie movies
Dane: I want to see what all the fuss is about
Reese's Pieces: I don't want you to be bored
Dane: you're gonna go alone?

"Are you gonna just stand there all day or what?" Eddie hollers. I turn my back to him and blatantly ignore anything else he has to say.

Reese's Pieces: I'll just wait to rent it at home
Dane: pick the last showing and I'll take you so you don't have to wait long to see it
Reese's Pieces: Dane it's okay
Reese's Pieces: I'm fine with waiting for it to be available online
Dane: then I'll just buy two tickets and go by myself
Reese's Pieces: Don't be ridiculous
Reese's Pieces: Don't waste your money
Dane: then take the other ticket
Dane: because I'll be there later tonight
Dane: it's your choice if you want to be there or not

A loud horn blares. My middle finger goes up. I stow my phone away, slam the hood down, and shove my helmet on as I slide behind the wheel.

When checkered flags ripple through the air, I'm already gunning it down the stretch of road. Goddamn, I fucking *miss* this. Even though I drive every chance I can get, I forget how much I enjoy the power. The speed. The acceleration.

It's the only time I ever feel in complete control. Knowing that the adrenaline, the rush, the *excitement* coursing through my every vein is all me?

Pure. Fucking. Ecstasy.

I DESERVE A MEDAL FOR BEING ABLE TO SIT THROUGH THE ENTIRE movie without glazing over, passing out, or spending the whole time checking out the brunette next to me who is much more enraptured by the plot than I am. She's fucking adorable.

I pay attention to the damn screen because I know the instant we step foot outside the theater, she's going to want to discuss the film, and glazing over while being subjected to the blandest flick I've ever seen won't do me any favors.

And I'm right.

The moment we're outside, Reese is already discussing the cinematography in extensive detail. I don't think she manages to take a breath. While I have no fucking idea what she's talking about when she starts to get really into the specifics of cameras and shots, my focus is solely on her as she visibly becomes more animated with her discussion.

Then, out of nowhere, she abruptly stops talking. Her excitement gives way to something sheepish. "I'm sorry, I'm talking too much—"

"Nonsense, Reese's Pieces." My words are met with a skeptical glance, and I shrug. I have no idea what to do with my hands, so I shove them into my pockets. "Keep going."

"No, I'm boring you," she murmurs, diverting her gaze to a nearby hedge. "Even Lili would have checked out by now."

"Well, good thing I'm not Lili," I remind her. *Or Blue Balls.*

Although, I'm dealing with a major case of the fucking blue balls.

Her attention pivots back to me, accompanied by this starry

look in her eyes. Fucking hell. Something squeezes tight in my chest, and I clench my jaw. Breathe through my nostrils. Think about literally anything that comes to mind just to stave off the fucking hard-on when she continues to peer up at me with the sweetest expression I've ever witnessed.

"What was it you were saying about the composition and lighting?"

Her mouth opens, but she holds up a finger when her purse buzzes. "Gimme a sec." She unzips it and shoves aside a few packets of trail mix. "I think someone just texted me."

"Your sister?" I ask. *I hope.*

"Caleb." With her phone in hand, she punches in her passcode, and a bright smile spreads across her face and gives my hard-on a swift death. "He wants to know what I'm up to?" Her eyes collide with mine, and the hopeful gleam in her gaze cuts through me like a knife. "I don't know what to say."

Tell Blue Balls you're with me.

"Play hard to get," I suggest instead.

"I don't want to play games," she mumbles. "And considering how many dates we've gone on," she adds, and my gut reflexively tightens, "where nothing happens? I don't know… What should I say to him?"

That you're with me right now.

"That doesn't come off as desperate or *hard to get,*" she tacks on and bashfully ducks her head as a dark shade of red blossoms across her cheeks.

"Tell him you went to see the movie without him." My voice is far too thick and gritty for my liking. "Maybe he'll take you next time." My stomach sours at the thought, followed by this plummeting sensation in my chest.

She pulls her bottom lip between her teeth and unintentionally snares my attention. Every ounce of my self-control is being tested while I try not to think about her mouth parting around a blissful sigh as I position myself between her thighs and slide—

"He said he wished he could have seen it with me."

"Then why the fuck didn't he?" The blunt edge to my tone causes her to look up from her phone.

"House meeting," she explains.

"Nice to see where the guy's priorities are," I deadpan with a scoff, crossing my arms against my chest.

Unsurprisingly, she comes to his defense. "Lili's sorority has mandatory meetings, too."

"Over what? Whose turn is it to do the dishes?"

She fights her snort with a mild cough. "I'm not an actual member, so I wouldn't know." Then her gaze returns to her cell. "Oh! He asked if I want to stop by—"

"The frat house?"

"Yeah."

Good God, the mental image that pops into my head ain't pretty. The last thing I ever want to think about is Blue Balls taking Reese back to his room. I bet he has a fucking lava lamp and a collection of whiny artists on vinyl he'll fucking go on and on about. Maybe he'll brag nonstop about owning cassettes or whatever hipster bullshit he's into. Perhaps he'll wax poetic about the importance of analog and how the sound quality is so damn superior to digital because the man is full of himself.

Reese will fucking eat this shit up because that's who she is. She's thoughtful and kind and always expresses interest in people's hobbies and passions.

Suddenly, my breath rushes out of my lungs. I feel like the world's biggest chump right now, even though I know I shouldn't.

Deep down, I've known all along I never had a chance with her. With or without Blue fucking Balls in the way.

A girl like her would never get involved with someone like me. I'm just along for the ride until she wises up, realizes I'm no good, and leaves like everybody else does.

She's not my type, I tell myself. *Not my type, not my fucking type.*

"And… sent." Her voice snaps me back to reality. I watch her hastily shove her phone into her purse and suddenly entertain the idea of dragging her back inside and subjecting myself to a hundred more bland movies. Anything to delay the inevitable.

"You're gonna go see him?" I ask gruffly.

"Hmm? No." She shakes her head. "That'd be rude."

"Rude?"

"I'm hanging out with you," she says, and my stupid heart swells into my throat. I don't know what to respond with. "It'd be rude of me to ditch you while we're hanging out."

For several beats, all I can manage to do is stare at her. I open my mouth, but can't get a single syllable out. Apparently, my tongue has quit on me.

With a rough swallow, I mutter, "Come on, Reese. Do Blue Balls a favor and put him out of his misery." My words sound so strange and far away to my ears.

She rolls her eyes and readjusts a butterfly-shaped clip in her hair. "No way."

"Damn, girl, you're really gonna let him die of a curable case of—"

"I'm hanging out with you," she repeats, and her nose scrunches up. "Don't make me regret it."

The teasing note in her tone is emphasized by the adorable smile at the edge of her lips—fucking hell. My heartbeat is way too loud and deafening. Then her eyes go a little too starry-soft and elicit an answering squeeze in my heart.

One I choose to ignore because there's no other alternative. Not with her. Not while she wants someone else.

She toys with the strap of her purse and casts a glance at the ground between our feet. "Thanks for going with me to see this. It… means a lot to me."

I suck in a sharp breath and play it off with a shrug. "If my little savior wants to go see a movie, we go see a movie."

"Little savior?" She makes a face. Already, I miss the starry-soft glow in her eyes. "Don't call me that. I barely did anything."

"Sometimes, the littlest thing can mean everything."

Her head tips back as she looks up at me. A slow and equally shy smile tugs at her lips and makes me feel pretty fucking stupid for saying those loaded words to the tiny girl before me.

"Tell me more about cameras," I suggest, a roughened edge to my voice. I need a distraction and will take anything I can get to stop fixating on the rapid rhythm of my pulse.

"Really?"

"Why the fuck not?" I shrug, feigning nonchalance.

She hesitates and gnaws on her lip. Before I can say anything else, I'm hit with the sudden impact of her grin. It's somewhat timid, but it's so damn sweet. "Okay."

"Okay."

With a nervous laugh, she finally dives into it and talks to me about the importance of framing shots. The words spill out of her in a breathless rush. Her cheeks are flushed by the time we get to my car, and I don't miss the fact that her eyes are extremely starry-soft and hazy the entire walk over.

17

———

REESE

WITH MY TUTORING SESSION DONE FOR THE DAY, I EXIT THE CENTER, wedge my notebook into my backpack, and sidestep to avoid the crowd of students rushing into the nearby language lab.

Just as I reach the stairwell, a throaty grunting sound breaks the silence, and I freeze in place. My brain leaps back to that night. My hand flies to my pepper spray. My breathing runs ragged.

"Hey, wait up, Reese." It takes a beat too long for me to realize I *recognize* the timbre of his voice. I *know* who's calling my name.

Yet my heart remains palpitating way too fast despite the deep breaths I take. I release the death grip on my pink can of mace before peeking over my shoulder and meeting Caleb's gaze.

"Jesus," he stammers, his green eyes wide. "It's just me."

"Sorry, sorry," I pant. Swallowing roughly, I paste a smile onto my face. Something calm and friendly to mask the overwhelming sense of panic gripping me by the throat.

Concern visibly doubles across his features. Acid churns in my stomach.

"Please, um, don't tell Lili about this."

"I won't." He mimes zipping his lips and offers me a kind smile. "So, I missed you."

"You have?" *Why do I sound so surprised?*

"I have," he confirms. "Sucks we couldn't hang out on Saturday—"

"It's all right," I assure him, and I'm unable to fight the grin as my thoughts go to Dane. It was really sweet of him to listen to me, even though I'm certain he had no clue about half the things I brought up.

"But I'm free this Wednesday," Caleb goes on. "Wasn't there this farmer's market you wanted to check out?"

Confusion knits my brows. "I told you about that?" I don't remember mentioning it to him. Usually, we talk about whatever he brings up, so our conversations often revolve around common interests, classes, or a band he wants to see.

"Yeah." He chuckles and rakes his fingers through his curly hair. "I'd never forget what you've said to me."

"Oh." My cheeks radiate with heat. Crap. I probably did tell him about it, and it must have slipped my mind. I *have* been preoccupied with a group project for my civil engineering class as of late. Maintaining my scholarships means staying on top of my assignments. "I didn't mean to imply—"

"It's all good, Little Vann." He waves me off. "I figured we could make a little date out of it. I wanted to surprise you, but I wasn't sure how busy your schedule is."

"That's really sweet of you." Realizing he's giving me an expectant look, I release a blustery laugh. "Oh, and I am free this Wednesday."

"Great. Shall I pick you up from the sorority?" His question is punctuated with his trademark dreamy smile, and I find myself staring at his mouth for a beat too long. Without blushing so hard that my entire body feels like it's been set on fire. I'm not flustered at all.

"Can't wait," I squeak out, then duck into the stairwell before the actualization hits me. I forgot to say goodbye. Whoops. I should double back, but my self-preservation kicks in and has me sending him an apologetic text instead.

Then I reach out to my sister, because I don't know what to make of my discovery.

Lilian: yay! this means you're comfortable around him!
Lilian: that's a good thing! you don't want to be nervous around the guy you like

Okay, she has a point. I'm definitely making a mountain out of a molehill.

Reese: I can't believe he asked me to go with him to the farmers market though
Lilian: better him than me
Reese: Aww but we talked about wanting to go to one for days
Lilian: and now you can go with Caleb instead
Reese: One of these days you and I should go
Lilian: one of these days

Emerging from the building, I immediately catch sight of Dane just a few yards away, treading across the campus walkway. With his backpack hitched over a tense shoulder. And a dark scowl etched on his face.

I've never seen him this pissed off—I don't think I've ever witnessed *anybody* walking as angrily as him.

It's as if he can sense me gawking at him, because his head whips in my direction with that hardened glare.

Instantaneously, it gentles and melts into something familiar.

"Mini Reese," he calls out with a wild grin.

A small thrill of excitement bubbles to the surface as I beam back at him and wave, and I swear, his features soften even more. My pulse speeds up when he makes his way to me, and before I can help myself, I blurt, "Guess who has a date this Wednesday?"

"Wednesday is the unsexiest day of the week," Dane argues and effectively ruins the shot I'm recording of the golden sunset with its pretty red hues.

A groan slips free as I stop the video and give him a sidelong glance. "The farmer's market only occurs on Wednesday. It's not like I can ask them to reschedule."

"Still the least sexy day of the week."

With an inaudible sigh, I take photos of the coastline instead and observe the glittering water as the sun sets into the horizon. After I've captured a dozen pictures, I roll the window up and lean back against my seat where the overwhelming scent of gasoline greets me.

Before long, the car merges into a turn lane, and I quirk my brow when it occurs to me that he's pulling into a plaza.

"What are we doing here?" I can't imagine him wanting to go on a shopping trip. Not when he practically wears the same threadbare shirt every time I see him. I wouldn't be surprised if he only has three white tees on rotation.

"Finding you onion rings for your fiesta."

The corner of my mouth sneaks up despite myself. "Finsta."

"That." He kills the ignition and quickly hops out of his car. I remain seated, somewhat bewildered by the last-minute plan. I thought we were just going for a ride to see if his engine was giving him any trouble.

My surprise amplifies when he opens the passenger door. Climbing out of the vehicle, I feel my cheeks go inexplicably warm. "I could have done it myself, but thanks."

He cocks his head, but before he can give me his trademark retort, a couple of elderly men approach us with questions about the car.

Soon enough, they're deeply engaged in a conversation about the make and model. It's like I'm not even here. I'm just silently observing them, if anything. Well, I'm definitely paying attention to Dane as he casually displays the extent of his knowledge. While I've got no idea what they're discussing, it's obvious he knows more than I expected.

At some point, Dane mentions that it still has its original engine from the sixties, and he receives a round of whistles. Then I get to witness a group of men fawning over shiny parts when he pops the hood for them to see what's inside.

It's kind of cute.

Cute?

Is that a word anybody would ever use to describe Dane Kingsley? I can hear my sister's voice screaming *no* in my head.

"All right," Dane says as he sidles to me once the car talk is over. He crams his keys into his pocket and tips his head. "Let's fiesta."

A challenge burns deep in his pointed gaze as if he's daring me to correct him, and it's so ridiculous that I huff out a snort. I'm met with what appears to be a rare smile from him, one that softens his eyes.

He clears his throat, and I realize I'm staring.

Blinking rapidly, I divert my attention to my purse as heat crawls up my neck. "Lead the way, Dane."

We check out every restaurant at the plaza before returning to the first one and settling for a blooming onion basket when we discover none offer onion rings on their menu.

Once we've situated ourselves outside on the deck, my attention goes to the décor, and I take in every little detail that catches my eye. I won't lie. It's a bit tacky, with lots of nautical decoration eating up the space—like the giant boat helm or the life-sized Kraken—but it oddly works.

"This is nice," I admit. Even though the temperature has dropped drastically and the marine layer has rolled in, I don't mind the cold. For once, my coat and sweater are practical. And I like the company.

"For how much this cost," Dane says dryly, picking up his soda, "it better be nice."

"I can split—"

"I'll pay. It wasn't a planned thing."

"Well, I'll tip then," I grumble.

"Snack Mix," he says, "don't worry about it. Save your money for your date with Blue Balls."

"Okay." I try my best to stop my mouth from tightening into a frown. "Do you like lavender?"

His head tilts to the side. "The plant?"

"Would you protest me buying you some lavender soap?" I explain. "Or maybe something with honey?"

"Are you trying to tell me I smell?" he asks, arching a brow.

"*No.*" Not at all. Sometimes, he reeks of the rich scent of motor oil, but usually, it's a subtle and pleasant mix of laundry detergent and aftershave clinging to his frame. Not that I'll say that out loud. Only a CIA agent can weasel that confession from me. "I just… If the farmer's market has them, I'd like to get you some as a thank-you gift. *For* helping me get the guy."

My embarrassment gives way to regret as I rub the back of my neck and try not to squirm underneath his inscrutable stare. Maybe I shouldn't have admitted that. What guy would want soap, anyway? He probably has one of those billion-in-one shampoo bottles that cleans you in every way imaginable.

"You're gonna buy *me* a gift while you're on a date with Blue Balls?" He whistles out a low note. "Don't think he would appreciate you thinking of another guy while you're out with him."

"He won't mind."

"You sure about that? If I seem to recall," he drawls, "he was mighty jealous when he saw you talking to me at the car wash."

"Caleb doesn't get jealous."

"Then he's a dumbass." Dumbfounded, I gape at him as he continues. "Any guy with anything other than rocks for brains ought to know they should be afraid of someone better swooping in and stealing you in a heartbeat if they could."

"There's one problem with that." I put on my most reassuring smile. "I wouldn't jump ship because *someone better* has come along."

"You'd rather stay on a sinking ship?" he counters.

"Well, no," I say hastily, slightly flustered.

"With a loser?"

"No," I splutter. "That's not—"

"And what if," he continues, "Caleb keeps wasting your time?"

"I'd like to give things a shot first," I admit softly. "And Caleb's not wasting my time. He's just taking things slow." *Really slow.*

"Really fucking slow," he utters, a frown flickering over his features. His mouth tugs into a hard line. His gaze burns into mine. "Why is that?"

The knot forming in my chest cinches tight. "What do you mean?"

"Well," he says slowly, shaking his glass in a circular motion. "If I were Blue Balls, I wouldn't be able to keep my hands off of you." He clears his throat. "Or any girl I'm seeing—as Blue Balls."

"He's very respectful?"

"You can fuck someone and still treat them respectfully," Dane says bluntly, and the tips of my ears go hot. "You can kiss someone and still treat them respectfully. You can tell them how badly you want them and it's more fucking respectful than acting like a stranger who takes you on these dates and leaves you confused about what the fuck is going on because he won't kiss you for what-the-fuck-ever reason that may be."

Wordlessly, I stare at him. It's the only reaction I'm capable of when a sudden mess of emotions unfurls deep in my belly.

"I don't fucking get it," he goes on, and the muscle of his jaw locks. "If I were in his fucking shoes, I would have told you from the very beginning that I'm into you and show it rather than just say it over and over and not make fucking do with my words."

My throat feels inexplicably hoarse as I watch him bring his glass to his lips.

"He's not like you," I say, and he sets his soda down with an audible *thunk* after draining a quarter of it.

"Pity," is his only reply, and that word seems to echo in the shocked silence blanketing us. I'm uncertain how to respond to that. Not when he refuses to meet my gaze. Finally, he pushes the basket toward me and rises from his seat.

"Where are you going?" I stumble through my words as my heart gives an unexpected lurch, and my eyes go round.

"To take a leak," he says dryly. "Unless you need to follow me to the little boy's room for visual confirmation."

The edge of his voice sends a sharp pang to my chest. I sit back and quietly watch him head inside the restaurant. *What just happened?*

Flummoxed, my bottom lip is pulled between my teeth. My stomach is swarmed with jitters. My appetite goes poof, and the greasy fried onions no longer look as appealing as they were just moments ago.

18

DANE

"Fuck you!" Wally screams and lays on the horn like the petulant child he is. Evidently, some people can't handle losing with grace.

I pucker my lips and blow him a kiss. He recoils in his seat and sneers when I send him another just to fuck with him some more.

"That good enough for you, baby?" A slow smirk works its way across my face. "Or should I give you another for good measure?"

Fury floods his features and convinces his pea-sized brain to jump out of his car. My grin broadens as I motion for him to step closer. If he wants his ass kicked, I'll gladly be the one to give it to him.

"Always knew you'd be back, Kingsley." Giancarlo's voice halts Wally in his tracks and brings a spike to my blood pressure. I barely look over and grit my teeth at the sight of him approaching our vehicles with his bodyguards in tow. "Could never resist the siren's call."

My scowl deepens with a scoff. *I've resisted just fine,* I want to snarl, because the alternative isn't better. *I need a fucking distraction.*

Admitting the truth won't do me any fucking favors. It never has. Keeping my trap shut has been my go-to method for a reason. People can't use your words against you if you don't give them any ammunition to work with.

"If you're ever serious about getting back into the fold," Giancarlo says, stressing out his words with a slow cadence, "you know how to reach me." There's a deliberate pause. "Unless you're finally cowering to your daddy's demand?"

My bad mood takes a nosedive. He's baiting me. You'd have to be born yesterday not to see it.

With a sharp exhalation, I stare straight ahead. My damn jaw is so painfully tight, it might snap like a taut rubber band.

I barely entertain the offer before a slither of reason cleaves through my derailing thoughts. I know better. The ounce of sensibility I somehow possess knows I need to keep my fucking head down. Lie low. Stay out of trouble.

Despite everything, I'm still itching for my next fix, for the rush of adrenaline, for the exhilarating sense of control when I'm behind the wheel and burning rubber against the asphalt. I know I'm on the edge of a slippery slope. I can sense my resolve crumbling every time I return to one of these races. If I'm not careful, this will blow up in my face.

Clarity sets in. The realization that this can end with me finally discovering what it's really like to get a crowbar to the head gives me the strength to decline.

"I'm. Good," I grit out and lean back against my seat, allowing myself a wry grin. I catch the glower on Wally's face in my periphery. I bet it hurts his pride to know he'll never be the best in Giancarlo's eyes. The daggers he glares at me pale in comparison to the envy coming off of him in waves.

He can trick out his vehicle. Buy all the tacky aftermarket parts he desires. Fuck with his exhaust system all he wants. No matter what he does, it'll never be enough. *He'll* never be enough, and we both know it.

"If you ever change your mind—"

"Pass."

"I'll be seeing you," Giancarlo says, and while I spare him a mirthless huff, unease takes rein in my gut. I hate that he's fucking right.

The best course of action is to leave, and for once, I follow through. My car pulls away from the crudely drawn finish line and grants some much-needed distance before I do something reckless or stupid that could land me in actual hot water.

Unfortunately, the night's still young. I need a distraction. One that doesn't involve me pissing off Father Dearest and also helps me get my mind off of what's been bothering me for a while now.

I decide to meet up with Marco and come to regret my decision when I walk through the door and immediately see *them* together.

Somehow, I forgot she's friends with the sorority girls who live here. My stance grows tense, and my hands ball into fists as good old-fashioned jealousy surges through my veins.

She's not my type. I don't chase the good girls.

Logically, my dick needs to get with the program and quit acting with a mind of its own. And my brain needs to stop presenting the idea of me marching over there, telling Blue Balls to fuck off, and taking his seat.

The air leaves my lungs when she leans into his upper arm and shows him something off her phone. She's wearing his beanie. Her chestnut brown hair hangs over her shoulder in loose waves. Her thigh is only a few inches from his instead of a healthy and appropriate twenty or thirty miles.

Doesn't distance make the heart grow fonder or some shit? He can set off for the North Pole for all I care. In fact, he can go one better and catch the red-eye flight out to the sun.

"Dane," Marco shouts over the Halloween music and slings an arm around my neck. "Let me introduce you to Karla."

Karla is this tall and tan sorority girl with a sinful smile that promises nothing but a good time.

And yet, I feel… nothing, which is concerning. How the fuck am I supposed to distract myself from what's happening on the couch if I can't even muster up a reaction?

"You know, my roommate thinks you're dangerous," Karla tells me while her eyes rove across my chest with the subtlety of a freight train.

I scoff. I don't give a fuck what people think about me. I've heard enough bullshit said behind my back that nothing fazes me anymore.

"So does everyone else, apparently." My words come out flat as I inadvertently redirect my attention to Reese, and my stomach clenches in a tight knot. All right, fine. So maybe there's one person whose opinion matters to me.

"But, like, the school wouldn't have let you back if you were *that* dangerous. *Obviously*," she continues. For a brief moment, I wonder how I can slink away before she rambles up a storm. "I think she has it out for you ever since you beat up the guy she liked freshman year."

The muscles in my shoulders go taut. I did *not* beat that fucker up. Believe me, I would have taken credit for it if I did. "And I should give a fuck about this because?"

"I'm just trying to make small talk." Annoyance flashes in Karla's eyes, and I don't miss the *asshole* muttered under her breath.

"Dane's just joking," Marco says lightly, pulling away from me with a reproachful glare aimed my way. I know he's trying to hook up with one of her sorority sisters, and the last thing he needs is me dampening the mood. It's not going to affect his game, though.

I should know. I've witnessed him pull girls with no finesse while we were growing up. He was always breaking hearts left and right; never one to settle down. He's too restless. We both are.

He's a good guy, though. Despite his shithead dad knocking him around and telling him he'll never amount to anything all his life, Marco got out of that hellhole relatively unscathed.

He enrolled at Belford U for a reason. He wants to break the cycle of fuckups in his family. Make a name for himself. Turn his life around for the better. Prove his old man wrong.

It's why he stopped racing before I did. Even though it's not the same without him around, I'm sincerely glad he called it quits. One of us should be able to look forward to the future.

Since I like the guy, I decide to peace out before my shitty mood ruins his chances with Stacy tonight. "I'm gonna get a drink."

Karla, thankfully, doesn't accompany me.

THEY'RE STILL ON THE DAMN COUCH.

I've caught bits and pieces of their conversation throughout the night, and watching ten coats of fresh paint dry is more entertaining than his story about meeting the lead singer to some obscure band I've never heard of.

Yet Reese finds it fascinating, but that's because she's too nice to realize he's duller than a butter knife.

She's laughing and smiling, and he's puffing his chest like he's telling her an anecdote about meeting God.

Then she scoots closer to him and twirls a strand of her hair, and a numbing bitterness takes root in my chest. I need to make myself scarce before she recognizes *the moment* transpiring between them and follows my stupid advice.

"Hey, you're still here." My frustration doubles as Karla sidles up to me and leans her weight into my shoulder. Her flirtatious smile shifts into a pout when I shrug her off of me.

"I don't hook up with drunk chicks," I state flatly. "Not my thing."

"So you're not that much of an asshole," Karla replies with a smirk.

I say nothing and exhale roughly when a familiar, husky laugh reaches my ears and captures my focus. Karla cocks her head and follows my line of sight before I'm able to reroute my attention to the expensive sound system nearby.

Karla brings her hand to her neck. "Have you heard about what happened to her?"

Suspicion narrows my eyes, but the sympathy shining in hers loosens the knot in my chest. With a shake of my head, I pretend to drink from my empty beer bottle.

She doesn't seem to notice as she launches into this long-winded tale about how her sorority hosted numerous fundraisers to help pay for Reese's medical bills two years ago.

Not going to lie, that earns them some respect in my books. Although it's depressing to hear that they had to resort to so many fucking fundraisers to pay off one person's medical debt.

The conversation sidetracks, and I don't know why she thinks I want to hear about her sorority sisters' petty drama over missing shoes. I'm not in the mood for small talk. She can gossip to anyone else here. It's not like it's slim pickings.

The house is so packed that one would think half, if not all, of Belford's campus is in attendance tonight. She's got plenty of options to choose from. Also, who gives a shit?

"It's so sad," Karla coos, and I offer her a noncommittal grunt. "If you were here last year, you would have seen how *terrified* she was of people."

I glance sideways at her when it occurs to me she's talking about Reese again.

"Or not," she goes on. "That girl always ran off and hid upstairs whenever people came over."

"So she's shy," I cut in, my teeth clenched in a growl. I have no reservations about calling her out if she starts making fun of Reese for that. She can't help who she is.

"Yeah, but… she's been having a rough time." She points to the base of her neck again.

My mouth pulls into a flat line. I don't like the idea of my little savior struggling.

Something guarded clouds her features as she glances around the crowded room. She leans in and drops her voice to a whisper. "That's why the girls and I have been trying to help her. See the guy she's with?"

My gaze returns to the couch, and my grip tightens around the glass bottle.

"She has a crush on him. A major one. Like, she's so smitten with him that she makes these heart eyes whenever he's around."

Well, isn't that a swift kick to the balls?

"What does that have to do with anything?" I grunt. If I want to feel like crap, I can always answer one of my father's calls. Anything is better than this particular brand of torture I'm being subjected to.

Karla gives the room another cursory glance and drunkenly stumbles closer. "Well, we thought it'd boost her confidence if her major crush asked her out."

Her words sink in slowly and fill my gut with unease. "So you told him to… go on a date with her?"

Karla's eyes twinkle. "We paid him to."

A lump chokes my throat. "Like a prostitute?"

"No."

"An escort?"

"*No.*"

"A gigolo?"

She huffs, exasperated. "Oh my God, stop it. He's none of those things. We only paid him to take her out on a few dates."

That would explain why nothing had panned out for her. The guy's not into her at all.

His loss. If he's not interested, he can step aside and graciously fuck off. Let her move on from his lame ass.

"But," Karla continues, tossing her shoulder in a casual

shrug. "If one thing leads to another…" She trails off with a meaningful smile.

Blood freezes in my veins. "The hell does that mean?" I almost snarl, and her grin drops. "You're literally pimping him out—"

"*No*, we're not," she protests. "We're only trying to help—"

"Help?" My tone is pure venom. I'm so fucking pissed on Reese's behalf that I forget what I want to say. "What's going to happen when she finds out he was paid to seduce her?"

The thought of Reese getting hurt by this fucker causes me to squeeze my bottle to the point where it's a miracle it hasn't shattered yet. She doesn't deserve this. On any other occasion, I might find it hilarious that the sorority girls are getting hustled, but not when Reese is involved.

"She won't find out," Karla insists. "We have a breakup planned—It's not *that* bad."

"Not that bad? Are you for real?" I scoff. "This is fucked up."

Karla sniffs, visibly offended. "We're only trying to help her out—"

"Right." Before I even think about it, I'm shoving my way toward the couch. Karla grabs my wrist with an alarming amount of strength.

"You can't tell her," she gasps, her eyes pleading. "It will break her heart if she finds out the first guy who's ever shown any interest in her never liked her all along."

I stop mid-stride and seethe. "She wouldn't have to experience that at all if you sorority girls didn't put her in this situation in the first place."

"*Please, don't say anything—*"

With a rough yank, I free my arm from her grasp and walk away.

Fury crawls through my chest as I reach the couch. I'm more than ready to grab the douchebag by the collar of his shirt and fling him onto the wooden coffee table. In fact, my hand forms a fist as Blue Balls looks over and his sentence tapers off.

Just as I'm about to swing my arm back, my line of sight slides to the girl beside him, and time suspends. My temper snuffs out like a candle.

The tacky string lights hanging around the house glow softly in those dark brown eyes, no match for how bright her face becomes when she sees me. She straightens, and without warning, she beams something so sweet and pure that I'm temporarily lost for words.

For a fleeting moment, I cling to the idea that she's happy to see me. That she's happy *because* of me.

And fuck me. It suddenly dawns on me that I can't hit the guy. I can't smack him upside the head, either. How will I ever explain that I want to sock him in the face *for her*?

I want to be the reason behind that sweet smile. I don't want to be the one who dims her sunshine by telling her this fucking prick has been pretending to like her for cash. I definitely don't want to be the guy who deploys a devastating blow to her already fragile confidence.

The last thing I ever want is to hurt her.

Her eyebrows scrunch as she looks on expectantly. My hand drops to my side, and my brain scrambles for something to say, but I'm coming up empty. Especially when she offers me another smile, and fuck. *Fuck me.*

How can a pair of lips cause that much shock to my system? How can one smile send my pulse into overdrive? How does *she* manage to make the world feel so much brighter with just her mere presence?

"Reese's Pieces." The nickname slips out as inspiration strikes me. "Blue Balls is not the guy for you."

He chokes, sputtering. "Who's Blue Balls?"

"What?" Reese stares at me with wide eyes. *What are you doing?* she mouths.

A crooked grin comes to my face as I move closer and set the beer bottle down on the coffee table. "Why settle for him when you can be with me?"

"*What?*" Reese wheezes.

"I want you." I gaze steadily into her eyes as my confession sets me at ease. "And I don't want to see you waste another minute with this tool when I'm right here, baby."

Her mouth parts in shock. "Is… Is this a joke?"

Blue Balls pushes to his feet. "Listen here, man—"

"You know where to find me," I plow on, "when you're done with this fucking loser."

With that, I turn around and make my exit. It's not until I'm outside that the reality of the situation sinks in, and I let loose a harsh breath.

I'm frustrated—beyond pissed—that I can't tell Reese anything about him leading her on or how the sorority girls have pimped him out. She shouldn't be kept in the dark, oblivious to everything going on behind her back. *That ain't right.*

But at least she knows one thing, which brings me some small comfort.

I'm dead serious about wanting her.

19

REESE

What was that? What was that?

My brain is screaming and unable to process, well, everything that has happened in the last five minutes.

There's no way. He did not waltz over to me and announce *that* for everyone and their mother to hear. He did not tell me to ditch Caleb for him. *He did not call me baby.*

Flutters awaken in my stomach, and I'm acutely aware of how breathless I feel. Of how fast my heart is racing. Of how warmth is spreading between my thighs—I exhale roughly.

He's messing with me. There's no other explanation. No other fathomable reason. It's not like he hasn't done it before. He likes getting a reaction out of me; only this time, he's taken it way too far.

That's why he called me baby, right?

Something unfamiliar stirs low in my belly. I suck in oxygen between my teeth and freeze when it finally dawns on me that *everyone* has witnessed this. Oh God.

Embarrassment unfurls through me like wildfire. I avert my gaze and catch sight of Caleb's expression. He looks half as flabbergasted as I feel.

"I… Um… He was joking," I squeak, because what else am I supposed to say? *He wasn't? He actually wants me?*

My pulse quickens at the thought, and I swear, every part of my body thrums with anticipation. But then I find myself wincing when I realize people are still staring. *And whispering.*

Flustered, my stomach starts to cramp. My nerves unravel. I hate this sort of attention. I don't want the spotlight on me. I never have.

Ducking my head, I turn and stare pleadingly into Caleb's eyes. "Can you take me home, please?"

***

THE SOUND OF MY DOOR BEING BANGED ON REPEATEDLY JOSTLES ME awake and shoves my heart into my throat. I go deathly still, my breath trapped in my lungs.

"*Reese.* I know you're in there!" Lilian's voice shunts me back to reality. "Let me in. *Let me in right now.*"

Crap. She's too loud, and the couple below me just had their baby. With a deep inhale, I rush to the door and unlock all the deadbolts with clumsy fingers.

She barges inside before I can say anything and stabs a finger in my direction. "*He. Wants. You?*"

Three words and my heart reacts instantaneously, drumming a relentless beat against my breastbone. I linger for a moment, then muster up an easygoing smile and redirect my attention to the deadbolts.

As I triple-check and make sure they're locked, I can feel the heat of her thunderous glare on the back of my neck. "He was joking," I insist, because that's likely the case. Dane didn't mean a single word he said last night.

Besides, I don't think guys like him go for girls like me. I'm too much of a hopeless and anxious ball of disaster, and he's… so self-assured. Brash. *Devastatingly good-looking.*

My eyes widen, but then I startle when my sister groans. I

peek over my shoulder and nearly flinch at the sight of her gritted teeth. Oof. She's definitely not happy. If she bares her canine, I'm in for a reckoning.

"Do you have any idea how dangerous he is?"

"Lili—"

"Do you?" She steps closer and rakes her hands through her blonde hair. *"He's fucking dangerous."*

It takes everything I have not to sigh as a hint of annoyance creeps to the surface. I love my sister, but there's no point in arguing with her. I know I'm not going to win here.

Even though I want to tell her to back off, I know how this will play out. If I give her a nudge, she'll push back even harder. I'm conflict-avoidant and too much of a people-pleaser. She's stubborn and will not let things go until she gets her way.

As frustrating as it is, I know exactly why she's like a mama bear on steroids. She's overprotective for a reason, and it's because she feels like she failed me.

"But what if he's not?" My tone is soft and placating in an attempt to calm her down. Only, it's not very effective.

"You can talk to Travis Walker if you don't believe me," Lilian snaps. "He broke his arm, Reese. *He broke his arm.*"

My reassuring smile evaporates, and I swallow thickly. The Dane Kingsley she talks about doesn't seem to align with the Dane Kingsley I know. Suddenly, I'm torn.

He told me he doesn't get into fights for fun, and I believe him. *I do.* But Lilian would never lie to me.

"Does it matter if he… wants me?" My pulse ratchets up a notch, and I draw in a lungful of air to steel my resolve. *"Caleb Marsden.* Remember him? I like Caleb."

The very same guy who has never kissed me or shown any remote interest in me. Okay, that's not a fair assessment. He has asked me out a few times. They might have ended on a boring note, but they were still dates he wanted to take me on.

Some guys like to take things slowly. Caleb is one of them.

Maybe a year from now, he'll finally have the courage to hold my hand.

My face almost scrunches at the thought. Do I really want to endure that for the rest of eternity? Wait with bated breath for him to take things a step further?

Or is it time for me to bite the bullet, figure out the *moment,* and finally get the guy I've been crushing on since last year?

I try to picture it, but it's not Caleb and his dreamy smile my imagination conjures up. It's... Dane. Dane and the teasing smirk he barely conceals as he gazes upon me with this... *look* of such sweet longing.

My heart takes off racing; my pulse trips over itself. I find myself irrevocably stunned. I shouldn't feel so strongly, *so intensely,* over him. Not when he only crashed into my life just a short while ago.

Not when we have so little in common.

Dane is not the type to take me to used bookstores, art galleries, indie concerts, or even the movies. And certainly not the museums. He's been *very* vocal about this.

And yet he's... already done most of that.

My heartbeat goes erratic, and my mind scrambles in every direction as it tries to make sense of it all. *Maybe he's just a really good friend?*

Underneath that rough exterior, Dane can be surprisingly sweet at times.

What about last night was sweet? Either he was messing with me... or he meant every word he said. The latter sends an electric current down my spine.

No. It's impossible. He doesn't seem like the type to do relationships. Heck, Lilian called him a skirt chaser, and he never denied it when I brought it up.

If anything, the truth is probably something very simple. Maybe he declared his supposed feelings for me because he owes me one. This is his way of repaying the favor: by letting

Caleb know the clock's ticking. It's… so far-fetched, but I wouldn't put it past him.

Would he do that, though?

Any guy with anything other than rocks for brains ought to know they should be afraid of someone better swooping in and stealing you in a heartbeat if they could.

Dane's words echo in my head and sear my chest, and an alarming amount of disappointment overwhelms me in the seconds that follow.

Before I can spiral any further, Lilian interrupts my train of thought.

"You need to steer clear of him." Genuine worry floods her eyes when I reluctantly find her gaze. "The guy is bad news, Reese." She pauses, then releases a shaky breath. "I don't want you to get hurt because of him."

An influx of emotions swells in my throat, and I force my lips into a soothing smile. "Don't worry about Dane." Before she can cut me off, I continue. "He was just messing around. He… wasn't serious."

She allows herself a quiet sigh and scrubs her hands down her face. "God, I hope so."

I know so. Something inside me deflates, and I struggle to ignore my heart as it hopelessly clings to the idea that maybe, *just maybe,* Dane wasn't messing with me.

2 0

—————

DANE

Ol' Reliable crosses over the crudely chalked finish line, bringing a smirk to my mouth as a green vehicle screeches to a halt moments later. I barely take my helmet off when Wally jumps out of his car and charges over to mine.

"Come out and face me, Old News!" he snarls. "You fucking cheated."

Scoffing, I roll down my window an inch and pucker my lips at him. "Baby, if you want to get your ass handed to you again, just ask."

His fist connects against the glass, and my grin drops.

I don't like people fucking with what's mine, so when his arm's mid-swing, I roughly shove my door open and let it smack into him. He's sent sprawling backward, sneering as he staggers to his feet.

"Baby, if you want to get your ass kicked, just ask." With one foot on the ground, I'm about to slide out and knock some sense into that brain-dead head of his when I hear it.

Sirens squawking in the near distance.

Fucking hell.

The local PD has been trying to bust these meets, which is

158

why false information is always floating around and why consecutive races are never held at the same place.

I can hear them closing in on us, and since I don't want to risk getting my ass hauled off to jail, I know I need to get out of here. *Fast.*

The last thing I need is my old man catching wind of this.

Without hesitation, I shut the door and take off, instinctively keeping an ear out for any signs of trouble. I know I have to be smart about this. It's not the first time I've had to shake the cops off.

Hopefully, it won't be too much of a challenge. My plate's bogus, and my car blends into the night, making it easier for me to evade them. I take a sharp right onto a narrow side street and then drop my speed to the posted limit.

For several seconds, it's just me cruising down the stretch of road. Then a pair of headlights appears in my rearview mirror and causes my mouth to curl.

Maintaining speed, I turn onto another side street and scowl when the cop car follows. The next intersection I come across, I take a left and suck in a sharp breath when it leads me through a residential area.

I'm going to be fucked if this turns into a dead end. My concern ebbs when I see a busy intersection just a few blocks ahead.

Steeling myself, I don't waste another moment. I gun it and blow through countless stop signs at breakneck speed, setting off numerous alarms. Sirens and flashing lights commence, and my pulse flares. My priority shifts to what's in front of me.

Traffic is heavy, granting me a small window of escape with a gap just wide enough for me to squeeze through. Gripping my hand brake, I tightly drift onto the main street and pray I didn't fuck up any of my tires when white smoke billows behind me.

Ol' Reliable whips around another corner, and I *floor it*. I don't see the squad car behind me, but I'm not taking any chances. Then I grit my teeth when I hit a pothole. Since I don't want to ruin my suspension, I slow down. Scanning the surrounding area, I take notice of a familiar run-down apartment and immediately pull into its parking lot.

Stashing my vehicle underneath a random carport, I throw a cover over it with feigned nonchalance and do one last cursory glance before I book it. Halfway toward the back, I let out a rough exhalation when my peripheral vision catches the cop car slowly coming into view.

Fuck. If they turn in here, I might have truly screwed myself over.

"Dane?"

I'd recognize that voice anywhere. I almost stop short as my line of sight shifts to Reese. She's holding a small bag to her chest, and her dark eyes are wide as she stares at me.

"What are you doing here?"

I could be honest with her, but I'm smart enough to know better.

"Still wanted to see if you're with the tool." It's not a complete lie. It's been a couple of days since I've last seen her. The radio silence has been a notch below excruciating.

She squints. "Are you messing with me?"

I shoot her a frown as I duck behind the building, then look back when I hear the distinct whoop of a siren. Sure enough, there's a police vehicle going at a speed of one mile per hour.

"You think I am?" I ask lightly, and my muscles tense when the cruiser slows to a stop. Right in front of the gate. *Fuck.*

The only response I get is *pspspsps.* Bewildered, I cast a glance over my shoulder. Reese sweeps her long hair behind her ear as she crouches low and pours a small mountain of kibble near the dumpster. Probably to feed that *chunky alleycat* she brought up once.

I'm defenseless against my smirk. It would have been a losing battle.

She peeks over, and I don't miss the slight frown forming above her eyes. "You are, and I don't appreciate it."

"Aw, Reese's Pieces. I swear to you, I'm not." My attention pivots back to the street, and a sigh of relief breaks free when the squad car finally takes off. *Thank fucking God.*

"Were you hiding from them?" Accusation rings in her tone as she shifts closer, and I wince.

"Not a fan of cops."

"I see." Her expression is nothing short of impassive, and I know I'm not doing myself any favors here with how dodgy I'm acting.

"I came here for you," I tack on smoothly, and she glances sideways at me.

Reservation sketches across her features, along with a gleam of hurt she can't quite mask. The wounded look gathering behind her eyes brings a crease to my forehead.

"Quit it," she whispers. "I know you like to mess with me, but I don't appreciate it right now." Her bottom lip pulls between her teeth. *"Please."*

"What's going on?"

She refuses to meet my gaze. "I... don't think I can handle it. Not right now. If you're going to pull something on me, you can leave."

"Why would you even think that?" It hits me just then. "You thought I was lying to you at the Halloween party? Is that it?"

She doesn't say a word. She doesn't have to. Even though we're standing under the dim moonlight, I can see her cheeks erupting in a deep shade of red.

"Reese. I wasn't lying to you." The edge of my mouth slants upward. "If you want, I can show you how much I want you right now."

Flustered, she lets out a cough, then another. "What? You? *What?*"

Something bold ignites in my chest as I step toward her, and her eyes widen.

"Caleb?" she squeaks.

I halt and level her with a frown. "What about Blue Balls?"

"Weren't you supposed to help me get with him?" she stammers.

"Why would I do that when you can have me instead?"

Her throat works with a rough swallow. "If you're messing with me—"

"Oh, Reese." I bridge the distance between us, and she drops the bag of cat food in surprise.

Within seconds, her back thumps against the side of the apartment building. Her rib cage heaves with her accelerating breath. Her lips part around a quiet gasp when I find myself between her legs.

Propping a forearm over her head, I have her small frame trapped beneath me and her hair in my other hand. Slowly, I wind the lock until the strands are taut and the curve of her neck is exposed, holding her gaze the entire time.

She goes utterly still before me, and I wait for a smile that never comes. Her confused little frown doesn't let up, either.

Well. If she doesn't believe me, then fuck it. I'll show her.

I lean in when her palm splays against my chest and her head turns to the side.

"You're taking this too far," she breathes.

I huff out a wry chuckle as I bring my face closer to hers. "I'm taking what's mine."

Since I tower over her, my options are limited. Either I bend my neck and back down extremely while she remains firmly on her feet, or I hoist her up. The latter won't end with me pulling a muscle. Clearly the superior option.

A startled yelp escapes her when she finds herself lifted, and her body is all but shaking as she clings to me.

Her legs instinctively wrap around my hips. My grip tightens on her thighs.

"If this is a joke—"

"Does it feel like I'm joking?" I grind against her, and she barely stifles her gasp as she peeks down at the point of contact between our bodies.

Her wide eyes broadcast her every thought. "Oh my God."

"If that's how you're reacting to my cock now," I murmur, and I can feel the hitch of her breath as her fingertips dig into my shoulder blades. "I can't wait to see how you'll react with my cock inside you."

Her mouth falls agape. "*Caleb*," she strangles, and I almost scoff.

"The name's *Dane*," I remind her with a gruff note in my tone. "Memorize it as it'll be the only name coming out of your lips when you're getting thoroughly fucked."

Her voice gets all raspy. "I—I think I'm with Caleb? I've—I've been going out with him?"

"Easy solution. Dump the tool."

"For a guy who chases skirts?"

"For a guy chasing *you*."

Something shifts in her features. It's barely perceptible but enough to elicit a startling pang in my chest.

"Tell me you're not messing with me."

"*Reese*." I readjust my grip, my blunt nails digging into her flesh. "I'm going to give you five minutes to dump the tool because I know it'll eat you up when I do whatever it takes for you to get the message loud and clear. *I'm not messing with you*."

To emphasize my point, I rock my hips up into the space between her thighs with an agonizing slowness. It takes every fiber of my being not to do it again. Especially when she drags in a ragged breath.

"Don't be presumptuous," she stammers. "I'm not breaking up with him because you told me to."

"If you want to cheat on the guy," I say bluntly, "then that's your call."

She recoils, offended. Hurt steals across her profile, and I wince as a sharp twinge of guilt slices through me. My gut reaction has made it clear time and time again that I don't like seeing her this way. I don't want to be the dumbass who makes her unhappy, either.

"Sorry, I'm being an asshole," I mutter, and she gives me a stiff nod while her bottom lip wobbles. "I'll give you a week to figure out who you truly want."

My hands are gentle as I set her down on her feet. Already, I miss the heat of her body and the scent of her skin.

"The tool with the shit music taste who has never made a move on you," I go on roughly. "Or me. And you know where to find me when you've made your decision. I know you'll make the right choice."

Her eyes leap to mine, imploring. Searching. "Th-this isn't a weird ploy to help me get Caleb?"

I give her an incredulous look. "What do you think, Reese's Pieces?"

Stunned, she peers at me as I back away, surprise registering across her face when I pick up the bag of kibble and tip my head to the side. She says nothing as I escort her back to her apartment.

Her chest rises and falls as she holds my gaze. Her lips part when I shift closer, and she goes still when I pass the cat food to her, letting my hand linger on her knuckles for as long as I dare.

"You know where to find me," I repeat, a gruff edge to my voice. "When you make the right choice and pick the right guy."

Before I do something reckless, like stepping inside the apartment, caging her against the wall, and kissing her until Caleb is nothing but a distant memory, I offer her a half-smile and force myself to walk away.

REESE

I'm t-minus ten seconds away from pinching myself. That did not just happen. He did not hit on me. He did not grind shamelessly against me with a raging hard-on. *He did not imply he was the right guy for me.*

Holy shit.

My back presses against the door, and I slide to the floor, eyes wide. I feel oddly weightless and shaky, abuzz with adrenaline. I try to slow my racing heart to no avail. It's beating so fast, so strong, *so sure* that I'm momentarily breathless.

Oh God, I want him. I want him to come back and kiss me like he means it. I want him to hold me up against the wall and murmur dirty words into my ear. I want to be pinned beneath him as he explores every inch of my skin. *I want it all.*

My eyes pinch closed as a thought strikes me out of nowhere. *Crap.* I still have Caleb to deal with. Guilt builds up inside me.

There's nothing wrong with him. We have similar interests, and we get along, but it feels like something is missing. Like something isn't *there*. It doesn't help that he's never once kissed me or made any move on me. I would have settled for a fleeting touch of hands.

Every date we've gone on feels like an outing with a friend.

Don't get me wrong, I enjoy hanging out with him. He's nice and sweet, but I don't see it going anywhere. *I don't even see him kissing me.*

Maybe he likes to take things extremely slowly, or maybe... he's not that into me.

A sense of ease spreads through me. There's no ache in my chest; my heart is not fracturing down the middle. I'm... okay with it.

Blowing out a breath, I know what I must do.

<hr>

I FIND MYSELF STANDING ON THE PORCH OF CALEB'S FRATERNITY ON a late Thursday afternoon. I wasn't able to meet up with him sooner. He had to take his sisters to a birthday party on Sunday and was busy with rehearsals on Monday. I had work and tutoring on Tuesday and Wednesday. Since I *didn't* want to end things with him via phone—it seems so callous and impersonal, and my conscience will never let me live it down—or have this dragged out for another day, I thought it'd be best to come here after my class let out.

As I'm in the middle of messaging him, panic sets in. *Oh God.* Do I really want to do it here where he lives? I don't want him to catch a glimpse of a pink lawn flamingo and flash back to the time I dumped him whenever he leaves the house. Should I have done this someplace neutral? Or an unpleasant place like the DMV?

The front door swings open before I can craft another text, and Caleb comes into view.

"You wanted to see me?" His trademark smile makes an appearance.

It's the same thing as last time. I don't feel anything. My heart isn't a fluttering mess. My stomach isn't swooping. My pulse isn't going haywire at the sight. If anything, I'm just nervous about the next few minutes.

Steeling my nerves, I force myself to look deeply into his eyes. "We need to talk."

"Isn't that… what we're doing?" he teases, and heat burns up the back of my neck.

"Right." An awkward laugh escapes me—my bravado with it.

"Do you want to come in?"

"No, I think we should break up," I blurt, and his body goes rigid while my eyes widen with abject horror. It takes a considerable amount of willpower not to cover my mouth with both hands. In my defense, I've never done this before. It's my first rodeo.

Something unreadable appears in the lines of his face, and the atmosphere becomes frigid. Suddenly, the DMV doesn't seem like the most unpleasant place on earth anymore. Not when this porch is a worthy contender.

"You want to break up?" he sounds out slowly.

I hesitate. Not because I'm reconsidering this, but because I don't want to make a bigger fool of myself. It's hard to believe I rehearsed something last night. To the stray tabby cat, but still.

"Yes?" I pause as it occurs to me we're not even exclusive. "We should stop seeing each other."

His eyebrows shift into a frown. "Is this because of Kingsley?"

"*Nope*. Not at all." Sweat prickles along my lower back as I try to stave off the flush on my cheeks and feign indifference at his name. I don't want to risk the chance of this conversation getting back to my sister. She cannot hear a peep about this. Not even a single syllable. "You're nice, but… I don't know. There was never any… spark between us. I think we're better off as friends."

There. I did it. It's over with. We can now shake hands and part ways.

He continues to stare. I wonder if I should soften the blow and flatter his taste in books when he finally speaks. "No."

"You don't want to be friends?" Disappointment cuts through me like a serrated knife. I don't know why I'm so surprised. Maybe it's because I did enjoy the conversations we've had beyond music and cinema. I liked hearing the things he'd tell me about his sisters. I *loved* it when he'd mention mine. Hearing what Lili did her freshman year while I was still in New Mexico always brought a smile to my face.

My sister *never* tells me anything. I think she feels guilty she was having a great time here while I was stuck at home. *Sorry I'm living my life while yours almost ended.*

I hate that she blames herself for what happened to me. It breaks my heart just thinking about it. I know she's always taken it upon herself to protect me—that's how it's been for as long as I can remember. But it's not her fault. I hope she doesn't blame herself, especially when I never have.

So, I enjoy hearing the things she did from her friends and sorority sisters for a reason. It's nice to know my sister is capable of letting loose.

"No, I don't want to break up with you," Caleb clarifies, and I let his words percolate for a few moments.

"But it's not going anywhere?" I stammer. Where was this energy weeks ago?

"Give me a chance."

"I'm sorry, but—" I break off with a shake of my head. "There have been enough chances. I really do hope we can stay friends. It would be nice to talk about the book once you finish it. If you don't wanna remain friends, that's okay. Regardless, it's over."

With that, I offer him a small wave goodbye and leave before he tries to change my mind.

***

THE BUS SCREECHES AS IT DEPARTS, AND SOON, IT'S JUST ME AND MY anxiety left on the side of the road. I don't waste another second.

My heart thunders against my breastbone; anticipation builds low in my belly. My nerves overtake me when the garage comes into view, and I catalog every detail. The door is up. Rock music pours out from inside. There's a car with its hood popped open. *He's standing right there.*

My body reacts instantaneously, and butterflies take off in my stomach. He doesn't notice me as I approach him. His head's tipped back as he drains his water bottle, and I run my gaze down the column of his throat, staring fixedly.

I barely manage to suppress the shiver racing down my spine, and my breath leaves me in a slow whoosh. *My God.* How can something so innocuous be so enrapturing to witness?

I wait until he's done. The last thing I want is to startle him and have him choking on water. The seconds extend into excruciating eternity while I linger nearby. Then I brace myself when he crumples up the plastic and tosses it seamlessly into a bin.

"Promise me you meant every word you said," comes out so softly, as if anything above a mere whisper will shatter the illusion. For a brief moment, I'm petrified. *Terrified* I've made a huge mistake.

But then he glances over, and time expands. The world grinds to a halt, and I lose all sense of my surroundings. It's just him.

Slowly, a lopsided smirk spreads across his face, barely outpaced by my intake of breath, and I almost double over when sheer relief pulses through my veins.

"Thought you were gonna keep me waiting until the very last second."

A quiet laugh slips free. I almost groan into my hands, sheepish.

"Well?" His brow lifts. "You still wanna keep me waiting?"

"Until the second to last second," I tease, and he snorts. My lips press together to smother my smile as I draw closer, stopping just shy of touching him. Only a few measly inches separate us. Just one more step and I will walk into the warm shelter of his body.

No one moves. There's a softness buried deep in the smolder of his gaze as he holds mine. Something unspoken simmers in the air. I feel ensnared by it. *By him.* The gradual shift in the atmosphere is so tangible that I pitch forward, only for him to hold his hands up with a low groan.

"I don't want my filthy hands all over you." He displays his palms. Sure enough, his fingers are covered in grime. Needless to say, they'll definitely stain the white skinny jeans and baby blue sweater I'm wearing.

And yet… "I don't care," I breathe out, and he snorts.

"You say that now." With a grin, he heads over to a small sink and turns his back to me. "But I'm not ruining your pretty clothes, Mini Reese."

Since he's not kissing me senseless, I take the opportunity to check out his butt. It seems like a fair trade. Then I avert my attention to the ceiling when he catches me ogling him, and my cheeks blaze.

He returns, and I practically throw myself at him. His sharp burst of laughter slides free as he deftly hooks his arms around my waist before I smack into his chest, and we nearly topple over. After he steadies us, I beam at him and soak up the idle tenderness of his hand stroking the small of my back.

Then I burst into giggles.

"Ticklish?"

"My eye didn't get poked out," I explain, as I stretch forward on my toes and press into him.

His brow shoots up inquisitively. "Do you want me to poke you in the eye?"

The teasing note in his words causes me to laugh into his chest. "No, it's…" I trail off as a flush of warmth goes through me, and I peel back to meet his gaze. I don't think there are enough words in the dictionary to describe how this feels so easy and right to me. "I think this is it."

"The moment?" He ducks his head closer to mine, bringing our faces so close that our noses are touching.

"The moment," I agree, as I tilt forward and meet him halfway. My eyes fall shut, and I all but stagger into his embrace as he drops his mouth to mine.

It's the most gentle kiss I've ever had, unhurried and thorough, as if he wants to make this last. As if he wants this to go on for an exquisite eternity. I don't mind. All I can focus on is his tongue and his impossibly soft lips to care about anything else.

An asteroid can hit the city, and I will not budge.

His hands move to my hips. My nails dig into his shoulders. His fingers press into my skin, and I whimper against him. His body tenses for a beat, and with a low groan from the base of his throat, he shoves his thigh between my legs and deepens the kiss.

His deliberate and slow pace gives way to an intensity I'm not prepared for. My gasp breaks free when he sweeps me up and drops me onto the hood of his car at an alarming speed. I'm momentarily blindsided and breathless before he climbs on top of me, caging me in against the cold steel metal. His mouth falls upon mine, all incessant and demanding, like he wants to claim everything I'm willing to hand over to him.

I want to give him everything. He can take it all.

My fingers tangle into his hair, and I greedily pull him in closer and arch my hips against his. A groan rumbles deep from his chest, an utterly guttural sound that sets me ablaze, and he grinds down in a slow, languid motion. I forget how to breathe.

In fact, I forget that I'm in the middle of kissing him. My brain errors out on me. There's a spinning loading circle where my executive function skills should be. He breaks from my lips, pushes up, and finds my gaze with heavy-lidded eyes and a heart-stopping smile.

"You good, Reese?" A knowing smirk follows his question.

In answer, my cheeks burn, and he chuckles while the rough pad of his thumb brushes over the rise of my cheekbone.

Wordlessly, my hand goes to the front of his chest and studies the rigid planes of his abs. My focus remains trained on his face.

The faded scar on his temple. The strong slope of his nose. The way his pupils have expanded to swallow up the frosty-blue color of his eyes.

His throat works with a rough swallow as I boldly venture lower. I barely tease his zipper when he pulls away completely and grates a string of curses under his breath. He seems at war with himself.

"You're not losing your virginity in my dirty garage." His jaw clenches tight as he exhales through his nose, and he all but ignores me when I frown in protest. "We're going back to my place, so I can shower and clean myself up real nice for you before I give you the sweetest fuck of your life."

DANE

I JUST DISCOVERED MY FAVORITE THING ABOUT RIDING A BIKE, AND it's Reese pressing up against me. Her tits are smushed against my back as she clings to me, and I have to remind myself constantly to maintain speed and focus on the road. Going any faster is out of the equation.

On any other day, I would gun down the scenic streets of Las Marinas and enjoy the euphoric rush when it feels like I'm flying, but not today. Not when I want to get us back to my place in one piece.

In a short while, my apartment complex swims into view. The engine's too loud, so I gesture to the right, wait for her to tighten her arms around my waist, and then swerve into the underground parking garage.

Once we've dealt with our helmets, she turns to me with wide eyes and flushed cheeks. "You really like to drive fast," she stammers, and I have to fight my laugh.

"That wasn't me going fast, Reese." And because I'm full of the adrenaline I always get from riding my bike, I curve my hands low on her hips and yank her toward me.

Within a heartbeat, she's hoisted into my arms. My blunt fingernails dig into her thighs. Her legs wrap around me, and her soft moans reverberate through her frame when I lick into her mouth.

She arches into me with more of these little noises, and I'm instantly harder than a hammer. I almost forget the plan to take her back to my apartment. I'm so keyed up that I don't think I can last another second. All I want is to fuck her against a car and hear her moans echo in this garage, but it'll defeat the purpose of why we're here.

Besides, I know better. I must behave. Just hold out a little bit longer. Her first time should be a little classier. And I'm still due for a shower.

With great reluctance, I set her down. It's a testimony of my restraint. Her eyebrows scrunch in protest. Her lips are kiss-swollen and bruised, and a flicker of smug excitement ricochets through me at the sight.

"Let's go," I say regrettably. "I need to shower, and you need to get yourself naked on my bed."

She puffs out a snort against her fist, but I don't miss the hint of pink dashing across her cheeks as her mouth curls into a shy little smile.

I flash her something reassuring in response, grinning harder when her blush darkens and the corner of her lips tips higher.

Finally, her hand slips into mine and squeezes tight. Believe me, I have no inclination to let her go.

We make it up to my place in record time. Kicking the door shut, I fling my keys onto the sectional and tug her toward the bedroom.

"Wait." She stumbles a few steps behind, and I stop short to steady her. "Lock the door."

"Afraid housekeeping's gonna walk in or something?" I tease, doubling back to twist the lock. "No one's here."

Which is good. The last thing I need is for Marco to scare her off. Especially with how nervous she is at the moment. I would have kicked him out without any hesitation. Anything to make her feel more comfortable with me.

"And the deadbolt."

"Bossy." I toss her a wink as she watches me intently. Her wary eyes soften into a gentle smile when I give her a thumbs-up, and she casts a glance at the kitchen.

As much as I'd love to give her a tour, I've got a one-track mind right now. My hands land on the small of her back as I steer her toward my room, and I snort when she thumbs the lock closed.

"No one's gonna interrupt us."

"It'll make me feel better," she replies, and I offer her a shrug as I haul my shirt off. If she doesn't want to risk the microscopic chance of someone walking in on us, more power to her.

I kick off my dirty jeans next, and I can feel the heat of her gaze on my ass when I'm left in my boxer briefs. Since I have no shame, I yank them down in a split second, and I crack a grin when met with a startled gasp.

"Like what you see?"

She sneaks a couple of glances at my cock and quickly feigns interest in the wall beside her when I flex my thigh. Her face is beet red as she stares attentively at the white paint. "Don't you have to shower?"

"Doesn't everybody shower naked?" I chuckle when she makes a noncommittal sound in response. "You better be undressed when I'm back."

"And you call me bossy."

"Hey." I level her with a solemn expression. "I'm just trying to be as efficient as you are."

That gets a laugh out of her, and she sticks her tongue out at me as I make haste and duck into the bathroom.

How I manage to scrub myself clean in the next few minutes is nothing but divine intervention. My hair is still damp when I return, coming to a complete standstill at the sight before me.

"Don't think you and I have the same definition of undressed."

She's wearing nothing but her pink bra and panties. Her

wavy tresses tumble over one shoulder. Her hand is splayed beneath her neck, covering her scar. Her nose scrunches up at me.

Even so, I'm rock-hard. She's got a pretty sweet body, and I possess functioning eyes. I take an unhurried perusal of her gentle curves and slim legs while I make my way over.

"I'm a little nervous," she confesses.

"We can put a pin on this. Say the word, and we'll watch a movie instead."

She swallows audibly and shakes her head, a gentle flush to her fair skin. "I want you." Her short confession is so soft and sweet that I almost groan.

Searching her expression, I wait for her to change her mind. When she gives me a bashful smile, I waste no time climbing on top of her and guiding her onto her back.

"You're going to have to move your hand." Unclasping her bra, I tug it down as far as I can and catch a glimpse of her dusky nipple.

"Please don't look at it," she whispers.

I spare her a reassuring grin as I reach for her panties, slide them carefully down her legs, and fling them over my shoulder. Something topples over with a thump; her mouth parts. I give her a casual shrug, and she dissolves into giggles.

Soon enough, the tension eases from her body. With a sharp intake of breath, she finds my gaze and shyly removes her hand from her neck.

Immediately, my head inclines. The line marring her skin looks just as harsh as I remember.

"*You promised* —" Before she tries to hide it again, I lean forward and press a kiss to her scar. She goes limp, only lifting her arm when I work her bra off.

"I didn't promise a thing. Besides, there's nothing wrong with it." Nipping at her collarbone, I trail a path of kisses across the hollow of her throat. Her pout gives way to a moan. "I've got plenty of 'em myself."

For emphasis, I take her hand and bring it to a specific one alongside my ribs. She quietly inhales as her thumb runs over the raised scar tissue. It was too big of a wound to heal properly. She doesn't need to know that, though.

"And I will find the shitbag who did this to you and fuck him up."

Her eyes pinch closed. "Please don't."

I will, I silently argue as I continue to work my way up to the side of her jaw.

My teeth scrape at a sensitive spot behind her ear, and her body instinctively curves into mine. Chuckling softly, I capture her lips with a slow and potent kiss she melts into.

She shifts beneath me and threads her fingers through my hair, tugging insistently. My stomach clenches tight as my hand travels down her chest to her navel. Soft curls brush my knuckles when my palm ventures south and settles on her clit.

Her kisses go sloppy. Her breathing becomes unsteady. She all but whimpers into my mouth as I tease her with tight, concentrated circles. For a long moment, it's all I do.

Then she bites down on my bottom lip when my middle finger pushes inside her. Her hips buck as a soft moan hums from the base of her throat.

Christ. She's so responsive. She's squirming underneath me, unraveling while I work her into a frenzy with just my hand and tongue. She breaks from the kiss and whines into the crook of my neck when another finger joins the first, stretching her. Filling her.

I don't ease up. I maintain pace as I chase her lips for another kiss, only to groan when she palms my cock and gives me a tentative stroke.

"A little harder," I grate out and clench my jaw. "Yeah. That's it, baby. Squeeze me just like that."

Her head tips back, and she peers up at me, her eyes all starry and hazy-soft. If she keeps looking at me like that, I don't know how much longer I'll last.

As it is, my composure's fraying. My heart beats off rhythm. Warmth spreads under my skin and infuses my chest, and I'm getting so embarrassingly close to coming in her fist when she shudders beneath me.

"*Oh God.*" Her eyes screw shut. Her breathing is shallow and desperate. She's the picture of pure bliss as she comes, utterly sated.

Fuck me. I almost follow her over the edge, and it takes a conscious effort to wrench away.

Confusion etches a small line between her eyebrows, and I nearly groan when her arms loop around my neck and she tries to pull me back in.

"Reese. I want to come inside you; not in your hand." With haste, I grab a condom from my nightstand. "Are you allergic to latex?"

She shakes her head.

"Thank fucking God." I tear the foil open and roll it on, keeping my gaze on her face the entire time. "You can still say no."

"*Please.*"

Fuck. One word and I stand no chance against delaying the inevitable and taking things slow.

I'm settled between her silky legs within an instant. My cock notches her entrance. My forearms are on both sides of her head, propping me up so I don't crush her with my weight.

"This might sting, but I'll take care of you," I tell her, a roughened edge to my voice. "I'll make you feel real good."

She finds my gaze once more. There's so much unwavering trust in her eyes that it does wonders for my ego. *She feels safe here. She feels safe with me.*

"Please," she repeats. "Don't treat me like I'm fragile. Don't treat me like everyone else does."

Tucking a lock of her hair behind her ear, I spare her a slanted smile. "I won't."

With that, I ease myself inside her, one unhurried inch after another. Her thighs split wide as I slowly bring our hips together, and the tight squeeze of her pussy has effectively turned my brain into mush.

I can no longer think straight. I can't even remember my name.

Abruptly, she tenses and lets out a pitiful whimper. *"I change my mind. This sucks."*

I snort against her hairline as my movement becomes arrested. "Thank you for your kind words."

"Sorry, sorry. I—" She breaks off with a harsh gasp. Her fingers press deeper into my back. Her nails bite into my shoulder blades.

"The pain will be gone soon, baby," I reassure her, peppering lazy kisses down her neck and jaw to distract her. Sucking a mark behind her ear, I carefully surge forward until our hips are flushed and I'm fully buried inside her.

My eyes shut as I groan something rough against the heat of her skin. Jesus fucking Christ, she's so warm and wet that it takes every ounce of my willpower to remain still.

I drop a string of kisses along her temple, then sneak one on her upturned nose. She bursts into giggles. I do it again before I track a path down her neck and shoulder.

Finally, she pulls back and takes her bottom lip between her teeth. Her expression softens into something sweet and shy when she finally meets my gaze. There's so much trust in her eyes that I want to bottle it all up and take it with me everywhere I go.

"Look at you," I murmur. *"Look at you, baby, taking all of my cock."*

A soft, fluttery whine parts through her lips; her body exquisitely arches into mine. Pleasure threads through me, and I fall into an easy rhythm and grind into her.

Boldly, she hooks her leg around me, anchoring me to her hips, and a deep, impatient groan takes hold of me. My tempo increases with each succeeding thrust. My jaw tightens with effort.

My thumb tucks under her chin and tilts her head back. "Lift your hips for me. I want you to feel every inch of me while I fuck you."

She complies, and I slide in so deep—so beautifully—that sweet satisfaction claims me. Her pussy's getting wetter, her moans louder. Her tits bounce with my every thrust—*fuck*, they're mesmerizing to watch.

I can barely focus. I'm losing myself in the feel of her body. The feel of her nails raking stinging lines down my back.

I wet my thumb with the flat of my tongue and bring it to her swollen clit, and she comes undone. Her small frame trembles beneath me as she cries out my name. I don't let up. I fuck into her deeper and faster until I meet my own release and empty inside her with one final thrust.

Immediately, I roll off of her before I inadvertently crush her with the heavy weight of my body. I sweep her into my arms, and she lets out a startled laugh when I pull her flush to me.

"Still think I'm messing with you?" I murmur into her hair. She offers me a shake of her head. Faint notes of coconut and sweat cling to her as she relaxes in my embrace.

"No, I think you kind of like me."

I barely hold back a snort and give her hip a firm squeeze. "Kind of?" My thumb goes to her clit, and I grin at her sharp intake of breath. "Let me show you how much I like you."

23

REESE

It's not my alarm that jostles me awake, but the distinct sound of something clattering against the floor, and panic grips me by the throat. My breathing escalates asynchronously to my skittish pulse.

Then I stiffen when a deep voice sounds from outside these walls. Hot tears prick my eyes as my hand smacks blindly into Dane's chest, and he jackknifes up with a start. His gaze lands on me, but I'm unable to look his way.

My whole body trembles as I claw at the covers and try to pull them over me in a futile attempt to hide and shield my neck, and I go deathly still when something touches my shoulder.

A knot of dread in my chest coils tighter despite every little reminder I run through in my head. I know the door to his room is still locked. I triple-checked it myself after staying up late binging mindless reruns with him. This building constantly has a security guard on site, which is probably a good deterrent—*no one can break in*. But I'm helpless against the fear bubbling up from the pit of my stomach.

"Reese?" My peripheral vision takes notice of him before his face comes into view. With furrowed brows, his eyes search mine. Somebody starts singing, and his scowl is instant. "I'll be right back."

I catch his wrist before he's able to pull away, and he gently wrenches his arm out of my grip.

"I'll be fine." He rolls out of bed and mutters something too low for me to hear.

I yank the cover over my head and try not to make any sudden movement when I hear the door creaking open.

"*Marco, will you shut the fuck up?*"

"Did I wake you up from your beauty sleep? Come here, baby. I'll give you a smooch to make up for it—"

A loud slam rends the air. I shrink as Dane's grumblings draw nearer, slowly peeking out from my hiding spot to see him running his hand down his face.

"Who's Marco?"

"An old friend of mine." He heaves out a long-suffering sigh. "I'm taking my damn spare keys back next week. He can sleep in his truck for all I care."

The mattress dips under his weight when I shoot him a pleading look.

"Wait. Can you make sure it's locked?"

He shrugs, unbothered. "You got it."

I watch him double back, and when I hear the audible click, the tension alleviates from my shoulders. Then I smother my giggle when he mimes a *ta-da* motion.

"Thank you." I muster up the biggest smile I can manage, taking in the sight of his body when he stretches his arms above his head and exposes the rigid lines of his abs.

Heat burns up to the tips of my ears when my mind wanders, and once again, I'm thinking about last night.

He knows it, too. A devastatingly handsome grin steals across his face, and he wiggles a brow. "What's up, Reese?"

"Not much," I say, feigning nonchalance. My voice is too pitchy to pull it off. I'm too busy daydreaming about his body—

broad chest and all. For posterity's sake, of course. "Just thinking about my physics assignment."

"Is that what we're calling it?"

I bury my face into a pillow and groan. Then I beam when he slides under the cover and gathers me into his arms. His nose pokes the back of my neck while he breathes me in, and he chuckles softly when I slip my hand into his and play with his fingers.

For someone who's allegedly dangerous, he sure likes to spoon. Not that I'm complaining.

"I have to get ready for school," I mutter regrettably.

His lips find my ear. "Ditch."

Snorting quietly, I glance over my shoulder. "Unlike you, I do enjoy going to my classes."

"Masochist," he teases, dropping a kiss on my temple. "Can't hurt to miss one day, can it?"

I'm maneuvered onto my back. He stretches his body over mine as he tugs the shirt I'm borrowing off me. For a millisecond, I almost reflexively cover my scar, especially when his gaze lingers and sears my soul in one fell swoop. Instead, I busy my hands with the ends of my hair.

His mouth curves into a faint smile, and my shyness heightens to a new level. I avert my gaze as my cheeks scald.

I know he saw me completely naked last night, but my anxiety has never been a logical beast. It never has been when it comes to my scar.

"Unfortunately," I stammer, "I have a quiz." My eyes shut as his mouth tracks a fiery path across the swells of my breasts. "Is there any chance you can take me home? I need a change of clothes."

While I can probably get away with wearing my sweater for the second day in a row, the same cannot be said about my jeans. There are smudgy fingerprints all over the white fabric, and I'm not *that* daring when it comes to fashion.

"I'll take you back." He presses one last kiss to the fluttering pulse point of my neck, then reluctantly pushes up and hands me back his shirt.

We fall silent as we get out of bed. I sneak a glance in his direction as he changes, and I swallow hard at the alarming amount of scars before me. He has so many, some of which are in very concerning places.

"My eyes are up here, Mini Reese," he teases.

Blushing, I snatch my bra hanging from a table lamp and hesitate. "Can we, um… keep this between us?"

"Don't want Blue Balls to know you've moved on so quickly?" He tosses me a wink, and my nose wrinkles.

Ugh. I haven't even considered that. I spent last night agonizing over Lilian finding out about us and, well, freaking the hell out on me.

"Or are you finally afraid to be seen with me in public?" His voice gains a playful edge.

"I don't want to hurt Caleb's feelings. I know you don't care much for him, but I can't do that to him," I explain, and his smirk melts into a stormy scowl. "Anyway, my sister's the one I'm worried about. I don't want her to know about this yet…" *Because she doesn't like you.*

He offers me a casual shrug. "Sneaking around to fuck and make out sounds fun."

I bite my bottom lip. "So this isn't… just a one-time thing?"

With a scoff, he zips up his jeans and strides toward me. Grabbing my hand, he guides it straight to his crotch. A little squeak escapes me.

"Does this feel like a one-time thing?"

"No." I expel a shaky laugh. "You are so crass."

"Blunt and abrasive, too, right?"

"And sweet," I tack on, and he makes a face. It's not like I'm wrong. He did kiss my nose last night.

Do dangerous people kiss noses?

Statistically speaking, some criminals are in loving relationships and perhaps enjoy displaying affection.

Oh God. I can practically hear Lilian screaming at me to run away. To not be fooled by him. To get out while I can. Swallowing hard, I peer in his direction as I recall everything she said about him. *It's a lot.*

"Do you know who Travis Walker is?"

There's an infinitesimal shift in the air, so subtle that I almost miss it. Something unnamed gathers in his eyes as he turns to face me, and I go stock-still.

"Why? Did that motherfucker say something about me?"

"No." I put on a reassuring smile and falter under his rapt focus. "I heard from… one of the sorority girls that you, um, broke his arm."

"Yeah, I broke his arm."

Oh. Okay. Wincing, I suck in oxygen at his blunt and clinical tone. I was honestly expecting him to deny it. I didn't want my sister to be right.

It's hard to grapple with the idea of him doing something that extreme. Maybe it's because my thoughts are fixated on his whisper-soft smile at the curve of his lips after he snuck a kiss on my nose.

"On purpose?"

"Yeah."

I try not to flinch this time. "Why?"

Dane casts another glance at me, and his cold demeanor gives way to something guarded. "Think that's the first time somebody ever asked me that."

A pang of sorrow tears into my soft heart. "Will you tell me what happened?"

He grates out a harsh scoff. "Fucker tried to get his frat brothers to jump me my freshman year."

Before I can respond, he lifts his shirt and twists his torso. My eyes land on a mess of scar tissue just a few inches above his right kidney, and the ache sharpens in my chest. *That could have been fatal.*

"This is the parting gift he left me with." There's no warmth in his tone as he shoots me a mocking grin. "It was either get shanked to death or get the fucking broken bottle out of his hand."

My palm covers my mouth, and despair sets in when he offers me a sarcastic shrug.

Everything about this is upsetting and confusing. Nothing aligns with what my sister has told me. *Nothing makes sense.*

"Why did Travis and his brothers jump you?" My heart gives an erratic lurch when my attention pivots to the jagged line. I'm beginning to reevaluate my feelings toward the fraternity members on campus.

"Beats me." His hand goes to the back of his neck. "Wouldn't be surprised if he was on something that day."

"Drugs?"

"No, he was high on life," he deadpans, then winces. "Sorry. I'm being an asshole." With a sigh, his defensiveness melts away. "I used to sell my services. Fixed cars, tricked them up, shit like that. Nothing too fancy. I'd leave the bigger things for someone else to handle, but I know a thing or two myself.

"Walker caught on that I was rolling in cash, so he and his shithead cronies not only stiffed me after I replaced an alternator for him, he tried to rob me. He said I didn't need the cash 'cause I had plenty to spare."

I draw in a steadying breath. "You're not lying to me, right?"

He frowns. "Reese, I would *never* lie to you."

Deep down, I believe him. I genuinely do. My only concern is my sister. I don't know how I'll broach this topic with her. I have a sinking suspicion she won't listen to a word I say. Not about him.

I'm the soft-hearted one. She's not.

"I believe you," I tell him, and I swear, the tension drains from his body.

He gives me a nod, along with a smirk that doesn't quite reach his eyes. He looks elsewhere and shoves his hands into his pockets, and I can feel my soft heart split down the middle.

Rushing over, I throw my arms around him and bury my face in his chest. He's as still as a statue while I hug him tight. "I know you don't fight people for fun. I believed you then, and my feelings haven't changed. How come… Why doesn't anybody know about this?"

"I'm not lying—"

"Dane." My head pulls back, and I lock eyes with him. "I know you're not."

His gaze sears into mine. "People believe what they wanna believe."

Lilian comes to mind. "You're not wrong," I whisper. "But if you tell them the truth—"

"It's a little too late for that." He shrugs. "Besides, everyone I care about knows the truth, and that's good enough for me."

"But maybe—"

"Come on. I know one of us actually gives a shit about going to class." He levels me with a pointed look. "Let's get you back to your apartment so you can change into something I'll be tearing off later."

My lips press together as I decide not to push it any further. I spare him a tiny smile, then scrunch my face when he gives my butt a rough squeeze, and I playfully shove him away.

He breaks into laughter. I stick my tongue out at him while I focus on wrangling my bra on.

Honestly, I have no idea how I managed to go from one extreme to another. From a guy who doesn't even hold my hand to someone who'll brazenly hit on me every chance he can get.

But then I catch a glimpse of that softness buried deep in his heated gaze, and already, I have my answer. I know how I ended up with him.

I simply picked the right guy.

24

DANE

Once Sergei passes me the keys, I hand him a wad of cash. My attention goes straight to my latest acquisition. It's a late-sixties white convertible that's seen better days.

The muscle car desperately needs a new paint job, but the real challenge is what's inside. The stock engine's completely jacked up, and there's a likely chance I'll have to gut the whole damn thing.

"Pleasure doing business with you, kid."

I grunt in acknowledgment as he swaggers off, and I'm quick to slide behind the wheel the moment he's gone. At least the interior has remained in pristine condition.

The girl's a beaut, but it's also an automatic. I've got nothing against them. I just like driving cars the way they're meant to be driven: by shifting the gears yourself.

The vehicle stalls when I start it. My second attempt doesn't fare any better. On my third try, the V8 engine sputters for a small eternity before a steady roar fills the air.

I breathe out a relieved sigh.

Since Marco dropped me off on his way to catch the waves, I don't have to deal with the logistical nightmare of transporting this beaut back to my garage.

However, it's the last thing on my mind. Taking a detour, I head straight to the other side of campus and pull into the staff parking lot. It's right in front of the Music Building, and the closest spot I can find to the bookstore.

Checking the time on my phone, I sit back and wait for Reese to emerge. I saw her schedule while dropping her off at her apartment the other day. Her whiteboard calendar listed closing shifts for the entire week. I don't like the idea of her waiting at a bus stop this late, especially with the number of campus crime alerts ramping up this semester.

She's too delicate and gentle to put up a fight, and she freezes up so easily when spooked. When it comes to defending your-self, every second counts.

Before long, she exits the bookstore. I immediately lay on the horn. She startles and casts a bewildered glance my way.

Right. I roll the window down and click my tongue twice. It's a long minute before she groans.

"Oh my God."

Waving goodbye to her coworkers, she jogs over to me and folds her arms across her generous rack. I silently thank the inventor of tight sweaters and shoot her my most charming grin.

She stares at me, unfazed. "What are you doing here?"

"Well, I go here," I tease.

She doesn't let up. Not a muscle in her face moves as she sighs. "I know that. Why are you here right now?"

"What else? I'm giving you a lift home."

"I can take the bus."

Frowning, I poke my head out and peer up at the inky night sky. It's so fucking dark that the dim campus lamps barely light up the area around us.

Someone could get away with lurking in the shadows. My chest constricts at the thought. More so when my gaze cuts back to her and lingers on her neck. I wish she'd tell me what happened to her, but it's not my place to ask.

Believe me, I'm the last person on earth to give her shit about it. If she ever wants to talk about her scar, I'll be all ears. But until then, I won't bring it up.

"As long as I'm in the picture, you can get a ride from me."

The innuendo isn't lost on her. With an exasperated laugh, she pokes my cheek, hitches her backpack over her shoulder, and flounces to the passenger side.

There's a flush to her skin as she shuts the door behind her. I'm about to throw the vehicle in reverse when she scoots over and plants a kiss on my temple.

"*Lower*, Reese's Pieces." I'm met with an instant glare.

"I have a bus pass, and I'm not afraid to use it," she threatens with an adorable little scowl. Then she yelps when the tires screech as I peel out of the parking spot. "Who taught you how to drive?"

"Self-taught." I ease my foot off the gas as we inch toward an intersection.

Clutching her chest, she gives me a sidelong glance. "Maybe you should teach yourself again."

I snicker. "Aw, baby, you wound me. I'll be the safest driver you'll ever ride with."

"*Within* the speed limit?"

I make a show of gesturing to the speedometer when the lights turn green. "Christ, that electric scooter is going faster than us."

"You'll thank me when we get there safe and sound."

"Even that bicyclist is faster," I cajole. "You think that jogger back there will beat us to the next stop?"

She barely conceals her huff of laughter and pokes me in the arm. "Is this car new?"

"You bet your sweet ass it is." I run my hand over the steering wheel. "Gonna fix her up real nice and get some chump change out of her."

"So, you *do* fix cars for a living." Accusation drips in her tone.

"It's more of a hobby," I correct. "A thing I do in my spare time. I don't have the space to keep every car I come across."

"Huh." She turns toward me. "How much spare time do you have, exactly?"

"Plenty when you don't worry about showing up for lectures." I flash her a wolfish grin and refocus my gaze on the crumbling road. There are too many potholes the city has done fuck all to fix, and I don't want to add suspensions to my list of things I need to deal with.

Far too soon, the convertible pulls up to the curb. It won't be long before she exits the vehicle and our short time together comes to an end.

"Any reason why they don't close the gates?"

"I think they're broken," she muses.

My forehead tightens with a frown. Sure, they were useful when I was ditching the cops, but still.

"This area is safe," she assures me. "It looks a little sketchy, but everyone leaves you alone. Just because it looks bad doesn't mean it is bad."

My brow slowly lifts. "We still talking about the gates here?"

Her mouth pulls into a sweet smile. "I hope you make some excellent chump change."

"It'll take some time before I'm able to get rid of her." I tip my chin. "You haven't seen what's under the hood. Lots of test drives await me."

"Ooh. Let me know if you'll be driving along the coast." She holds up her phone. "I'd love to ride shotgun."

"For your fiesta, right?"

"Finsta."

I grin. Messing with her has become my second hobby. "Something about the golden shower?"

She splutters and playfully nudges my arm. "Golden *hour*. Good*bye*, Dane."

With that, she pockets her cell. She glances back at me and hesitates before she leans over to kiss my cheek. I curve my palm around her wrist and tug her closer, bringing my mouth to hers without a second to waste.

She melts into me as she takes my lower lip between her teeth, teasing me with a tantalizing flick of her tongue. Abruptly, she pulls away before it can escalate further, and I groan something feral at the ceiling.

"I'm sorry. I have an engineering project due, or else..."

"Say no more, Mini Reese." I slide my hand behind her neck and draw her back in. Her breathing hitches as my teeth scrape a sensitive spot behind her ear, and she clutches the front of my shirt while I suck gently at the tender skin.

I want to hoist her onto my lap. See how loud she can get with just my mouth and tongue. Christen every inch of this vehicle. Instead, I reluctantly let her go, then glance down when I feel her trace something on my chest.

A heart. She's drawing a heart over my heart.

"Again, Reese is my nickname," she whispers and sneaks a kiss on my lips. Her eyes have that starry glow to them when she finally pulls away.

Oddly dazed, I barely register my intake of breath or the steady thrum in my ears as she climbs out and shuts the door behind her. She spares me a sweet smile before she heads off to the gate.

That sweet smile brightens when I scramble out of the car and quickly catch up with her, but it's no match for the look she gives me as she steps inside her apartment. It takes every last ounce of my self-control not to do anything more than bend down for one last kiss.

She offers me a little wave and shuts the door.

Crossing my arms, I wait sixty seconds just to ensure there aren't any creeps lurking nearby. Once I get visual confirmation that nothing appears out of the ordinary and my chest feels at ease, I return to the convertible and set off for my garage.

2 5

REESE

With Thanksgiving next week, Lilian has been blowing up my phone. Her sorority is hosting Friendsgiving again, and she wants me to confirm for the nth time I'm coming. It's not like I have anywhere else to be. Back in New Mexico with our mom and her boyfriend? No thanks.

I send my sister a text promising I'll be there with sparkling apple cider, then lean back in my seat and enjoy the scenery as the convertible flies down the road. It's exhilarating.

With the top down, the engine thunderous, and the air salty and rich with gasoline, I feel… very much alive. Adrenaline courses through me as the car takes a sharp turn at high speed. I'm not a thrill seeker, but… I can see the appeal.

In my periphery, Dane is the definition of confidence. It's not from a place of arrogance. He's the most relaxed I've ever seen him. There's no point of tension in his body. He's just so undeniably assured and calm.

His black hair rustles with the wind. His blue eyes have a serene quality to them. His broad shoulders casually lean into his seat as he drums his fingers along the top of the steering wheel.

He is in his element.

I silently watch him. For a short spell, it's all I do. There's no point in talking. When he's going this fast, he's not much of a conversationalist. He's too focused on the road.

All of a sudden, his demeanor shifts. He's no longer smiling. His teeth grit as he sits forward and strangles the steering wheel.

"She's gonna cut us off," he growls, jamming his foot on the brakes as a red sedan barrels into our lane. Time slows down into frame rates. My heartbeat is in my throat as the other car narrowly avoids being clipped by the convertible. There's only a fraction of an inch between both vehicles. My soul has shriveled up and died faster than a houseplant under my sister's care.

Screeching tires rend the air as Dane swerves into the bike lane.

"*Learn how to use your fucking mirrors!*" he snarls, flipping the bird.

Trembling, I stare ahead as the sedan maintains speed at what must be twenty under the posted limit. I'm squeezing my phone so tightly that I wouldn't be surprised if it fused with my hand.

"Sorry." Dane's face comes into view. "You all right?"

"Yeah." I let out a shaky breath. "I promise," I tack on when a small divot forms between his dark brows. "Swear on my pinky."

His expression doesn't ease up. His throat works with a rough swallow before he streaks his fingers through his hair. "You can be the best driver in the world and still be at the mercy of some fucking dumbass on the road."

"That is *totally* reassuring," I deadpan. "I definitely cannot wait to learn how to drive with these inspiring words."

"You don't know how to drive?" He feigns offense, splaying his hand against his heart.

"I never had the opportunity to learn. Or the time," I stammer. "And with what car? What's the point of learning if I don't have one to practice with?"

With a shake of his head, he pulls over completely. "That has to change."

"Wait. Are you kicking me out because I don't know how to drive?"

"No." He fights his grin. "We're switching seats."

My throat closes up. "Do you want me to crash into that pole? Because this car has a date with that pole in the next thirty seconds."

He snorts as he cuts the engine. "You'll be fine. I'll have my hand on the emergency brake the entire time."

"But—"

He hops out of the vehicle before I can get another word in. Bewildered, I say nothing when he opens the passenger door.

"Come on, Reese. You'll never have a better teacher than me."

"I've seen how your other student drives," I say flatly.

"And he's fucking good at it," Dane replies without missing a beat. "Now, come on. Let me show you a thing or two before daylight's over."

"Are you gonna teach me how to *Tokyo Drift*?"

His mouth twitches at the corner. "No. I'll teach you how to drift one of these days if you want—"

"I'm good." I swallow past the small lump in my throat. Knowing my luck, I'll somehow launch this convertible into the ocean instead of pulling it off.

"All right. Let me know if you change your mind. I'll have to get my other car—"

"Why not this one?"

He chuckles as if it's the funniest thing he's ever heard. "If it's got a carburetor, it ain't drifting well."

I've got no idea what he means by that, but I offer him a small nod, regardless. This must be what it's like to be in his shoes when I go on and on about how camera lighting can contribute to visual storytelling based on its balance and depth.

"Ol' Reliable can handle the maneuver," he continues. "Her front camber's fixed for it."

Again, I have no idea what any of these words mean.

"Anyway, let me give you the basics." He extends his hand, and I reluctantly take it after I unbuckle my seatbelt. "Lucky for you, this girl's an automatic. It'll be easy."

Trepidation floods my bloodstream as I meet his gaze. "Say goodbye to your car."

He slips into a smirk. "I have plenty more back at my garage."

All too soon, I find myself behind the wheel. I pull the driver's seat all the way up—which he ribs me for good-naturedly—then readjust the rearview mirror. My peripheral vision spots him holding up my phone. I twist to gawp at him, then recoil slightly when the flash goes off. I'm pretty certain I was mid-blink.

"For your fiesta."

"Finsta," I correct, reaching for my phone. "Gimme that—"

"It's not safe to text and drive." He pockets it and hikes his chin. "Now, put your left hand here."

For the next ten minutes, he gives me a rundown on the levers, brakes, and pedals. He does not leave out any details.

"Don't be *that* idiot who uses both feet," he explains. "You don't want to accidentally hit the gas and get into a collision."

"Got it. Hit them both at the same time," I tease, and I freeze in place when he levels me with a dark scowl.

"We do *not* joke about car safety," he growls.

Oof. "I was just being silly," I mumble, and the hard lines on his face give way to something softer. "I won't say another word."

Remorse shines in his eyes, and he allows himself a quiet sigh. "Sorry, it's a touchy subject," he replies gruffly. "You're good." Clearing his throat, he goes over the levers near the steering wheel.

I pay extra attention just so he knows I'm taking this seriously. I can feel his gaze on me the entire time, and my heart twists when he puts a tentative hand on my shoulder in a small act of comfort and apology.

"And there you have it," Dane wraps up. "Now start 'er up."

My bottom lip worries between my teeth as I twist the key, and my breath freezes in my lungs when the engine rumbles to life. *Was it always this loud?*

Instinctively, my fingers tighten around the steering wheel. My pulse has rushed into my ears. I feel like I'm going to puke. I can practically taste the club sandwich threatening to make a reappearance.

"Reese, you'll be fine," he assures me.

"I'm not fine," I squeak.

"If anything, you're sexy."

Despite myself, I burst into giggles. "I'm *trying* to take this seriously, Kingsley. Now's not the time for you to be silly."

"I was being serious, too," he says, and I glance sideways at him. Something gentle takes over his features as he holds my gaze. "I promise you, everything will be okay. I won't let anything happen to you."

With a terse nod, I redirect my attention to the gear lever. I don't think I'm breathing as I run through the steps in my head. Unease plagues me as I stare ahead.

I've had a good run. Nineteen years is pretty great, considering it's two more than I ever expected.

My foot hits the gas, and Dane shouts immediately as the car shrieks to a halt. I think I am, too. Shrieking, that is.

"*Easy, girl, easy!*" His hand is white-knuckling the emergency brake, whereas both of mine are clutching my chest.

"*I'm sorry,*" I gasp, rattled. "This is why I don't drive. *I'm a menace behind the wheel.*"

He snorts, then brings a fist up to his mouth and snickers into it.

"All right, menace," he sounds out slowly, and I choose to ignore that. He hacks out a bunch of coughs and thumps his sternum. "Think of it as sex. You need to ease into it the first time."

My eyebrows scrunch. "Is sex always on your mind?"

"That and cars," comes his response, and this time, his laughter tears loose from him. It's a nice laugh, even though it's at my expense. There's a subtle warmth to it.

"Oh my God," I mutter, pressing my finger against my brow bone. "You are such a guy."

"Go slow," he reminds me. "*Ease* into it."

I spare him a tight-lipped smile. "Got it."

Finally, he removes his hand from the emergency brake. With a steadying breath, I *ease into it* with a gentle tap.

"All right," he says, whistling out a low note. "Attagirl."

My neck erupts into flames, and I nearly squeak. I'm suddenly too aware of how blazing hot my cheekbones are.

"Aw, you like that," he says, ever the freakishly observant guy.

"Shut up," I wheeze as I bring the car's speed up to thirty miles per hour.

"You're doing such a great job, baby girl," he drawls, lowering his voice to a husky whisper. I would glare daggers at him if I weren't busy trying to make the turn around a bend. "Keep going, baby—"

"Swear to God, Kingsley," I choke out, then startle when a horn honks behind us. Suddenly, a minivan swings into the opposing lane. The driver flips the bird before he cuts us off, and I shrink.

"Ignore him," Dane says. "And don't take your eyes off the road."

"I don't like being an inconvenience."

"Then drive at the speed limit."

I get the convertible up to fifty, then squeeze the steering wheel in a death grip for the next stretch of road. Thankfully, he directs me to a nearby lot. It's a good call on his end. Any longer and I might inadvertently snap the metal wheel in half.

"Are we done now?" Every fiber of my being winces when the car hits the sidewalk and mounts the curb.

"Not yet," he answers. "You need to learn how to park and reverse before we wrap things up."

"Do I have to?"

"Reese. Reversing is fun," he says. "It really is."

"I'll take your word for it." I suck air between my teeth when I somehow manage to take up two parking spaces. "Was your experience anything like this the first time you drove?"

"Nah. I knew how to drive at the posted speed."

I finally get the chance to glare daggers at him. "Wow, look at you, Mr. I Know How To Drive Cars So Fantastically."

He snickers and claps his hand on my shoulder. "Reese, you did an *okay* job."

My eyebrow lifts. "Oh? What happened to *such a great job, baby girl*?" I retort, and his grin broadens.

"*Aw, baby, you did so well for me.*" His voice sinks into a husky murmur, and my whole body feels like it's been set ablaze. "*I am so proud of you—*"

My finger smushes against his lips. I level him with a warning look and pry my hand away.

"Glad to know Mr. Self-Taught did so well his first time," I mutter, and he chuckles roughly.

"Yeah... That was not the case." He leans back in his seat and scrubs the line of his jaw. "My first time ended with three totaled cars."

"*Three?*" I yelp, and I swivel toward him with saucer-wide eyes. "How?"

"I was being stupid."

"Were you texting—"

"No. Nothing like that. I was the only one driving that night."

My eyebrows knit together. Maybe it's me, but it's hard to imagine him—the guy who complains about people not using blinkers—causing that much damage. "You don't have to tell me anything if you don't want—"

"I was a dumbass kid who stole my father's car and took it for a joyride." His gaze bores blankly into mine, his words unnervingly clinical and matter-of-fact. "Lost control of the vehicle and overcorrected it like an idiot. I pummeled two cars whose only crime was being parked outside."

I blink, stunned.

His throat bobs with a rough swallow. "Not my proudest moment."

"Were you hurt?"

"Just my pride." He folds an arm behind his head. "I didn't get off easy, if that's what you were thinking. My father flipped out. Threatened to have my ass hauled off to juvie." His sentence dwindles as a pensive look flits across his profile. "He wanted to lay down the law. It didn't pan out the way he wanted it to, though.

"See, those two cars I hit were getting work done at this mechanic's shop. The owner felt bad for me and offered to let me work there to pay off all the damages I'd done."

Bitterness creeps into his tone. I reach over and squeeze his knee.

"Was the guy a jerk to you?"

"Who, Sal? Nah. Sal and his wife… they're good people. They moved to Texas shortly after I graduated high school, but they were good people."

The fondness in his voice brings a smile to my face before I register his words. "Were?"

"Sal passed away last year, and his wife died a few months ago."

"I'm so sorry," I whisper. "Um… I'm glad they were nice to you."

"Yeah." He falls silent. "Doesn't mean Sal didn't get on my ass, because that man did. We could never go more than a week without him calling me out on something." He chuckles wryly. "I don't think I'd be here if it weren't for him."

"You'd… be in jail?"

"Nah. Probably dead, if anything."

My heart squeezes painfully as a wave of distress takes root in me. Before I can say anything else, he clears his throat.

"All right." His eyes flicker toward me. "We've had enough touchy-feelies for today. How about I get some touchy-feely action in return?" With a plastered grin, he brazenly drops his line of sight to my breasts and lets out a low whistle.

"You are so romantic," I state dryly.

"That's not a no."

"*No*," is my resounding response, and he snickers.

"Damn. And here I was," he drawls, "bleeding my heart out for you, Reese's Pieces." He hits me with a somber stare. "Should I sprinkle in some praises for you—"

"*You said reversing is fun, right*?" I reach for the keys left in the ignition and ignore his smoldering gaze. "Let's see how fun it can be."

DANE

For the past two hours, I've been subjected to nonstop bubblegum pop. It's not the music I'd jam to in my garage, but Reese asked if she could stream her playlist after discovering I tend to listen to the same song on repeat.

I'm not listening to the lyrics. I just need background noise while I work.

As it is, I'm taking inventory of what I need to order for the beaut: filters, fuel pump, and spark plugs. It's a damn shame. Replacing assembly line parts with aftermarket always kills me, but it must be done if I want this car to run smoothly.

Taking a step back from the engine, I catch sight of Reese removing her sweater right then and there. As if she can sense me shamelessly checking her out, her eyes narrow in suspicion. Her hand goes to cover her scar.

"Don't mind me. Feel free to take it all off—"

She shoots me a baleful glare, but at least she's no longer trying to conceal her neck. I'll count that as a win. "It's a bit hot in here."

She's not wrong. It's stuffy in here with the door down. I have the windows cracked open, but they can only do so much.

"Want me to get you some water?" I offer, and she shakes her head.

"I'm fine, but thank you." Smiling, she spins around on the barstool and returns her attention to her engineering project. Whatever's on her laptop screen looks mighty confusing. I can't blame the frown she's got going on. I'd be pissed, too, if I had to deal with this while other Belford U students got to mix colors for a grade.

My focus goes back to the engine, where countless stripped bolts taunt me with their presence. Out of nowhere, Reese leans forward in my periphery, and I fight my groan when her tiny top slides up and reveals a glimpse of her skin.

Then I actually groan when I smack my head into the hood. She peeks over her shoulder, concern etching across her features.

"Are you—"

"Wasn't looking where I was going." I tense up when she rushes over, willing myself to relax as she stretches on her toes and examines me. "I'm experiencing some déjà vu from this."

Her eyebrow arches. "Which time?"

Right. She's fussed over me twice now. I quietly chuckle. "Both, I guess."

"Do you need ice?"

"I think I need a kiss to make it better."

She dissolves into laughter as she gives me a playful shove. "*I* think you'll be fine."

"Damn, you're cold, Reese's Pieces."

She sticks her tongue out at me and returns to the workbench.

***

THERE'S NO MORE BUBBLEGUM POP PLAYING, SO I CAN HEAR THE crickets chirping outside and the occasional car driving by. We're both sitting on the floor with takeout from the local Thai spot. Reese is leaning into my shoulder as we wolf down the food.

Well, I am. She's all manners with her stir fry, and she's too damn sweet offering me pieces of chicken in between bites.

"Are you heading home for Thanksgiving?"

It's an innocent question, but it dampens my mood. I can already imagine the nightmare awaiting me if I dare show up. Easily picture the unhappy faces. "Nah, fuck that."

"You're not close to your parents, either?"

"*You're* not close to yours?" Between us, she seems like the type to, I don't know, have a good relationship with her family. Hell, she's always reaching out to her sister whenever we're together.

Her expression falters as she grumbles, "I asked you first."

"Are we in middle school?" I counter. "Nah. I'm not close to that prickhead at all."

"What about your mom?"

With a shrug, I set my carton down and grab a napkin. "I'll stop by the ocean or some shit."

"The ocean?"

"That's where her ashes are scattered."

"*Oh.*" Her voice is soft.

"Save your tears, Reese's Pieces." Looking over, I find her giving me sad eyes. "Don't worry about me. Everyone's moved on already."

Her stare becomes pensive and makes me feel scrubbed raw from the inside out. "Define everyone."

"Every person, everybody—"

"*Dane.*"

"Why don't you like your folks?"

Immediately, she ducks her head and pokes at her food. "They're not good people."

"Did they do something to you?" My gut clenches as I look at her scar.

She glances sideways and balks. "What? *No.* They didn't cause this. They were just mean and bitter... Always had an opinion about something."

"You know, your parents don't define who you are," I tell her, and she spares me a smile that doesn't reach her eyes.

"I know." She bites her bottom lip. "What are you doing for Thanksgiving, then?"

"Probably be here. Fixing the Nova. You?"

"Hang with my sister. I think she's gonna drag me to the mall on Friday."

"For the love of God," I interject. "Don't buy yourself another sweater. We're in Southern California, not Vermont. Unless you enjoy being in a state of constant sweating, get yourself more of these."

I reach over and tug on the thin strap of her top.

Her nose scrunches. "You should paint the Nova purple."

I decide to go along with the change of topic. Give her an out. "Why purple?"

"Okay, well… Whenever I hear Nova, I automatically think of supernovas." Something sheepish flits across her profile. "I know they're composed of different colors, but I always think of purple first."

I grimace. "For the car, though? *Really?*"

"It's not a bad color," she insists somewhat defensively.

"I've never once seen a purple that's not a bad color."

She gasps. "Well… I like this one particular shade… which happens to be the color of my name."

Furrowing a brow, I give her a slow perusal. "Your name is *Purple?*"

She pulls away slightly, stunned. *"No."*

"Wait." I straighten my spine. "What is your name?"

She offers me a shrug, feigning nonchalance. "Wouldn't you like to know?"

"Aw, baby. Don't do this to me," I protest. "Don't ruin my Christmas gift for you. I wanted to surprise you so badly, but how will I get my back tattoo done if I don't know what it is?"

"What?"

"Yeah. I wanted my first piece to mean something. I guess I'll have to settle for *Reese's Stuffed*—"

Her palm spreads across my mouth; her gaze narrows in warning. "I know it's your body, but *no*."

My eyes crinkle as I peel back and settle against the car. "You've got nothing to worry about."

"Don't I?"

"I don't care for 'em," I explain, and I'm met with a heavy dose of skepticism. "Let me guess. A dangerous guy like me should be covered in them?"

Her face falls. "Dane—"

"It's okay, Reese's Pieces. I know you don't think I'm that bad, or else you probably wouldn't have fucked me."

She splutters as her cheeks become splotchy red. "I don't think you're as bad as people make you out to be. You're a bit rough around the edges, though."

"Yeah. I know. You said that about me before. I remember everything you tell me." I tap my temple, registering her surprise. "Just because I ditch class doesn't mean I'm dumber than a bag of rocks. I'm capable of recalling things."

Flustered, she folds her arms. "Even from that night?"

"The night we fucked?"

"The night we *met*," she clarifies.

I hesitate as vivid flashes of a swinging crowbar come to mind. "You thought I had a bicycle." With a shake of my head, I snicker. "And you didn't even buy me dinner before my shirt went off, which *you* demanded. You couldn't even keep your hands off of me once I stripped for you."

"You were bleeding everywhere," she points out, unamused. "And I thought sushi counted."

"People tend to wine and dine *before* they get to it," I tease, and she narrows her eyes.

"Speaking from experience?" she asks dryly.

"Nah. I never bothered." Christ. I sound like a major tool.

"They were just meaningless hookups." Great. Now I sound like a complete douchebag.

"Oh." She goes silent. "Am I—"

"*No.* Do not finish that sentence."

"But you haven't wined and dined me before we…" She trails off and picks at her nails.

I wince. I should have seen this coming. She likes the *museum*, for crying out loud. And she endured Blue Balls for weeks while he took her to places like that nasally concert.

Knocking her thigh with mine, I wait until she looks my way. "You want me to take you out on dates?"

"It doesn't have to be anything fancy," she says softly. "I'd like to go out with you."

"You got it," I say. "I already know where to take you."

Suspicion gathers behind her eyes. "Should I be worried?"

I toss her a wink while I grab my soda. She quietly sighs and returns her attention to her stir fry.

"How many?"

I crack a grin. "Damn, you expecting me to take you on ten dates in one day or something?"

"How many girls have you slept with?"

"Reese, I don't keep track of that. I'm a dumbass, not a sleaze."

"But if you have to ballpark?" she prods, and I don't think she's going to drop the subject any time soon.

"All right, I'll be honest with you." I turn toward her. "I've been around a few times. Back in high school was the brunt of it." *Before the Walker incident.* "I went through a stupid phase where I believed I was hot shit and could get away with anything."

"And you've… *matured* since then?" I don't miss the slight tease in her voice or the hint of concern in her gaze. It's her expressive face. It betrays her every time.

"People can change." I bring my hand to her cheek, and she reluctantly leans into it. "Promise you, there's nothing to worry about. I know I'm a handful and my past is… checkered, but I'm… all in with you."

"You are?"

A sharp exhalation escapes me. "Yeah, so don't leave me hanging, Reese," I say teasingly. "Tell me you're all in, too."

"And you say I'm bossy." She stifles her laughter with her fist and peers into my eyes. "I guess I'm all in with you, too."

"Wow. You *guess*?"

"I'm worried about where you plan on taking me for our first official date, and I kind of want to wait and see—" She shrieks and tries to shove me away when I bury my face into her neck. "*Ew. You're sticky—*"

"Come on, Reese," I wheedle. "Tell me what I want to hear."

"I won't buy another sweater." She yelps when I nip at her collarbone. "Okay, okay." She nudges me back before I can venture any lower and barely manages to suppress her giggles, her palm pressed flatly against my chest. "I won't leave you hanging."

"You sure about that?" I tease, and her finger pokes the spot above my heart. I don't have to look to know what she's tracing as she holds my gaze.

"If it's not that obvious by now," she says softly, her mouth sneaking up at the corner. "I'm all in with you, too."

REESE

I wonder if it would be rude of me to sneak off to the kitchen and scarf down a bowl of mashed potatoes like a rabid raccoon. I'm *starving*.

Lilian has been busy posing with her sorority sisters for the last hour. Friendsgiving dinner has yet to commence. My breath is beyond fresh with how many mints I've sustained myself on. There's a questionable half-eaten granola bar in my purse I might devour if this doesn't wrap up soon. So what if it appears to be covered in lint? Fiber's good for us, right?

Oh God. I look up and glimpse the girls blowing kisses for the camera. Behind them, gold tinsels stream down from the ceiling. Stylistic cutouts of pumpkins and autumn leaves are placed purposely across the wall. It's very festive, but I might gnaw on a plastic vegetable prop in the next five minutes if push comes to shove.

"Shit, it won't focus. It's too dark," Peyton says, and I eye the kitchen longingly. The turkey will decompose before this finally ends.

"You should let Reese do it," Lilian volunteers me. "She's good with cameras."

I reluctantly put my granola bar down.

Luckily, it goes by quickly. Peyton's phone is much newer than mine and doesn't freeze up when taking photos, so I have it done in no time. Handing it back to her, I take a single step toward the cornbread that awaits me when Karla hollers for me.

"Come on, Little Vann! You should take one."

I make a face. Listen, I love taking pictures, but not of me. It's a funny conundrum, but I'm too self-conscious about my scar. "I'm good."

"You don't want one for Caleb?"

"Caleb?" My brow furrows. Why would I do that?

"Don't tell me forgot the boy you're seeing," Lilian says, her words heavy with a tease.

I freeze. *Oh crap.* Did I never tell her I broke up with him? In my defense, we've both been busy with midterms, but still.

"Oh… We're not seeing each other anymore."

Everyone turns to stare at me as if I just announced I'm going to hock knives for a pyramid scheme.

"Wait, what?" A frown forms between Lilian's brows. "Why not?"

"Did you guys break up today?" Karla gasps, and I barely manage to brace myself when she tackles me with a hug. "I'm so sorry."

"Um, no." I splutter as I try to spit her hair out of my mouth. Blessedly, she releases me before the air entirely depletes from my lungs. "We ended things about two weeks ago?"

Again, I'm hit with varying looks of shock and surprise. Maybe I should give a sales pitch on hocking knives to break the tension, but I offer them a reassuring smile instead.

"It's okay, though." Dane comes to mind, unbidden, and I chew on my inner cheek to fight my blush. "I'm fine."

"But…" Chrissy—or is it Jenna?—blinks and folds her arms. "Caleb said you guys went out yesterday."

"He said what?" Stunned, I gape at her. *Wait, Caleb talks to the girls about me?* Oh God, what has he told them? How boring I am because all I do is—surprise—talk about books, movies, and my sister? "Well, we did not. I'm not seeing him. I broke up with him two weeks ago."

"*You* broke up with him?" Lilian gasps.

"*Two* weeks ago?" Lauren repeats.

Something inside me shrivels up from their disbelieving stares. Is it that hard for them to believe I dumped him? "Yes? I ended things with him."

Karla frowns. "Does this have to do with D—"

"Things with Caleb weren't going anywhere," I squeak. If she mentions Dane's name, my sister will spend the entire dinner lecturing me about him. "He never once tried to kiss me or..." Gosh, this is embarrassing. My neck scalds while I try to find my words. "It just wasn't going anywhere. We're better off as friends."

Silence seems to echo in the foyer as I wait for a reply. No one says anything. It's getting more awkward by the second. A redirect is clearly in order.

Pasting on a giant grin, I point toward the kitchen. "Should we go eat? I'm starving."

Unlike my sister, I do not enjoy shopping. The penny pincher in me will splurge every now and then on a book or organic crunchy tuna treats for the stray cat, but I would rather save in case of an emergency. Lilian, on the other hand, loves buying things to make up for how we didn't grow up with much.

It's why she's dragging me around the outlet mall. Personally, I would have just looked at deals online, but she'll prattle on about in-store exclusives again if I bring it up.

Currently, we're inside a boutique where I can't go two steps without getting an elbow to the face or a purse to the chest. I'm trying my best to keep up with my sister as I haul her shopping bags after her.

"I can't believe you broke up with Caleb," Lilian says, and I bite back my sigh. I naïvely assumed the moment she found out things between us were done, she'd stop bringing him up. "I thought you liked him."

"I did, but…" My words dwindle as my attention snares on a cute floral dress nearby. "You should try it on."

She gives me a look. I get it. My sister likes her clothes to be a bit more on the clubbing side. The only time she'll wear a dress is for a sorority event.

"It's more your style," she points out, and she's not wrong.

It's in a lovely shade of baby blue, and the sleeves are my favorite part, but the issue is the square neckline. There's no point in buying something I'll never wear.

"And don't change the subject," she adds. I purposely divert my focus to the rack behind us. "You don't have to hide your scar. If you want, we could save money to get it removed—"

"It's okay," I cut in. "Do you think the food court has root beer soda?" I paste on the brightest smile I can muster, and her lips remain flat.

"Of course, but—"

"How is your presentation going, by the way?" I came to this prepared. I will lob as many questions at her as possible, so I'm not the one in the hot seat. "Aren't you supposed to meet with Jesse this weekend to work—"

A long-suffering sigh slips free from her chest, and she marches over to the dress and snatches it. "Try this on. It's half off."

My head shakes, and she groans.

"Okay." Throwing it over her shoulder, she glances sidelong at me. "Don't come complaining to me when the dress is too tight and your boobs are popping out."

"What?" I follow her to the other side of the shop. "Lili—"

"My treat." She plucks a sheer top and adds it to the never-ending pile on her arm. "I'm sorry about Caleb, by the way."

"I'm not." I offer her a shrug when she frowns. "Believe me, I'm okay."

"You don't have to put on a brave face."

"Trust me, I'm not." For a brief moment, I let my mind wander, and it goes back to its favorite hobby as of late: daydreaming about Dane getting all sweaty in his hot garage, taking his shirt off in slow motion, and then railing me against the hood of his car.

"Maybe Chrissy knows someone you can rebound with." Lilian's voice snaps me back to the present. "No one from Caleb's frat, for obvious reasons—"

"I still don't understand why he said we're still dating," I interject, frowning. I ended things. With no panache, but still. He can't be *that* interested in me. There's just no way.

Our outings together were so… *mild* and lackluster that if the standard for attraction is that low, then I can say there's more chemistry between me and half the sorority girls by that logic.

"Maybe he wants you and he's saving face?" she suggests. "Are you sure you don't want to give him a second chance?"

Lili, that ship has sailed. I'm all in with someone else.

Why would I want to go back to a guy who'll never confess his feelings for me until he's on his deathbed?

"I'm fine." Since I don't want to keep talking about the guy, I point to another top. "That color would make your eyes pop."

She hits me with an inscrutable stare. A pulse of unease flickers into my chest as her shrewd eyes narrow. My neck starts to prickle when she offers me a terse nod and grabs the shirt in her size.

Her gaze never tears from mine. "It so would."

2 8

DANE

WITHOUT READING IT, I DELETE THE SHORT TEXT FROM MY OLD MAN and toss my phone onto the driver's seat. Yanking my protective goggles down, I secure the respirator over my mouth and return to what I've been working on all morning.

Sanding the beaut down.

I'm not one to stand outside for hours on end, but this project is an all-day ordeal I want to be done with before it turns into a two-day hassle.

As soon as the body has been completely sandpapered, the paint stripper is applied next. It's an easy task, but time-consuming. It needs to sit under plastic after it's been spread everywhere, and then I have to scrape everything off with my putty knife once it sets.

The sun dips toward the horizon as the hours drag into the evening. Aggressive rock pours from my phone's shitty speakers. My brain is silent. My hands are busy. I'm at peace.

Abruptly, a loud straight pipe pierces the air and drowns out my music. In my periphery, a sleek blue car flies up to the curb and screeches to a grinding halt.

My hackles rise. I've never seen it before. A muscle in my jaw clenches as I brace myself for whatever bullshit is about to go down.

The door flings open, and I nearly chuck my putty knife at his damn head when he exits the vehicle.

"Like what you see?" is the first thing out of Marco's mouth.

Almost immediately, the tension dissolves from my chest. I offer him a snort. "I've seen better." Then I smirk when he grabs a pair of goggles from the workbench.

With another set of hands, everything moves faster. We're making actual progress. Something sentimental pulses in my chest when it occurs to me that we've fallen into a rhythm. It's been a while. I can't remember the last time we worked on a car together. A burst of nostalgia fills my veins when he tosses me a replacement putty knife the instant mine breaks.

We get everything done before midnight. Once I have the Nova stashed in its usual spot, I turn to face him.

"What's with the new set of wheels?"

The corner of his mouth tips up, and he casts a glance toward the empty street. "Won it fair and square. Figured you could help me add an under-glow."

"Should've known there'd be an ulterior motive," I deadpan as I follow his line of sight and check out his car. Personally, it's not my style. I prefer my vehicles on the older side while Marco's always been the one who likes them angular and low. I wouldn't put it past him to wide-body it at some point.

Shaking his head, he lets out a quiet laugh. "You still have that clunker?"

I chuckle wryly. I don't even have to look to know which car he's talking about. "Sal, you know? He'd crawl out of his grave and drag me to my doom if I even *think* about getting rid of it."

"You don't even like the headlights," he teases, and it's not like he's wrong. For this make and model, I prefer the vertical ones.

With a snort, I raise my brow at him. "Would *you* want to risk your ass getting haunted by Sal for the rest of your life?"

"I could take that old man on."

"If anything, he'd be too busy rolling in his grave," I remark. "Disappointed we're falling back into our old ways."

His gaze cuts to mine. Visible concern flits across his features. "You're racing again?"

"You're gambling again?" I counter, and we stare each other down. No one speaks. No one moves. It's a long minute of silence before he huffs out a scoff and spares me an easygoing smirk.

"Not all of us are born with silver spoons in our mouths," he says dryly. I've been around him enough to know he's just ribbing me.

"You need money?" I fold my arms and frown. He could've come to me any time for that. He knows about the trust fund my mom left me. I don't mind tapping into it for him. But I'm well aware of his pride. He wouldn't be able to handle it if I helped him out like that. His ego wouldn't let him.

"Nah." He waves me off. "I got it handled."

"All right, but don't come crying to me when your cousin tears you a new one." I tip my head to the side. "I should have a kit lying around somewhere." After the hours he's spent helping me with the Nova, it's the least I can do. "You still know your way around a garage?"

Marco glances over his shoulder as he heads to his car and breaks into a grin. "It's in my fucking blood."

***

Marco's not crashing on the couch tonight, so I have my place to myself for once. I'm too tired to go to some party Shyla's hosting, and I want to get rid of all the filth and grime on me before I hit the hay.

After showering, I retrieve a glass of water and settle in the living room. It's a sweet setup, everything paid for by Daniel Kingsley since it'd look bad if I'm living in squalor while he's residing in the American Dream home with the white picket fence and his do-over family.

At least the apartment is nice. Charcoal and gray furniture are sparsely placed throughout the place. Floor-to-ceiling windows provide the best view of the beachy coastline. It's a minimalist's wet dream; utterly devoid of life.

Leaning back against the sofa, I ignore the missed calls from my father and check the unread texts from Reese. I had sent her a picture of the Nova's current state before I left the garage.

Reese's Pieces: Ooh!!!
Reese's Pieces: Have you picked a color yet?
Dane: if you tell me your name, I'll tell you the color
Reese's Pieces: It's more fun to see you guess :)
Dane: likewise, mini Reese
Reese's Pieces: Maybe green?
Dane: why green?
Reese's Pieces: A green convertible seems like something you'd do.
Dane: you want to know something I would do?

It takes three rings before she finally picks up. Her face appears on the cracked screen, grainy and barely illuminated.

"It's late," she murmurs.

"It's only two in the morning." I smile crookedly at her. "Why are you still up?"

"One of my professors had online homework due today," she explains. "I just turned it in."

"Why are we whispering?"

"I'm still at the sorority house," she reminds me, "and every-one's asleep."

"After a long night of pillow fights?"

She snorts, and even though it's dark on her end, I can sense the dry look she's giving me.

"So…" Propping an arm behind my head, I crank up the volume. "What are you wearing?"

"Oh my God. I'm wearing my PJs."

"Sexy ones?"

"Oh, yes," she says blandly. "I'm totally naked under my sexy PJs."

"*Aw, fuck yeah, baby.*" I exaggerate a groan, and she breaks into giggles. "You are so fucking hot fully dressed and cozy for me."

She fights the twitch to her lips and gives me a playful frown. "Why are you up?"

"'Cause you're not wearing anything underneath those layers."

She barely smothers her laugh with a sigh. "I'm serious."

"Me too." I toss a wink at the camera. "Wanna see?"

"*See?*" she chokes out.

"*Si* is Spanish for yes." With a slanted grin, I switch to the rear-facing camera. She squeaks as I give her a sneak preview of my body. It's nothing indecent. It's just a glimpse of my long legs crossed on the coffee table while I'm dressed in gray sweatpants. The only time she sees any skin is when I briefly show off my naked torso.

"I'm *on* the couch," she rasps.

"So am I."

"I'm… I can't…" Her teeth sink into her bottom lip. "My sister's upstairs."

"You don't have to do anything you don't wanna do," is my immediate response. Her eyes are round as saucers while she visibly contemplates and then offers me a faint nod. "Oh, come on, baby. I need a yes in English if you want to see how up I am."

"*Yes.*" Her word is punctuated with a rustling noise as she pulls a cover over her head. She clears her throat and tries to school her features into something neutral. "As you were, soldier."

Chuckling, I loosen the drawstrings and draw my cock out.

I'm rewarded with a breathy whimper, which brings a smirk to my face. "You sure know how to make a guy feel like God."

"Are you…"

"Gonna jack off?" I supply. "Only if you tell me what to do."

She expels a slow exhale. Her voice is barely audible when she replies. "Touch yourself?"

"Isn't that what I'm already doing?" I give my dick a quick, featherlight stroke, and another whimper escapes her. "Now, tell me what to do."

"Please touch yourself."

"Aw, you're so polite," I tease. "How's this?" My index finger pokes the crown of my cock, and she heaves out a strangled huff.

"You know what I mean."

"Do I?"

"Put your hand around—" Her gaze darts up, and she freezes.

"Aw, don't get shy on me now."

"I think someone went to the bathroom," she mutters, hunching her shoulders.

"Don't give a fuck about that," I grunt. "Now, come on, baby. Tell me what you'd be doing if you were here touching me yourself."

"Oh." She lets out a blustery laugh. "I'd wrap my hand around…"

"My neck?"

"Your *cock*."

"Now we're talking." I grip the base and give her an expectant look. "And then what?"

"I'd move my hand."

"Away?" I tease, and she wrinkles her nose.

"Up and down." Her face is barely visible under the cover, but I don't need to see it to know she's beet red.

Slowly, I stroke myself for her. "Just once?"

"Until you come," she replies boldly, and I grin. "I think I'd go a little faster, though."

With another chuckle, I lazily lean back into my seat and quicken my pace. "You wanna know what I'm thinking?"

Breathlessly, she nods. "W-what?"

"I'm thinking of how sweet it'd be to have you here," I groan out, and already, I'm picturing her generous tits bouncing while she's on top of me. "Riding my cock. Screaming my name. Taking every fucking inch of me."

Her breathing stutters. "Really?"

"Yeah, baby. Just thinking about what a little mess you'll become. How fucking wet and greedy you'll get just for me. How that sweet ass of yours will go up and down while you fuck yourself with my cock."

She exhales sharply, watching me intensely as I fuck my fist and think about her in various positions. Straddling me and playing with her clit. Spreading her legs wide on her back. Desperately begging for more on her hands and knees while my come drips down her tits.

Fuck.

The idea alone tips me over the edge. My muscles tighten. My jaw locks. Pressure builds against my spine, and a guttural sound rips up my throat as I spurt into my hand.

"Oh my God," Reese gasps. "Did you—"

"The next time I come," I grunt, "will be when I'm buried deep inside that tight little pussy of yours."

Her breath catches; her chest hitches.

"And that's a fucking promise."

2 9

REESE

Every time I sneak a glance in his direction, my body reacts straight away. My neck blazes. My cheeks flush. My heart gives a rapid flutter as my mind hightails back to the other night and sets up camp.

Dane catches me with my next not-so-subtle peek and lifts a brow, and I divert my attention to the convertible. I don't miss the suggestive smirk forming around the corner of his mouth. I feign extreme interest in the paint swatches spread out before us and squint in determination when he lets loose a raspy chuckle.

He hasn't decided which color to go with yet, but he's set on burnt orange or neon green. I think both sound atrocious, but it's not my car, so I'll keep my opinion to myself. Still, I tactically nudge my favorite color toward him. It's a pleasant periwinkle blue. And it's not offensive to the eyes.

He gives me an amused look in response. "Keep going for me, baby," he husks out, and every inch of my skin is set on fire at the graveled edge of his tone. "That can't be it. I know you've got more to show me. I can take it."

My lips clamp tight as his teasing grin makes an appearance. Abrupt thoughts about him being buried deep inside me come to mind and stoke a flurry of awareness low in my belly. I'm about to be very forward for the first time in my entire life when he tilts his head to the side.

"Eh, you can show me all the purples you like later," he deadpans, his voice no longer rough and low. "Ready for the date I promised you?"

I'd rather we fuck on every car. The tips of my ears are red hot as I offer him a bright smile.

Once the garage is locked, we're winding down the coast in his Mustang. His gaze is solely focused on the road, while I'm all but watching him drive.

"Reese, if you want me to pull over and fuck you right here, just ask," he teases.

I bite back my whimper as heat solidifies between my thighs. It's so tempting of an offer that I want to say yes. Every ounce of me wants to scream the word from a rooftop.

If public indecency weren't a thing, I'd be all over him in an instant.

"So, where are you taking me?" I ask instead.

He winks. "Wouldn't you like to know?"

I would, but the fun is in the surprise. "I get to veto if this is something weird."

"It ain't a museum."

My eyes narrow in his direction, and within a heartbeat, his shoulders shake with his laughter.

Soon enough, he pulls into the parking lot of an arcade. I'm mildly surprised—until he cuts the engine and I hear the sound of cars whizzing by. My focus cuts to the sign blinking to our right, and my lips press together to suppress my amusement.

"You took us to a go-kart place?"

"Hey now. I took you to check out that Ferris wheel." He gestures to the giant attraction blinking neon colors against the darkening sky. "It just so happens that this place has an indoor racetrack."

My arms fold across my chest. "What a coincidence."

"Very much so." He maintains a straight face. "Serendipity is quite a marvelous thing."

Rolling my eyes good-naturedly, I flash him a half-smile. "Can I at least get some funnel cake first?"

"And onion rings for your fiesta."

"It's *Finsta*."

Inside the main building, bells and whistles chime from the arcade games. Pop music from the last decade plays from hidden speakers. The scent of deep-fried carnival food wafts in the air. It's a bit of a sensory overload, but I snap out of my slight daze when Dane twines his fingers with mine and steers me to the walk-up counter.

He slaps a hundred onto a counter. Before I can protest, he orders, "Root beer soda, funnel cake, and onion rings."

"We don't break—"

"Keep the change. Or whatever."

"You know, you'd probably have smaller bills at your disposal if you take the change," I whisper the instant we're out of earshot. I don't want the teenager to overhear me and spit in our food.

Dane shrugs a shoulder. "I'm not hurting for cash."

"Making that much money from the cars?"

"Nah. Mom left me everything from her estate."

Surprised, I fall silent. There's a lot to unpack there. He doesn't like bringing his mom up, which is a no-brainer. But I'm also hit with the realization that he's loaded. *He lives in Las Marinas. Of course, he's got cash to spare.*

Suddenly, I'm too aware of our class differences, and unease fills my stomach. If my mom knew about him, she'd make a snide comment about how her youngest brat is trying so damn hard to claw her way out of the trailer park and turn her back on her roots.

No. She'd probably encourage me to use him as a meal ticket.

Unfortunately, it's not a foreign concept. She used to do it all the time with Lilian. Whenever our mom was home—if she ever was—she always encouraged my sister to sleep with the rich men in our towns, even the guys old enough to be our dad. She tried to do the same with me. I developed early, and she would drop a comment about how *my girls* could bring in the cash we needed, but Lilian would step in and effectively kill the conversation before it could even take off.

A wave of shame scours my throat.

"Earth to Reese." Dane's voice draws me back to the present. "You okay?"

"I'm not into you for your money," I blurt.

He blinks, then snorts and ducks his head to my ear. "Yeah, I know. You're in it for my cock."

My neck smolders into flames, and I shoot a sidelong glance at a mother standing nearby with her two children. "You're going to get us kicked out," I hiss, poking him squarely in the chest.

"I know you're not in it for my money." He tugs me flush to his body. "You're not like that. You're too kind and sweet with that goody-two-shoes heart of yours."

I glare up at him. He chuckles and holds me even tighter.

"But, really, I don't give a fuck if you were," he goes on. "I'll spoil you with all the onion rings and root beer soda you want."

Before I can respond, I hear our order being called. Peeling myself out of his embrace, I erupt into giggles when his mouth presses to the curve of my neck.

"Wait," he growls against my skin. "Rub yourself up against me once more—"

"*Behave.*" I shove him playfully and head to the counter.

So far, the date has mostly been a lot of trash-talking with a smidge of flirting sprinkled in. We made out on the Ferris wheel. Sabotaged each other during mini-golf. Played a lot of skeeball and took it to the extremes. Throw with your nondominant hand. Stand on one foot. Spin in a circle with eyes closed.

Somehow, we didn't maim ourselves with the last one.

Once Dane pawns off our tickets to a little girl we come across on our way out, we sprint to the indoor racetrack. Since it's almost closing time, it's glaringly empty when we step inside.

It's for the best. I don't think it'd be a good idea to have a bunch of witnesses around when Dane gets behind the wheel.

"Are you even tall enough for this, Mini Reese?" He gestures to the height requirement sign near the entrance and is met with my cool stare.

"You're going to regret your words, Kingsley."

"Just remember one thing," he says gravely, the lines of his face go taut as he holds my gaze. "Ease into it."

Then he rockets forward with a screeching lurch and leaves me in his dust. I splutter and chase after him at half his speed.

My hair whips behind me. My pulse thrums in my ears. My adrenaline spikes when the kart accelerates faster, and it's oddly freeing. Exhilarating, even.

I kind of get it. To a certain extent. I won't dive off cliffs tomorrow or sign up for skydiving any time soon, but I understand why Dane likes to drive because, at this moment, I feel... invincible. Limitless. *So very much alive.*

My thumb barely locks the door before he hooks his arm around my midsection and tugs me away with haste. I tumble backward onto my mattress, and wild laughter escapes me when he stretches his body over mine and captures my lips.

Our hands are everywhere. Our fingers flirt with anything we can touch. Our kisses become a little uncoordinated and clumsy while we fumble with each other's clothes until we're skin-to-skin.

I can't stop smiling. I can't stop my heart from beating oh so fast. I can't do anything but allow myself to let go and fall in deeper. It's all I can manage. My body feels so fluttery and fizzy and vibrant and bright and a whole list of words I can't even think of because I'm still riding out the high that's yet to fade from our date.

Tracking a path to my scar, his unshaven jaw tickles my sensitive skin and ignites embers deep in my belly.

"Wait," I gasp, and he tenses as I nudge him back. He blinks down in confusion, tightening his grip on my hip bones when I give him another gentle shove. "You wanted me to ride your cock, right?"

My words bring a flush to my cheeks and a smolder to his eyes. Then I yelp when he flips us over in one fluid motion and hoists me onto his lap.

His mouth quirks up at the corner as he peers up at me. His palm idly strokes my back. His lips part as I swivel my hips, my pussy a slick and slow grind against the length of his cock. A gritty sound rips up his throat.

"Baby—" He groans in protest when my movement comes to an abrupt stop. "What are you doing to me?"

"Just taking my time with you." With a smile, I slide up to his waist and lean in, sneaking a kiss on his lips. Then I pull away before he can deepen it and draw a heart on his chest. "Thank you, by the way."

He lifts a quizzical brow. "No, *thank you.* I'm enjoying the view. And everything you've been doing so far."

Despite myself, I snort. *"For the date."*

"You're telling me that every time I take you out, it will end like this?" His fingers delve into my hips, digging deep. "Are you free tomorrow?"

"I have a group project to work on."

"Blow it off," is his response.

"I'd rather blow you," I say boldly, and he lets loose a rough exhalation. "Was that a little too corny?"

He snorts. "Baby, I'm a little too horny to care."

Giggling, I climb off of him and feel his heated gaze follow me as I settle between his legs. I'm suddenly too aware of him and my pounding heart as I sit back on my heels.

A low and gritty breath escapes him when I pitch forward and take him in my mouth. He immediately clenches the sheets and rocks his thick, heady weight against my tongue, hitting the back of my throat.

Reflexively, I gag, and his entire frame tenses. Embarrassment scalds my cheeks as I peek up with wide eyes. Only the tip remains between my lips.

"Sorry," I muffle, and he chuckles as he tucks an arm behind his head.

"You don't have to deepthroat me," he murmurs. "Just do that thing you did with your tongue."

I have *no* idea what he's talking about, but I give him a tiny nod. Hopefully, he'll clue me in on what *that thing* is when I take him in again.

"Fuck. Yes. Like that, baby," I can feel him straining beneath me to keep his hips still. "Just like that."

His moan is pure gravel. Rough. His fingers twine into my hair, fisting the strands in a tight, almost-stinging grip, and fizzling heat races down my spine.

My mind is suddenly swirly; my entire body is abuzz with incessant need. My concentration is dwindling by the second.

"Fuck," he repeats. "Touch yourself for me while you suck me off."

I whimper and bring my thumb to my clit, and he groans so loudly that goosebumps ripple across my skin. My eyes pinch closed, and my breathing runs ragged.

Without warning, he jerks himself out of my mouth, and I startle.

"I didn't say to stop playing with yourself." He hoists me up onto his lap. "Do you need a hand?" he teases, punctuating his words with a smirk.

"I wasn't finished," I mutter weakly, then bite back a moan when he slides two fingers deep inside me. My palm smacks against his broad chest for purchase. My pulse goes haywire.

"I don't want to come down your throat tonight," he grunts, and my thighs tremble as he strokes me at a faster pace. "I want to come inside this pussy of yours like I said I would."

A fluttery gasp escapes me, and I grind against his hand. "Do you have a condom?"

"Got one in my wallet with your name on it," he replies brazenly, and I snort.

"Just one?"

"Well, I didn't think an entire box would fit in there," he says with a sly grin. "Give me a second." With one last stroke, he removes his fingers, and I hold back a whimper at the sudden loss.

Leaning over, he retrieves a foil from his jeans, tears it open, and rolls the condom on so quickly that I think he may have set a world record. Then he finds my gaze as I move to straddle him, his pupils eating up the color of his irises.

My knees spread wide across his muscular thighs. My hand splays across his ribs as I drag my pussy against his length and coax out a low, gritty moan from the base of his throat. My hips lift, and after I line him up against my entrance, I sink down.

His head tips back as his mouth falls open in sheer bliss. I swallow a breath and squirm from the sudden fullness.

"Oh. Fuck. *Yes*. There we go." The rough feel of his hands slides up my thighs and grasps my hips. "How does that feel?"

Biting my bottom lip, I take in his hazy eyes and slightly flushed cheeks. A sudden thrill runs through me at the sight. "Like you're very hard for me?"

He chuckles hoarsely as he pulls out halfway and rocks into me, and my fingertips press into his skin. "I would have taken *good* for an answer."

I say nothing. My eyes flutter shut. My legs slide wider apart. My body arches forward as I settle into a gradual, steady rhythm and chase every exquisite slide and stretch of his cock splitting me open.

"Oh, look at you," he murmurs. "So fucking greedy. You like riding me that much?"

"Mmhmm." A hum is all I can respond with as I push against his thrusts.

"Yeah? Then keep fucking me." His grip tightens on my hip bone, and I can feel the deep imprint of his blunt nails. "Show me how much you want this."

Warmth builds low in my belly. My nails bite into his pecs as I ride him faster. His hands go to my breasts and squeeze, and my hips stutter. Then he slides one palm down to our point of contact, and my movement becomes choppy with every flirt of his fingers against my swollen clit. With every dirty word muttered in the air.

He doesn't ease up. He's relentless with his touch as he picks up the pace and fucks into me harder.

"Oh God, Dane," I moan, and he lets out a raspy chuckle.

"Fuck, yes, baby," he grunts. "Say my name. *Say my name louder.*"

It hits me so suddenly that a sharp gasp breaks free while I shatter. My thighs tremble. My vision blurs. I'm blissed out. Completely, utterly, wholeheartedly spent.

He keeps pace while he continues to chase his release, thrusting over and over until he finally tenses and groans something so exquisitely choked off at the ceiling when he comes.

Without notice, he reaches an arm around me and pulls me into the warm shelter of his body. Already, I'm curling into him, breathing in his familiar scent, and listening to his heartbeat echoing mine while his fingers trace random shapes on my side.

Burying my face against his chest, I melt when his lips press into my hair. I want time to freeze. I want to lie here forever in his embrace.

And, as his arm wraps around my waist, I just might.

30

DANE

Her gaze flicks up from her textbook, and her pale face turns white as she drops her pencil. "*No.* You're going to paint it *that* color?"

I slide the swatch of the ugliest yellow-green shade I've ever seen closer to her, and she masks her whimper with a cough. "I think it'll look nice," I hedge, "with the flames I'll add to the side."

Pure devastation floods her eyes. "What has that car ever done to you?"

I almost break as I offer her a casual shrug. "You don't think it'll look badass?"

"Believe me, that's not at all what I'm thinking," she rasps, and I can't help it. I burst into a fit of laughter, and she straightens and squints at me. "I regret asking you to come and hang out with me at work."

"I'll make it up to you," I say, and her brow quirks with interest. "How about a kiss—"

Her finger presses squarely against my forehead, halting me from leaning any closer. "One, I'm still on the clock. My boss only lets me get away with so much. Two, there's someone in line."

230

An exaggerated groan escapes me. "You owe me a kiss later."

She splutters. "I do not. Now…" She makes a shooing motion, and I oblige. "I'm not off for another twenty minutes."

"I'll fuck around with the displays until then."

"Please don't," she calls after me, and I toss her a wink over my shoulder.

Soon, I'm pacing around the bookstore. Just as I'm checking out the laptops, my phone buzzes. I fish it out and frown. On the screen is a text from an unfamiliar number providing coded details for the next meet.

I lean against a nearby display and delete the message, leaving me with hundreds of unread ones to deal with. While I couldn't care less if they remain unanswered, the notification bubble drives my girl nuts. I thought she'd be secretly pleased none of her texts have ever been included in that number.

She's not.

Since I've got some time to kill, I go through them. Most are just phishing scams about unusual bank activities. Then I pause on one from a few days ago. The area code isn't familiar, but the number has to belong to someone who knows me. Whoever it is, they want my assistance with a cylinder issue.

Instead of replying, I ignore the text and move on to the next one. They'll take the hint. Thanks to Walker, I don't sell my services anymore. The only person I even interact with is Sergei, who's more of a middleman for me than a customer.

He's the only one I trust to find cars for me and buyers once I fix them up. Not only that, he deals with all the paperwork nonsense. I don't make much profit, but it's not like I'm hurting for money.

"I think those would bring out your eyes." Reese's voice is a gentle tease as she sidles up to me. I glance over my shoulder and spot a pair of tacky blue earrings.

"And I think this one would look hot on you." I tip my chin toward a clunky-looking necklace. It's the ugliest thing I've ever seen.

"How so?" she asks dubiously. Evidently, I'm not the only one who thinks it's hideous as fuck.

"If you wear just that with nothing else on?" My mouth curves into a wolfish grin. "*Hot.*"

She sticks her tongue out at me as she hoists her backpack over her shoulder. "Come on. I need to make sure the cat's fed before we head to your place."

Her hand slips in mine as we step outside, and she abruptly stops in her tracks. With wide eyes, she yanks me toward the nearest hedge.

"Is this your way of telling me you wanna fool around in the bushes?" I snicker. "We—"

"*Shh.*" Her profile tightens with visible distress. "My sister."

"Right." I crouch to the ground and turn toward her.

With a ragged breath, she nibbles on her bottom lip. "I don't think she saw—" She shrieks and claps her palm over her mouth when a buzz sounds from her back pocket.

I reach for it and give her ass a quick squeeze in the process, and she glares.

Taking the device, she brings it to her ear. "*Hi,*" she squeaks. "No, I already left. Yeah, I'm on the bus—No. It's fine. I'm meeting a friend for dinner."

While she's floundering with her excuses, I take the opportunity to slide my hand up the curve of her waist. She bats me away. I trace random circles on her knee instead. She swats at my touch and flushes when I catch her wrist and intertwine my fingers with hers.

"No, it's okay. I'll see you tomorrow. Love you. Bye." Blowing out a shaky breath at the night sky, she slams her eyes shut. "She didn't see me."

"That's good." I bring my mouth to her ear. "Wanna fool around in the bushes now?"

With a quiet laugh, she reaches over and pulls a twig from my hair. "No."

"Oh, wow. I can't believe it."

"Believe it."

"You're actually studying?" Reese gasps, clasping her hands to her cheeks in mock surprise. Her eyes glitter. Her mouth twitches. "You?"

I'm unable to fight off my snort. With a shake of my head, I bring my attention back to my textbook. "Unfortunately, I have to pass my classes to get that stupid finance degree."

"Why don't you tell me what you've learned," she asks, and the edge of my lips curls into a half-smile.

"That I'll look like a tool if you ever see me in a suit—" A flash of bright light goes off, and I freeze. My gaze tears from the current chapter I'm on and lands on my girl. Her mouth parts in horror as she carefully sets her phone down and covers her face.

"You didn't see a thing," she wheezes, and I press my hand to my heart.

"It's all right, baby," I say solemnly. "We both know you wanted that for your spank bank."

She peeks between her fingers. Her withering stare tugs at the corner of my lips.

"Yes, seeing you study is *such* a turn-on," she says dryly. "Now, if you'll excuse me, I'll be studying, too."

With that, she returns her attention to her laptop. It's hard to ignore the small grin touching her mouth when she steals a peek at her cell. Every fiber of my self-control prevents me from climbing on top of her, tugging her bottom lip between my teeth, and discovering new ways to brighten that smile.

I know better than to keep bothering her. Between us two, she's the only one invested in getting A's in her classes, and the engineering shit she's working on right now looks complicated as fuck.

So I swivel in my chair and face my desk again. Queue up the cheesy indie and pop music she's subjected me to in the garage, so there's background noise. Resume working on my long list of overdue assignments.

In my periphery, Reese dangles her legs over the side of my bed, swinging them back and forth. I don't miss the fact that she sneaks another picture of me. This time, with the flash off.

WHAT FEW WOULD DESCRIBE AS SINGING STARTLES ME AWAKE. I barely sit up when Reese blinks her eyes open and goes utterly rigid beside me. Her face contorts in sheer terror. Her hand strangles her pillow. Her breathing runs ragged and cleaves through my heart.

Just as I'm about to roll out of bed and put an end to Marco's one-man concert, she gasps and finds my gaze. There's a flicker of confusion in them as some color returns to her pallid cheeks.

"You all right?" I murmur, pressing my palm to her jaw, and a knot forms in my chest when she leans into my touch.

Despite the tears shining in her eyes, she spares me a nod.

"Want me to tell him to shut the fuck up?"

She releases a slow exhalation and shakes her head. "That's rude."

I almost snort. I should've seen it coming from a mile away. It's such a good girl response from her.

"What's rude is subjecting us to this at an ungodly hour," I say, my voice dropping to a quiet note while I trace aimless zigzags across her cheekbone.

Her breathing evens out as time slips by slowly, and the tension subsides from her frame. "Does he always sing?"

"Unfortunately." Tugging my shirt on, I make my way over to the door and yank on the handle, only to remember it's locked when it doesn't give. Right. Reese did that last night. As she does every time she's over.

With a furrowed brow, I unlock it and poke my head out to see two chicks hanging out in my living room. I step halfway out and spot Marco in the kitchen, and I find myself regretting my decision to give him a copy of my keys when he starts belting the high notes.

"Kingsy," he hollers, tipping the spatula in my direction. "Want some pancakes? I made extra."

"*Fuck no—*"

"Wait, don't be too hasty," Reese chirps from behind me. I glance over my shoulder as she gathers her hair into a ponytail and peeks out, only to freeze. Something shy steals across her features, and she edges backward.

It's hard to believe this is the same girl who screamed at the two dickheads to stop kicking the crap out of me the day we met.

"Fucking keep it down," I grunt to Marco, then shut the door. Amusement curves the edge of my lips when Reese locks it.

She swallows audibly and offers me a bashful smile. A flush darkens on her cheekbones when I slide my forefinger under her chin and bring her gaze to mine.

"Sorry, I'm nervous around strangers," she says softly. "Do you think they'll be there all morning?"

"Knowing Marco? All day."

"But I have a lab later today," she mutters.

"They won't bite," I tease. "Aren't you friends with an entire sorority?"

"It took a while before I got comfortable around them." She nibbles her bottom lip and averts her gaze to the floor. "I don't want to make a terrible first impression."

"Don't worry about it," I tell her. "Make the worst first impression."

"But—"

"You'll *likely* never see them again." I'm met with another frown. "They're one-night stands."

"Oh. *Oh.*" Surprise gathers behind her eyes. "Have you ever done that before?"

"Bring a girl back to my apartment?" I squeeze her hips and grin. "Looking at her right now."

Reese huffs out a snort. *"Girls."*

"Nah."

"Really?"

"Reese," I say, pulling her body flush against mine, "the hottest thing for me is when I'm getting a girl off. Knowing that I made her come on my cock?"

"I mean," she hedges as a blush crawls up her neck, "you could get *two* off at the same time."

"Eh. Not my thing. If I want to disappoint multiple people at once, I can always go home." My words elicit a confused stare from her end, and I let out a self-deprecating chuckle. "I like to focus on the one I'm with. Give her all of my undivided attention. I guess I'm a one-girl kind of guy."

She regards me inquisitively. "Not even during your *hot shit* phase?"

"Nah. Most of that time was spent doing donuts in an empty parking lot at, like, three in the morning."

A peal of laughter escapes her. "Wait, really?"

"*And* taking advantage of empty streets," I add as I head toward the bathroom.

"Is that where you did all the racing?" Reese asks while she follows me in and grabs her toothbrush. "You and Marco?"

I hesitate and glance at her reflection in the mirror. "Yeah," I say, keeping my voice low and measured. "We loved speeding through the city when everyone's dead asleep. If you ever want to give it a go—"

"Absolutely not." Her attention snares on the half-remaining bar of soap and slants her mouth. She got it for me during her farmer's market date with Blue Balls.

Now my hands smell like lavender instead of the usual mix of gasoline, grease, and other stuff I work with in my garage. Listen, soap's fucking soap to me, but she gets excited every time she sees me using it. So whenever I can, I make a big show out of it. Without fail, her eyes light up like twinkling stars, and her smile becomes sweeter than air.

"How about—"

"I'm not doing anything illegal," she gasps. Even with a toothbrush in her mouth, she manages to level me with an adorable scowl.

Spitting my toothpaste out, I grab the soap, which brings a delightful curl to the corner of her lips. "Have some faith in me. I just wanted to know if you wanted to grab breakfast from the pancake house nearby."

Her face brightens. "Oh. I could go for some."

"If we hurry, we could get some before your classes today."

She gives me a sidelong glance and tilts her head. "Do you think they have chocolate chip?"

My brow lifts. "What kind of pancake house would they be if they didn't have any?"

With a laugh, she beams at me. "Good point."

3 1

REESE

If I have to choose between analyzing spatial data for my engineering project or watching Dane tinker with a new vehicle he got this morning, I'm going with the latter.

There's a matte black pony car where the Nova used to be. It's a little jarring not to see the convertible in that spot. He dropped it off at an auto body shop a few days ago, but I'm not used to it being gone. I keep catching myself looking for it every time I glance over my shoulder to see what Dane's up to.

Currently, he's... I have no idea what he's doing. He mentioned something about a stressed component in the engine earlier, but I only understood each word separately when he first explained it to me. Still, I find it riveting. I like seeing people get super invested in their hobbies. Also, his back muscles ripple every time he leans forward, props one hand on the metal frame, and uses his wrench.

With utmost reluctance, I return my focus to the workbench. Half-eaten Chinese takeout and Mexican Coca-Cola bottles are strewn across the counter behind my laptop. I steal another piece of broccoli from his carton, and just as I swipe a piece of orange chicken, my phone lights up. As I read the first word from

Lilian's message, Dane stalks over and eats it from my chopsticks.

"Hey," I gasp, and a peal of laughter tears loose when he presses a sticky kiss to my hairline. "*Hey.*"

He snickers as he returns to his car.

Lilian: event ended early so I'm coming over with leftover cupcakes and face masks
Reese: Raincheck? I'm studying at a friend's place

Guilt settles heavily in my heart. I'm not technically lying to her, but I feel terrible, nevertheless. We haven't seen each other in a while, save for the few times we bump into one another on our way to class.

She's been busy with her internship and sorority fundraisers, and I've been hanging out with Dane whenever I'm not working. Our schedules haven't aligned to the point where I can't remember the last time we had breakfast together or even did our campus picnic by the duck pond.

Lilian: you don't have time for me anymore :(
Reese: We'll hang out this weekend :)
Lilian: we better! I feel like I haven't seen you in forever
Reese: I saw you earlier at the library!
Lilian: not the same
Reese: I'll stop by the house with some awesome pancakes tomorrow to make up for the long lost time :)
Lilian: I can hear the sarcasm
Reese: Good :)

A sharp bang rends the air and startles me, and my phone clatters onto the workbench. My heart rockets into my throat; my fingers scrabble for my mace.

Gulping a lungful of air, I hop off the barstool. "Did you hurt yourself—" My words catch in my throat.

Dane's no longer bent over the hood of his project car. He's standing at full height with narrowed eyes and lips pulled into a grim line.

I follow his gaze and stare at the garage door. My pepper spray has been released from its keychain and is held tightly in my hand. "Is it someone you know?"

A deep wrinkle forms between his eyebrows as he wipes his fingers with a rag and shoves it into the front pocket of his jeans. "No. Only Marco and Sergei know where my garage is. And you."

"Should I call the cops?" I wheeze. My heart won't stop skittering. My pulse is racing at an all-time high. My nerves are beyond shot. I can't stop trembling. The sound of shattering glass keeps ringing in my ears.

"Nah. Fuck them. They won't do shit." His words break through my daze. My foggy thoughts give way to sheer panic when it occurs to me *he's walking toward imminent danger.*

A whimper of protest breaks from me, and he halts.

"What if they're dangerous?" I croak, my voice too soft, too muted.

He cracks his knuckles and clenches his jaw. "Only one way to find out—"

"*Dane,*" I rasp, and I am near tears when he swivels toward me and sears me with the harsh intensity in his gaze. He blinks, and his features soften immediately. The tension in his every taut muscle fizzles out.

He keeps his focus on me and puts on a reassuring smile. It doesn't reach his eyes. "You know what? It's probably nothing."

"It doesn't sound like *nothing.*"

"Might just be the wind." He takes one step toward me when an eerie silence fills the garage, and my attention swings to the door. *The banging has stopped.* "Or maybe it's just some dumbass punk trying to break into here. It happens all the time."

"That doesn't make me feel any better," comes out hoarsely

as I drop my mace onto the counter and press the heel of my palm to my cheek. I go still as a statue when he closes the distance between us. "It doesn't."

Tears burn my throat while I sniffle. I hate how small and pathetic I feel right now, and I want to disappear when he grabs a napkin from the takeout bag and carefully holds my shoulder with it.

"Don't wanna ruin your sweater," he grumbles, and I let out a shaky laugh. With a gentle squeeze, he crouches slightly until his face is level with mine. "They can try all they want, but no one can get it."

"I know," I wheeze. The rational part of my brain is well aware of the fact that the garage is deadbolted from the inside. I literally watched him secure the place when we got here. But my anxiety won't let up.

"I promise you, it's nothing. No big deal," he continues. I'm sure he's trying to reassure me, but downplaying it is only spiking my panic, if anything. "They can't get it. They just know there are cars in here that can net them an easy thirty k—"

"They cost thirty thousand dollars?" I choke out.

"Well, that one over there costs ninety," he comments, and I squeak and stagger backward.

Holy crap, I think every vehicle under this roof can pay for my entire out-of-state tuition. It never once occurred to me how expensive his hobby is.

"Wanna take it for a spin?" he offers, straightening his posture. "Might take your mind off of things."

Shaking my head, I hug my arms to my chest. "I think I'll sit there." I shoot a sideways glance at the workbench. "And not touch anything in here."

"Not even me?"

"You know what I mean," I stammer, finding his gaze. "Are you still going to check what that was?"

He shrugs. "Nah. If my girl doesn't want me to kick some

dumbass in the ass for trying to rob me, I'll stay right here." His features soften as he offers me a crooked grin. "But there's nothing to worry about, Reese. I'll be your getaway car if anything happens. Not that it will, but…" He taps his chest. "Your getaway car."

My mouth twitches as a raspy laugh escapes me. "Really?"

"Yeah," he murmurs. "I won't let anything happen to you. If anyone tries to pull something? Well, they'll be on my list after I get you someplace safe. I mean it."

I give him a wobbly smile and dry away the tear tracking down my cheek with a knuckle. "Yeah, I know."

THE NEXT MORNING, I STROLL UP THE DRIVEWAY TO THE SORORITY house with a takeout box filled with coconut pancakes and chocolate crepes. It's still early enough that Lilian shouldn't have class yet. The sun has barely burned through the fog, and while it's warm, it's also startlingly windy.

I regret my scarf when it tangles up once again with the breeze. It pairs well with my periwinkle coat, but wanting to look cute should not be this frustrating.

After shooting my sister a text, I lean against the porch railing and wait. Before long, Lilian emerges and frowns at me.

"You know the door's unlocked."

"Yes, but…" I shrug. The girls don't lock the place during the day, so everyone can come and go as they please. But I don't want to come in unless someone invites me in.

Following her into the foyer, I freeze at the chorus of *Little Vann*. I shyly wave my fingers at all the familiar faces, then join my sister in a secluded corner of the living room.

"What's going on here?"

"Cram-fest for finals." She snatches the box before I can set it down on the coffee table and tears into it. "Oh my God, this looks good."

"Wait until you try the syrup. It's to die for." I take my seat and cross my legs beside her. "Actually, no. The pancakes are so good, it's like eating a cloud. They're not too sweet, either."

"Ooh." Piling her blonde hair into a topknot, she grabs a plastic fork and hands me the other. "Oh my God, this is good."

"It's better freshly made." I grab the container of maple syrup and pass it to her. "One of these days, we should take the bus to Las Marinas again and go there. They have all these artisanal jams and jelly, too."

Lilian frowns. "Las Marinas? What were you doing out there?"

"I… wanted to take a picture of the sunrise," I hedge. I do, in fact, have one from today.

A vastly perceptible shift occurs to her features when she hits me with a hard stare. "You went there by yourself?" It's both an accusation and a question.

"Oh, um…" I trail off as my mouth curves into something nervous. I'm not sure what to respond with. I was hoping she'd drop it, or be too distracted by the food to give me the third degree. Before I can think of anything, her attention darts away from me, and her face lights up.

"Travis," she calls out. "You *have* to try this."

I tense up immediately as a lean blond guy approaches us. He's not part of Caleb's fraternity, but I've seen him around before. And the moment my eyes land on his face, I want to close the takeout box in protest. He doesn't deserve magical pancakes.

"Reese, this is Travis," my sister introduces, and the way her voice knocks up a pitch twists my stomach into a knot.

"Is it true you got your arm broken?" I blurt, and my hands ball into fists when he has the audacity to take a bite of the crepe off of her fork.

He coughs and swallows it down. "Yeah. During my sopho-more year."

"*Reese*," Lilian interjects, but I ignore her as I forge on.

"And how did it happen?"

"Forgive her," Lilian cuts in with a strained laugh. "I told her to ask you about your arm if she was curious—I didn't think she'd *actually* do it." She punctuates her statement with a thunderous glare aimed directly at me.

"It's all right." Travis shrugs, unbothered. "Some lunatic tried to jump me."

My nails dig deeply into the flesh of my palms. My molars grind. It takes every last bit of my self-restraint to stave off the scowl threatening to appear. "Why?"

His forehead suddenly creases. "What do you mean *why*? He's psychotic."

Lilian's head whips in my direction. "Happy?"

No. Not at all. My sister believes my boyfriend is psychotic. Of course, I'm not happy. Frustration sets in as I stare at them.

Dane is not psychotic. He's not a lunatic, either. He's kind. Loyal. Fiercely protective. Despite everything I've heard about him, he's proven to be the sweetest guy I've ever met.

He cuddles me and gives me nose kisses after sex. He picks me up after work so I don't have to wait for the bus when it's super dark. He tries so hard to boost my confidence about my scar. He respects the time I carve out to study.

How can I tell my sister this when I know she won't believe a word I say? I know she'll call me naïve or say that I'm far too trusting of people after everything I've been through. She'll definitely flip out on me, and that conspiracy theorist brain of hers won't let her back down until she's made her point clear regarding Dane.

If I want to get through to my sister, I'll have to choose my words carefully. Let her come to her own conclusion and see the guy that I see.

"How did he end up breaking your arm?"

"What?" Travis turns toward me, clearly taken aback.

"Did he just walk up to you and decide, *I'm going to break this guy's arm*?" I forge on, keeping my tone measured and carefully light. "Or was it out of nowhere?"

"*Reese*," my sister snaps.

"No," Travis growls. His lips curl into a sneer. "The psycho came straight at me with a glass bottle and smashed me with it. When I tried to stop him, he broke my arm."

"Oh." My palm rests against my chest. "I didn't realize… I'm so sorry."

"Travis got hurt pretty badly," Lilian hisses to me with a withering glare.

I don't let her deter me. My eyes remain trained on Travis. "And what happened to him?"

"Don't know." He shrugs a shoulder, his expression impassive. Indignation pulses through me, and I blink back my tears of frustration. "He walked away that night with barely a scratch on him."

I nearly seethe. *That scar is not a scratch*, I want to scream. Not when I can easily picture it; not when I can vividly recall every little detail. *He could have died.*

Anger blazes through my every vein. I still my fists as I rein in my emotions. I cannot lose my cool. *I cannot grab the takeout box and dump it on his head.*

"We both went through something similar," I say, voice sotto voce. "It's always nice to meet a fellow survivor." Acid crawls down my throat, and my chest coils tight. My fingers tremble as they brush against my scarf. "I can't even look in the mirror without thinking about how I almost died. I'm still coming to terms with it."

With that, I lift my head and stare him down. It takes all of my efforts to refrain from averting my eyes and cling to my false bravado for as long as possible.

His gaze bores into mine as he wears a haughty expression.

"But it lets me know I survived, as much as I hate it," I continue, and I'm clutching the thin fabric like it's a lifeline. I'm so close to breaking. Lilian grabs my forearm, but I barrel on. "Was yours as bad as mine?"

"*What?*"

"You know." Adrenaline kicks in. I'm all but shaking as I pause for breath. Anything to steady my erratic pulse. "Was yours as bad as mine?"

My scarf slips off my neck and balls into my hand.

And he winces.

There's a squeamish quality to his features as his gaze drops to my collarbones. A cloying sting fills my heart at the face I've seen countless times.

Not from Dane. Never from Dane.

"You didn't walk away without a scratch," I say flatly. "Neither did I."

The shift in the air is palpable. It's so painfully fraught with tension that the breath leaves my lungs.

"What's it to you?" Travis asks, a sharp edge to his tone, and Lilian tugs at my wrist.

"I want to know I'm not alone. It's always nice to meet someone else who's gone through something similar," I state. "As a fellow survivor, it would mean so much to me to see it. It would make me feel better, you know? Seeing a testimony of your strength and perseverance will… let me know what's in store for me when it comes to healing and moving on."

"I don't have any." He shrugs. "Look, I just want to forget that night ever happened," he tacks on.

"And you know what that's like," my sister hisses at me.

I *do* know what that's like. Believe me, I do. But this guy is clearly lying. It's so glaringly obvious that it's painful to see my sister fall for it. She's letting her bias cloud her judgment, and it's so damn frustrating that I have to chew on the inside of my cheek to hold back my scream.

How do I get it through to her that Dane is not the bad guy she makes him out to be? I know he's flawed, but so is everyone else. Nobody is perfect. He's far from it, but that doesn't make him a monster.

The real monster is the asshole standing in front of us. Travis

Walker. He is a fucking liar who hurts people and gets away with it.

And Dane deserves better than everything he's endured because of him.

3 2

DANE

The car stalls. Reese dissolves into laughter, the sweet and husky notes filling the small space as she struggles to stop. "This is why manuals are being phased out."

"That's because people these days have no appreciation for how a car is meant to be driven," I retort, and amusement tugs at my lips when she tips her head back and cackles harder.

Her eyes have a glittery quality to them as she finds my gaze. Her cheeks possess a healthy glow. Her mouth spreads into a wild grin when the seconds slip by without either of us looking away.

At last, she swivels forward and starts over. With her hand on the gearshift, she shifts into first gear only for the engine to abruptly stop turning again.

"Baby," I say, "release the clutch slowly."

"Are you talking to me or the car?" she teases, then bursts into giggles when I run my hand across the dashboard in a slow caress.

"She doesn't understand what we've been through, baby girl," I drawl, and my girl huffs out a snort.

"Shall I leave you two alone?" Reese asks dryly.

"How about we get her to the other side of the parking lot?" I lean back and smirk at her. "Now, release—"

"Yeah, yeah." Her brows knit with concentration on her next attempt, and suddenly, she shrieks. "*I did it!*"

"Fuck yeah, you did!"

"Your bike's next!" Reese sings, beaming so brightly that I'm momentarily transfixed by a specific crinkle forming around her mouth. It remains there as she takes a ridiculously slow lap around the abandoned lot.

I chuckle. "You should worry about getting your license first."

"That's almost a month away," she reminds me. "It's only the written test this weekend."

"Soon, you won't need me to drive you home," I remark, and she shakes her head.

"I mean, I still have a bus pass," she says matter-of-factly. "Oh, before I forget, thanks for trusting me with your *baby girl*."

"Everybody should know how to drive a stick shift," comes my immediate response, and she snorts as she takes the vehicle out of gear and switches the engine off.

Before I can say a word, something drops in my lap. My peripheral vision observes her shoving her hand back into her coat pocket and feigning interest in the material of her dress underneath.

"An early Christmas present." Her voice is a notch below a whisper. "It's nothing flashy."

I pick up the Hot Wheels: a Chevy Nova painted in a familiar yellow-green color. I automatically lose the fight against my crooked smile.

"It's a thank-you gift for everything," she continues, letting out a soft exhalation. She still won't look at me. She's tracing a star on her knee. "I know it's not a convertible—"

"I'll keep it on me." The toy car is pocketed within a heartbeat, clanking against my janky phone. "I'll take it everywhere I go."

"You don't have to." She glances over. "It's nothing special."

"It's from my Reese's Pieces," I say. "Therefore, it's pretty special to me."

Her breath hitches as her features soften into that sweet, shy smile.

"Unfortunately, what I have for you isn't on me," I continue, and I'm met with a frown. "Figured it'd be a good way to celebrate you kicking the final's ass, too."

Technically, the semester hasn't ended yet, but there's no point in bringing that up. Not when she's peering at me with those starry-soft eyes.

"Really, Dane." She leans over and presses a gentle kiss to my temple. "You don't have to get me anything. *Especially if it's a back tattoo.* Teaching me how to drive is more than enough."

I don't get a chance to respond when she pulls away and hops out of my Mustang. Without having any trouble with the handle. There's a first for everything.

Releasing a sigh, I exit the vehicle and catch her in my arms before we can trade back seats. My lips find hers before she can even blink, stealing her gasp with an urgent and incessant kiss. Her fingers twine in my hair, and she giggles when she finds herself caged beneath me on the hood of my car.

***

"FOR YOUR FIESTA." I GESTURE BROADLY WHILE REESE TAKES IN THE lobby with wide eyes. Red and gold ornaments glitter on a massive two-story Christmas tree in the center of the room. The walls are adorned with tinsel. Above us hangs a crystal chandelier. It's not my scene by far, but I knew Reese would get a kick out of it.

"My fiesta is gonna have so many amazing pictures," she agrees, tilting her phone back to capture the star on top of the tree. Then she leans even further back to snap a photo of the chandelier.

Instinctively, my arm hooks around her waist and tugs her to me before a kid knocks into her. The place is crawling with people trickling in and out of the place, which isn't a surprise. The Westbrook Resort has always been one of the fanciest joints I've ever stepped foot in.

Her breathing is a little unsteady as she gives me a sheepish smile. "You didn't just bring me here to take pictures, did you?" She's not exactly subtle when she sneaks one of me.

I pluck her phone, blatantly take a photo of her while she splutters, and pass it back. "Nah. We're here for what's outside."

"The beach?" She lifts a brow. "We're not skinny dipping."

"Aw, fuck, I should've thought of that." My hand goes to the small of her back. With a gentle nudge, I steer her toward one of the exits. "In fact—"

"It's December. We're not risking hypothermia," she hisses, only for her eyes to go wide a beat later.

"But any other month is fine?" I tease, but she remains rooted to the spot.

Finally, she swivels toward me, her mouth falling ajar as she meets my gaze. "An ice skating rink?"

"Do you know how to skate?" I ask and smile crookedly when she offers me a tiny head shake. "Perfect."

"How is that perfect?" Her attention pivots back to the attraction. The glow of the lanterns strung above the beachfront rink shines like stars in her eyes.

"Two hours of a pretty girl clinging to me sounds like a perfect time. Fantastic, even." With a grin, I steer her straight to the gate.

Once we've swapped our shoes for rental skates, I help her onto the ice. Her arms shake the whole time.

"You know how to skate?" she marvels, and a startled yelp escapes her when she wobbles.

"Who doesn't?" I tease, eliciting an exaggerated scowl from her. "Played some hockey when I was a kid."

"You played hockey?" she gasps. "Why did you stop?"

My shoulder hitches in a shrug. "Got pretty hurt one year and didn't feel like it anymore."

She nods, then sucks in a breath when a few kids nearly careen into us coming from the opposite direction. I think she's cutting off circulation in my hand with the viselike death grip she's got going on.

"You won't die if you fall on the ice," I tell her. Never mind, she's definitely cutting off the blood flow in my fingers now.

"I wouldn't fall on the ice if I weren't on the ice," she wheezes.

"I won't let you fall."

"Swear on your life." Somehow, she squeezes me even tighter as I guide her toward the center where there's less traffic.

"I swear on my life, my bike, and my cars," I say. "Here, let me teach you the basics."

Her bottom lip worries between her teeth as she peers up at me. Soon enough, her hesitation gives way to an unwavering amount of trust. It steals across her face as she allows her fingers to flex and slip from mine.

A startled shriek breaks free as her arms immediately flail. My reflexes kick in instantaneously, and I catch her by the elbow.

"See?" I steady her and offer her a half-smile. "You're a pro already."

"Wait." She whips her phone out. I don't get a chance to blink when the flash goes off.

"You know, I'm curious here." I readjust my hold so that I'm not wrinkling her coat sleeve. "What do you even do with all the photos you take of me? Because I know it's not going on your fiesta, where your sister might see it."

"I don't post every picture I take," she states. "Most of them are just for me."

"Got it. They're all going into your personal spank bank."

She nearly topples over, but I catch her again and bring her body closer to mine.

"*No.*" She pockets her cell and spares me a tiny frown. "I just like having them. They're memories of things I can always come back to. And it's nice to have pictures of you looking…"

"Sexy?" I supply.

"Happy."

My breath stalls in my lungs, and my heartbeat echoes in my ears as she carefully straightens herself.

"Anyway," she continues, "I'm ready to knock my teeth out when I fall."

My voice is gruff when I find it. "You won't fall." I clear my throat. "I won't let it happen."

Slowly, I let her go. For the next half hour, I show her the ropes. Catch her by the elbow or the material of her coat if needed. Spin her around once like we're a pair of figure skaters. I even demonstrate how to properly fall and lose the fight against my grin when she breaks into a husky peal of laughter as she lands ungracefully on her ass.

She's still giggling when I skate backward, showing off some impressive skills for someone as rusty as me. Skidding to a stop the instant I'm on the other side of the rink, my arm stretches wide.

"Come on, Mini Reese! Let's see you fly!"

I'm unable to keep the corners of my mouth from tipping up at the sight of her moving at the speed of molasses. She's fucking cute.

"I'm doing it!" she shrieks. Her pace barely picks up by a small margin.

"Fuck yeah, you are!"

There's the sweetest beam I've ever seen on her face as she comes within reach. At once, her smile falters. "Wait, how do I st—"

She smacks into me. Instinctively, I brace my arms around her and let myself fall backward. My ass hits the ice first. My head thumps against the cold surface next.

"Oh my God," she wheezes, prying her cheek from my chest to find my gaze. "I'm so sorry." Her expression is nothing but worry as she searches my eyes. Her body goes stock-still when the rough pad of my thumb runs across her temple.

I brush the loose strands of hair out of her face and register her soft intake of breath.

A stupid grin breaks across my face as my hand slides to the back of her neck and tangles in her wavy tresses. Lanterns twinkle behind her, bathing her in a warm, atmospheric glow.

"You're so beautiful," I whisper, and she lets out a shaky laugh as I draw her in.

"I think you have a concussion," she protests with a smile, and her nose brushes against mine before our mouths slant together.

I tug her closer, and she melts into me. My other arm barely circles her waist when a chorus of high-pitched heckles startles her, and she pulls away. Children scatter when I shoot them a withering glare.

"Damn brats," I grumble as she sheepishly untangles herself from my embrace. The fragrance of her coconut shampoo lingers while she carefully rises to her full height.

"Can you teach me how to stop this time?" she asks, and I look up and find myself ensnared.

I wish I could grab her phone and capture a picture of her at this very moment, with the lanterns still backlighting her in a hazy-soft glow and her eyes glittering more beautifully than the night stars above us.

Instead, I memorize every little detail, push up to my feet, and skate a lazy circle around her. "You got it."

33

REESE

ONCE MY ENGINEERING PROJECT IS TURNED IN, I AM FREE. I WON'T have to look at geographic information systems for the next four weeks. Raster data is no longer something I must think about until the spring semester starts. Winter break is finally underway.

Dragging my feet out of the Science Building, I come to a complete stop when I spot a familiar cherry-red Mustang parked by the entrance.

Even though I'm bone-weary from back-to-back all-nighters, I perk up. "What are you doing here?"

Unlike me, Dane has been done with finals since Monday. Instead of working on his cars, he'd been helping me study for my physics and calculus exams at his apartment. It's a shame he's not considering mechanical engineering. He knows more than he lets on.

"My Reese's Pieces is finally done," he says, "and we're celebrating."

"Aren't you done, too?" I climb into the passenger side and brush my lips against his cheek, bursting into laughter when he turns his head and captures them in a searing kiss.

"Eh. Only one of us put in any effort." He pulls away, and I refrain from sighing. There's no use debating with him over this. Maybe he's not as studious as I am, but he *has* cracked his text-books open a few times and pored over his slides. An attempt is better than nothing.

"Since you're here, I have your actual Christmas gift back at my place."

It's a professionally printed and framed picture I'd taken of his Mustang parked at the beach, with the streaky sherbet sky in the background. It was the only thing I could think of that was thoughtful and not too cheesy. Also, his apartment could use a splash of color. It's so drab and depressingly vacant.

"I have a gift for you, too." He pats his groin area before I can utter a single word.

My eyes narrow. "Do I even want to know what it is?" I ask dryly, and his grin turns devious.

"Get your mind out of the gutter, Reese." This time, he thumps his thigh. I'm not sure what to guess from that, and I don't think I want to know.

"So," I hedge, averting my attention to the passenger side window. "Where are we going?"

"It's a surprise," comes his response.

Biting my inner cheek, I mull it over. "Go-karts again?"

He chuckles. "Passing the written test turned you into a speed demon?"

"Ha. Good one." Unlike Dane, I wholeheartedly believe in driving at the posted limit. Mostly because I'm terrified at the idea of crashing one of his cars. I know how precious they are to him. I don't want to be the reason why he loses any single one of them.

Since I'm running on fumes, I drain the remaining coffee from my thermos, then watch him drive.

He's so casually confident every time he's behind the wheel. His mouth is pulled into an easy smile and sends a buzz of awareness to my chest. I love his smiles. All of them. I like when he doesn't look so broody all the time, as if he's carrying the weight of the world on his shoulders.

Retrieving my phone from my pocket, I snap a photo of him while he's running his fingers through his hair.

His grin broadens. "For your spank bank?"

"Yup. My spank bank needs new material," I deadpan, the edge of my lips curling as I observe the picture and save it to my private album. It was created in case Lilian snoops through my cell.

We would never do that to each other, but still. It's better to be safe than sorry.

The last thing I want is to risk any chance of her finding out about him and freaking out on me. Some selfish part of me wishes she'd give him a chance. Or at least trust my judgment.

Just then, my stomach twists into a knot. With a defeated sigh, I force myself to think about something other than her. Now's not the time to bum myself out.

Soon, pine and palm trees pass by in a blur as he guns it and expertly weaves through traffic. When he takes an exit, I still don't know where we're going. We're in a city I've never even heard of.

However, it's not hard to figure out whether this area is wealthy. It practically oozes wealth. Pristine boutiques display luxury goods in their windows. The sidewalks are spotless and practically glittering. Trees and flowers are neatly manicured and maintained.

While I'm certain my sister would love it here, I've never felt more out of place in the secondhand sweater I've had since the seventh grade and well-worn jeans.

Abruptly, he pulls into the first parking spot that he stumbles across. Unless he took me here for salvaged driftwood furniture or designer handbags, the confectionery shop is probably what he had in mind for our little date.

"Did we come here for chocolate?" I ask incredulously.

"I go here every year," he explains as he climbs out of his car.

"Didn't know you have a sweet tooth," I murmur while I reluctantly exit the Mustang and follow him through the door.

Inside, a sweet fragrance lingers in the air. Ornate decorations hang from the ceiling. Black and white portraits of celebrities who've visited the candy shop neatly line the walls. Carved wood displays are strewn purposely across the store, boasting countless truffles in various flavors.

I sneak a peek at a price tag, and my soul shrivels up at the amount printed in a loopy script. A lollipop should not cost that much money.

Roaming around aimlessly seems like the only thing I can afford in here. While I browse the seasonal confectioneries, I read the names of actors and musicians. I don't recognize most of the faces.

Dane sidles over to me and picks up a box of artisanal chocolates wrapped in glittery foil. "You want anything?"

"I'm good." I shake my head immediately when he grabs another and points it at me. "You don't have to."

"Eh. I won't be back here 'til next year." He wanders off, and I release a quiet sigh.

Redirecting my attention to the wall, I continue to scan the autographed pictures. One thing I've noticed so far is the transition of fashion styles over the decades as I venture deeper into the shop. *The hair. Wow.*

A photograph from seventeen years ago snares my attention. Standing fully in the frame, a gorgeous woman with a light-colored bob and a brilliant smile poses by the register with two employees. Finally, someone I recognize.

Katherine Ellis, an English actress who starred in this epic romantic drama I adored and watched multiple times as a kid. It was the last film she starred in before she retired and stepped away from the limelight.

She looks a little bit older here. It must have been taken a few years before she passed away, though. Lilian gently broke the news of her untimely death to me, and Mom's boyfriend thought it was funny how devastated I was over the news.

My heart gives a little twist when my focus shifts to the toddler on her hip. I can't even imagine how her passing must have affected him. Wait.

With my pulse thrumming in my ears, I stretch on my toes and lean in for a better look. He has chubby cheeks, and his grin for the camera is wide and crooked and familiar. *Oh my God. Is that—*

"Reese!" Dane hollers, and I glance over my shoulder to see him motioning for me from the register. "Did you find something?"

"No, I'm fine." I take one last glance at the photo before I make my way over to him. He immediately hooks his arm around my waist, pulling me flush to his side. I want to take another peek so badly when he points to a pile of handcrafted peanut butter cups.

"I bet they're not as tasty as you."

A loud snort escapes me, then I erupt into a peal of laughter when he ducks his head and nips at my ear. *"Behave."*

In response, he squeezes my hip and then pays for his purchase. I try not to balk at the digits flashing on the tablet.

As we move away from the register, he pushes the bag into my hand. "For you."

"Me?" I gawp at him. "I can't accept this—"

"Sure you can." He folds my fingers over the handle and offers me a smirk. "See?"

Before I can respond, he's already heading toward the exit. Swallowing hard, I peer at the crowded shop once more and scramble after him.

34

DANE

Daylight sifts through the window and drenches the bedroom in a soft orange glow. Reese is plastered against me on her small bed. I don't think she's even aware of how often she reaches for me while asleep. As it is, her fingers are clinging to my arm.

I woke up early because I heard a car backfiring nearby. I haven't gotten any shut-eye since. Just as I'm about to doze off, a loud, rattling knock jolts me awake like a shock to my system.

I groan. Bringing my mouth to the shell of her ear, I gently shake her shoulder. "Reese. I think someone's outside your apartment."

"Hmm?" She slowly blinks at me with bleary eyes and a wrinkly nose. There's no doubt about it. This girl is dead tired. She's not wearing a look of panic as she comes to. It'd be a boost to my ego if finals weren't the reason for her exhaustion.

"Sounds like someone's at your door." I smooth a strand of her frizzy hair behind her ear, and every inch of her face turns pink.

"Oh." I don't miss how her shoulders hunch as she curls into me.

My head tips to the side. "Want me to tell them to kindly fuck off?"

"No, no," she breathes out. "It might be my sister."

"Want me to kindly fuck off?"

In answer, she pokes my nose as she sits up and crawls over me. A protesting squeal tears from her chest when I catch her with my hands low on her hips, holding her in place.

"I need to get my phone," she gasps.

"You could always just ask." I blindly reach for it from her nightstand, then pass it to her. While she remains on top of me and checks her cell, my palm skirts under her oversized shirt and tracks a line up the heat of her body.

"It's not Lili," Reese observes, yawning. "She would text me when she's coming over."

"Offer's still on the table," I remind her, and she touches my chest, stilling me.

"It's probably my neighbor." She leans in, and her hair sweeps across my collarbone as she presses her lips to mine. Instantly, my arms wrap around her and draw her in for a deeper kiss. She bursts into giggles as she breaks away. "One, morning breath is a thing. Two, I need to see who it is."

"It's Christmas Eve," I mutter in protest. "Can't they wait until after Christmas?"

Shrugging, she slides off of me and reaches for her coat and can of mace. I hope whoever's at her door isn't in for a rude awakening. "I'll be right back."

"I'll scare them away if needed."

With a sigh, she glances at the door. Then she darts back to me, sneaks another kiss, and grins brightly when she steps out of my reach before I can wrap my arms around her.

"Let me know if you need backup," I tell her, and I reach for my shirt when she exits her room. I barely grab my jeans when I hear her voice through the wall.

"Caleb?"

Every muscle along my spine tenses. *What the fuck is he doing here?*

I can't hear his response. Even when I'm leaning against the door, his words are muffled. I'm unable to discern what Reese is saying, either. I'm about to head out when I hear the telltale slam, followed by the audible clicks of her deadbolts.

Soon enough, Reese returns and locks her doorknob behind her. Her eyes collide with mine, and her brows knit together in confusion.

"Was that Blue Balls?"

"*Caleb*," she corrects. "And yes."

I frown. "Why was he here?"

"You have nothing to worry about." Her mouth curves into a sweet smile as she plants her hands on my chest and leans into me. It takes a beat to realize she thinks I'm jealous, and I fight my scoff. "I'm with you."

"I know that." My palms rest on the small of her back. "I meant, why was he here on Christmas Eve?"

"Oh. His family has a party this evening, and he wanted me to come as his date." She puts on a thoughtful frown, one that mirrors mine. For different reasons, I'm sure.

I've got no idea why he'd want her to attend something as intimate as *that*. Not when he hasn't talked to her since she ditched his lame ass. She hasn't brought him up since, and I can't imagine her keeping his pursuits a secret from me.

Could the sorority girls be involved? Or has the dumbass finally realized what slipped through his fingers?

"You said yes, right?"

She huffs out a snort and peels away from me. "Of course not." Shrugging her coat off, she drapes it over the back of her desk chair. "I told him we were better off as friends. That was pretty much it."

With that, she crawls back into bed and pats the space beside her. A shy smile touches her lips.

I don't hesitate. Sliding under the cover, my arm tucks around her waist and anchors her to my chest. It doesn't take long before she nods off. Her head droops into her pillow. Her breathing softens into something even and steady. Her hair tickles my nose and envelops me with the faint scent of coconuts.

Shutting my eyes, I don't move another muscle. Not even when my phone starts buzzing. I don't give a rat's ass if it's my old man calling me. As of right now, there's no one else I'd rather talk to than the one in my arms right now.

I BARELY ANSWER THE VIDEO CALL, AND ALREADY, I'M SUBJECTED TO a frown.

"You shouldn't have," is the first thing she says. She must be hiding in the bathroom at the sorority house. I know she's spending Christmas with her sister, and there's a bathtub behind her.

My shoulder lifts in a casual shrug. "It's just a necklace."

Her gaze sharpens. "It's a *key*—"

"On a necklace."

"I know what a car key looks like."

"Now you'll have something to drive with for your driver's test," I say coolly, and her lips purse in annoyance. "Hey, if it'll make you feel better, it's an old car."

She huffs and rakes her fingers through her hair. "All of your old ones cost way too much—"

"This one barely cost a thing," I insist, and a lazy smirk tugs at the corner of my mouth. "Don't worry about it. Consider it a thanks for saving my ass that one night."

The lines of her face tighten with protest. "I didn't do anything," she whispers, and that couldn't be farther from the truth. "And you know I'm not the type to expect something in return for helping—"

"Reese. If you don't want it, you can sell it. Scrap it for parts. Do whatever the fuck you want with it."

"Give it back to you?" she tries, and I smirk.

"It'll be in my garage, waiting for you," I go on. "Or collecting dust. One or the other."

At once, her expression falters, and my stomach clenches tight. "It's just…" She trails off and gnaws her lower lip. "I feel lame. I didn't get you anything as fancy—"

"You got me a car." Switching to the rear-facing camera, I make a show of pushing the little Nova against Ol' Reliable's dashboard. "I got you one, too. Seems like an even trade to me."

She groans. "They're not the same, and you know it."

"Look, I have to go." My words are steeped with reluctance as my focus goes over my phone. Up ahead, Shyla is sashaying toward the starting line. "Have a good Christmas, Reese."

"I hope you do, too. I'm sorry we couldn't spend it together…" Her sentence dwindles, and something bittersweet paints over her features.

"It's fine. We'll see each other tomorrow."

"Yeah, I know." Finally, that sweet smile of hers surfaces and abruptly dims. The car key comes into the frame as she frantically waves it. "And this isn't over."

"If you say so," I reply. "Enjoy your new set of wheels."

She sputters. I end the call before she can get another word in, jam my phone into my pocket, and then yank my helmet on.

To my right, a lime-green coupe is revving like a jackass. Before me, is the sweet open road.

Cracking my knuckles, I roll my shoulders and stare straight ahead. It's been a good minute since I've driven the streets surrounding the county reservoir, but anticipation surges through my bloodstream, nevertheless. I miss a good challenge and the heady rush of dopamine when I overtake another vehicle and win by the skin of my teeth.

The second the checkered flags whip through the air, I leave

Wally behind to play catch-up when I accelerate across the starting line and fucking floor it.

35

REESE

Karla's jaw drops. "You turned him down?" Her voice pitches high with shock. "Seriously?"

I blow out an exasperated breath. As much as I love Lilian's sorority sisters, my social battery depleted a long time ago. Five sorority sisters ago.

They're friendly, don't get me wrong, but they're so nosy. And I can only explain so many times that I don't want to give Caleb another shot. If I could name-drop Dane and be done with it, I would.

"I don't wanna go out with him," I reiterate, and the silence that follows is extremely awkward and tense. I guess I can understand her surprise. From her and everyone else. They made a huge deal about my crush on him last year. Sometimes, it felt like they were more invested in my relationship with him than I was.

"Are you sure?" she asks, and I spare her a tight-lipped smile that borders on a grimace. "Lilian said you were still... you know, struggling with..."

My stomach sinks. "Oh."

"*And* wouldn't Caleb be a great distraction from that?" she continues brightly. Her attention flits to my exposed neck, and there's something so gentle in her gaze that makes me feel very small and scoured from the inside out.

I glance elsewhere, busying my fingers with my hair. Anything to distract myself from her look of pity. I should've just put on my sweater. Sure, I spilled soup on it, but I'd rather wear last night's dinner than subject myself to this for any minute longer.

"I…" I hold back my grimace. I can't tell my sister's roommate I'm currently seeing someone. Word will get back to Lilian before I even take one step out of the guest room's door, and I would like to leave this house without another person commenting on my love life. "I don't need to distract myself with a guy."

"But it's so fun, though."

Shoving the duck plushie Karla got me for Christmas into my backpack, I flash her a wan smile. "Thanks for the advice, but I'm good. *Bye*."

Before she can continue this excruciating conversation, I bolt out the door and cling to the desperate hope no one else will utter Caleb Marsden's name to me while I rush downstairs.

He's a nice guy, but he's *not* the one for me.

"Lili, I have to leave." I poke my head into the kitchen and freeze at what's transpiring before my very eyes.

There's a list of things I never want to experience. This is up there between getting rabies and stubbing a toe every day for the rest of my life. No one in their right mind would ever want to see their sister getting felt up.

Especially when it's by the one and only Travis Walker.

My mouth tightens into a grim line. My stomach roils. My focus cuts to the ceiling as I try to purge this horrifying incident from memory. This is unexpected, unsettling, and most of all, *ew*.

Staring fixedly at the red tinsel dangling above me, I clear my throat. I do it again, louder this time, and then I hack my lungs out with a series of coughs.

"Lili," I hiss. "*Lilian*."

She jerks away from him as if scalded by hot water, and a splash of pink colors her round cheeks when she swivels toward me. There's no trace of embarrassment in her expression. If anything, she's breathless, which would be easier to digest if it were caused by literally anyone else.

My line of sight slides toward Travis, and I don't miss the vehemence gathering behind his eyes. Or the fact that he placed his hand directly on my sister's ass.

"What's up?" Lilian asks, smoothing away the disheveled strands of her thick hair.

"Can you walk me to the door?" I clip, my voice tight and bordering on shrill. With a rough inhalation, I flash her an even tighter smile.

"Sure." She leans over to murmur something into Travis' ear, and my grimace doubles when he draws her in for another kiss. I peer intensely at a coffee pot.

Soon, she extricates herself from his limbs and accompanies me toward the foyer. A frown furrows between her eyebrows. "Are you okay?"

"Couldn't. Be. Peachier," I rasp, and she squints at me. I paste on a stiff, friendly, *everything's fine* smile and speedwalk to the front. Sensing her shrewd gaze on me, I shoot her a *nothing's wrong at all* grin and wish my nerves would stop cresting.

Her eyes bore a hole through the side of my head. "Are you sure?"

Crap. She knows me well and can easily read my tells. It's why I never lie to my sister. Up until the last few months, I haven't had any reason to keep secrets from her.

My stomach gives a sharp twist as guilt assails me.

"Can we talk out there?" I whisper, tipping my head to the side. Wordlessly, she nods and follows me through the door.

Outside, the wintry air is crisp and chilly. The sun's breaking through the morning clouds and foggy marine layer, warming the earth. Yet it does nothing to calm down the swirling mess of emotions warring inside me.

Shoving my fingers into my hair, I pivot on my feet to face her. I don't know how to broach the subject. Racking my brain, I try to figure out how to get the ball rolling as eloquently as possible.

"Travis Walker?" I hiss.

Her weight shifts onto one leg. "What about him?"

"I…" There are so many things I want to say. So many things I want to point out. But we both move to the side of the porch when the front door swings open and another sorority sister exits the house, and I lose my train of thought. "Lilian… Him? Seriously? *Why?*"

She frowns. "Because he's cute?"

"B-but…" What am I supposed to say? *He's dangerous, Lili?* I'd laugh at the irony of the situation—at how the tables have turned—if this wasn't a serious matter. Blowing out a quavering breath, I forge on. "Doesn't he come off super sleazy to you?"

"Sleazy?" Her arms cross as she slices me with a hard glare. "Because he's a frat guy?"

"What?" I gasp, stunned. "No."

"He's actually nice if you get to know him. In fact, you should get to know him," she states. "This Saturday, we can go to that pancake place you've been raving about."

No freaking way. I resist the temptation to scowl. "I have work."

Her posture straightens. "You always have work." Accusation rings in her tone, and her amber eyes sharpen into steel as silence weighs down on the space between us. "And FYI, I dropped by the bookstore last weekend when you were supposedly working, only to find out from Mandy you had an earlier shift that day."

My breath catches, and I'm frozen under her blazing gaze. *She did what?*

"I stopped by last Wednesday, too. Oddly enough, you weren't around even though you told me you were covering for one of your coworkers." Her teeth grit in a mean growl. "So, are you actually working this weekend or are you gonna lie to me again?"

The air painfully leaves my lungs. "I'm not—"

She huffs out a scoff, bringing her hand to her temple. "I know you. Don't fucking lie to me."

My lips clamp shut. Crap. I don't want this to spiral into an even bigger fight, but I can't think of a thing to say. My brain is reeling, and I'm overwhelmed as I try to figure out how to defuse the situation and calm her down.

"Okay," I hedge, "I've been busy."

"Doing what?" she cuts in.

Doing my boyfriend. The words almost slip off my tongue. Oh God, I've been around Dane a bit too much lately.

"Homework," I explain, and she rolls her eyes. "I've been busy with my physics assignments—*and engineering projects.* Lili, the course load for my major is hard."

"And yet I haven't seen you at the tutoring center." Her disbelieving stare causes me to flinch. "And don't say you've been at home, either. You're never at your apartment whenever I stop by."

Well. *Shoot.* I gnaw on my inner cheek. This isn't how I wanted to break the news to my sister about Dane, but if push comes to shove, I'll... tell her about him. Especially if it means I can bring up everything he's said about Travis and provide her with some much-needed context.

"I... I have my reasons—"

"You have *reasons* to lie to your sister?" she seethes, and I almost clutch my forehead as a throbbing ache overtakes my skull.

This is so like her. I can never get more than a few words in before she goes on the offense.

"I *wouldn't* have to keep things from you if you'd give me a breather!" I bite out, and she falters back a step, stunned.

"You want a breather?" she repeats slowly, sounding out each syllable, and hurt flashes across her profile. "From me?"

"I didn't mean it like that," I begin, only for her to cut me off.

"Reese—" She exhales sharply and stares up at the sky. A frostiness settles across her features as her attention pivots to me, and her nostrils flare. "You know what? Forget it. Have fun working or doing your homework or whatever it is you're actually doing. I'll give you the breather you want."

"Lilian," I protest. "That's not what I meant."

"Never mind that I've been sick and worried about you," she plows on as she edges away from me. "Worried that something could have happened to you again—" She redirects her focus to my neck, and her eyes shine brightly with unshed tears. "Go have your breather, okay? I'll leave you alone, so you don't have to keep lying to me anymore."

My chest tightens. "Lili—"

"Here's your fucking breather." She yanks the door open and slams it shut after her, leaving me standing there, gawping at the Christmas wreath in absolute shock.

Tears keep prickling my eyes despite my attempts to quell them. I hate fighting with my sister. We rarely get into arguments to begin with. Whenever there's ever any tension brewing, my people-pleaser tendencies kick in, and I try to keep the peace by any means necessary.

Even when I'm in the right, I prefer peace. I hate conflict, and I've never liked being in a hostile environment to begin with. But it's not healthy or fair that I'm always the one who has to cave and let her get her way. Just because she doesn't like to bend or fold or apologize doesn't mean I always have to be the one who extends the olive branch.

I love my sister, but she can be frustrating. Her temper and mean streak come out in full force if she thinks she's been slighted. While her fierceness, fiery personality, and ability to stand up for herself are admirable to an extent, it *sucks* when she refuses to consider any accountability or accept that sometimes *she* can be in the wrong.

It's not entirely her fault what happened between us, but her hotheadedness is not helping at all.

My chest aches as I pace the footbridge of the campus pond some more. I don't want to look like I spent the last thirty minutes crying, but my sadness hangs over me like a rainy cloud. Not even the pintail ducks are cheering me up.

When my phone buzzes, my hope spikes and fizzles out within a beat as I check the message. Hugging my arms to my chest, I set off toward the parking structure.

Before long, the concrete building comes into view. I drag in a deep breath and freeze when I spot Dane walking over with his hands shoved into his pockets. Just as he's within reach, his grin turns into a frown while his eyes rove across my face. His stance shifts, and his muscles tense as if he's priming for a fight.

"What's wrong?"

"It's nothing." Blinking rapidly, I duck my head and retrieve a key from my backpack. "You need to take this back."

"Do *not* feel guilty about the car I got you," he says, sliding his knuckles under my chin. "You haven't even seen it yet. I got it painted in both orange and yellow just for you, with *Reese's Pieces* detailed on the back bumper."

An inhuman sound of sheer horror squeaks out of me.

There's a ninety-nine percent chance he's messing with me. I know that. But the horrifying image that pops into my head is enough for me to be terrified of the one percent chance he actually went through with it.

"You did not."

He offers me a slanted grin and leisurely strokes my cheekbone with the pad of his thumb. "And the plate spells out *Big Cups—*"

"Swear to God, you're the worst," I grumble, pulling away from him.

He chuckles. "At least see it before you decide that you don't want it."

"I don't want it," I say immediately, and he sighs.

"Will you at least humor me a little?" he asks, then pauses. "Unless… Are you that upset over what I got you?"

"Huh?" I go stock-still when he dries a tear off my cheek. "Oh no, I wasn't…" My words stick in my throat as I find his gaze. I don't want to tell him about the fight and have him blame himself for what happened between me and Lilian. "Did you really paint it orange?"

"And yellow." He tosses me a wink, and I laugh for the first time today despite myself.

"If I don't like it, you said I could sell it, right?" I ask softly, and his mouth twitches with amusement.

"Trust me, Reese," he says. "You'll fucking love it."

<hr>

AFTER HE CUTS THE ENGINE, I PASS HIM MY HELMET AND COMB MY fingers through my messy, windswept hair.

Dane hops off his motorcycle and glances over his shoulder. "Need you to look the other way."

"What could this car key possibly be for?" I ask dryly, turning around to face the street. It's currently empty, save for us two.

"The fun part"—his boot crunches the gravel as he approaches me from behind—"is getting to see the look on your face."

"Oh God." My nose wrinkles. "Should I be worried?"

He lets out a raspy chuckle. "Nah. Now, cover your eyes, Mini Reese. If you're peeking, I'll do it myself."

With a sigh, I oblige and startle a beat later when I feel his hands on my biceps. He carefully spins me around twice, and I'm dizzy when I come to a complete stop. Hopefully facing the garage.

"You can look now."

Slowly blinking my eyes open, I peek through my fingers and brace myself, only to see the usual suspects. A flashy black coupe hangs to the left, tucked behind the vintage red and blue muscle cars. Then there's the pony parked in the middle. Further back is the newest addition he got last week: a green fastback with a cracked windshield that needs to be replaced.

There is nothing remotely yellow or orange under this roof. As I squint, my peripheral vision finally takes notice of a vehicle to my right. My eyes widen as it slowly dawns on me I recognize the shape of the taillights. And the tailgate. Of the convertible. Which is now painted in a light purplish-blue shade.

The air whooshes from my lungs, and I stand there, rooted to the spot. My heart thumps in my ears; my hands shake. I can't breathe. I've forgotten how to.

It's the dreamiest color I've ever seen—something close to pastel—and pairs well with the white interior.

Breathless, I swivel around and peer up at him. He shoves his hands into his pockets and offers me a shrug. My lips part.

"Is that the Nova?" I choke out, my words barely a scratch above a whisper.

"A Nova for a Nova." He fishes out the Hot Wheels I hand-painted for him and spares me a slight grin. I'm vaguely aware of how my feet are moving until my knees bump against his shins, and the distance between us ceases.

"Oh my God."

"You know," he continues, placing his hands low on my hips. "I do hope you don't get rid of it. The color alone was a pain in the ass to customize."

"It was?" I wet my bottom lip with the tip of my tongue. My heartbeat is frantic and wild and beating oh so fast. I thought he sold it. At least, that's what he told me.

"But iris is such a nice color that it was worth it," he continues, punctuating his words with a gentle squeeze. "You feel me, Charisse?"

I'm helpless against the beam overtaking my face. Overwhelmed, I glance elsewhere as a flush of heat crawls up my neck. "You know my name."

"No shit? Charisse?" I can hear the smirk in his voice. "I got it right the first time?"

Peering sideways at him, I catch sight of his unabashed smile, and my pulse trips over itself. "It's—"

"I know." He winks. "Give me some credit."

Biting my bottom lip, my attention returns to the car. I don't know what to say. I don't even know how to thank him. I'm speechless. Utterly so. Because *oh my God*?

My brain has officially short-circuited on me. It cannot form any words. It is simply a pile of mush.

This has to be the sweetest gesture anyone has ever done for me. My stomach gives a warm flutter, and tears begin welling behind my eyes.

"This is your car," Dane says finally, tucking his head into the crook of my neck. "Unless you happen to know another Iris out there who'll appreciate this beaut more than you."

"I…" I let loose a hoarse laugh. "It's so weird hearing someone call me by my given name."

"I feel ya, Reese's Pieces."

"Daniel?" I guess. I mean, what else could it be? *Danish*?

A shudder racks through his frame, and he pulls back and levels me with a hard grimace. "Don't think I like hearing that from you, Reese."

"How did you even figure out my name?"

"Well, I Googled *shades of purple* after our conversation and saw it on a list." He offers me a smug little grin and shrugs. "Was torn between *raisin* and *iris*, so I flipped a coin."

I snort before I can help myself. "You didn't have to. I—I thought you didn't like purple?"

"Well, some girl I know suggested painting it purple," he says. "I decided to go through with her advice."

"Must be some girl," I whisper, as he tugs me in close to his body.

His expression softens while he peers steadily into my eyes. "She is."

DANE

Her hair ribbons and billows with the breeze, and her smile takes on an excited edge, as the Nova flies down the scenic route I've driven countless times. The golden hour is upon us, and hazy orange sunlight casts over us and bounces off her skin.

Retrieving my new phone from my pocket, I take a picture of her behind the wheel. My girl's the photographer, not me, so it comes out blurry. The next one I capture has her sticking her tongue out at me. It's extremely out of focus and my favorite photo of her by far.

Since I don't want to distract her, I stow my device away and provide her with directions needed to get to the hidden beach. Only locals know about this spot, and even then, it's a pain in the ass to find.

Soon, we find ourselves in a residential area, and Reese puts on a frown when she circles the block for the third time.

"I don't see any parking," she mumbles, heaving out a quiet sigh.

"There's one right there." I gesture to my right, and she blanches.

"It's too tight."

There are plenty of innuendos I could make right now, but I

decide to behave for once. Especially when she's finally comfortable on the road. She's no longer holding the steering wheel with a death grip, and her shoulders aren't pulled taut when she brings the vehicle to the speed limit.

"Don't even sweat it, Snack Mix," I assure her. "You got this."

The corner of her mouth twitches a beat, and then she blows out a breath. Trepidation gathers in her eyes when she stares ahead. With a nod, she throws the vehicle in reverse and carefully tries to parallel park.

If we could even call it that. I resist the urge to snicker, staring pointedly at the side-view mirror and pressing my knuckles to my lips when I sense her scowling beside me. A smart man knows better than to laugh, but I can't help it.

My girl's terrible at this, making more than a twenty-point turn without any real progress.

"All right," I say finally. I don't think I'll be able to maintain a straight face if this becomes a *fifty*-point turn. There's only so much self-control I can exert. "I'll give you a refresher tomorrow. Let me park the car for you."

A groan of relief breaks free, and she thumps her head against the headrest. "Thank you for putting me out of my misery."

With the brakes on, she jumps out of the convertible like a bat out of hell and scrambles for the sidewalk. I quickly climb into the driver's seat, and my knees bang against the steering wheel. Right.

Pushing the seat all the way back, I readjust the rearview mirror, then peel away from the curb.

With ease, precision, and speed, I quickly back the Nova into the tight spot in under ten seconds and kill the engine. Parallel parking is a fucking breeze for me. It's one of the first things I learned just a few months into working at Sal's. Marco wanted to see who could do it better, and I wasn't going to let him beat me at it.

Hopping out of the car, I glance over and catch sight of

Reese gawking at me. More importantly, she's biting her bottom lip. My amusement only grows. "Aw, that turned you on, didn't it?"

A heavy blush blooms across her face. "Shut up."

"Oh? On second thought, I won't give you any refreshers," I tease. Before she can say anything, I throw my arm around her waist and wrench her to me. "I like the idea of my Reese's Pieces getting all hot and bothered because I can park like a champ for her."

"You are *so* embarrassing," she chides, pulling away before I can hoist her into the air for a well-earned and *much-deserved* kiss. "I think we should save the kissing for midnight."

"Aw, baby, you're gonna make me wait until next year?"

"Never mind. You are *so* cheesy." She rushes back and rises on her tiptoes to sneak one on my jawline.

My hands drop to her hip bones, and I tug her in close. "You like it, though."

"I like everything about you," she corrects with a gentle laugh. Her smile broadens as she reaches up and brushes aside a strand of my hair that's fallen over my forehead, her touch lingering.

For an instant, all I can think of is the night we met. The first time those dark brown eyes peered into mine in a moment just like this. The first time in ages since I've let anybody into my personal space like that.

"You'll definitely like me more tomorrow when I parallel park like a champ for you," I say, and she lets out a long-suffering sigh.

Wriggling herself out of my embrace, she offers me a tiny smile. "I like you the best when you're softer around me."

"Baby, I'm hard around you all the—"

"I walked myself into that one, so that's on me," she laughs, tugging on the sleeve of her sweatshirt. *A regular, navy blue Belford U sweatshirt.*

It's nothing fancy—it's clearly well-worn and two sizes too

big for her—but the scoop neckline does little to hide the harsh scar between her collarbones.

I avert my gaze elsewhere, suddenly invested in the craggy shoreline that awaits us. I know better than to be a dumbass right now and make a big deal out of it. I will be on my best behavior. I won't draw any attention to her willingness to go out in public—*with me*—without hiding any part of herself.

My girl trusts me.

She fucking trusts me.

Sure, we're at a hidden beach—a small, secluded cove shrouded in tidepools. I know we're most likely the only ones here tonight since the residents who live in this area are wintering someplace else for the New Year, but still.

It fucking means a lot to me.

My heart swelling with pride, I take her hand and run my thumb over the bumps of her knuckles. As I carefully guide her down the sandy stairs, my focus remains on her.

There's a wintry flush to her cheeks and upturned nose while she studies the cliffs with genuine interest. Her eyes crinkle when she catches me staring and beams. Her giggle is low and husky while the rising tide laps at our feet.

"Did you find this place joyriding?"

"Nah. I've known about this place my whole life." Amusement threads through my veins as she tilts her head back to peer up at the evening sky. "Take a picture. It'll last longer."

With haste, she whips her phone out, turns on selfie mode, and lets out a cute laugh when I crouch on the sand and tug her onto my knee. She's all smiles and sunshine as she finds my gaze, and then she breaks into a grin when I capture her lips with a kiss she eagerly responds to.

"It's New Year's somewhere," I murmur, stealing another one.

"Probably in Australia," she agrees, shifting closer.

"What I meant"—I groan into her mouth—"is that you should take a photo of the sky."

"This is better." She tugs my bottom lip between her teeth, and my eyes pinch closed.

As much as I want this to continue—and God knows how much I want it to—I reluctantly break away. A protesting whimper sounds from her throat, and she buries her face in my neck and nips at my pulse point.

All the blood rushes from my head. "You don't want a picture of the stars and the moon for your fiesta?"

"I want a picture of us for me."

"Damn, Reese," I grumble. "Make it a little easier for me to give you a gift."

"A what?" She rears back a few inches, furrowing her brows. "Why? It's New Year's Eve."

"Then consider it an early Valentine's Day present." How I manage to shrug my backpack off while my girl's still on my knee is nothing short of a miracle. Grabbing the box inside, I hand it to her.

Her mouth parts on a soft inhalation. "Did you wrap this?"

"I'm not that talented," I snort. "I got the lady to help me with it. This was the closest shade to iris she could find."

She swallows audibly. "You shouldn't have—"

"You haven't seen it yet."

"It's heavy," she observes tentatively. "It better not be something expensive."

"It didn't cost as much as the Nova," I confirm, and her frown doesn't let up. She squints at me for a drawn-out beat before she tears into the wrapping paper.

Immediately, she shoves the box toward me, and I catch it before it topples into the sand.

"Dane, I can't—"

"Sure you can."

"*This* is expensive," Reese protests, springing to her feet. Her fingers delve into her hair as she paces, refusing to meet my gaze. "I can't accept this."

"Baby, it's for Valentine's," I say, and in answer, her nose wrinkles at me. I suppress my chuckle. "We have to register for classes soon. I figured you might wanna try photography or something this semester. Or take high-quality pictures of onion rings for your fiesta. Either way, it's yours to do whatever you want with it."

Contemplative silence falls between us. She reluctantly glances over, her eyes stormy with emotions.

"I can't get you anything as nice as this," she says, her voice low and rough. Suddenly, I want nothing more than to chase away the flicker of guilt shining across her slender face. Do what I can to hear her husky laughter sweetening the air and see her starry eyes and sweet smile out in full force.

"Reese's Pieces, it's not about the cost; it's the thought that counts. You like photography. I like seeing you happy," I assure her. "If you want to make it up to me that badly, take a photo of the golden hour every day for me."

Her gaze continues to hold mine. The guilt is still there, but it's gradually growing duller by the minute. "Like a New Year's resolution?"

"Well, no," I say flatly. "Like a plan people actually follow through with."

A husky laugh slides free, and the corner of her lips tips up into a wobbly grin. I'll take whatever I can get.

"I don't want to get sand all over it, so I'll look at it later." Her expression gives way to something bashful, and her voice lowers to a whisper. "I can't believe you got this for me."

"Oh, come on," I say gruffly. "Don't make this a big deal."

"To me, it is." The gentle vulnerability working across her features makes my throat feel tight. "I like this softer side of you. I wish everyone else could see it, too."

"Nah, Reese. I'm a fucking dickhead."

"No, you can be very sweet," she insists, and her sincerity has me rooted in place.

The thing is, I want to believe her. I want to see this version of me she wholeheartedly believes in. Maybe she's reading too much into every little detail, or maybe… that side only exists for her. If that's the case, she's the only person I want to be *that* guy for, anyway.

Neither of us says a word. It's just the sound of the ocean waves crashing against the shore in the background.

"Can you hold on to it for safekeeping?" she finally whispers, bridging the distance between us. "My pockets aren't big enough for it."

"Say no more." Unzipping my bag, I fight my smirk when she takes the camera and handles it like a precious newborn as she places it inside.

Her brow immediately hikes up an inch. "What's with the… Pinot noir?" With wide eyes, she snatches the bottle and squints at the label in the dim moonlight. "I know we're ringing in the new year, but we're *not* getting publicly drunk. We have to drive back to BU."

"Always gotta be a good girl, huh?" I tease with a wink, and my heart takes a sudden nosedive when the air turns palpably rigid. The bottle slips from her grasp, and she goes utterly still. "Reese?"

Genuine panic clouds her eyes. Her hand flies to her neck, her fingers clutching the material of her sweatshirt like it's a lifeline in a turbulent sea. Her breath comes in shallow pants.

Dread grips me by the throat as I take one step closer, only to halt mid-stride when she visibly shrinks before me. "Reese, baby?"

It demands all my conscious effort to keep my voice soothing and low. To refrain from letting my emotions show. I want nothing more than to pull her to me. Promise her she's safe with me. Swear on my life I won't hurt her.

But she keeps retreating into herself. And it kills me to see her like this. It fucking kills me.

"I'm okay." She gasps raggedly for air. "*I'm okay.*"

"Oh, fuck, baby. I'm so sorry," I breathe, and my movements are deliberately cautious as I close the gap between us and bring my hand to her face. She tenses, then trembles as the pad of my thumb wipes away the tear tracking down her cheek.

What the fuck happened to her? My stomach tightens as my thoughts go to the worst-case scenario. One where *good girl* could even come up. One where those words could be uttered.

My blood pounds deafeningly in my ears. Anger claws through me, vicious and raw. I want to find the fucker who did this. I want to make him hurt. I want to make him *twice* as afraid of his own pathetic shadow. But there's nothing I can do at this moment. The only thing I can do is remain calm and try my fucking best to help her ride out her panic.

"Did he say—"

Her whimper splinters my heart, and every muscle in my body screams in protest as I force myself to remain still. Resisting the urge to ball my hands into fists, I gently stroke the line of her jaw with my palm.

"Never again," I swear to her. "I won't say those words ever again."

"I almost died." Her voice is so soft that I almost don't hear her over the water.

Any few inches higher and… I might have lost my voice or…

My lungs give out on me as her words echo in my head like a broken record and reroute my focus to her scar. The gentle moonlight catches on the harsh line, sparing no details.

"It was my senior year of high school. Lili was away at college," she says, the words merely a decibel over a whisper. "It… was really hard not having her around when she was there for me my entire life. Our childhood wasn't the best, but she did everything she could to take care of me and protect me.

"Dad left us when I was three, and Mom was never home. She'd disappear with her boyfriend, and we'd go an entire week or two before she showed up again."

Jesus. "You don't have to tell me anything you don't want to." It doesn't take a rocket scientist to know how difficult this must be for her. Especially when she won't look me in the eye.

Her lips press together, and she shakes her head. She doesn't say anything else, though. She remains silent for a long, long minute. I patiently wait, regardless. It's all I can give her.

"With Lili gone, I was by myself a lot," she finally continues. "People… caught on. Someone must have been waiting for my mom to run off to God knows where before they…"

Her voice breaks, and my heart sinks like lead. Suddenly, it all clicks. All those times she'd freak out over the locks and deadbolts make too much sense, and I find myself overanalyzing every detail—poring over every little moment and wondering if I've ever fucked up. Or rather, how many times have I fucked up already.

"Do you want me to hold you?" My gruff words nearly stick in my throat.

"Please." She doesn't have to ask twice.

Keeping my movements slow not to spook her, I draw her into my arms. Her cheek nestles against my chest, and she shakes when I soothingly stroke her back.

"T-they broke into the trailer," she stammers. My shirt's getting soaked with her tears, but I pay it no mind. "I-I was asleep when it happened. There were two of them ransacking the place and looking for anything valuable. I woke up when I heard glass breaking and—*There was this man. In my room. He had a hoodie on and a knife in his hand.*"

The reality of her words set in. My chest coils tight. So fucking tight that I can't breathe. I have to remind myself over and over to remain calm, but I'm struggling as it is. I'm barely keeping myself together, clenching my jaw to stave off the overwhelming amount of anger surging through my every vein.

"I panicked and b-bolted for the bat Lili kept under her bed, and he"—she breaks into a low sob—"g-grabbed me from behind and p-put the blade to my throat. T-told me if I stayed still and remained q-quiet, I'd live."

"Baby, if this is too much," I begin, and she clings to me harder. There's nothing I want more than to find this bastard and give him a taste of his own medicine. I want him to cower in fear —to piss himself when he hears the fucking wind blow; to breathe through a fucking straw—for the rest of his pathetic life, but that's not the pressing matter at hand.

My girl needs me. She's opening up to me. Right now, I have to focus on her. I must make sure she knows I'm here for her. I'll *always* be here for her.

"No. I want t-to tell you," she sniffles. "I—I just remember freezing… and him whispering…"

Good girl.

"W-what they didn't know was t-that my neighbor had j-just gotten home," she continues. "She saw t-them breaking in, so she c-called 911. They were spooked by the sirens, and he…" Her hand presses against her neck. "He c-cut me by accident, and I was left bleeding on my bedroom floor while they escaped through the window."

"Tell me they found them," I growl.

In response, she offers me a strained smile. "My mom was pissed—"

"That they did that to you?"

"That I got hurt."

"*Good*," I say bluntly.

"*Because* I had to go to the hospital," she tacks on. "Not only were the medical bills outrageous, but she was mad the doctor reported the injury. It got her in a whole lot of trouble with the state."

"What the fuck?" I exhale sharply. "You went through some-thing terrible—Shit. *Fuck.*"

"W-what?" She jerks back, her eyes flying wide with alarm and concern.

Fuck. Way to fucking go, dumbass.

"I shouldn't have done that to you." I swallow thickly, and my guilt is insuperable and scours me raw. "Behind your apart-ment that one night. Holding you up against—"

"Oh." A faint blush creeps onto her cheekbones. "I didn't

mind. I mean, I trust you." The words come out so irrevocably firm and sure that my heart squeezes tight.

"Didn't people tell you I was dangerous?"

"You've never hurt me before," she whispers. "Why wouldn't I trust you?"

Aw, hell. Her earnest sincerity has me in a fucking chokehold.

I will find whoever hurt you and make him pay, I silently promise as I look steadily into her expressive eyes. *I fucking swear on it.*

With a quiet sniffle, she musters up a tiny smile—something reassuring, as if she's trying to appear brave. My heart pangs.

She's so fucking strong. I should know.

I know how fucking terrifying it is to be attacked and left for dead. I know how long it takes to put yourself back together, and all the bullshit you do to cope. You don't fully move on from your trauma and all the shit that comes with it; you learn to live around it the best you can.

I just *hate* that she's gone through it, too.

"Your mom sounds like a fucking piece of work," I grunt. "High offense to her."

"It's okay. She's not in my life anymore," she admits. "The second I got my high school diploma, I took a bus out here and never looked back."

"My girl's a fighter."

"I don't think cutting people out makes me much of a fighter." She taps her forefinger against my knuckles. "I'm kinda conflict-avoidant."

"My girl's so fucking strong."

"I don't feel that way most of the time," she whispers, peering up at me through her wet eyelashes.

"My girl's so damn brave."

A dry, shaky laugh bursts free from her. "You don't have to do this."

"Do what?" I feign confusion, and she pokes my nose.

"I know I'm being a buzzkill." Before I can object, she pulls away from me, drying her tears with the sleeve of her sweater. "Let's go get drunk and liven up the mood."

"I didn't bring you here to get drunk," I tell her. Genuine concern courses through me as I gauge her profile. I know my girl doesn't drink. It must have taken a huge toll on her to tell me about her past. Hell, it's taking all of my conscious effort to remain calm and be her steady rock after everything she revealed to me.

She blinks slowly, as if she's having trouble processing my words. "You didn't?"

"Nah." I hesitate for a moment. "This is for my mom."

"I thought your mom—" She sucks in a quiet breath, her gaze drifting to the ocean. "Oh, Dane."

"It's-it's nothing," I say gruffly. "It's just something I do every year."

"On New Year's Eve?"

"She, uh, died on New Year's morning," I admit, and her attention snaps back to me. "Car accident."

Her long, sorrowful gaze pierces me down to the marrow of my bones, and my chest winds tight with every second that lapses between us.

"Not around here." I swipe the bottle from the ground and roll my eyes with a scoff. "This was her favorite. Always ended a night with a glass of this. Figured it'd—Never mind. It's stupid. Let's just forget about this and—"

"*Dane*. It's not stupid." Her words are utterly gentle as she closes the distance between us and buries her face into my chest. "Thank you for letting me be a part of this."

"It's nothing," I mumble, swallowing roughly as I prop my chin against the crown of her head.

She only hugs me tighter in response. I don't push her away. Instead, I breathe in her familiar shampoo and listen to the incessant thrum of my heartbeat in my ears. Then I slowly wrap my arms around her with no intention of letting her go.

REESE

"I'LL HAVE TO ENROLL NEXT SEMESTER FOR PHOTOGRAPHY. OR maybe I'll take a class at the community college this summer for fun?" I muse. "Oh, I could always look at tutorials online."

While I'm broadcasting my thoughts, I mess with the camera's settings and adjust the lens. Peering through the viewfinder, I carefully aim it in Dane's direction, only for him to extend his arm out and block his face before I can take a photo.

"Don't you have a million pictures of me by now?"

"None from this camera," I say sweetly, and he sighs something deep and long-suffering.

"In another life, you'd make a great lawyer." With a shake of his head, he returns his attention to the fastback. "Want me to pose for you like one of those ridiculous calendars?"

"What do you mean?" I snap a picture, then frown when he picks up a wrench, leans over the engine, and lifts his shirt up halfway to expose the hard planes of his abs. He gives me a smoldering gaze, and my teeth sink into my bottom lip to smother my laughter. "You're ridiculous."

Tossing a wink, he yanks his shirt down. "Your loss."

With a snort, I capture another shot of him while he nods along to aggressive rock music and tinkers with his latest project car. I can't think of a better way to spend a day off than hanging out and doing nothing together.

The stereo abruptly stops, snaring my focus. Dane groans and drags his fingers through his tousled hair.

"Want me to get that for you?" I offer, and he waves me off.

"Fuck no." He retrieves his phone from his pocket, and seconds later, the music resumes. "Only two people call me, and I don't wanna talk to either of them."

"What if it's an emergency?" I ask. My sister rarely calls me unless there's an urgent matter. Not that we're on speaking terms right now. She's still pissed about the whole *breather* thing, and she's leaving me on read.

I won't lie, it's actually very frustrating. I'm genuinely upset that this is all happening because of Travis Walker. I left her a message about him being a creepy liar, but her phone's been set on *do not disturb* since.

We've never gone this long without talking. Our longest fight lasted half a day, and the more I reflect on it, the harder it becomes to ignore the glaringly obvious truth. That argument— like all the others—ended because I caved just to keep the boat from rocking. There's never been one disagreement where Lilian ever admitted she was wrong.

"I'm the last person you'd want in an emergency," Dane says dryly, jolting me back to reality. "It's nothing serious. Just my old man checking in to see if Junior screwed up some more or something, and it'll be a cold day in hell before I subject myself to that again."

My brows draw together. It never occurred to me that he's named after his dad. Before I can respond, he clears his throat.

"You ready to pass your driving test?"

I heave out an inaudible sigh. It's such a blatant change of subject, but I decide to humor him and go along with it for his sake. "What if I forget to keep clear of a keep-clear zone?"

"Baby." His arms fold over his chest. "I'm insulted you don't think my teaching's good enough—"

"Oh my God," I gasp, covering my mouth. "What if I drive like a maniac on the road and give the evaluator a heart attack?"

Something unamused flits across his features, and I bite back my laughter and offer him a cheeky grin.

"You're gonna ace it," he says firmly. "Then you'll drive us out for dinner, where we'll celebrate your accomplishment."

"It's just a license," I begin, and he huffs out a snort.

"Just a license," he echoes, shaking his head in exasperation. "One month ago, you were too scared to drive. Now look where you are."

My cheeks blaze. "Still afraid to drive?"

"That's fair," he says. "A car's still a car. It will cause a lot of damage if you're not careful." He glances sideways. "If you're that worried, we could do what Sal told me to do."

"Obey traffic laws at all times?"

"Go for a spin around the DMV," he says with a casual shrug. "Familiarize yourself with the area. That way, you'll know what to expect when it's time for the test."

"That's... actually not a bad idea."

"Not a bad idea." He does the sign of the cross and points skyward. "Hear that, Sal? You would have loved having my girl around, inflating your ego." A half-smile forms on his lips. "Give me ten minutes to replace this starter, and then we'll see what you're dealing with."

<hr>

CONTRARY TO WHAT MY BOYFRIEND BELIEVES, PARALLEL PARKING IS A pain in the ass. I'm wholeheartedly convinced it's the tenth circle of hell.

"You know what I think?" I grit out, breathing through my nose. I spin the steering wheel rapidly to one side, trying my best not to become overwhelmed when a massive truck appears in the rearview mirror. "The city should invest in public transportation."

Dane keeps his knuckles pressed firmly against his lips. He thinks he's being slick, but I'm not oblivious. I know he's struggling to maintain his composure. His eyes always give him away. *Always.*

"You got this, speed demon," he says, then coughs loudly to mask his laugh, and grinds his fist to his mouth.

"I'm just saying." With a hoarse exhalation, I ease my foot onto the gas pedal. "Having additional modes of transportation available would make this city more bearable to live in. *And* it's better for the"—I hold my breath while I pull into the spot, and the muscle in my jaw clenches as I quickly straighten the tires— "*environment!*" I shriek. "I did it!"

"Holy fuck," he grunts, bringing his hand to his ear. "I mean, *fuck yeah, you did.*"

I twist toward him, and my heart hammers against my rib cage, as a too-bright grin breaks across my face.

"Think you could take us back to the garage in one piece?" he teases, and I shoot him a playful scowl. He gestures to the fuel gauge. "Might need a refuel first, though."

"Of course, *Daniel.*" Within seconds, I peel away from the curb and head west. Then I pull into the first gas station I see, barely killing the engine when Dane climbs out of the vehicle.

"I'll be right back, *Iris,*" he responds. "With lots and lots of gas station sushi for you."

"Don't forget the mozzarella sticks, Daniel."

"Who could forget the appetizers?" he deadpans, and I snort as he rounds the convertible, drops a kiss on my hairline, and grabs a pump. Then I watch him fill the tank. Honestly, I'm ogling him. Shamelessly so.

He looks like a heartthrob straight out of a sixties car flick, so effortlessly timeless in his threadbare shirt, ripped black jeans, scuffed black boots, and dark sunglasses. A fluttering hits my chest as I keep my eyes on him. *That's my boyfriend.*

He catches my gaze, and his knowing smirk only heightens

my awareness. "Jesus. You find me hot parallel parking and pumping gas for you. What's next? Oil changes?"

I roll my eyes good-naturedly as heat rises in my cheeks. "I've seen you do that before. Many times."

"Damn. How do you control yourself around me?" he teases, and I stick my tongue out at him.

"With ease," I retort, and he cuts me a smug grin and thumps the side of my car twice.

"We'll see if you can still control yourself *with ease* around me while I fix a flat tire." His smile broadens. "Or install a kill switch."

I sigh, then startle when he sneaks another kiss to my hairline. Wrinkling my nose at him, I wait until he returns to the passenger side, then poke his bicep. His laughter stokes a flurry of warmth low in my belly, and I'm unable to resist my beam for another second.

With an uncharacteristically small amount of traffic for a city in Southern California, it's a short drive to his garage. I'm more than grateful when Dane stashes the Nova in its cramped spot for me. I've already tested my luck with parallel parking today. I don't need to push it any further and see how much damage I could actually cause.

He hops out of the convertible and lifts his sunglasses. "Ever want to see the golden hour from my room?" His lack of subtlety is punctuated with a quirked brow.

Folding my arms, I pretend to mull it over. "Has that line ever worked on anybody?"

"I'll let you know in a second," he says, and I giggle before I can help myself.

"I'll need *two* seconds before I give you my answer," I say, schooling my expression into something bland and serious. "Well, Daniel? Has that line ever worked on—"

A loud shriek expels from my lungs when he grips my hips and hoists me into the air. My legs instinctively wrap around his waist, and I level him with a playful scowl.

Amusement crinkles his eyes. "It works."

"Does it now?" I breathe, dipping my head forward. Peering at his chest, I trace a small heart over his heart.

"It works," he repeats, then crushes his lips to mine.

Our bodies stagger. In the next instant, my spine presses against the cold steel frame of a nearby car. My fingers cling to the soft material of his shirt for purchase, and I draw closer when he abruptly breaks away and brings his mouth to my ear.

"Now, let's go see the golden hour from my room."

I blink, then burst into laughter when he unveils a mischievous grin and tips his head toward his motorcycle.

Before long, we're flying down the side streets toward Las Marinas. Anticipation catapults through me as we near his apartment, and my impatience nearly takes rein the moment we're all but rushing to his floor.

"Marco's out," he confirms, kicking the door shut behind him. His eyes lock on mine as he twists the deadbolt, gestures to it with a tap, and flashes me a thumbs-up. My heart squeezes tight. "We have the whole place to ourselves."

"It's so cute how you let your best friend come and go like a cat," I observe, and his expression gives way to confusion. It's not like I'm wrong.

"A cat?"

"The chunky stray in my neighborhood keeps sneaking into my apartment if I open the patio door for more than a second," I explain with a smile. "He refuses to leave when I try to shoo him out. He comes and goes as he pleases."

With a shake of his head, he chuckles lowly. "I can't believe you compared him to a cat."

"Am I wrong, though?" A soft giggle tears loose from me when he hoists me into his strong arms. My legs reflexively lock around him. My hands frame his jawline as I peer deeply into his eyes.

"Guess not," he says, and then his mouth covers mine, the

pressure of his lips all incessant and demanding, as he carries me toward the bedroom.

We tumble onto his mattress, and heat simmers between my thighs when his kiss slides to the pulse point of my neck. His grip on my waist grows rough. His hips fit against mine as he bears the full weight of his body down in a slow grind. A quiet moan dispels from me, giving way to a whimper of protest when he pushes up.

"Baby, as much as I'd love to continue this, I'm dirty from the garage." He sneaks a kiss on the hollow of my throat, eliciting a sharp peal of laughter straight from my heart. With a boyish grin, he pulls away and sweeps his gaze across my body in an unhurried perusal.

"So you… decided you're just gonna stand there?" I tease.

"Give me a sec. Just trying to appreciate a work of art. I'm sure you're familiar with the concept."

I cackle into my palms. *"Go shower."*

"Bossy." Kicking his jeans off, he tosses his keys, wallet, and phone onto the nightstand. "Better be fucking naked when I'm back."

"Mmkay." I shrug my knit sweater off and let out an undignified snort when he wolf-whistles. Quickly peeling the rest of my clothes off, I riffle through his drawer for condoms when his cell buzzes.

Peeking up, I spot *Daniel Kingsley* flashing on the screen. Curiosity flickers through me as the call goes to voicemail. Dane doesn't tell me anything about his dad. Then again, he never says much about his family, to begin with, and my brows furrow at the thought. Well, at least I've got visual confirmation that neither one of them is named Danish, so that's something.

Soon enough, the bathroom door swings open, and Dane comes into view. Shaking his wet hair, his cocky grin surfaces as he takes another long look at my body. My neck blazes hot at his expression while he makes his way over.

Within a heartbeat, his hands hook around my calves and tug

me toward him. Silky sheets bunch up beneath me as he guides one leg over his shoulder. His blunt fingernails gently dig into my skin, and every thought leaves my head.

"Not gonna lie." A featherlight kiss is pressed to my knee. "Seeing you naked in my bed has given me a great idea."

"Hmm?" My eyes sink closed. "What's that?"

"You should be naked in my bed at all times." His voice turns gravelly and teasing. "Sounds like a great idea. We should commit to it right away in my completely honest, *unbiased* opinion."

I huff out a groan, then sigh a little dreamily as he nips at a sensitive spot on my inner thigh. He takes his time, trailing a path of kisses to my hip bone with painstaking slowness. Impatience takes hold, and I shift beneath him, wordlessly urging him to go where I need him most.

Instead, he continues with his torture. His mouth goes to my navel, then up to my breasts. His hands slide to my pelvis and pin me in place as he flits his tongue around my nipple, then licks an obscene line across my skin toward the other. My chest heaves. My breath stutters.

Slowly—so, so *slowly*—he nips his way down my stomach, inching closer and closer to my clit when he presses a kiss to my other hip bone.

I almost snarl in frustration. "*Dane,*" I whine, desperately pushing my hips against him, and he chuckles roughly against my skin.

"Just messing with you." Before I can grab his hair and guide him to me, his shoulders wedge my thighs apart, and his tongue sweeps across my swollen clit. A moan leaves my lips, and my fingers curl into his shoulder blades.

The familiar feel of his calloused hands sliding up my inner thighs ejects all thoughts from my head. He spreads me wider. I feel exposed and boneless as he anchors me down with a firm grip and buries his face into my pussy. It's exquisite—the slow drag of his tongue. The teasing, broad strokes. It's as if he's taking his time. As if he plans on doing this for hours. *For days.*

If he keeps licking me like that, he can do this for the rest of eternity for all I care.

Glittering heat coils deep within. Pleasure rockets through me. My skin feels ablaze; every nerve ending is set abuzz. My eyes screw shut, and my heels dig into his lower back while my fingernails drag incessant lines across his shoulders as I come.

His head lifts, and he finds my gaze, a wild smirk playing at the corner of his lips. His focus never wavers as he climbs on top of me, stretches his body over mine, and splits my legs wider around his hips.

Ducking his head, he presses a startlingly gentle kiss to the edge of my scar. Then another. And another. It's as if he's trying to worship every inch of it. Soon, his hand slots between my thighs. His thumb flirts with my clit, and I whimper when two fingers slide in deep. Just then, he captures my lips and sends a pulse of need through me. The urgency of his kiss is all-consuming and overwhelming and too much.

I need him close. I need him so impossibly close that I can feel his heartbeat in my chest. Feel every inch of his soul entwining with mine.

My arms loop around him, and I draw him in until we're skin-to-skin. Still, it's not enough. It's simply not enough.

"I want you," I moan into his mouth.

"You have me," he growls, tugging my bottom lip between his teeth. Before I can deepen the kiss, he breaks away and pushes up onto his elbows.

A protesting whine breaks free. I nudge him with my knees, and he lets loose a throaty chuckle.

"Aw, baby." Grabbing the condom I left out, he's quick to roll it on, then rewards me with the press of his erection between my legs. "Is this what you want?"

With a tilt of his hips, he fucks into me in one smooth thrust, and my lips part at the sudden stretch. My head tips back as his breath hits my neck, and my heart gives an easy rhythm. Clutching onto his shoulders, my dull nails bite into his flesh as he fully buries himself inside me.

A low groan comes from the back of his throat. I hum a sound of agreement. It's all I can manage. I'm too dizzy with the feel of him to form a coherent thought.

For a moment, neither of us moves. It's as if we're trying to draw this out for as long as possible. Like we're trying to let time suspend. I peek up at him and catch the softness embedded deep in his gaze, and my smile is imminent. His eyes crinkle in response, but he doesn't move another muscle. Not even when I rock my hips against him in a futile attempt to seek my release.

"*Please*," I grumble, and his grin grows crooked.

"Aw, baby. Always so polite," he teases, skating his nose along my collarbone. He all but ignores my next suggestive grind as he plants a kiss on the curve of my throat. "So damn greedy, too. Just give me a minute."

I shake my head and hook my leg around his waist, pulling him closer. He lets loose a rough-edged chuckle against the crook of my neck.

"Baby, I don't wanna come until I fuck you thoroughly," he groans. "Give me a minute or I'm not gonna last."

"I don't mind."

He snorts, and his face comes back into view. Warmth spreads through me as his adoring gaze holds my breath captive. My pulse kicks up a few notches when he brushes a stray lock out of my face.

"You're so beautiful," he whispers, and my laughter bubbles up in my chest. His mouth curves, and with that, he slides out and rocks back into me so slowly, so devastatingly tender. My heart is aflutter.

The headboard thumps as his rhythm builds. My breasts bounce and snare his focus, and he husks out a full-bodied groan.

"Fuck." Pitching forward, he wets his thumb with a slow lick and brings it to my clit, and I squirm. "Squeeze your tits for me."

Heat ripples through me instantaneously. My hands fall from his back to my breasts, and he grates a harsh breath against my temple when I pinch my nipples.

"So fucking hot," he grunts, then nips at the pounding pulse point of my neck. "I didn't tell you to stop."

Oh God. It's becoming hard to concentrate on anything but the weight of his body pressed against mine. The feel of his tongue when he claims my mouth. The relentless pace of his movements as he drives into me and teases my clit.

It's overwhelming. Magnificently so.

Without warning, he pulls out of me completely and grits his teeth. Shoving his fingers through his hair, he breathes hard through his nose and ignores my noise of protest. "I don't wanna come just yet."

"I want you to." My heart beats impossibly fast with anticipation as I find his gaze, and my expression gives way to something shy. "Fucking me from behind?"

He blinks out of his stupor and groans. "Baby, I don't want you to freak out—"

My heart takes flight at his words. "Please?"

With my back to him, I shift onto all fours. My pulse thrums with need. My breathing picks up as glittering heat rushes over every part of me. My skin buzzes with awareness under the slow perusal of his gaze.

"I trust you," I add softly. It's the truth. While it's very sweet of him to worry, I trust him completely—with every inch of my soul.

"Okay," he says finally. "But if it's too much for you, let me know. Say *museum* and I'll stop."

I snort before I can help myself. The mattress shakes with our laughter in the beat that follows.

"Really, Dane?" I almost drop my face into my hands. "*The museum*?"

"It's the perfect safe word," he insists, and his chuckle relieves the small knot of tension in my stomach. Soon, he settles behind me. He wastes no time kissing the line of my shoulders. His hand falls to my hip, and he gently wrenches me against him. My cheek softly lands on his pillow, and my breath stalls in my throat as his erection teases the sensitive heat between my thighs.

Finally, he eases into me, and my eyes squeeze shut.

"You good, baby?" he utters, his voice a gritty whisper.

I nod, speechless, as I push against his grip, desperately seeking every slide of his cock he's yet to give me.

"Fuck. *Yes.*" His thumb teases my clit. His other arm tucks around my waist and anchors me flush against his chest. "Come on, baby. Squeeze your tits for me while you come on my cock."

Oh God. His words ignite a fire inside me. My mouth parts on a sudden gasp as my hands clumsily palm my breasts. He leans forward, the movement causing my knees to spread further apart, and everything builds as he fucks me into his mattress. As he takes me and claims me and every last piece of my heart. I would irrevocably give myself over to him. *I'm his.*

His name barely escapes my lips when his teeth graze the curve of my neck, and the tautness in my belly grows even tighter.

"Don't get shy on me now, baby. Louder." He sucks a mark at the tender skin, and I'm unable to hold back any longer.

I moan and tremble beneath him as I ride out my release. He doesn't ease up. If anything, his pace quickens into something feverish and relentless. He rocks into me over and over until he pulses hard inside me as he comes.

His breathing slowly evens out against my neck. His fingers trace aimless zigzags across my ribs as the warmth of his sweat-sheened body bleeds into me. Without a word, he rolls us over so that we're lying on our sides. His arms are still around me, but I wriggle even closer into the shelter of his embrace.

"We should probably go wash up," I mumble absent-mindedly.

"In a minute," is his response, which doesn't sound so bad. Not when he presses a kiss to the crown of my head, and a sense of awareness strikes me all at once. I didn't have to use the safe word. *I didn't panic.* At the realization, my heart kicks up a few beats.

I stare ahead at the window, my lips sneaking up at the corner when he reaches for my hand and laces his fingers through mine. "I think we missed the golden hour."

He laughs into my hair. "Yeah, we did. We can always try again tomorrow, the day after—however long it takes until we finally see it."

I barely suppress my snort. "Has that line ever worked on anybody?" I ask monotonously, and a peal of laughter tumbles out of me when he nips at a sensitive spot behind my ear.

"I'll let you know tomorrow."

"Oh, Dane." My voice takes on a solemn tone. "I forgot to mention I'm suddenly busy from here on out to ever come over to your place again."

"I'll let you know tomorrow," he repeats, then kisses my neck. I try to contain my smile and automatically lose the battle.

Damn my soft heart. It folds so easily for him.

"Yeah," I finally agree. "You'll let me know tomorrow."

38

DANE

I DON'T DO SMALL TALK, SO I STAND FAR AWAY FROM THE SECURITY cop posted outside the entrance, hands shoved into my pockets as I wait. And wait. And wait.

Checking the time on my phone, I refrain from sighing. I don't know what's taking so long. Just as I'm about to pace around the building, I spot a purple car pulling into the lot.

With a brief *thanks for not subjecting me to fucking small talk* nod, I make my way over just as she gives me a tiny wave and ducks inside the DMV with her evaluator. It's a good sign. She's probably getting her photo taken since we get our license in the mail, but I wait until she returns and get my confirmation the moment I see her face.

Her eyes brim with excitement as she shrieks, "I passed!"

"Fuck yeah, you passed!" I snort when she high-fives me. "I'm a good teacher, huh?"

"The best, Mr. Self-Taught." Her excitement is immeasurable. Her beam is brighter than the summer sun and elicits a stupid grin from me in response. She's so ecstatic that she bounces on her feet and captures the attention of the man exiting the building just then. Her tight sweater leaves nothing to the imagination, and the dumbass has the audacity to ogle her instead of walking off the curb and straight into oncoming traffic.

I level him with a hard glare, and he has the smarts to divert his gaze to his wristwatch when he notices my expression. I'd rather he look directly into the sun until his retinas burn out, but at least he's not perving on my girl anymore.

Reese touches my arm, snagging my focus. I glance sideways to catch the delicate frown forming between her brows.

Abruptly, I clear my throat and steer her toward the convertible. "Ready for your victory celebration?"

"You don't have to spoil me," she grumbles.

"You deserve all the onion rings and root beer in the world."

With a sigh, her mouth tips up at the corner. "Well, at least my fiesta will have new material."

"Then let's look for the best onion rings in the county."

Soon, the car's barreling down the street at the posted speed. The top is down, the stereo is blasting cheesy bubblegum pop from her playlist, and Reese is singing along to the track.

Out of nowhere, she hits me with a pleading look. I immediately shake my head.

"I have to clear out my unread messages," I hedge, and she snorts.

"One day, you're gonna sing a Hollandale song with me," she says, and I make a face while I unlock my phone. "You'll become their biggest fan."

A chuckle slips from me. My brow lifts a beat later. There's a voicemail from Giancarlo, which I delete without hesitation because no fucking thanks. I've been tempting fate by risking my neck whenever I show my face at a meet.

I know I have. I've been playing with fire when I should have called it quits long ago. Walking away now before I'm inevitably dragged back into the life of street racing is the correct choice. The only way forward where I don't get fucked over by Giancarlo at some point.

With money always on the line, Giancarlo wouldn't hesitate

to double-cross me. Not just him. There's got to be a list of people trying to screw me over for a quick buck. Like Wally.

Definitely Wally.

I can easily picture that boot-ass motherfucker hitting his breaking point and taking out all that pent-up rage on me. Especially if he loses another race to me. His pathetic ego wouldn't be able to handle it.

Look, it's not my fault he's done a shit job maintaining his vehicle. It's as if his obnoxious car is assembled with stolen, incorrect parts welded together. You can hear how fucked up his engine belt is. A novice mechanic could do better than him.

Truth be told, he might have a chance of winning these races if he took better care of his coupe. Not that I'll ever point that out. It's been fun watching him fuck himself over. And he's one of those whiny dickheads who can't receive any advice without taking it personally. So I'll keep my trap shut, even if it pains me deeply to see a car in that state.

Just then, a coded text pops onto my screen. I delete it, and a sense of ease dulls the restless itch ebbing within. *This is a good thing*, I remind myself. My girl wouldn't be thrilled if I came back from a meet with a busted mug.

Hell, I got a bruise on my elbow the other day, and she wouldn't stop fretting over me. Even when I swore up and down it was a dumbass move on my part. The hood of my fastback swung down on me, and I tried to block it instead of getting out of harm's way.

So, there's one very good reason why I have to end this now. It's not like I need the money. Nor do I owe Giancarlo anything.

He just misses me because I was his best driver. A sure bet.

Most of the people he's collected over the years for his races are either in jail or dead. There are rarely any in-betweens. Nobody lasts long in this world, especially those whose track records carry more L's than W's.

And I've got a girl who—for reasons that make me count my blessings—cares about me. I'd like to live long enough to enjoy every waking second with her before she comes to her senses and moves on.

Abruptly, my train of thought derails. Wally returns to mind as I recall his idiot friends trying to cut me off in their piss-poor attempt to help him win. Could that fucking tool be the reason why I got the crap kicked out of me in the alleyway that night?

Were they trying to rob me? Swipe my keys to get complete access to my cars?

I need to ask around and see if anybody knows something I could work with. My best bet is to reach out to Eddie. Shyla's got her ears everywhere, but I don't want to chance it and accidentally get dragged into whatever game she has going on with him.

Releasing a sigh, I craft a short message, then glance sideways at my girl. She's still beaming, and her mouth curves into something bashful when she catches me staring.

She bats her lashes as she sings along to the current pop track, and I sigh. Then she hits me with that sweet smile of hers. A groan escapes me, and after several, *several* seconds, I half-heartedly mumble the chorus.

"Yes!" she squeals, shimmying in her seat. "You're the best."

Two excruciatingly slow ballads later, we find ourselves in the parking lot. As she pulls into a spot, her expression is all sorts of shy when she realizes people are gawking at the car. I mean, it's a purple muscle car. With a pair of fuzzy dice hanging on the rearview mirror. And the V8 engine is loud as hell.

Even so, I glower at them. They all have the self-preservation to mind their own business.

"I can take you someplace else if you're not feeling it," comes a soft voice, and I look over to see a startling expression of apprehension across her features.

My glare melts into a soothing grin. "I've already had plenty of pet store sushi for you. You know I'm down for anything else you wanna throw my way."

She playfully swats my shoulder. "Even mozzarella sticks?"

My stomach roils at the thought, and I grimace. She breaks into giggles as she hops out of the convertible.

Inside, a wall of red roses greets us. Among the plastic flowers, gaudy neon signs blink the restaurant's name in different cursive scripts. It's not my scene at all.

"I can see why you like the place," I observe, and she spares me a bright beam.

"Lili and I went here a couple of times," she says offhandedly, and her smile falters. A note of sadness clings to her voice. "The last time we were here was for my birthday in August."

I give her a sidelong glance. "You two still haven't gotten over your fight yet?"

She hesitates and shakes her head, her expression turning forlorn. She hasn't told me much about what's going on—just mentioned that her sister wasn't talking to her—but I figured they'd patch things up by now given how close the two are.

As it is, I want nothing more than to see her visibly vibrating with excitement again. To see that sun-bright smile overtaking her face once more.

The thing is, she won't tell me what's causing their riff, but I'm no fucking moron. "Is it me?"

"No!" she blurts. A little too quickly, I might add, and I bite my tongue before I call bullshit. "She still doesn't know about you. *About us.* It's… about the guy she's seeing."

I want to pry, but our hostess appears just then and shows us to our booth. The moment we're seated and she's out of earshot, I ask, "Who's she seeing?"

Reese huffs through her nose. Her lips curl into a deep scowl as she levels an adorably menacing glare at the menu in her grasp. "An actual jerk."

A beat skips. I prop my chin on the heel of my palm, gradually tipping my head to the side. "Now hear me out, Snack Size. I think you could find some common ground there with your sister—"

"You're not a jerk," she grumbles. "My sister assumes I believe all frat guys are sleazy—"

"Aren't they all?"

"Caleb isn't," she insists, and I open my mouth only to catch myself in the nick of time. Shit. My dumbass almost revealed what the sorority girls had done.

"I don't know, Reese's Pieces," I hedge. "He gives off a sleazy energy to me." Personally, I consider him to be the fucking jerkoff extraordinaire. Tricking a sweet, harmless girl into thinking he's into her for money is the sleaziest thing I can think of, but it's not like I can say that out loud.

"You don't have to be jealous of him." Reese's words snag my attention, and she leans over the table and presses a kiss to my cheek. "I don't like him that way anymore."

"I'm not threatened by him at all." For emphasis, I scoff. "Why would I be jealous of his unremarkable ass?"

"*Dane*," she chides. "That's not nice. I picked you; not him. *You*. I wouldn't be dating you if I were still into him."

"I know." I can't help the smug half-smile at the edge of my lips. "But he's still a sleaze."

She heaves out a quiet sigh and settles back in her seat. When she tugs at the collar of her turtleneck sweater, my gaze flies up to the ceiling. The A/C doesn't seem to reach us.

After a moment's hesitation, she peers at me and nibbles on her bottom lip. "Can you help me with my shirt?"

"Off?" I tease, bringing an infinitesimal twitch to her mouth.

"Hold it down while I take my sweater off," she clarifies as she comes over to my end.

"Offer's always on the table," I say slyly, allowing my hands to skim her hips for a lingering beat before I rein it in and behave. My smirk broadens at the sight of staticky hair the moment she shrugs her turtleneck off.

"Thank you."

"No, *thank you*," I behaved long enough. Running my thumb

along the lacy hem of her top, my fingers flirt with the strip of soft skin revealed. "Do you always wear something like this?"

"Hmm?" She peeks down and smooths out a wrinkle on the thin fabric. "I guess? Most of my clothes are from high school—"

"Good thing we didn't know each other back then," I comment. "One look at you, and I would have followed you around—"

Her snort is anything but dignified. "One, I'm from New Mexico. We weren't even in the same state, let alone the same zip code. Two, I wear them under a jacket or a sweater. Three, you wouldn't have noticed me."

"That's like saying a flower wouldn't notice the damn ass sun." When she rolls her eyes, I tack on, "I'm not blind, baby. I would have noticed the hot babe on campus."

With a tittering laugh, she returns to her seat. It doesn't last, though. Trepidation forms in her eyes as her gaze flits around the restaurant. Her hand toys with her necklace. It's not hard to miss her trying to shield her scar from plain sight.

"My girlfriend's a smoke show," I say, and her focus snaps to me. "Goddamn, I could look at you all day like a painting in one of those museums you like."

A slow-breaking smile takes to her face, and she ducks behind her menu. "You are *so* cheesy."

"Like those awful, greasy cheese sticks, baby." I toss her a wink when she peeks over the cardstock, and she giggles.

"Which they do not have."

"Pity. Guess we'll have to settle with pet store sushi," I tease, and she snorts again. Soon enough, her body no longer appears stiff. The tension subsides from her shoulders and is long gone by the time our waitress arrives.

After ordering a bunch of appetizers, I pretend not to notice her sneaking a picture of me. She can take hundreds of them if it'll keep that smile on her face. Unfortunately, it dims far too quickly.

"You thinking about your sister again?" I ask, and she nods. "If she's anything like you—"

"She's not."

"Because she's a social butterfly?"

"She is, but..." Her fingers drum on the counter as she considers her words. "Lili's kind of... a hothead. Very headstrong. A bit temperamental. She can really hold a grudge, so you never want to get on her bad side."

"And you two are related?" I deadpan, earning a disapproving frown.

"She can be sweet, in her own way," Reese says, coming to her defense like the nice girl she is. "She's always been a mama bear, but it's been so much worse since..." Her hand touches her neck. "I don't like how she flips out over everything I've done. It's just... I can't even blame her. I know she's just worried about me. It doesn't help that she thinks I'm too trusting and naïve."

"Yeah, you are a little too trusting and naïve," I say bluntly, and a flash of hurt etches across her features. "Do you make it a habit of letting strangers crash on your springy futon?"

With a sniff, she looks me dead in the eye. "Would you have rather I called the cops?"

Well, damn. "Touché."

"My sister would have if she were the one who found you that night..." Her sentence dwindles. "But I... I guess... I figured the moment I dialed 911, you would have bolted or something and gotten more hurt..." She swallows thickly and picks at her nails. "You could barely stand. And... I... took your keys as insurance so that you wouldn't hurt me."

"Maybe I was acting?" I counter. "What would you have done then?"

"You were bleeding pretty badly. I don't think anyone can act out a bunch of flesh wounds," she says flatly, and a look of genuine worry makes a reappearance and goes straight to my heart. "I wish you went to the hospital—"

"I know a guy." I offer her a casual shrug, but her expression doesn't let up.

With a slow intake of breath, she fixes me with an inscrutable stare. "Be honest with me," she whispers, taking hold of my gaze.

Something prickles along my neck as she says nothing. It feels like I'm under a spotlight with how inquisitive her eyes become as they search mine. My spine straightens the longer the silence swells between us, and I don't know if I should be worried she might ask something I can't answer truthfully.

Swallowing audibly, she drops her voice to the lowest register. "Are you in a gang?"

I blink out of my thoughts, and she winces. Then I let loose a roughened laugh as my relief almost tears me in half. "Fuck. You think I'm in a gang?"

A hint of red splashes onto her cheeks. "I just need to know if I'm dating—"

"Baby, you're hilarious." I wipe away an imaginary tear. "You really thought I was in one? I can barely stand to be around people. What makes you think I would want to work with them?"

Her flush darkens. Leaning forward, she clears her throat. "Then why are you afraid of the police?"

"I'm not afraid of the police." She raises a brow, and I hesitate, then sigh. "My father. Let's just leave it at that."

"Is he a cop?"

"Nah. Lawyer."

"For criminals?"

"For anyone who can afford him," I say blandly, flashing her a wry grimace. "He knows a lot of law enforcement through his line of work."

"Oh." She wears a thoughtful frown. "What about your mom?"

"Are you asking if she was a criminal lawyer?"

"What was she like?" Reese clarifies.

"Like any mom." I lift a shoulder. I want to redirect the conversation, but it's clear from her expression that she wants me to continue. "She was a good mom. She went to all of my hockey games and volunteered for plenty of bake sales. Sometimes, she'd take me on late-night drives to get chocolates when she thought I was having a bad day. Every summer, we'd go to London to visit family."

"London?" Shock colors her tone as she gasps.

"Yeah. Hammersmith," I confirm. "My mom's English."

"Your mom?" she echoes. "Not *mum*?" Her grin is heavy with a tease.

"Forgive me, Reese, you're right," I reply, slipping into an English accent, and her eyes glitter with delight. "Nah. Mom. I'm, first and foremost, an American. Besides, she lived in the States for quite some time before I was even in the picture."

"When was the last time you went to London?"

"It's… been a while," I admit. "I haven't been there since she…"

"Oh." She reaches over and grabs my hand. "I'm sorry. Your dad never took you back?"

"Nah." I watch her stroke my knuckle and try not to clench my jaw. "He never went with us—even back when she was still alive. My father was always too busy with work. I don't think it ever occurred to him we weren't home for *weeks* until we called him for a ride home from the airport. Even then, he'd send someone else to fetch us."

"I'm sorry." She links our fingers together and offers me a remorseful smile.

"It didn't bother me as much as it bothered my mom. You know, she gave up her career for my father. Ignored her family's warnings and stayed here for him. She did *everything* for him, and he—" A dry laugh escapes me. Something bitter worms its way through my chest when I remember all the countless nights my mom would drink her sorrows away. "Reese's Pieces, don't you *ever* settle for someone who won't make the fucking time for you."

"I don't think—"

"Promise me that. Never fucking settle for anyone unworthy of your presence."

Finding my gaze, she taps her ankle against mine. "As I was trying to say, I don't think that's gonna be a problem." Her lips curve into something sweet. "I'm all in with you."

My throat closes up tight as I take in the gentle flush spreading across her cheekbones. The way her eyes crinkle. The tendril of hair that always needs to be clipped back or else it falls into her face.

"That's fair." My voice is low when I find it. "You could have settled for Blue Balls and his whiny music."

With a long-suffering groan, she unhooks her ankle from mine. "He has a name."

I flash her an innocent smile. "Blue—"

"I've seen your mom's movies before," she interjects, and my brow raises. "Um... I recognized her face at the bougie shop you took me to."

Huh. I forgot they had a picture of her on the wall. I guess I should be surprised, but I'm also not shocked by her confession. My girl likes to watch the most random movies. She once gave me a detailed recap of a historical lesbian drama she watched, only to then follow it up with an essay-worthy amount of information about some zany Western comedy she wanted me to see.

"You have?"

"Yeah. She was in a couple of these period films I watched multiple times growing up," she explains. "I always wondered what happened to her—*before* she passed away. I was sort of bummed when I found out she stopped making movies."

"Gave up her career for a man who couldn't even wait to marry someone else the moment her ashes were scattered," I supply flatly.

Sympathy etches into her features. "How long did he wait?"

"A year," I grit out. "Fucking disrespectful." My gaze cuts to the ceiling as a wave of bitterness ripples through me, and I pull in a sharp breath when she squeezes my fingers. My line of sight shifts to her face as the pad of her thumb circles my knuckles.

"You really do love her," she begins, her attention raptly focused on our joined hands. "I think your mom would be so happy to know what a great guy you turned out to be."

"I thought I was dangerous," I mutter, my words rough. It feels as though the inside of my throat has been sandpapered dry.

Her head shakes. "You're many things, Dane Kingsley. Dangerous isn't one of them. You're supportive. Protective. Selfless—"

"I'm selfish as fuck."

"Dane, you let your friend crash at your apartment," she points out. "You let him come and go as he pleases."

"Like a cat," I deadpan, and the corner of her lips tilts up.

"You watch movies I *know* you don't like for me," she continues. "You willingly enter an art museum without complaining—"

"So, I'm nice to the two people I care about." My shoulder hitches. "Marco and I go way back. You're my girl. Of course, I'm gonna treat you two better than everyone else."

"You're a great guy," she says softly, her unwavering gaze chipping away my resolve. "If I have to spend the rest of my life proving to you how great you are and how lucky I am to have met you? I can think of worse things than that."

My chest coils tighter than a rubber band. My heart gives a little thump. As I take in her sincere expression, I can't think of anything to say or do to alleviate the tension. I can't think of anything but how much her words mean to me. How much *she* means to me.

The last time I saw my father, he told me not to take for

granted how lucky I am to not be dead right now. That I have more in life to be thankful for. *Grateful* of.

He's right. As much as it pains me to admit, I'm looking directly at it. *At her*. Until she wises up and leaves me for someone better, I'll never take any moment with the girl who saved my fucking life for granted.

39

REESE

With the spring semester underway, I'm picking up more hours at the bookstore to make use of my free time. There's a lengthy gap between my morning and evening classes, and I could use the cash.

"Little Vann." Those two words bring a grimace to my lips, and when I glance up from my notebook, I freeze.

Pure dread steals up my spine at the sight of Travis Walker standing right before me. The seconds that follow are excruciatingly long, and my nerves abound.

His dark gaze never wavers as he slaps a blue book onto the counter and slides it to me. "Thought that was you."

Reaching for the book, my lips press together when his forefinger keeps it pinned to the wooden surface. Swallowing hard, I tug it free with more force than anticipated. To my immense relief, it doesn't tear. Thank God.

"Was expecting you to be a no-show," he goes on. "Given how many times your sister bitched about you—"

"Don't talk about my sister like that." Without hesitation, I lift my head to glare at him.

"Don't talk to a paying customer like that," he mocks, his mouth curling into a sneer. "You should know better than that."

This is the guy my sister likes? Him? How does she not see what a complete asshole he is? He comes off as a stereotypical villain in an eighties flick. He looks like a guy who'll complain that his father will hear about this.

Lilian has dated her fair share of awful guys, but I never thought it would be this bad.

"Well," I say, wetting my bottom lip, "I know you're a liar."

"I'm lying about the customer is always right policy?"

"No." The slight tremor in my voice sends a pulse of frustration down to my stomach. I hate it. I wish I felt as brave as I'm pretending to be. Or that my nails aren't digging crescent moons into the flesh of my palms. "I know you lied about what happened between you and Dane."

Somehow, the air becomes impossibly colder. His gaze narrows into slits. I swallow past the lump in my throat and steel my shoulders.

"Is that so?"

"You were never injured—"

"My *broken* arm that the psychopath gave me paints a different picture—"

"You were never injured *intentionally*," I hiss. "It was done in self-defense. And I know you don't have a scar, either. You were the one who attacked him with a bottle—"

A loud slam halts the rest of my sentence. With both palms on the counter, he leans in until our faces are merely an inch apart. My pulse becomes skittish. My heart skyrockets to the moon. His eyes are impassive as ever while he studies me like I'm some sort of bug he can't wait to crush.

Even so, I refuse to flinch. I won't move a muscle even if it takes every last ounce of my willpower. He shifts closer, and I can smell the gum he's chewing. It's spearmint.

Still, I remain firm. That is until his breath grazes my cheek, and he's getting too close for comfort. I stagger back a step for some much-needed space between us. Before I can reach for my can of pepper spray, he lets out a dry chuckle.

"It's your word against mine." His voice gains a mordant edge. "And nobody's gonna believe the sad little charity case who's easily scared of her own freaking shadow."

Every muscle in my body seizes. Tears sting behind my eyes. "You're an asshole."

"Never stopped your sister from slobbering all over my knob before," he states coolly.

Taken aback, my grimace is inescapable. "Lili has higher standards than that—"

"Please," he scoffs. "I can tell her to get on her back like a—"

"How dare you? Don't talk about her like that," I cry out as my rage blossoms within like an open flame. No one talks about my sister that way. No one should ever talk about *any* girl that way.

"You can take a girl out of a trailer park, but you can't take the—"

"Shut—"

"Back the fuck off," comes a menacing growl. I wince and scramble backward as Travis holds up his hands. Marco shoves his sleeves up as he strides over and smacks his fist into an open palm. "Unless you need some fucking help with it."

"Chill out," Travis sneers. "We were just talking."

"Doesn't look like it to me." A muscle in Marco's jaw ticks. "You gonna back the fuck off now, or do you want your arm in a cast and sling again?"

Stunned, my breath leaves my lungs in a sudden whoosh while I remain rooted to the spot. I'm uncertain what to do. I should call Dane and let him know what's going on, but the tension in the atmosphere is so thick that any abrupt movement might set them off.

Right now, they're both just glaring at one another. Sizing each other up. Priming for a fight I don't want to happen. I don't like violence. Also, there are so many displays nearby that if they escalate further, my coworkers and I will be saddled with cleaning everything up.

"You threatening me?" Travis hisses.

"I'm promising you," Marco retorts, and Travis puffs his chest. I don't know why he's entertaining this pissing contest. Marco has at least fifty pounds on him.

It must have finally dawned on him, too, because his expression shifts with a nervous swallow. "Whatever," he sneers, snatching the blue book from the counter. "Go threaten someone else like your buddy does. I'm out."

My anger sparks up, but he storms out the door before I can get another word in.

"You good?" Marco's words snare my attention, and my mouth flattens into a frustrated scowl.

"He didn't pay." Why am I even surprised? This is the same guy who was saying all those degrading things about my sister just minutes ago. *What does she see in him*?

"Don't worry about it." With a weary sigh, he places his Scantron down. "I got it."

"Oh, no. It's fine." I wave him off and put on a light smile. "We have change left out for a reason."

His brows furrow as his tongue clicks a beat. "Always annoying when they think they can get away with anything, huh?"

I sneak a peek at the sliding door, and my shoulders sag. "It is."

"He didn't give you that much trouble, did he?"

Something watery graces my lips. "Nothing I can't handle."

He cracks a grin. "No joke, you sound just like Dane right there."

A soft peal of laughter bubbles out of me. "Guess he's been rubbing off on me, huh?"

"I think you're rubbing off on him, too," he muses with a quiet chuckle. "Didn't realize he was capable of smiling for more than a second."

My heart beats erratically faster, and I don't bother fighting the dorky smile flitting across my features while I ring him up. "If you stay around, Dane should be here soon to pick me up."

"Nah, that's all right." He shakes his head. "I've seen his cranky ass more than enough times now. I can go one day without it."

I snort before I can help myself. "What was he like? Back then?"

"Loyal," he answers without missing a beat. "If I had to use one word to describe him."

The corner of my lips tips even higher. After hearing my sister rant my ears off about what a bad guy he is, it's nice to hear something kind about Dane for once. "He is loyal."

"Like a damn dog," Marco teases, his brown eyes crinkling at the edges. "If you're worried he'll step out on you or—"

"Oh, I'm not worried about that," I say. "I don't wanna come off too presumptuous, but I think he has a soft spot for me."

"He cares about you," Marco says, and it's evident my joke went over his head.

"Yeah, I know." A fluttering warmth unfurls in my chest as my thoughts go to Dane, unbidden. "Would you mind telling my sister that?" At the sight of his confused frown, I laugh it off. "I'm just kidding."

Although, it would solve many of my problems if my sister heard from someone else how great Dane is. Then again, she would probably shut it down before a single syllable is uttered. The only person who can even get through to her is me, and we're still not on speaking terms. She'll just keep leaving me on read, and honestly, I don't really want to deal with that right now.

LIKE CLOCKWORK, DANE'S CAR IS IDLING IN THE FACULTY PARKING spot when I exit the bookstore. I rush over before he honks and draws the attention of every student nearby.

Wedging my backpack into the backseat, I'm quick to remove my sweater before I climb inside. I'm instantly met with a sharp-edged whistle, and I peer sideways to see him lifting his sunglasses.

"Damn, Snack Mix," he says. "How am I supposed to drive with you looking like the world's best distraction?"

"It's just a dress." It's the ditzy floral number Lilian got for me. The square neck displays my scar, practically accentuating it. I give him a reluctant glance, only to realize he's not looking at it exactly. His gaze is a bit further south.

"Just a dress," he echoes. "Did you always wear something like this?"

"Sometimes," I admit, and he lets out another whistle. "When the weather calls for it."

"The forecast calls for clear skies for the weeks ahead." His pale blue eyes twinkle with mischief. "Feel free to leave your sweaters at home and wear all the short little dresses you want around me."

Amusement zips through me. "Let's not get carried away."

"How you've managed to go nineteen years without a boyfriend…"

My mouth flattens into a grimace, and his playful grin drops. His expression shifts; the level of concern in his gaze sends a spell of weariness through me.

Leaning back in my seat, my eyes pinch shut. "I never really… liked that kind of attention."

"No?"

"It's…" With a shaky exhalation, I distract myself by thumbing the seatbelt. "Guys back home thought I was easy because my boobs came in when I was twelve." A flicker of embarrassment I'm all too familiar with takes root in the pit of my stomach. "And because my family lived in a trailer. I was known as the *RV* slut. I'd get all these comments. Like, Mom's boyfriend said… it was a good thing… my attacker didn't, um, slice my boobs because that would have been… a waste."

"Fuck him. Fuck all of them," Dane growls, his brows slashing into a harsh line. "They're all going on my list."

I blink against my stupor, then groan into my palms. "Don't tell me that list actually exists."

He lifts a shoulder and shoves his sunglasses back on.

"Dane." I frown when he doesn't say anything. "*Daniel.*"

"It doesn't," he promises, drawing a small cross over his heart. "I swear on my life, my bike, and my cars." My lips twitch. "I'd never lie to you. But the moment you point out your mom's shitty boyfriend to me, I will not hesitate to kick his ass."

"I don't want you to get into fights," I argue, only for him to cut me off.

"Baby, I'm not getting into fights. I'm kicking ass."

Heaving out a blustery groan for a long second, I resist the temptation to drag my hands down my face. "It'd be easier going to bed at night without worrying about my boyfriend getting hurt."

"Have some faith in me." He husks out a rough chuckle. "I can handle a little sting to my knuckles—"

"*Daniel.*"

"Damn, you're really going to keep weaponizing my government name against me, huh?" He reaches over and runs his thumb over the hill of my cheekbone. "Promise you, if anything happens, they had it coming."

I give him an unamused stare.

"Now, come on," he says. "Daylight's burning, and my girl threw a wrench in my plans for today when she decided she'd rather work than hang out with me."

"And what exactly do you have planned?"

In answer, he winks at me. With a sigh, I lean back in my seat and try to figure it out on my own. Nothing comes to mind. All I know is that he's driving toward my apartment, but then he passes by the building, and I'm stumped.

My phone dings just then, and I perk up, only to wilt when I see that it's a scam text for vague remote work opportunities filled with grammatical errors and weird jargon.

"What's wrong, Mini Reese?"

My lips wobble before I can help myself. Of course, he'd notice when I'm feeling down. He's always been freakishly observant. "It's my sister."

"She finally texted you?"

"No." I blow out a breath and drum my fingers against my upper thigh. "This is the longest we've ever fought." And I feel troubled at the thought; a blizzard of emotions clashes within me. "I was hoping she'd at least respond when I messaged her about what he said earlier." At this point, I'd have an easier time convincing a brick wall that Travis is a slimeball. With just the right amount of peas, I can perhaps persuade the pintail ducks on campus to make him public enemy number one.

"What did he say?"

Tears burn a fiery trail up my throat. "Just some awful things not worth repeating."

He sighs, then takes a left turn into some random parking lot. I've never been to this plaza before, but the sorority girls swear by the Korean barbeque place up ahead.

Once he cuts the ignition, he gives me a thoughtful glance. "I don't get it. How have you not made up with her yet?"

"What do you mean?"

"Well, for starters," he hedges, "it's you." His hand goes to the back of his neck. "Besides how you're usually the type to smooth things over, for obvious reasons." He pauses. "I can't imagine anyone holding a grudge this long against you. Hell, you're the last person on earth I'd ever want to lose. You have so much kindness in that heart of yours, and you still manage to see the good in everyone after everything you've been through. You're an amazing girl, Reese, and anybody with a damn brain cell would recognize that and not fuck things up with you."

Heat touches my cheeks as warmth settles deep in my belly. My heart thumps sporadically against my rib cage, kicking up a notch when he squeezes my knee.

"I hope she comes to her senses and fixes things with you,"

he adds, and I crack a tiny smile. "Until then, let's enjoy picking up the ingredients needed for our own gas station sushi."

"Excuse me?" I rasp. A gradual flicker of horror works through my veins as I swivel forward and gawp at the pet shop before us. "Oh my God, Dane. I'm *not* eating a goldfish."

Wild laughter erupts from his chest. His shoulders shake as he theatrically wipes away an imaginary tear. "We're not, but the cat might—"

"What?" I interject, bewildered. "Wait. Are you getting a cat?"

"We're rescuing one," he amends. "Orange. Chunky. Likes to sleep on the hood of my car when I stay the night at your place 'cause the engine's still warm."

My mouth falls open. It's the only response I can make.

"Reese's Pieces, we're getting Onion Rings flea meds and a collar." He breaks into a grin. "You have a habit of taking in strays, and I know you've been feeding him. Might as well make it official."

I take a slow breath. I'm speechless. Utterly so. "What if he belongs to someone else?"

"And they just let him roam around?" he asks incredulously. "It rained last night."

"I know. That's why I let him in… *We* should check if he's chipped first," I stammer. "Before we make any rash decision. And… *Onion Rings*?"

"Open for suggestions." Amusement gleams in his eyes. "Root Beer's a good name for the tabby, too."

"How late are they open?" I peek at the storefront, then drop my gaze to my chest.

"I can grab your sweater for you," he offers. "Or lend you my jacket if you want."

With a slow exhalation, I turn toward him. "I'll be fine." My voice is a soft rasp and brings a flush to my cheeks.

"Fuck yeah, you're fine. Fine as hell," he says, and before I can even groan into my palm, he catches my wrist. "Now, come on. Let's go inside before they close."

Neither of us moves. We both remain seated, facing one another as he slips his hand in mine. Slowly, a beam overtakes my face.

"What's making you smile, Snack Size?"

"You."

"Me?"

"Yeah." I bite my bottom lip while I trace aimless patterns around his knuckles. "You. You're the best boyfriend ever."

He snorts. "Not much competition there."

"Still the best," I insist. "You've done so much for me." My smile abruptly fades when Travis' words spring into my head like an unwelcome guest. *Charity case.*

Dane frowns and straightens his spine. His gaze rests on me as he draws nearer, and I go still when he slides his thumb underneath my chin. "Baby, you all right?"

I swallow hoarsely. Hesitation floods my system. "Be honest with me."

"Always," he responds right away.

"How much did it cost to"—I crinkle my nose when he emits a loud groan—"fix the Nova?"

His focus pivots toward the windshield. "I don't remember."

"*Dane.*"

"Reese's Pieces, I promise you," he says, his tone gentle and soothing, "that money is of no concern to me. I have plenty to spare. I made some nice pocket change from my short stint with flipping cars. Besides, my mom left me everything. I'm one of 'em filthy trust fund brats."

"I can't have you spending all of your mom's—"

"She left me a lot." He gives my hand a reassuring squeeze. "Don't worry about it. I'm not hurting for cash. I'll get another huge chunk of my trust fund when I turn twenty-five."

My attention cuts to the center console as uncertainty racks me.

"Mini Reese, I don't want you to feel guilty about any of this, all right? My father got on my ass once about investing the cash I came into. He didn't think I'd be responsible with any of it," he explains. "If I'm not spending it on things you deserve"—his forefinger presses against my lips before I can interject because *deserve* is a strong word—"I'd be blowing it all on cars, anyway."

A snort breaks free. "You would," I tease, and he chuckles. "You so would."

"If I can treat a girl like you the way she deserves to be appreciated," he continues, "then I'll do just so."

"A girl like me?" I echo.

"Someone who's kind, compassionate, and"—his gaze flits to my scar—"*strong.*"

My breath hitches as I peer deeply into his eyes. "I'm not strong."

"You're plenty strong," he whispers back. "You're the strongest girl I know." His hand goes to my arm, and he tweaks my biceps. "If I have to spend every day of my life reminding you of how strong you are? Well, baby, you better buckle up and prepare for the ride."

An answering warmth blooms in my chest. My heartbeat stumbles over itself. My stomach swarms with a kaleidoscope of butterflies. If only Lilian could see how great he truly is, she'd understand why I love him so much.

My lips part around my silent gasp as my thought strikes me speechless. I love him. How can I not?

Before I can say anything—before I can tell him those three words—he leans over the center console and brushes a kiss on my forehead.

"Now, come on," he murmurs. "Let's go find Onion Rings the most badass collar."

I smother my snicker, only to burst into sharp laughter. "I draw the line at studs, Dane."

Amusement breaks out across his face. "So, we're going with Onion Rings?"

"We're going with Onion Rings."

40

DANE

It's hard to miss the lime-green car parked beside mine in the crowded parking structure. Not when the fiberglass hood is totaled. A headlight is caved in. One tire is missing a rim. In other words, it's a fucking mess.

How it got up to the fourth level without falling apart like a terribly wrapped burrito is nothing short of a miracle.

A vein in my forehead pulses. Anticipation tightens my muscles while I scan the surrounding area with keen eyes, gearing up for whatever bullshit awaits me. The rush of traffic sounds in the far distance. Idle chatter rises from the ground floor. Wisps of smoke float in the air and drag my attention westward.

Within seconds, Wally steps out from between two random vehicles and crushes a cigarette beneath his boot. He doesn't say a word. He just stands there and sneers at me. The atmosphere hangs heavy with silence. Tension simmers in the air.

It's on me for hoping that I could go one semester without any bullshit happening. After all, hope is a dangerous thing to have. Especially for someone like me.

"I'd ask what you're doing here," I say, my voice gaining a

caustic edge, "but I think the bigger question is, *do you know where you are?*"

His scowl deepens. "Do I what?"

"Because there's no way a place like this would let you in," I continue. "Unless Belford lowered their admission standards. If that's the case—"

"Why were you asking about me?"

I grit my teeth. Fucking Eddie. I should have known better than to assume my talk with him would stay between us two. Unlike his lady, he can't keep his mouth shut.

Wally draws nearer, and I shift my stance. Abruptly, he halts.

"Just wanted to see if… we had any mutual friends," I say blandly.

He scoffs. "Can't imagine anyone being friends with you." His mouth tilts into a slight smirk. "You thought I got my guys to jump you? Well, maybe I did. Maybe I didn't. Who knows? Maybe I know something you don't."

Skepticism courses through me as I give his busted headlight a sidelong glance. "Doubt that."

"And I'll tell you what I know," he continues, "if you hear me out. I've got a business project for you."

"*Proposition.*"

"Does it look like I have girls with me, Old News?" he demands. Like all the teachers in his life, I decide not to bother cultivating the only two brain cells rattling inside that empty head of his.

"Listen, Wallet—"

"*Wally.*"

"I'm not interested in whatever bullshit you're spewing my way," I maintain. "You'd have a better time convincing me to get rid of my cars—"

"I need you to lose."

With a huff, my attention slips sideways to his shattered side-view mirror. "Yeah, you'd have a better time convincing me to—"

"If you lose to me at the next race." He pauses for a dramatic breath. "I'll give you a cut of my win."

"Yeah, hard pass," is my immediate response. To spare us both from the dumbest idea I've ever heard, I barrel on. "What do you think will happen when Giancarlo finds out we fixed it?"

"He won't." The smug, cocksure grin working its way across his face tells me this plan is going to end up with us being paid a visit by Giancarlo's goons. Forgive me if I don't want to find out what it's like to lose a kneecap once and for all.

My arms cross my chest. "Pass."

I don't want to know what would encourage his two brain cells to seek me out in broad daylight. Especially at Belford, of all places. I have no clue how he found me to begin with. I just want him gone.

"I only need to win a couple of them. All you have to do is drive—"

"GC isn't on the same level of intelligence as you," I say dryly, and he nods in agreement. "He'll find out. He *always* finds out."

"He won't," Wally insists, and I give him a wary stare.

He's… too persistent. This could be a trick Giancarlo cooked up for me. Something to see if I'd take the bait and try to screw him over. Loyalty is a big thing for him. But the idea alone is insulting to Giancarlo's intelligence and mine.

Not only that, Wally's the last guy Giancarlo would ever want to work with. Wally's simply too volatile. Impulsive. This is the same guy who once branded his chest at a meet just to impress a girl he didn't even know.

Regardless, I know how this will end if I get involved. Double-crossed and screwed over isn't a prediction. It's a guarantee. Like his car, this has trouble written all over it.

"Fuck off," I grunt, and his nostrils flare.

"Whatever." He glowers. "You'll regret it when I beat your ass next time—"

"I know *statistics* is too big of a word for you," I deadpan, and his expression darkens. "But given the fact that you've won a sum total of zero races in all of our matches, the odds are stacked against you."

I barely take a step back, dodging his right hook. Before he lands a blow to the side of my head, I duck and grab his arm mid-swing. With a rough shove, he stumbles onto the asphalt.

Breathing hard as he scrambles to his feet, he spares me an agitated glare. Christ. If he's willing to attack me in broad daylight, he's *that* stupid. And desperate. It doesn't bode well for me.

I need to put an end to this. I don't want to give my girl another scare by acquiring a brand-new shiner on my mug. And nobody in their right mind enjoys getting their face pulverized.

"I'm gonna give you the chance to go." The muscles in my shoulders grow tense as I ball my hands into fists. "Try to hit me again, and I'll fucking rearrange your face."

His jaw tightens. "You're gonna regret this. I'll make sure of it. I'll make sure you lose—"

"I won't lose a damn thing to you," I state flatly. Does he think I'm scared? Shaking in my fucking boots? Even a basket of kittens is scarier than this. He can keep dreaming all he wants, but there's never going to be another race between us.

I meant every word about calling it quits and walking away from this life. I cannot risk getting dragged into more bullshit like this.

"Now get the fuck out of my sight."

He says nothing, so I brace myself for whatever bullshit his petulant ass will pull. Only, he doesn't swing at me. He doesn't lunge at me, either.

Instead, he stalks off to his vehicle. His baggy jeans swish loudly with each stomp. His jaw is clenched in a harsh scowl. Reaching his door, he yanks it open, then slams it into the side of my fastback.

His blank eyes lock on mine over the roof of my car as he does it again. And again. With no sign of stopping.

I want nothing more than to repeatedly slam his head into the side of his coupe until he's knocked out cold, but I remain rooted in place and school my features into something blank. Breathe through my nose. Silently meditate for the first time in my damn life just to remain calm. He's fucking up my paint job, but that's an easy fix. So long as I'm not picking my girl up from the bookstore with a black eye, he can bash in one of my headlights for all I care.

Clearly, my lack of a reaction wasn't what he wanted. With a frustrated snarl, he kicks at my side-view mirror. "You're gonna lose, Old News. You're gonna lose everything. I'll fucking make sure of it."

He punches my passenger window, then jumps into his coupe and slams the door shut. A smug little smirk pulls at my lips at the sound of his engine failing to turn over. It's music to my ears.

He cuts me with a sneer before his shitbox car finally comes to life. Flipping me the bird, he peels out of the parking spot and sets off a cacophony of alarms.

"Dumbass." Unclenching my jaw, I glance skyward for a minute and wait for my annoyance to subside. Once the tension no longer lingers in my chest, I head over to the fastback's hood to see if he tampered with anything before I arrived.

"He did what to your car?" The look on Marco's face brings a wry grin to mine. He drags his fingers through his wet hair, then wedges his surfboard into the sand. "You don't fuck with a man's car."

"No fucking shit." My line of sight goes above his shoulder. Reese is standing near the shore with her camera in her hands, capturing shots of the surfers riding the early morning waves. "But if my girl asks—"

"You backed into a pole like a dumbass," he supplies innocently. "Sideswiped it, too."

"—some dumbass hit it while I was in class and left behind some bogus insurance info."

"Do you really think anyone's gonna believe that?" He gives me a dubious glance. "Your ass rarely shows up to lectures—"

I show him my middle finger, and he snickers.

"I got your back," he says, and I nod. "Can't believe he did that, though."

Me neither, but I tip my head and sit up straight just as Reese snaps a photo of us. Soon, she's stashing her camera in her bag while she makes her way over.

Her arms wrap around her stomach the moment she's within reach. Her cheeks are mottled red from the blustery chill of the wind. Stray flyaways of her hair catch on the breeze.

"Oh my God," she rasps, peering up at Marco. "How do you get into the water *willingly*? It's *freezing* out here."

"You cold?" With a grin, I pat my thigh. "Come here."

"Aw, baby, thanks." Marco bursts into a hearty guffaw when I shove him away from me. Hand to the face. "You gonna do me like that?"

"You're not my girlfriend," I deadpan, hoisting my girl onto my lap. She wriggles her sweet ass into my crotch as she settles into my arms, and I bite back a groan.

"I'm your best friend, though," he says. "We've known each other for how long now? You'll just let me freeze to death despite everything we've been through? Fucking cold-blooded, man."

Groaning, I shake my head in exasperation.

Reese giggles and leans into me. "I'm curious. How long have you guys known each other?"

Marco beats me to the punch. "For a long time. I've known him since the night he crashed his daddy's car into my uncle's shop."

"How exactly is that a long time?" I counter, and he snorts.

"It won't ruin your street cred to admit you have friends, Kingsy." He takes a seat beside us on the hood of my car. "You know, as his oldest friend, I'm surprised Sunshine over here got himself a girlfriend. He never tells me anything."

"I tell you enough."

Marco ignores me. "How did you two meet again?"

"At a cafe—"

"When my ass got curb-stomped," I say at the same time, and Reese tosses a frown over her shoulder.

"Shit, you got your ass kicked at a cafe?" Marco howls with laughter. "What did you do, Kingsy? Said that you preferred almond milk to oat milk? Asked them to grind some coffee beans by hand, one at a time?"

"GC," I grate out, and his expression sobers within a split second. Understanding fills his gaze. We haven't discussed my attack since the morning he picked me up from Reese's apartment.

Truthfully, I'm going out on a limb here. Grasping at straws. It's a reach, but it's something, which is better than nothing.

Eddie doesn't know why I was ambushed that night. Shyla's got no clue, either. For all I know, they could be lying to protect Wally, but that's an even bigger reach. Wally's too dumb to orchestrate anything like that.

Reese turns her head and finds my gaze, her eyes inquisitive. Searching. "What's GC?"

"Some guy I no longer associate with," I reply slowly, stealing a glance at Marco. The weight of my words lingers in the air.

"No?" While his face gives nothing away, the hint of infliction in his tone betrays him.

"Nah, I'm done."

His surprise is evident in his arched brow. His expression smoothes into something neutral when Reese refocuses her attention on him. "Right on, man. You're way too good to be rolling with him." My chin hikes in acknowledgment when he continues. "So, what do you plan on doing?"

I nearly draw in a ragged breath. Besides the obvious— buying cars and fixing them—I haven't got the faintest clue. The idea of sitting in all those finance lectures makes me itchy already. A familiar restlessness takes hold of me without a moment wasted.

"Help Snack Mix catalog onion rings from every restaurant along the coast for her fiesta."

Confusion passes over his profile as he slowly blinks, then releases a cough at the sentence I delivered with a straight face. "Uh, have fun? Or you could finally learn how to surf?"

My features pull taut with the grimace forming around my lips. Surfing is his thing, not mine. I don't want to wake up at an ungodly hour every morning to catch some waves at their peak. I'd rather stay in bed with Reese plastered to my side, clinging to me.

"You're missing out, Kingsy." He hops off my hood and stretches his arms over his head. "If you ever want lessons..." His offer isn't directed at me. He spares Reese a nod, and she immediately shakes her head.

"I'm busy as it is. I have *way* too many science classes I need to stay on top of this semester," she stammers. "But thanks."

With a chuckle, he grabs his board. "Have fun with your... onion rings."

"See ya later, man," I tell him, and a snort slips out when he does a mock salute while he treks backward toward the ocean. Then I sneak a kiss on Reese's temple, grinning when she squeals. "Still cold?"

"I've forgotten what it's like to feel my arms."

My head ducks, and I bite the pulse point between her neck and shoulder. "Think pancakes will warm you up?"

"With a nice cup of coffee, perhaps." Her breathing hitches when I scrape my teeth against her soft skin. "Coffee and pancakes sound pretty great right now."

"Then let's get out of here."

"You don't want to watch him surf?" Abruptly, she straightens herself and frowns.

"We came here for the sunrise," I remind her. "The sun has risen. Now let's go."

A soft laugh dispels from her chest. "At least watch him take on one wave."

I exaggerate a groan, and she giggles even harder. "All right, fine. You drive a hard bargain, Reese's Pieces." Tightening my arms around her, I rest my chin on the crook of her shoulder.

After we've witnessed him catch at least a dozen waves, we finally leave the beach. The one thing I love most about the weekends is how empty the streets are. No nine-to-five traffic. No morning gridlock. It's nothing but the clear, open road before me.

I'm not gunning it, though. Times like this call for a slower cruise, so I can savor the morning sunlight burning through the fog and brightening the sky.

"Speaking of onion rings," Reese says. "The cat has been clawing up my futon."

"Put the damn thing out of its misery," is my immediate response, and she gasps. My hand lifts in defense. "It's on its last leg, and it's springy as fuck. It poked the shit out of me."

"Let me guess," she says dryly. "The only good poking is of the penis variety."

"Penis variety?" I chuckle under my breath. "You're not wrong—"

A loud revving sound cuts me short. My spine goes ramrod straight as some orange sports car pulls up beside me. My peripheral vision takes a quick inventory. It's last year's model with illegally tinted windows and a wide-body kit installed. The exhaust's got a muffler delete. A spoiler wing is mounted to the trunk, complete with vortex generators attached to its roof.

Whoever's behind the wheel revs his engine again. I grit my teeth and pointedly keep my eyes trained forward while my mind whirls. I need to determine the best course of action here. Take a right at the next stoplight or drop my speed.

"Do you know the guy?" Reese shouts.

The prick won't let up with the revving. I hope he fucks up his valve.

"Nah." Easing my foot off the gas pedal, I watch the vehicle from the corner of my eye. "No clue who he is. Just 'cause he's got a stupid car doesn't mean I know him."

Tension drains from my body when the guy finally takes the hint and plows ahead in an orange blur.

"You didn't want to race him?"

"Fuck no." My tone is blunt as I relax my grip on the steering wheel. "Not with you in the car."

"What?" she breathes. "I wouldn't mind."

A deep growl sounds from my chest. "I would." My foot taps the brakes when we reach an intersection. "One, civilians are driving at this time of day. Two, this street is notoriously crawling with cops. It's practically a speed trap." As if on cue, a patrol car makes a left turn ahead of us. "Three, I don't want anything to happen to you if something goes down." My words dry up in my throat, and I clear it. "Four, the last thing I want is to deal with my father if he were to catch wind of this."

The lights change, and I step on it. Reese remains silent beside me. Just when I think the conversation is over, she speaks.

"I thought you liked to race, though?" Notes of genuine curiosity fill her voice.

"I do," I answer truthfully. God knows I do. "But I like to go against people who know what they're doing. In an area cleared of civilians—" A smug grin breaks across my face. Up ahead, the orange sports car has been pulled over.

"Can I watch you?"

"Nah, Mini Reese," I tell her. "No fucking way."

"What? Why not?" she asks. "You always do things I want to do. I want to support your interests, too."

The idea of bringing her to a meet sends a wave of dread

through me. No self-respecting car guy would take his girl to that kind of scene. Not only that, I don't want to run the risk of anyone finding out about her and trying to fuck with me through her.

It's for her safety and my peace of mind. The last thing I need is for her to be more worried about me as well.

"I'm not about that life anymore."

"So you're giving it up? You don't want to do it for fun?" she tries, and I refrain from groaning.

"Go-karts are perfect for that."

"Race *cars*."

"Go-karts are a type of car."

A weary sigh escapes her. For a moment, neither of us speaks. It's just the hum of the engine as I cruise down the stretch of road. My fingers drum a quick beat on the steering wheel. Her knee bounces while she hits me with puppy-dog eyes.

This girl, I swear to God.

"If you want to support my interests," I begin, my words heavy with reluctance.

She nods and breaks into a beam, her enthusiasm permeating the small space between us. Dammit. She's making it hard for me to say no. Especially when she's practically vibrating in her seat.

I pinch the bridge of my nose. "I can set something up for next weekend." I pause. "But, baby, you don't have to turn yourself into a car girl for me. I don't want you to go through all that trouble. Just because I like 'em doesn't mean you have to."

"It'd be nice to have something in common."

"We hate shitty music," I deadpan. "Isn't that enough?"

"It would be nice," she reiterates. "So, what's happening next weekend?"

"There's a track more inland where they let you drive—"

"With go-karts?"

"With any car," I correct. "There's no speed trap—no tickets for speeding, either. We can take Ol' Reliable out there—"

"Really?" She abruptly stops bouncing. "What about your motorcycle?"

"We don't need to go to a track for you to learn how to ride my bike," I point out. "You just need to wear something that'll protect you in case you fall."

"You don't mind me crashing your bike?"

"Well, I'd much rather you didn't," I tease, tapping the brakes at the next red light. "I don't want to see you hurt. That's all."

The moment my Mustang comes to a complete standstill, she scoots over and presses her lips against my cheek. A stupid grin plasters across my face when she peels back, but it falters when my gaze flies over her shoulder.

To the shiny white hybrid, where two chicks are gawping at us with wide eyes and slacked jaws. They look familiar, but I can't place their names.

"Friends of yours?" I ask, and Reese furrows a brow while she follows my line of sight. A squeak escapes her while her entire frame goes stiff as a board. "*Not* friends of yours?"

She wheezes while they make a right turn. The moment they're out of sight, she sinks into her seat and shoves her hands into her hair. "They're Lili's sorority sisters."

"Maybe they didn't recognize you?" I suggest, and she lifts her head to spare me a funny look. In my periphery, the lights turn green, but my focus remains on her. "Guess we don't have to sneak around anymore, huh?"

With a quiet exhale, she casts a glance out the windshield. Her fingers play with the hem of her sweater. Something a lot like apprehension flickers across her slender profile.

Pasting on a reassuring grin, I reach over, take her hand, and give it a gentle squeeze. She tries to smother it, but a small, tentative smile plays at the edge of her lips when she finally meets my gaze.

"Guess not."

41

REESE

Statistically speaking, there's a hundred percent chance my sister is going to flip out on me. It will happen. I know this. At this point, I just need to figure out how to calm her down when I tell her about Dane and she inevitably loses her cool.

Hopefully, it's me who's breaking the news to her and not the sorority girls.

Anxiety settles low in my stomach, and I bite my bottom lip. The idea of texting her the truth and then powering my phone off for the next decade seems very tempting.

Sensing my distress, Dane puts his hand on top of mine. "Are you sure you don't want me to go with you?"

I spare him a brittle smile. "I think it's best if it's just us." I don't want to ambush my sister. Having a heart-to-heart seems like the better alternative. And I don't want Dane to hear the things she'll say about him.

I'm already stressed about what awaits me. I don't need to worry about keeping the peace between them as well.

Suddenly, a horrifying thought pops into my head. What if she makes me choose between them? Insist that I break up with him?

My heart sinks a little as my attention cuts to the sorority house across the street. There's no sign of my sister being home at the very moment. I texted her half an hour ago asking if we could talk. She didn't leave me on read, but she also didn't respond to my messages, either. She's most likely busy.

Some part of me hopes that Chrissy and Jenna didn't relay a single thing to her, but they're notorious gossips. It'll be foolish of me to go in without bracing myself for the worst.

"Let me know if things go south," Dane says, drawing my focus. "I'll be here. Your getaway car."

My mouth tips up into the barest hint of a smile. There's nothing I want more than to sit here with him and pretend life doesn't exist outside of this car.

With extreme reluctance, I unbuckle my seatbelt. "I'll see you soon."

"Your getaway car," he repeats, sparing me with a reassuring grin. Some of my nerves melt away under the level of focus in his gaze.

I kiss his cheek and breathe in his familiar scent, erupting into laughter when he tugs me closer.

"Everything will be fine," he promises. "And if it's not?"

"You're my getaway car," I mumble into his chest, soaking up the familiar feel of his embrace. As much as I want to continue pushing this off—as much as I *really* want to stay here indefi-nitely—I pry myself out of his arms and climb out of the vehicle.

With a steadying breath, I make my way over to the house. It's not Lilian who answers the second I ring the doorbell, but Peyton, who gasps excitedly as she draws me in for a hug.

"Little Vann!" she squeals. "I haven't seen you in *forever*."

Wincing, I let out a nervous chuckle. "I've been busy. Is Lili around? I need to talk to her."

"She's at her internship," Peyton says, checking the time on her phone. "But she should be back soon. Maybe in ten minutes or so. Want me to get you anything? Sparkling water? Seltzer—"

"I'm good, but thanks. I'll just wait for her in her room." With that, I head for the stairs. Since I've last been here, the girls have taken the Christmas decorations down. The place looks... emptier without them. Almost ominous, if anything.

Lilian's room, on the other hand, is actually empty. I step inside, wishing my nerves would subside, as I take a seat on the edge of her bed. Unfortunately, my anxiety seems to climb higher and higher with every second slipping by slowly.

Flopping back on the mattress, I shoot Dane a text.

Reese: It might take a while
Dane: don't mind waiting for you
Reese: I do. You don't have to stay
Dane: I'm your getaway car, Reese's Pieces
Dane: I'm not going anywhere

Time is moving at the speed of snails crawling through molasses. To keep my mind busy, I scroll through my photo album and send him all the pictures I love. The slight blur of him skating across the ice. The Christmas tree at the hotel. The shot of him holding Onion Rings in his muscular arms. The crinkle of his eyes when he drives. The grumpy expression on his face when he's trying to bite into his sandwich. The messy hair late at night when his hair gel's worn off.

There's a high chance I'm sending him everything in the album.

Dane: heads up
Dane: I see your sister

Oof. With a rough exhalation, I tuck my cell into my back pocket. My palms press against my upper thighs in my attempt to still them, and just when I wonder how long it'll take for my sister to come up to her room, the door flies open.

Her gaze collides with mine as she bares her canines, and I flinch.

Sitting up slowly, I offer her a tentative wave. The tension between us doesn't ease up. "Before you freak out—"

"Tell me something." She angrily yanks her purse off of her shoulder. "*Are you insane?*"

"Lilian—"

"*Are you?*" She flings her bag onto her desk, and it knocks into her pencil holder, spilling pens everywhere. "Do you need me to remind you how *dangerous* he is?"

"He's not—"

"He broke Travis' arm!"

"He—"

"*Do you lack self-preservation and common sense?*" she snarls, and I recoil.

Something inside me twists painfully at her words, and I blink away the start of prickling tears welling behind my eyes. "I have self-preservation—"

"*No,*" Lilian snaps. "No, you don't."

"*I do,*" I protest.

"*You let a complete fucking stranger into your apartment!*" she sneers, and I pull in a sharp breath. I don't have any counter-arguments there. I *know* that was a terrible judgmental call. "*Dane fucking Kingsley, of all people. What would have happened if—*"

"He's really nice," I cut in.

"How is breaking someone's arm nice—"

"He didn't—Okay, context is important," I bite out, pressing my hand to my brow bone when she scoffs and rolls her eyes.

"What's going to happen when he loses his temper and decides to take it out on you?"

My temple pulses irritably as my frustration blooms hot in my chest. Of course, she wouldn't let me expand. A brick wall would literally be easier to talk to. At least it wouldn't interrupt me before I managed to get more than ten words in.

"You don't know him like I do," I argue. "And he would *never* hurt me—"

"You'd have to be the most gullible idiot in the world to believe that—"

"He's the sweetest guy I've ever met. *He is*," I insist when she snorts resoundingly. "He picks me up from work—"

"*Oh, so you don't lie to* him *about when you're working?*" Her upper lip curls. "*Just me?*"

A renewed sense of annoyance overtakes me like a thick fog. Despite my feelings, I swallow hard and keep sweet. "*Because* he doesn't want me to take the bus back—"

"Sounds pretty controlling to me."

"I *won't* let you twist everything he's done for me because you assume the worst of him," I hiss, shoving to my feet. "He's kind. *Considerate*. He makes it a point to let me know when he locks the door—"

"So you know you can't escape?"

"So I can sleep knowing no one is going to break in!" I cry out, and the color leeches from her sun-kissed skin. "He sleeps closer to the window for me. When I'm having panic attacks, he comforts me the best he can because he cares about me." My hands clasp over my heart. "He's never once made me feel lame or boring for my hobbies and interests. Even though they're not his thing, he supports me regardless. He got me a camera and—"

"He got you a camera?" Her face screws up intensely with shock.

"And a car," I admit.

"Oh my God, I thought you were better than that," Lilian hisses. "You sound *just* like Mom right now. Ignoring all the red flags because a man buys you things. *Wow*. She would be so proud of you for being a fantastic gold digger—"

"I'm *not* a gold digger." Mortification blazes across my cheeks. Raw hurt takes root in me as I shoot her a disbelieving stare. I would never compare her to our mom. *Never*. "He gave me the car he taught me to drive in."

"Oh, wow," Lilian deadpans. "So, you're his sugar baby? Is that it?"

"Because he gets me nice things? So do you—"

"Not a car!"

"It has never stopped you from dipping into your student loans to buy me things *outside* your means," I remind her. "You bought me a dress—"

"Do you seriously think a dress compares to a car?" she screeches. "Are you fucking kidding me?"

"You buy expensive things for everybody," I say. "You spent *three hundred dollars* on a rave suit for Jenna, which she'll only wear once because she doesn't do repeat outfits."

She gnashes her teeth in a vicious growl. "Do you *honestly* believe he got you a *car* and—what?—a fancy camera because he *likes* you? Be real here. *He likes you because of these.*" She gestures to her breasts. "He's a guy, Reese!"

My face flames as the ache sharpens in my chest. "Do you truly think that little of me to believe he only likes me because of my body?" My words are so painstakingly soft that the question nearly sticks in my throat.

Despite her huff of breath, remorse etches across her profile. "That's not what I meant."

"So you can twist my words all you want, but I can't interpret yours?" My jaw sets as I glare at her. "You don't know a single thing about him—"

"You're deluding yourself," she cuts me off. "He's a dirtbag."

"No, *you're* deluding yourself," I reply hotly. "You're completely wrong about him. You only know what *Travis* said, and that guy is a liar, a sleaze—"

"Because he's in a frat?"

"Because he is a major sleazeball." My voice gains an edge. "I texted you about it—He made degrading comments about you. He called me a charity case. He basically confirmed that Dane broke his arm—"

"Because he did—"

"In *self*-defense," I snarl. "Travis was the one who *shanked* him, and you're too dickmatized to realize the truth."

"You're the one too dickmatized to accept the truth," Lilian retorts, her mouth twisting into a hard sneer. "A rich guy gives you some attention for once and—"

"Don't be an asshole."

"Don't be naïve."

"I didn't fall for him because he gave me attention," I snap. "I'm in love with him because he's kind and thoughtful and sweet to me—"

"No, he's not kind or sweet or whatever nonsense you think he is." A humorless laugh escapes her. "You wanna know who's actually kind and sweet?"

"Swear to God, if you say Travis," I begin, only for her to roll her eyes.

"Caleb," she spits out. "The actual nice guy you dumped."

"Caleb?" My brow scrunches at the thought of him. I mean, she's not wrong. He's always busy taking his sisters to their gymnastics routine. He'll rescue spiders from their doom. He never has a mean thing to say about anybody. "Sure, I guess—"

"And he's respectful—"

"So is Dane—"

"*Caleb* would treat you with genuine respect," Lilian barrels on. "And you have a lot more in common with him—"

"I have a lot in common with the friends I make online," I say blandly. "That doesn't mean anything—"

"Yes. Yes, it does. Because Caleb would never hurt you—"

"Dane wouldn't." I will *not* let her steamroll the conversation. "And you're the last person to talk. You think Travis is innocent when he's a total slimeball—"

"Caleb would *never*—"

"You don't know that. Maybe Caleb's a slimeball, too?" I suggest, incensed. "He's not infallible. He could have ended up hurting me—"

"He wouldn't!"

"That's the point. You don't know that—"

"Yes, I do!"

I want to drag my fingernails down my face. Can she go one minute without cutting me off? This is so like her. I just want to be able to get in more than three sentences without her interrupting me incessantly like an annoying smoke alarm in dire need of a battery change.

"Lilian—"

"He would *never* hurt you—"

"Oh, I didn't realize I was talking to a psychic." My glare turns withering. "How can you be *so* freaking sure he'll never hurt me?"

"Because we paid him to!" she snarls.

"You—" The rest of my words die on my tongue as the world comes to a screeching halt.

Her anger gives way to horror as her hand slowly rises to her mouth.

"You..." The air drags raggedly through my lungs. "You... paid him to?" *To what? Be friends with me?* Or... No. *Please, no.*

A lump lodges in my throat. She won't meet my gaze. She refuses to as I desperately search her face for *any* other answer, and time expands. No, it *freezes.*

Oh God. No. A sharp ache twists painfully between my ribs. My chest constricts. My pulse rings in my ears. My face goes hot, as do my eyes when it occurs to me that my sister—my best friend; someone I've looked up to my entire life; someone who's always sworn she'd never let anybody hurt me; someone I've always trusted with every inch of my heart and soul—has... paid a guy to go out with me.

Sudden tears blur the edges of my vision.

"Reese," she rasps, but my head shakes as nausea threatens to overtake me. "*Reese*, please listen—"

I shoulder past her and break into a sprint. Scrambling out of her bedroom, my rib cage heaves with every labored breath as I rush for the stairs. Reaching the main floor, I skid to a halt when my neck prickles with an alarming amount of awareness. It feels as though I've been thrust under a spotlight.

Swiveling to my right, I'm rendered stock-still. Frozen in place at the sight of Lilian's sorority sisters. All staring at me. With varying expressions of stricken shock on their faces and— *Oh God.*

"Little Vann," Jenna stammers, but hurt propels me forward. I'm out the door before they can shout for me to wait, my heart fracturing down the middle when I hear my sister calling for me.

The heel of my palm presses hard into my cheek as I rush across the street. My nail almost breaks against the handle as I yank the passenger door open, and Dane jolts, barely glancing at me before the muscles of his jaw go taut.

"Reese?" He sits up straight. "What's wrong?"

A tear slides down my cheek, and his frame goes utterly rigid. Concern gathers in his eyes, and devastation claims me. A whimper slides free, and my throat closes tight.

I try to find my words, but I can't. I simply can't. Nothing comes to mind. Everything just… hurts. The sting in my chest sprawls deeper into an overwhelming ache, and I break into a sob before I can help myself.

"Can we please get out of here?"

42

DANE

THE CAR EASES TO A STOP, AND REESE LIFTS HER HEAD TO PEER OUT the window. I pretend to observe the scenery until she glances my way. Her bottom lip trembles. She sniffles, then rubs her eyes with the inside of her wrist.

She's been doing that the entire drive.

It took all of my willpower to focus on getting us here in one piece without pulling over to the shoulder once. I don't know what happened with her sister last Saturday. She hasn't said anything since she left the sorority house crying her heart out. While it kills me to be left in the dark this past week, she'll tell me when she's ready. I know she will.

Now that we've arrived at the track, the gut feeling to do whatever I can to figure out what's wrong is barely outmatched by the need to put an end to those tears.

"Reese," I say, drawing her attention toward me. "We don't have to do this if you're not feeling up to it."

With another sniffle, her watery smile gives way to a sad, mournful grimace. "I'm up to it," she insists, as her shoulders droop. "*I am*. I swear."

"Baby, we can always reschedule and come back another day—"

"No." Her head shakes vehemently. "We're going to have fun. I'm not going to be a buzzkill, so move aside, Danny boy, and I'll prove it to you."

Her eyes glitter through her tears when she finally meets my gaze.

"Danny boy?" I huff, the edges of my mouth tilting up into a smirk. She blinks innocently at me, and I chuckle. "You're lucky I find you cute."

"Enough to let me get away with singing about how the pipes are calling?"

"Baby, I will turn the car around the second you belt out the first word of the song," I warn her and break into a lopsided grin as a full-blown smile steals across her face. Then she laughs for the first time in days, and it's so damn sweet. "There she is. There's my Reese's Pieces."

Her expression softens into something bashful. Ducking her head, she plays with the material of her sweater. Then she inhales softly when I reach over and wipe away the stray tear trickling down her cheek.

She redirects her focus toward me as I leisurely stroke the rise of her cheekbone.

"I hope she stays around a little longer," I continue, "but I understand if she needs some more time to herself."

Her eyes alight with amusement, and after a drawn-out beat, she leans into my hand. I wait for her to say something, but she doesn't.

She doesn't have to. We sit there in comfortable silence. My thumb continues to caress her cheek while she holds my gaze. Her eyes are starry-soft, her lips curved into a gentle smile.

With an audible swallow, her hand wraps around my wrist and gives me a gentle squeeze before she pulls away from my touch. "Let's drive."

"*Let's*"—I reach into the backseat—"make sure you drink some water first." My heart swells at the immediate grin pulling at the corner of her mouth. "What kind of boyfriend would I be if I didn't make sure you had some water after you cried?"

Taking the plastic bottle, she beams. "You should consider getting a reusable one. It's better for the planet."

"With the cars I have?" I deadpan. "Don't know if it'll do much, but I'll get right on it." I hike my chin toward the window. "You wanna take the first lap?"

Twisting the cap off, she shakes her head. "You should go first." She pauses, sheepish. "I kind of want my eyes to stop feeling so scratchy before I drive."

"All right, Snack Mix." I lean back and grab the helmets stashed in the backseat—her brows furrow when I hand her the smaller one of the two.

"We have to—"

"We have to."

"Really?"

"*Yes*." My voice is firm.

"But the movies—"

"I'm *not* driving over eighty without you wearing one," I growl. "The movies are bullshit. This is real life. I'd never forgive myself if you got hurt because of me."

"Okay, okay." She giggles softly and drains the rest of her water. "I was just surprised, that's all."

With a lopsided grin, I help secure her helmet over her head, check her seatbelt, and chuckle when she hooks her pinky around mine before I'm able to settle back in my seat.

Once I've secured mine on and readjusted the side-view mirrors, I look ahead. The ribboning track sprawls before us, every inch of tarmac being mapped out under my direct gaze.

The rush of anticipation greets me when I turn the key. The instant the clutch engages, I let off and give it plenty of gas, met with the gratifying rumble of Ol' Reliable's engine.

With one hand on the steering wheel and the other on the gear shifter, the scenery fades into the backdrop as my vehicle sets off and accelerates down the stretch. Screeching tires fight for traction and bite into the paved surface as the vehicle swings along the hairpin turn.

My adrenaline builds; my pulse thrums. My heart soars as the air turns charged within an electrifying moment. It's heaven. Euphoria. Fucking exhilarating.

It's just me and my girl, and I wouldn't have it any other way.

***

"YOU DON'T HAVE TO DRIVE FAST, SPEED DEMON." I CHUCKLE WHEN Reese shoots me a sidelong glance and sticks her tongue out. "You know it's just us right now. We've got the track to ourselves for another hour, so feel free to go slower than an electric scooter if you want."

"I will be faster than that," she replies, leveling me with an utmost solemn expression. "I'm thinking of coasting along at e-bike speed." At once, something serious flickers across her features. "Do you really trust me with your car?"

"Do my carburetors have a return spring?" When I'm met with a blank and confused look, I hold back my snort of amusement. "I trust you with all of them."

"But what if I—"

"You're *not* going to crash it," I assure her. "You can go as slow as you want. There's no shame in that."

Her gaze softens, and I grin. "Before I forget," she whispers. "Can I go fifty-five in second gear?"

My smile takes on a very strained edge as my brows slowly crash together. "Well, yes."

Amusement tugs at her lips as she leans in closer, a mischievous glint in her eyes. "Should I go fifty-five in second gear?"

In response, my face becomes utterly impassive, and I give her a humorless stare. "What do you think?" I ask blandly, and she dissolves into giggles.

Picking up her helmet, she adorably taps it against mine. "I got this."

I don't respond. I just look at my girl and take in the sight of her steeled shoulders, her furrowed brows, and the way her lips twist into a determined grin.

Right then and there, my pulse kicks up a few notches, as if my heart's firing on all cylinders. "Fuck yeah, you do."

"Fuck yeah, I do." She beams at me something brighter than the sun while she lifts her helmet above her head. "I so got this."

"I MEAN IT. YOUR MOTORCYCLE IS *NEXT*," REESE SINGS WHILE SHE enters her apartment first. Her hair is slightly wet from the sudden rain we were caught in, and her cheeks are still flushed with the afterglow of adrenaline.

"You got it." I flash her a thumbs-up after I twist the lock and secure the deadbolt, and her eyes crinkle. The second she steps away, my arm hooks around her midsection, and she shrieks when I hoist her into the air. "How does next week sound?"

"I'll have to see if I'm working." Her forefinger traces a heart over my chest, then another. "I should feed the cat."

She captures my lips with a kiss that ends far too soon when she peels away and wriggles herself out of my embrace. I reluctantly set her down.

"Thank you again for today. It really took my mind off..." Her sentence peters out as she grabs the bag of kibble.

"Glad it did."

"You don't have to keep doing this." Her rasp deepens her husky voice. "Taking me out on these expensive dates or getting me expensive things."

"Root beer dates are expensive now?" I tease, eliciting a weak smile in return, and my smirk fades away. She won't meet my eyes. She peers at her shoe rack for a long minute before her gaze snaps to mine.

"I don't want to be your sugar baby," she blurts, and I bite back my groan of frustration. The entire purpose of the racetrack today was to cheer her up; not make her feel more guilty.

"You're not my sugar baby." My voice is firm and unwavering while I bridge the gap between us. She hugs the cat food to her chest and reroutes her focus to her coffee table. "You're my girlfriend. Someone I like to treat to make up for all the bullshit she has to put up with 'cause of me. I'm kidding. I just want you to be happy. That's all."

She spares me a rueful glance, then pulls her bottom lip between her teeth. "I... I'm sorry. I know. I appreciate everything you've done. Everything you've gotten for me. I..." She trails off, and her cheeks turn splotchier. "Thanks for being a great boyfriend."

Her words would be more convincing if she weren't on the brink of tears. It doesn't help one bit that her voice breaks at the end of her sentence.

"I love the enthusiasm," I say teasingly, only to frown when she hastily wipes at the abrupt tear streaking down her cheek. "Will you tell me what's actually upsetting you, Reese?"

"I... found out..." She hiccups. "I found out that Caleb was paid to go out with me."

A hoarse exhalation slips free. "*Fuck*," I mutter, and she doesn't resist when I fold her easily into my arms and stroke her back. "When did they tell you?"

"*They*?" She tenses against me and jerks her head back, and her teary eyes collide with mine.

Fuck. I try to backtrack, but the words stick in my throat. Air seizes in my lungs as horror slowly dawns across her face.

"You... knew."

"Baby—"

She wrenches herself out of my embrace and frantically scuttles backward. I move one step forward, only for her to add more distance between us until her back thumps against her bedroom door.

"You knew?" Her visible distress is eclipsed by the hurt inflicting her tone. Pure devastation racks her small frame, and she whimpers when I try to draw nearer.

Flinching, I stop partway. "I can explain—"

"*You knew*?" she cries out. "Since when?"

I hesitate, and my throat bobs with a rough swallow. The few seconds bleed into endless eternity. "For a while."

My admission is met with radio silence and wounded eyes. My gut clenches at the sight, and guilt settles thick in my heart when they start to glisten in the dim apartment lights.

"Since. When?"

Panic grips my chest. I don't want to lie to her—I don't want to be the one who hurts her—but it's too little, too late for that. I fucked up. I fucked up big time. Anything but the whole damn truth would just be me digging a deeper grave.

"Before we started dating."

The living room falls into heavy silence. It's so unnervingly quiet that you can almost hear the low purr from the tabby as he slinks over to the food bowl.

"Did they pay you to go out with me, too?"

I almost frown. "Does it look like I need the mon—"

"Or are you, like, only dating me because I'm a charity case—"

"A *what*?"

"—and you feel bad for me?" she stammers. "Is any of this even real?"

The sting in my chest gives way to an overwhelming ache. Disbelief clouds my features. "How could you even ask that? Of course, it's real."

"You're lying. Nothing about this is genuine. You just feel bad for me like everyone else and-and—Oh God." Her focus slices to the whiteboard beside her, and something stricken washes over her profile and crushes my heart into a pulp. "You owe me a favor—"

"I'm not with you because I owe you one," I insist, and she

shakes her head in response. "Baby, I know you're upset, but what we have is real. I promise you—"

"*Leave.* Please go." Her despair comes off her in waves, hanging palpably in the air. "I want to be left alone—"

"Baby—"

"*Please.*" The raw anguish settling on her face kills me. It fucking kills me. "I can't look at you right now."

My breath freezes in my lungs, and I'm terrified at the path lying out before us. I'm fucking terrified this is how it'll end.

This isn't what I want. Not in any shape or form. I don't want it to end like this. I don't want her to be left alone when she's on the verge of breaking down into tears. I don't want to give her up.

But I've already caused enough damage.

"I'll leave," I begin, shoving my hands into my pockets and ignoring how every part of me is silently screaming in protest. "If that's what you want—"

"It's what I want." She hiccups just then and presses her palm to her cheek as a tear spills freely down her face.

I suck in a sharp breath. "But I promise you," I swear, "that everything I've felt about you—everything I've done for you— has always been sincere. It has always been real."

Her lower lip trembles, but she doesn't respond. She just sniffles and casts a glance at the floorboards by her feet.

"I'll give you some space," I add, even though my heart drums incessantly in objection. I *can't* leave her here by herself. Not while she's upset. Especially not while she's crying.

I want nothing more than to comfort her. Cheer her up. Do everything that I can to put an end to her pain. But nothing comes to mind except her one request, as much as I hate to admit it. As much as I know it's the right thing to do.

"And you know that I'll be here for you the moment you need me," I continue roughly. "You know that. You have my number. Doesn't matter if it's three in the morning. Text me when you need me, and I'll be right over."

Still, she doesn't say a word. The silence is killing me, along with the very fact that she refuses to look me in the eye. I can feel the one and only good thing I have going for me slipping through my fingers as I force myself to walk away.

I've barely taken two steps toward her door when she wheezes.

"I thought you said you'd never lie to me?"

"*Never.*" At once, I regret that word as I swing around to face her.

"Why didn't you tell me the truth?" comes out in a mere whisper.

A pang of regret ricochets through my chest. I wish I knew how to answer that question without fucking things up like I always do. "I didn't want you to get hurt."

"I thought you said I was strong."

"You are strong."

"Do you even believe that?" Her choked sob breaks free and shreds my heart into pieces. I barely edge forward and halt mid-stride when she holds her palm out. "Are you just making things up for me because you feel bad for me—"

"No."

"We don't have anything in common," she rasps. "Why are you even with me—"

"You see the good in me." My voice holds firm, and her breath hitches. It takes every ounce of my willpower to remain rooted in place. "You've always seen the good in me, even when no one else did. Even when you heard that I was dangerous, you looked past that. You *never* believed that. You're so damn kind and sweet and good to me, and you've never once made me feel like crap about myself." I pause. "Except for right now, of course, for obvious reasons, which I deserve."

A quiet snort escapes her. The corner of her lips twitches as she fights her smile. "Don't make me laugh, Kingsley," she grumbles. "I'm mad at you."

"You have every right to be," I reply. "I feel like absolute shit for not telling you the truth about Blue Balls sooner. I should have told you the moment I found out what was going on."

She hugs her arms to her chest and casts a sidelong glance at the cat. "And… when did you find out?"

"Right before I hit on you," I admit, rubbing the back of my neck.

She blinks against her shock and furrows her brows while she processes my words. "In the back?" Her thumb goes over her shoulder. "While you were escaping the cops?"

I open my mouth to object, but she fixes me with an incredulous stare, and I wince. Yeah, I was trying to ditch them that night. There's no point in denying it.

"At the party. One of the sorority girls told me what they did. How they paid him to go out with you," I clarify. "Why'd you think I made a jackass out of myself in front of everybody that night?"

"Oh my God?" she strangles out. "*That's* what that was?"

With another wince, I scratch the back of my head. "If it makes you feel any better, I was *pissed* when I found out about their plan. I wanted to tell you right away, but… *fuck*. She didn't want you to be devastated. I didn't, either. And you looked so happy with him—"

"Who, Caleb?"

"You wouldn't stop smiling and laughing at all the boring ass shit he said," I mutter. "You just looked so damn happy with him, and I didn't want to be the guy who took it away. I like seeing you happy. The world feels brighter when you're happy. It always has."

Holding my gaze, she brings her wrist to her cheek and dries her tears.

"If I could go back to the night of the party," I go on, "I'd give you a heads-up about him."

Her hand stills. "Like how you went up to me and loudly—"

A long groan expels from the base of my throat, and she

presses her lips together to smother her laugh. "I'm *never* going to live that down, huh?"

"I don't think so." Her mouth hitches at the corner, and I let loose a chuckle.

"I wouldn't be that tactless. I would have texted you to meet me outside so I could tell you to dump the loser."

"You did tell me to dump him," she mutters, clearly lost in thought.

"Reese, I swear to you," I continue, "it was *never* my intention to hurt you. I wanted to tell you, but Kayla—"

"Karla?"

"Her," I confirm. "I wanted to tell you, but Karla said it would devastate you, and I didn't want to do that to you. I didn't want to be the asshole who broke the news to you and hurt you in the process."

Her attention drifts to her fridge. To the fucking *I OWE YOU ONE* message still scrawled onto the whiteboard. "You weren't in on it?"

"Paying fucking Blue Balls?" I scoff, and she redirects her focus toward me. "Fuck no. I would have told the girls to get the fuck out of here with that nonsense and gave you the real first boyfriend experience you deserved."

"I mean... you are my real first boyfriend," she points out softly as her lips wobble. "If you think about it."

My mouth curves into a hesitant grin. "I'm honored to be your only boyfriend."

She snickers and shakes her head. Her smile lingers for a fleeting moment before it fades away. She peers at the floor.

I wait patiently for her to say something else, but she doesn't. When an entire minute passes, it's obvious she's got nothing left to ask.

Reluctantly, I break the silence. "Still mad at me?"

She swallows audibly. "Not really? I don't know. I'm so overwhelmed," she admits. "I'm hurt you didn't tell me, but you were caught between a rock and a hard place. I can see why you didn't tell me… I wouldn't know what to do if I were in your shoes."

The knot in my chest begins to unravel. She's too damn reasonable and kind. She always sees the good in people— always sees the good in me. "That's fair, Snack Mix. Take all the time you need." I hesitate. "Do you still want me to leave and give you some space?"

Her response is instant: a quick shake of her head. It relieves some tension from the line of my shoulders.

"Do you want me to stay?"

"I don't know," she whispers, and I don't miss the reluctance in her voice.

"I'll sleep on the springy futon if it comes down to it," I offer, grinning when she spares me a snort. When I take a step toward her, she doesn't seem to recoil or flinch, which is a massive improvement from a few minutes ago.

"I'm extremely embarrassed right now," she admits as she walks into my embrace.

"That's okay—you can feel however you want to feel."

"You must think I'm such a loser—"

"Hey, don't diss my girl by calling her that," I say, looping my arms around her waist. "I won't allow any more slander to happen on my watch."

"But I am one," she mumbles into my chest. "My sister and her friends *paid* a guy to go out with me."

"You're not a loser," I argue. "They're losers for doing that to you. They had no right to do that to you."

Her head pulls back, her long hair brushing my knuckles while she scans my face. Uncertainty creases the lines of her eyes. "You didn't date me because you feel bad—"

"Baby, I've wanted you for much longer than that," I cut in. "Before I even found out about him."

"You did?" Surprise registers on her face. "Really?"

"I'd never lie to you." I flinch at my words, and my body becomes taut while she pulls away completely. Even though my statement is nothing but the truth, now's *not* the time. "I mean it. I would have pursued you relentlessly if things had been different. If you never had a crush on Blue Balls in the first place? I would have been *all over you*."

Her brows knit together. "Really?"

"Cross my heart. I didn't want to get in the way of what you wanted, even if it sucked. You asked for my help to get some idiot who couldn't recognize how great you are. His. Fucking. Loss. You're the best thing to happen to me. You're a great girl, Reese. I'm lucky as fuck just to have you in my life."

With a soft inhale, she offers me a watery smile while her eyes begin to glisten.

My throat tightens as I reach up to gently wipe her tears away. "I mean it. As fucking ridiculous as it sounds, I'm glad I met you that night behind the coffee shop, even if it meant getting my ass curb-stomped by two whack jobs. If that night had never happened? If they had never chased me into that alleyway? We might not have ever met and, well, that'd be a crying shame."

My grin is tentative, but it broadens when she leans into my touch.

"You're really sweet," Reese whispers, and she gnaws on her bottom lip for a contemplative moment. "You don't have to leave, Dane. You can sleep on the springy futon if you want."

I eye the furniture warily with as much reluctance as the cat did with the bell collar. It beats going home. Even if it means my back will become reacquainted with that damn spring. "Really?"

"No." She lets out a dry laugh. "I'd like some cuddles from my boyfriend. I feel extremely lousy right now, and he's the only person in the world who doesn't make me feel bad at the moment."

"I'll give you all the cuddles you want. We can even watch one of 'em movies you like, too."

"I'm not really in the mood for that." Even though she hasn't cried for a short while now, her voice is still huskier. At a lower register. "Can we watch a movie you like?"

"Don't really have one," I say, eliciting a horrified gasp from her, and I snort in response.

"We can watch car flicks then."

"I'll complain the whole time," I warn her.

"That's okay," she says. "I'll complain about the bad acting and the terrible amount of camera cuts the films manage to have in under half a minute."

I'm unable to hold back my smile. It graces my lips as something sweet crinkles the corners of her eyes. She doesn't flinch or pull away from me when I draw her into my arms. In fact, she falls into my embrace so easily that my heart gives an easy beat.

"Sounds like a date."

43

REESE

My eyes are scratchy and dry when I wake up tucked into Dane's side. I don't remember going to bed or putting on his shirt over my thin camisole. He must have put it on me when I fell asleep during our movie marathon. Something inside me warms at the gesture.

For a short spell, I stare at the wall and watch the gentle shades of the pale yellow sunlight drench the room. Unbidden, my breath catches in my lungs as the Caleb situation comes to mind. Mortification grips me once more. Hurt floods my system.

I don't know how to feel about it. I don't know if it's possible to get over how humiliating it is.

Stinging tears blur my vision just then. I suck in a lungful of air and bite back my sob when Dane slings his arm around my waist and draws me into the warm shelter of his body. His coarse leg hair is scratchy against my thighs. His breath hits my neck as his fingers link through mine.

"I know, I know," he murmurs into my hair. "It's a crying shame his Charger got totaled."

A stifled snort escapes me. My eyes squeeze shut as a stray tear rolls down my cheek and splatters onto the pillow.

"At least it wasn't a Stang," he continues, and my shoulders shake with quiet laughter. "That would have been the real tragedy."

Carefully peeling myself out of his embrace, my elbow nearly connects with the wall when I turn around to meet his gaze. His oversized shirt bunches up awkwardly against my hip and spine in the process.

His sharp features tighten with concern, and his mouth pulls into a firm line. With measured slowness, he brings the pad of his thumb to my cheekbone and dries my tears. "Hey, come here."

"This is a twin bed," I grumble, bridging the inch between us. "I'm already here."

With a low chuckle, he somehow manages to tug me in closer to his hard chest. Even though I know the weekend's over and that I have a calculus quiz in an hour, I cling to him and listen to the steady rhythm of his heartbeat.

"I'm so embarrassed," I admit.

"That's okay."

"I'm *really* embarrassed."

"That's fair." He begins to stroke the line of my back.

I swallow roughly. My voice is small when I find it. "I hate that they did this."

His response is immediate. "I'll put them on my list."

"There shouldn't be a list," I mumble, and a soft laugh breaks free while I rub my bleary eyes.

"Then they shouldn't have done this," he grumbles, "if they didn't want to go on my list."

Despite myself, I rasp out a chuckle. "I wish I could continue calling out sick," I admit. "I don't want to see any of them."

I haven't shown up to work since my fight with Lilian. Knowing my sister, she'll camp out at the campus bookstore and wait to corner me into a conversation I don't want to have. Not right now. Not ever, if I had a choice. Why would I subject myself to another argument where she won't let me get in a single word?

"I'll be your bouncer," he offers. "I'll turn them around. If they refuse, I'll scare them away, yeah? How does that sound?"

"Like you have too much time on your hands," I say without missing a beat, and he snorts.

Before he can respond, my alarm goes off. With a groan, he reaches blindly for my phone, and the buzzing sound halts a few seconds later.

"What if we stay in today? We can attempt to make our own copycat pancakes from the pancake house." He pauses. "Learn how to make artsy ones for your fiesta."

"I wish," I murmur. "I have a quiz worth five percent of my grade, and I don't think my professor will let me retake it because I'm hurt that my sister paid a guy to go out with me."

"You don't know that," he says. "Check the syllabus before you jump to a conclusion."

I let loose a soft peal of laughter, my eyes sinking closed while his lips skim against my hairline. "I'm pretty sure it won't be in any of them." Reluctance weighs heavily on my mind as I detangle myself from his embrace, and my shoulders immediately hit the wall with an audible thump.

This bed is not meant for two people, especially those as tall as Dane, who always sleeps with his legs curled into mine whenever he stays over. Even so, I love the closeness it grants us.

His hand slides to my upper back and gently kneads away the faint sting, and his voice breaks my train of thought. "You okay, Reese?"

"I will be," I whisper back and reroute my focus from his chest to his eyes. I know we're not talking about my shoulder.

The corner of his lips tilts up while the rough feel of his palm trails to my jawline. "Fuck yeah, you will be."

"I will be," I repeat, steadily holding his gaze. Determination sets in and straightens my spine. Even though I'm not fully certain I'll get over my mortification right now, I've dealt with much worse. If I can survive nearly dying on my bedroom floor almost two years ago, surely I can handle what Lilian and her sorority sisters did.

I EXPECTED TO RUN INTO MY SISTER AT THE CAMPUS BOOKSTORE; NOT while I was heading out of the Science Building. Maybe I should have seen it coming. With all the STEM courses I'm taking this semester, I have a lot of lectures in this building. Heck, I have a late class tonight in the same classroom I just left.

"Reese," she calls out.

Indignation hardens my mouth into a harsh slant, and I stare ahead. My pace quickens, and I'm power-walking away from her like she's one of those pushy solicitors on campus trying to get people to sign an obscure petition. It's no use. With legs much longer than mine, she easily falls into step beside me.

"We need to talk," she continues, and her words are enough to put a pit in my stomach.

"We do not," I counter, growing stiff when she grabs the bend of my arm. "Let go of me—"

"I'll let go when we—"

"*No*," I bite out and shrug her off of me. Her stiletto nail snags onto the knit material of my sweater and unravels the yarn when I roughly pull away. "I don't want to talk to you right now."

"I need to explain—"

"I don't want to hear it," I reiterate, heatedly swiveling toward her. Our eyes collide, and her breath hitches. "What I want is some space—"

"Will you let me explain—"

"Seriously, Lilian? *Save it*," I hiss. "You've *never* given me the chance to explain anything, so why should I give you the same courtesy?"

Taken aback, she opens her mouth, only to catch herself at the last second. She presses her lips together and tersely nods.

My jaw becomes tight as I forge on. "You wouldn't talk to me for *weeks* when you found out I lied to you a couple of times about when I was working, so why don't you give me the same amount of time now that I've found out you *lied* to me for *months* about Caleb?"

It takes everything I have to keep my frame from trembling while I level her with a reproachful glare. It takes twice as much effort not to crumble like a sandcastle and apologize for my petty remark. The people-pleaser in me wants to smooth things over, but I will *not* have my feelings dismissed anymore.

"I'm hurt by what you did. I'm beyond hurt. I'm *humiliated*." My hand flies up when it's clear she's about to respond. "I don't want to hear your excuses. Give me some space if you want me to get over this. I can't heal or move on from this if you're always steamrolling me into forgiving you because you decide that now is the time to resolve things between us. That's not fair."

"I'm sorry," she whispers. "For everything. I truly am—"

"Save it," I wheeze, hugging my arms to my chest. "Please don't ask for my forgiveness, because you're only going to make things worse. Just *go*. Please."

"I didn't mean to—"

"You didn't mean to pay Caleb?" I almost explode. My face blazes as I stare at her in disbelief. I don't want to hear her rationale as to why she paid him to go out with me in the first place. "It just accidentally happened? Money somehow slipped into his hand and he instinctively knew what to do? Just—*Leave me alone*."

Pivoting on my feet, I stalk off before things get worse between us. She doesn't follow. Thank God. In a desperate attempt to distract myself, I try to fix my sweater while I head toward the tutoring center.

I wish I could feel vindicated. I wish I felt happy or justified I stood up for myself, but I'm just sad. Irrevocably so. My heartache hangs over me like a gloomy cloud. My mind is foggy, my eyes are still puffy and sting with fresh tears, and my throat is so dry that it hurts to breathe.

Sniffling hard, I only jolt out of my little pity party when my name sounds across the quad. Embarrassment flushes across my cheeks the second I spot Caleb jogging toward me, and despite turning the other way, he easily catches up.

"Are you being paid to talk to me right now?" The words hiss between my clenched teeth.

He halts, wincing. "You have every right to be mad—"

"I *am* mad." A mix of fury and disbelief spears me while I level him with an agitated glare. "How could you?"

"If you'd let me explain—"

"Go ahead," I grit out. "Explain how you pretended to like me for money."

His throat bobs reflexively. "You have every right to be upset, Reese. I'm pissed the girls forced me to go out—" He expels a hoarse breath. "That sounds way worse out loud."

"It really does," I confirm with a too-bright smile, then tread toward a different walkway and glower at the palm trees nearby when he matches pace with my strides. "Do I have to pay you to leave me alone?"

He flinches. "The girls paid me, yes, but I would have turned them down if I didn't need the money."

"Nice to know where your principles lie," I say flatly. "Thank you for the truth. You can leave me alone now."

"I think I told you that my dad got injured at work," he goes on, and dammit, my brain is quick to snag onto the fact that he has two younger sisters he's been taking care of in his free time. His mom's picking up more hours to make ends meet, and his dad still hasn't returned to work after a scaffolding accident last summer. Rent's been increasing, too. "My sisters have gymnastics—"

"I know." *Because I genuinely cared about you while you pretended to like me for cash.* My eyes prickle with tears I don't want to cry. Not over him.

"Savannah and Quinn had all these fees my mom couldn't afford, and—" He blows out a weary breath and streaks his fingers through his hair. "That's just me trying to justify it. I agreed to do something awful to you. I shouldn't have; not even when the girls strong-armed me into it."

"Your sisters?"

"No. Peyton, Karla, Jenna, Chrissy—all of them," he clarifies. "They told me you had a raging crush on me." He cringes when I squeak in horror. "And that I should ask you out. I didn't want to—*because there's someone else,*" he tacks on quickly. "But they all gave me crap about it and said I was an awful human being—called me the worst guy on earth for not giving you a chance because of your scar."

"And you thought being the awful guy who *pretends* to like me is a better alternative to being known as the awful guy who's superficial about my scar?"

"I know. I'm sorry. I didn't want to piss off the girl I like and—"

"The girl you like?" I echo, and my brow shoots up while he shakes his head.

"It's nothing," he splutters, but my mind is racing with the process of elimination of who would be most offended, and my eyes go wide. His ears tint red as he clears his throat and aims his line of sight directly above my head. "You've been nothing but nice to me. I'd always feel shitty after every date the girls would help me plan."

"You never liked any of that stuff?" I whisper, and he blinks.

"Well, no, I do," he stammers. "I think we would've become friends if not for their meddling. We like the same stuff. Lili Pad used to talk about you to me all the time. She would always ask me for movie recs for you."

"Oh." My eyes suddenly sting with tears.

"Honestly, though," he continues. "I was kind of hoping you'd realize there was nothing there between us and end things with me."

"You were?"

"I never made a move on you for a reason," Caleb says.

I swallow hard. My brain can't stop overanalyzing every meandering date of ours and how they all felt like friends hanging out. *Because that's what they were. Just two friends hanging out.*

He expels a wry chuckle. "I even took you to see this band I hated because I was hoping the date would be so bad, you'd end it once and for all."

I blink, stunned. He made me endure avant-garde experimental screaming for that? "But… you tried to get me to change my mind when I said we should end things," I remind him. "You asked me to take you back."

"I was just covering my tracks. I didn't want the girls to accuse me of sabotaging things again," he says. "They got on my ass and told me to try harder after the concert date, and I didn't want to risk them blowing up on me if I didn't try to fight for you or something."

"Seriously?" I gasp, and he reluctantly nods. "But you showed up at my apartment right before Christmas."

"The girls were pushing me to *step up* and *be the man* they paid for, since you were still having a hard time with your attack," he mutters. "I knew you weren't going to take me back. I just wanted the girls to stop pestering me once you turned me down."

My brow lifts. *Was this after my attempt to call Travis out at the sorority house?* "You knew I wasn't going to take you back?"

"I mean, yeah?" he chuckles. "I know you're dating Kingsley. I've known for a while. I've seen him pick you up while I was leaving practice for months now. He's, like, right there in front of the music building every night. It's kind of hard not to notice his loud cars. Also, he did make an ass out of himself at the girls' Halloween party for you, and that guy hates everybody he comes across."

I gawp at him like a fish. "Did you tell anyone about us?" I gasp, and he shakes his head. "Why not?"

"Lili Pad doesn't like him," he says, and that's the understatement of the year. "Figured I'd give you the chance to tell her about him yourself."

"Oh." My voice tapers off, and he shrugs. "Thank you for that."

He gives me a nod. "I understand if you want nothing to do with me ever again," he says. "I'm genuinely sorry for my involvement in this—"

"Did the girls really push you to do this?"

"Yeah. They dogpiled the crap out of me," he says. "Kept accusing me of being shallow, mean, cruel, and all these things for not wanting to date you."

"And… you didn't want to piss off my sister," I hedge, and his ears go red again. "Or have her think you were shallow and cruel to her sister?"

He releases an awkward cough, then another, suddenly invested in the succulent nearby. "If I could do anything to make it up to you, let me know. But I won't blame you if you never want to talk to me again."

I hesitate. For a contemplating moment, I rock on the balls of my feet, then chew on the inside of my cheek. I feel bad he was pressured into this, but it's not like he couldn't decline or back out at any time. My thoughts become muddled when I think about his sisters and *my* sister, which makes me realize how messy this is. Not only is this a weird moral dilemma, but it's such an absurd situation either one of us has found ourselves in.

Sucking in a lungful of air, I meet his gaze. "Can you tell me something?"

"I didn't date you to get closer to your sister," he says, and I blink in confusion before my nose wrinkles at the horrifying idea. "I swear on my guitar. I haven't talked to her in months."

"It's not about her," I whisper, although I'm surprised to hear that. "It's about Travis Walker."

His expression turns inscrutable. "What about him?"

"I know he's a frat brother," I begin, only for him to cut me short.

"He's not in my fraternity."

"Yeah, I know," I whisper. "But, um, do you know anything about his fight with Dane? Or anything useful about him?"

"We're not really in the same circle," he says, "but I might have some information about that night."

"You do?"

"Yeah. I wasn't there when it went down. I had just dropped my sisters off at a sleepover and was heading back to the house when I saw him," he explains. "Kingsley was just lying there in the middle of this street. I almost didn't see him. I actually considered going a different route that night, since I only took that street whenever I wanted to avoid traffic during the day."

My breath halts in my lungs. "Did you… leave him there?"

"What?" Something a lot like offense shines in his disbelieving stare. "No. Of course not. I called 911 and almost left my car rolling in neutral when I ran to check on him." His voice lowers to a rough-hewn note while he shuts his eyes. "I stayed with him until the ambulance arrived. I applied pressure to his wound."

Nerves tighten in my stomach at his words. I'm shocked, to say the least. "I can't believe you did that."

"But I did," he says. "I don't think he remembers me—he was in pretty bad shape, Reese. I was just fucking relieved he didn't die on me and later—*much later*—I heard that he got into a fight—"

"No," I interject. "He didn't get into a fight. He got attacked by a couple of frat guys."

He nods straight away. Some part of me is grateful he's not sticking his neck out for Travis simply because he's also a fraternity member.

"I didn't know that," Caleb says. "At the time, all I heard was that Travis wrestled a bottle out of Kingsley's hand and defended himself with it."

"But that's not the truth." Sheer anguish nearly breaks me while I find his gaze. "Travis left him there to bleed to death in the middle of the street?"

"I think so," Caleb replies, and acid creeps up my throat at the horrifying realization.

My sister is dating him—the guy who left my boyfriend for dead. A growing dread churns in my stomach, and my mind whirls.

"I can always ask around," he offers, "and see what his brothers could tell me. See what anybody knows. I might not get anything, but—"

"It's better than nothing," I finish. Swallowing past the lump lodged in my throat, I glance sideways at him. *Dane might not be here right now if it weren't for him.* "I can't believe you saved him that night. He never brought you up."

"To be fair, I didn't stick around. I left after I gave the cops my statement." He pauses. "I did check in on him once at the hospital, though, but he told me to fuck off."

"That... sounds a lot like my boyfriend." My focus goes to the middle ground. It's a lot of information to receive—a lot to digest. I don't know how I'll break the news to my sister that her boyfriend is the scumbag of the century without risking the chance of her bulldozing me into forgiving her about the Caleb situation.

"I'm sorry for everything," Caleb says, snapping me back to the present. "For my involvement with the girls' plan. I told them many times it was fucked up, how I wanted no part in this, and how it was gonna hurt you." His green eyes fill with regret. "They kept insisting and... There's no excusing it. I should have told them no."

A dull sting twinges in my chest, and I draw in a shaky breath. "I... I understand... but I need some time."

Both of his hands lift. "Say no more." His expression is nothing but remorse. "Again, I'm sorry."

"Me too." Readjusting my backpack over my shoulder, I spare him a sad smile. "I should go. I need help with my physics homework, and the tutor I like is only there for another hour. But, um, let me know if you find out anything about Travis Walker."

He nods without protest. "Will do."

With one last look at him, I amble off to the tutoring center and cling to the desperate hope that I'll be left alone from here on out.

IS THERE A SIGN ON MY BACK TELLING EVERYONE TO APPROACH ME and apologize for paying Caleb to go out with me? I half expect to run into another sorority sister when I emerge from the Science Building, so I'm extremely thankful to see no one there.

Huffing out an irritable breath, I trudge back to the center of the campus. I still haven't decided if I truly forgive Caleb, and he's the one who was browbeaten into going out with me. The sorority girls were the ones who paid him to go out with me in the first place.

Objectively, that's worse. They're the ones who came up with the idea. They're the ones who schemed to have a guy I had a *raging crush on* go out with me.

They've overstepped so many lines I never knew existed, and all I want right now is to be left alone. I'm still trying to come to terms with this, and they're not helping their case at all when they keep bombarding me with explanations or apologies. I don't care. As it is, I don't want to hear why they came up with this crappy idea in the first place.

It makes me feel worse, regardless of their intentions, and I'd rather have the earth open up and swallow me whole than die of utter mortification.

Blowing out a lungful of oxygen, I avert my focus to my knit sweater. Pinching the unraveled yarn, I try my best to fix it when I hear my name being called.

Almost immediately, my lips flatten into a thin line. Dammit. I'm tired of being forced to go on the *listen to a flimsy apology* tour.

It's late. I'm exhausted. My environmental engineering class just flung a bunch of new information I need to go over for the upcoming quiz.

Whatever excuse they have for me this time, I don't want to hear it. I simply want to go home, study, and snuggle with my boyfriend and cat. Is that too much to ask for?

My name is shouted this time, and I heave out a quiet sigh as I come to a complete stop. Damn my soft heart.

With a put-upon frown, I glance to my right, and instinctively, my hand flies to my pepper spray as a hooded figure steps out of the shadow.

My breath runs ragged. My hands are clammy. My heart is skittish as blinding terror seizes me in a viselike hold and keeps me frozen in place.

"You're Old News' bitch."

I can barely hear over the incessant thrum of my pulse in my ears, and it takes me way too long to parse his words. *Old News?*

"Stay back," I whimper. My fingers are clumsy as I release the pink tube from its keychain. "I will—"

My sentence catches in my throat when a strong pair of arms grabs me forcefully from behind. My brain hurdles back to that awful night in my childhood room—to the dark, overwhelming feeling of helplessness and defeat. Hot, desperate tears well up behind my eyes at once as I try to shield my neck.

Frantically squeezing the can of mace with my other hand, I barely let out a terrified scream for help when something is yanked over my head and envelops me in pitch darkness.

4 4

DANE

As much as California needs all the rain it can get, I'm the chump who thought it would be great to take my bike for a spin tonight. It's on me for not checking the weather in the first place.

Pushing my damp hair out of my face, I take another glance at my lock screen. It's almost nine-thirty p.m., and my girl still hasn't texted me that she's heading to the bookstore.

I know her last class of the day lets out at eight-forty and that she has a habit of sticking around to ask professors questions since she's trying to keep her grades up for her scholarships. But even then, she'd usually text me a heads-up. She always felt bad about making me wait, even though I never minded.

As it is, there's no message about her running late. There's a high chance her phone died. She has an old model, and the battery doesn't last long once the temperature drops below sixty degrees. I might get her a replacement if that's the case.

Ditching my bike, I head over to the Science Building on foot. There's nobody in sight. It's practically a ghost town. The whole area would be dark if not for the faint orange glow from the few lamps strewn across campus and a hint of blue light from the emergency phone box in the periphery of my vision.

It's still deserted when I reach the west end of campus. My

frown deepens when the front doors won't budge. Not even the other entrance will let me inside. It never occurred to me until now that Belford locks everything up for the night.

Filing that under useless information I'll never think of again, I observe the area and retrieve my phone. Small droplets of water bead on the screen while I message her.

Dane: hey, did your class end early or are you at the bookstore?

I check out the twenty-four-hour floor at the library next, but she's not there, either. Circling back to my bike, a sense of foreboding sets in. It's almost ten. There's a small chance she's at her sister's sorority house, but I highly doubt it given how upset she's been these past few days.

Just then, my phone buzzes. A flicker of relief spreads through me, giving way to annoyance when I read a coded text from an unknown number. The undeciphered coordinates taunt me and provide information about the car meet happening at midnight.

It's cute that Giancarlo thinks I blocked any of his burners. Or that I'd ever want to come back. He can try all he wants, but I'm done. Sure enough, I get a couple of messages this time, and a scoff escapes me while I scan them.

Unknown: bring $100000
Unknown: u better show up
Unknown: unless u wanna say by by

I snort at the audacity, then feel the air rush out of my lungs as a grainy picture appears on my screen.

A grainy picture of her.

They have her.

With her body crammed inside a car trunk, her arms and legs bound behind her back, and a sack pulled over her head—*They have her.*

My blood runs cold. I recognize the sweater she put on this morning, the flowery skirt, the long brown hair—*They. Have. Her.*

Dane: don't you fucking dare hurt her
Unknown: midnite or she goes by by

Fuck. *Fuck.* How am I supposed to get a hundred thousand dollars right now? It's fucking ten p.m.

I don't even keep a fraction of that much cash on me. Not unless I plan on buying a car from Sergei, but even then—My hands delve into my hair. I can't breathe. Panic engulfs me and scours me raw. I have to get my girl out of there before they do anything else to her. Before she gets hurt because of me.

Swinging my leg over my bike, I barely secure my helmet and immediately take off. No matter which route I take, the roads are too slick. The sky is too dark. Visibility is piss-poor right now with the heavy rain, and I'm going way over the speed limit. There's no doubt about it. This night won't end well for me if I stick with my motorbike.

If I'm about to willingly walk into a trap—if I want to rescue my girl—I need to swap it for Ol' Reliable.

My heart lurches into my throat as I bulldoze through a red light, narrowly dodging a sedan blaring its horn at me. It's a close call. *Too fucking close.*

The rain lessens into a drizzle as I reach the outskirts of the city, and I all but abandon my bike the instant I pull up to my garage.

Thumbing through my set of keys, I hastily look for the specific fucking piece of metal that'll let me inside. My fingers scrabble the bulky padlock while I jam the key in and—after much resistance—unlock it. It feels like I'm racing against a clock. I *am* racing against a clock.

I still need to get the cash. I still need to get to the fucking location. I still need to rescue her.

The lock clicks open, and my wet, frigid hand grabs hold of

the door and hoists it up with extreme force, only for my entire body to freeze at the sight in front of me.

At the lack of cars in front of me.

All of my vehicles are gone. My Mustang, Ol' Reliable, Sal's Pontiac, and the two project cars I've been working on since the semester started. Even Reese's Nova isn't in its usual spot.

Everything's gone. They're all gone.

Taking an inadvertent step backward, I glance around and get visual confirmation I'm still the only person here. My throat runs dry while I reach for my phone.

Something glints in the streetlight and snares my attention as I scramble toward my bike. I barely make out a familiar green rim lying on the curb when he answers.

"I need your help. They have—" My hand chokes the device while I stare up at the night sky, my voice nearly breaking as brutal desperation racks me. "You're the only one I can turn to. *They have her.*"

THE OVERWHELMING SCENT OF WET ASPHALT GREETS ME WHEN I arrive, accompanied by dead silence the moment I cut the engine. My muscles grow tense as I climb off my bike and survey the surrounding area.

The water treatment plant is empty. There's no one in plain sight. Besides the few puddles rippling while reflecting the yellow glow of nearby street lamps, the whole place lacks any movement, any activity.

"*Wally!*" My words are a near growl, echoing throughout the empty street. "Come out and show your fucking face!"

This is a trap. I know it's a fucking trap. I know my ass is going to get kicked. At this point, it's undeniable. *Inevitable.* Written in the damn stars. I showed up with a heavy as fuck backpack and no backup. If I make it out of here alive, it'll take a fucking miracle to end all miracles.

Where are you, Marco?

"It's fucking midnight!" I snarl. "Quit fucking with me!"

A revving sound floods the air. For once, it's not music to my ears. My hands ball into fists as a vehicle slowly creeps toward me. It's not a green, clapped-out shitbox that pulls into the flickering streetlight.

It's a Mustang. A late-sixties model, exactly like the one I hitchhiked to Arizona to buy shortly after my eighteenth birthday. Painted bright red, as Marco dared me to the moment I rolled into Sal's shop. Windows barely tinted, so my father wouldn't bust my balls about California's tint laws, but dark enough for me to catch my reflection and see the wet hair plastered to my forehead.

After an eternity passes in the long few seconds, the glass pane finally rolls down at a measured pace until my eyes connect with Wally's.

"Like my new ride?"

The muscles in my jaw set. I'm barely breathing as I glance inside the coupe. There's no sign of her anywhere. "Where's the girl?"

"Uh, uh, uh." He tuts, baring his teeth with a smug grin. "We're doing this on my teams."

Does he mean terms? I'm having trouble wrapping my head around what's happening right here, right now. Wally's not the brightest lightbulb to begin with. I can't even see him masterminding tying his own shoes.

"You better let my girl go—"

"Say another word," he sneers, "and you'll never see her again."

I go still as his gaze slides to the backpack hanging on my shoulder.

"That's better," he says, and it takes all of my strength not to send him crawling home with a rearranged face. "This is how we're gonna do it. You're gonna give me your money." He pauses. "And your motorcycle."

"Show me the girl first."

"On your hands and knees," he continues. "I want you to crawl to me on your hands and knees and beg me to take your money and motorcycle from you. If you want your bitch back—"

"Where is she?" I demand, my tone caustic as hell while I take a step closer. "Where the fuck is she?"

"With one of my guys." As if on cue, I hear an engine backfire on my right and the sound of the brakes squealing to a stop on my left. His lips split into a sinister sneer. "Now get on your hands and knees, Old News. For everyone to see."

"Show me the girl first!" I growl, tearing my gaze away from his to look at both cars behind me. One's yellow and the other's purple. I don't recognize either one of them.

"We're playing on my teams!" he snarls. "My teams—"

"Show me the girl and I'll do whatever you want."

"*Fuck*. Fine!" He snaps his fingers. "Let him see her."

Anger radiates through me as some unfamiliar douchebag hops out of the yellow fastback and takes his sweet ass fucking time swaggering to the back. The trunk pops open, and my heart pounds with twin spirals of relief and fury the moment he hoists a small, wriggling body out the back of the sports car.

"Get that fucking thing off of her—"

"On your hands and knees," Wally cuts me off. "Get on your fucking knees now—"

"If you don't get that thing off of her head right now." Venom fills my voice as I turn to face him. "It will become your fucking body bag—"

"On. Your. Fucking. Hands—" His head jerks back when the backpack whams into his face. Without hesitation, I take off running toward my girl. Hands balled into fists. Muscles taut in the set of my shoulders. Jaw clenched in sheer determination.

Pure adrenaline propels me forward as I drive my knuckles into the first face I see. I swing at him again, landing a blow just below his eye, when someone slams into me from behind and sends me staggering forward.

The sharp taste of copper fills my mouth and mixes with my saliva. I spit out blood and twist on my feet, barely dodging the right hook when Wally socks me squarely in the sternum.

"Where's the fucking money?" he screams. "You could have made it easy for yourself—"

A feral sound ruptures from my throat, and I charge him. His body slams into the pavement. He grapples me down to the ground with him.

My fist connects with his temple. His knee goes into my ribs. Our hands are flying wildly as we thrash and jab and sneak in every below-the-belt hit we can get. Every second counts. There's no such thing as honor.

Before his dirty nails can claw at my eye, I jackknife my knee into his groin. He grunts, momentarily blindsided by the pain, and I deck him hard in the nose, instantly met with a sickening crunch that mingles with his anguished scream. Blood gushes everywhere. His eyes pool with tears.

There's no such thing as honor.

I strike another devastating blow to his face, and he howls in pain, unable to weasel away in time from the next jab that goes straight to his bleeding nose. His forearms fly to his mug, but I don't give a shit about him anymore.

Staggering to my feet, I crack my jaw and turn around to see who's next. I'm angry. Beyond pissed. They kidnap my girl and think I'm going to cower, bend over, and play on their fucking terms?

Panting heavily, I spit out the blood pooling in my mouth. My hands curl into fists. My legs shift. My stance squares. I know I'm about to get my ass handed to me. The odds are stacked against me when there are still three of them standing and we all fight dirty.

The chances of me getting out of here with just a couple of bruises are low. My girl won't like that one bit, but she'll be safe and sound, and more importantly, she'll be far away from these assholes. That's what matters most to me.

With ruthless intention, I charge at the one on the right. I don't have the element of surprise on my side, but I manage a blow to his jaw just before one of them yanks me back and hooks an arm around my neck, crushing my windpipe. Someone sucker-punches me in the gut, and the air whooshes painfully from my lungs when he lands a harder blow to my ribs.

I thrash and kick wildly, managing to elbow someone before I get a hard uppercut below my chin, and my tongue gets sharply bit in the process. A fist slams into my left eye. A boot connects with my abdomen, and I wheeze through my bloodstained teeth.

I jerk my head back and headbutt the guy holding me. He makes a startled noise, abruptly hacking a hoarse wheeze a millisecond later, and his grip slackens out of nowhere.

"Let go of him," comes a dark growl.

I nearly crumple to the ground while I wrench myself out of his grasp. Coughing up blood, I find myself looking Marco directly in the eye. He nods at me, barely shifting his stance when his body tenses at the sudden sound in the distance.

Sirens. Fucking sirens.

It's a symphony to my ears. Relief uncoils in my chest, barely outmatched by my amusement when Wally's friends bolt for their cars. It only lasts for a second before my exhaustion kicks in. With a low groan, I clutch my aching ribs and try not to drag my feet to the small body abandoned on the wet pavement.

"It's me," I wheeze, my heart sinking into my stomach when she recoils and jerks away from my touch. "Iris, baby, it's me." My movements are slow as I carefully gather her into my arms and yank the sack off of her head.

She won't stop shaking. Her eyes are squeezed shut in distress, tears tracking down her cheeks. Her disheveled hair sticks to her clammy temples. Wet leaves cling to her sweater in random spots, and her bare knees and shins are streaked with dirt.

"You're okay, you're okay." I ignore the wailing sirens as I gently tug down the gag around her mouth.

A rough sob works through her frame and tears my heart into shreds. I breathe deep through my nose—through the agonizing pain of my stinging rib cage when my chest expands —and bring my hands to the binding around her wrists.

She goes rigid as a stone.

"It's okay. It's okay," I whisper. "I'm only removing—"

She weeps something incoherent, her body trembling even harder in my arms.

"I got you," I continue. "I'm here. I'm right here."

I free her wrists and fight the heavy ball forming in the pit of my stomach when she immediately clings to me, her fingers clutching onto my torn shirt as if it's her lifeline.

"You're okay," I promise, bringing her ankles onto my thigh. I tug at the tight, intricate-looking knot and bite back my frustration. Fuck. It's too tight. My fingers are stiff and raw and stinging as I yank and pull on the rope, trying everything I can think of to get the knot loose.

It won't give. The rope cuts into the pads of my fingers. Bites into the flesh of my palm. I tug even harder, but it won't fucking give. *It won't fucking give.*

"Baby—You're going to be okay, but I need to get someone—"

"No," she sobs. "*Please.* Please don't leave me."

My heart squeezes tight while I swallow thickly. "Never. I'd never."

She doesn't say anything else. Her face buries into my shoulder, her tears soaking up what's left of my shirt. My arms tighten around her as I press my nose into her matted hair. It takes a long while before my heartbeat slows down. Before I can accept the fact that she's safe.

I lift my head when I feel something splatter against my forehead, then look up as the rain starts up again. Around us, it's... chaos. Pandemonium. Lights flashing everywhere. Cop cars blocking both sides of the street. Wally's idiot friends resisting arrest. Wally screaming nonsense while his arms are pinned and zip-tied behind him. Marco standing near my Mustang with his hands up.

My lungs heave against the biting, wintry air as I bury my face in her hair. My pulse slows down a notch when I breathe in her familiar scent. "I won't leave you. I promise."

FROM WHAT I CAN MAKE OUT IN MY REFLECTION, MY FACE HAS SEEN better days. My boot taps incessantly against the linoleum floor. My fingers drum against the steel table.

I don't know what's taking so long, or why they haven't let me go yet. These bozos have already taken my statement. I've answered every question they had, even the ones about people who weren't at the scene. What else could they want from me?

Minutes of my life are being wasted away when somewhere outside this interrogation room, my girl is waiting for me. I don't want to be away from her for another second. Not when she hasn't stopped crying since I got her back.

My fingers thrust into my hair. I'm on my last nerve and it's being tested. I know my fucking rights. I'm not arrested. I don't have to stick around until someone comes around to dismiss me like it's a classroom.

Before I can push my seat back, the door swings open. And right there, standing in the doorway, is my father. The tightness in his jaw is no match for the tension in his neck. Whatever he says to the officer, it's too low for me to hear.

I sit up tall and brace myself for yet another lecture about what a disappointment I am to him, the family name, my dead mother, and whatever else he wants to throw at me.

We've had this dance before. Two years ago. I'm not in the mood to do it again.

The instant the officer leaves the room, my mouth curves into a grim line.

"Just can it, all right?" I grunt. "I know the drill. Disappointment. Screw-up. Taking shit for granted—Spare me the theatrics."

"Daniel."

"I'm going to take my girl home now." The chair screeches against the linoleum as I stand. "I know *loyalty* to the girl you love is unheard of for you—"

"You called me." His eyes sharpen. "I helped you—"

"Because it'd look fucking bad if the great Daniel Kingsley's fuckup son was found dead in a ditch?"

"Because I love you," he snarls, and I spare him a leveled stare. "I'm tired of you treating me like the bad guy—"

"Are you not the bad guy—"

"I was *terrified*—"

"You never cared about me," I plow on, "so spare me the waterwork—"

"How could you—"

"How could I?" My jaw aches as I glower at him. What I would give for another painkiller right now. "You know what? I'm leaving. If it'll make you feel better, I'm not gonna get into any more trouble, so you can stop pretending like you give a damn. You won't have to worry about me sullying your family name any longer."

"I don't give a damn about that," he gripes, anger furrowing his stern brows. "I give a damn about you. I always have."

"Right," I say dryly, punctuating the word with an eye-roll. "Let's be honest with ourselves. We both know you wished I died that night with Mom."

The room falls into dense silence, and horror slackens his features. "Daniel, how could you say such a thing?"

"Because it's the truth?" I seethe. "Once I'm out of the picture, you'd have a clean slate with your do-over family and your perfect new sons—"

"I've never wished for that," he interjects.

"It's the truth, though!"

"It's not the truth!" His nostrils flare. "Never in my entire life have I ever wanted you dead or wished for you to die."

"Just Mom, though, right?" Bitterness drips in my tone, and tension simmers in the air.

For a long moment, he fixes me with that familiar disappointed stare. He lets out a rough exhale. "I never wanted her dead. I never wanted my wife to die or for my son to resent me for something she did—"

"For something she did?" I echo, and it takes what's left of my depleting energy to remain rooted to the spot. I don't need to be a rocket scientist to know socking my old man in the face at a police station is a bad call.

"She almost got you killed," he grates out through gritted teeth. Never mind. We'll both be walking out of this room with black eyes. "Instead of taking a cab home, as I had insisted, she drove you home way over the legal blood alcohol limit."

All at once, the anger leeches from my body while it feels like I've been sucker-punched in the gut again. What is he talking about? They said there was a drunk driver at the scene, but... Nausea threatens to tear through me.

No. He's wrong. He has to be.

"You nearly died because of a bad judgment call on her end," he goes on, and somehow, he looks twice his age as he wearily looks me in the eye. "I was beside myself when I got the call— when I thought I lost my entire family that night."

I want to chew him out. I want to tell him he's fucking wrong. I want to stop him from dragging my mom's good name through the mud.

She's not here to defend herself, but... I can't either. Not when I have so many memories of her drowning her sorrows late at night. Of her telling me to keep it a secret between us when she sneaked a flask into one of my games. Of all the wine she'd drink on flights to Hammersmith.

Icy dread floods through my veins. I gape at the man before me. At the man with a history of using his money and connections to keep the skeletons in the closet when it comes to our family.

"In a way," he says, after a strained minute of silence, "I did. Because you blamed me for what happened, even though I wasn't there. *Because I wasn't there.* I wasn't there for you when you needed me, Daniel. You were grieving, but so was I. I lost my wife. I nearly lost my son. You hated me, and I could never do anything right. I tried so hard to fix things, but you kept pushing me away.

"Then you told me you wished it had been me who died in that accident, and it destroyed me. It absolutely destroyed me to see you hurting, and no matter what I did, you saw me as nothing but a monster." He pulls in a deep breath. "I know you'll always hate me. I've accepted that. Even if it kills me, I've made my peace with it. But I want you to know I'll always love you. I will always be there for you however I can. When you called me for help, I came—"

"I called you for help before," I remind him bluntly. "Two years ago, when the Walkers threatened to sue me. You *paid* them off even though I was innocent. I told you what happened that night. Every little detail. I told you the bastard and his friends attacked me. I swore to you that I only broke his arm in self-defense, but *you didn't believe me.* You really thought I beat him up when I didn't. *None of his other injuries were from me.*"

To my surprise and his credit, he flinches. "I'm sorry," he says. "Daniel, I truly am. I was only trying to look out for you—"

"You paying them off only made things worse for me," I growl. "Paying them off was practically an admission of guilt. I was *innocent.* I told you they ganged up on me, but you automatically assumed the worst. You've *always* assumed the worst in me. All because I fucked up once when I was a kid and took your car for a joyride while you were too busy playing father of the year with your do-over family."

Frustration stirs in my chest, and my hands scrub my bruised jaw while I stare ahead. Every muscle in my body is coiled up so damn tight, I know I'm on the verge of snapping. I need to get out of here before I reach my limit.

"Believe me, I regret everything. For not being there when you needed me." Remorse clouds his profile, and his shoulders sag. "For not trying harder to repair our relationship. Know that I would give anything to fix things between us."

My line of sight cuts to the table. I can't look at him. Not right now. Not while it feels like the walls are about to close in on me.

All my life, I wanted his approval. His love. Any fucking sign that showed he cared about me. Anything that proved he didn't think of me as a burden or see me as an ugly reminder of his first marriage. Something that corroborated the fact he didn't want me out of his life for good so he could have a clean slate with his picture-perfect new family.

Now here it is. Here's everything I've ever wanted my entire life… and I don't know what to do with it.

A weary sigh escapes me. "My girl's waiting for me, and I don't want to keep her waiting."

He hesitates. His expression is nothing but anguish and causes a sharp pang in my heart, and I avert my attention to the door. "Is she okay?"

Reluctantly, I redirect my focus back to him, and my throat becomes tight at the touch of concern in his pained gaze. I'm not sure if she's really who he's asking about. Not while he surveys my busted lip and swollen left eye with this look that depletes the rest of my energy. Exhaustion sets in. I've never felt this… drained in my whole life.

"She will be," I say finally. "She's the toughest girl I know."

4 5

REESE

The golden hour is quite lovely to witness in Dane's room, as it has been for the entire week. Curled into a ball, I watch the sunset and draw comfort in the steady thrum of his heartbeat. At my side, my boyfriend provides me with the warm shelter of his embrace. At my feet, the cat sleeps contently.

Today marks the first day I've gone without crying. If I can manage more than two hours of uninterrupted sleep tonight, it'll be a welcome reprieve.

A shuddering breath works through me, and I squeeze my eyes shut when the mattress dips. Dane gently murmurs something against the crown of my head I can't discern. Soon, a reusable bottle nudges the palm of my hand.

Reluctantly, I sit up, and Onion Rings mewls in protest at the sudden movement. After draining half the water, I give Dane a sideways glance and swallow hard at the sight of discolored bruises spread across his profile.

"Hey, hey," he whispers and slowly slides his thumb under my chin. "I thought chicks dig scars."

Despite my misgivings, I snort. "I don't like seeing you hurt."

He huffs, offering me an imperceptible smirk. "This? It's nothing."

My gaze diverts to his jaw, where yellow edges the ghastly black-and-blue splotch, and my heart plummets as everything sinks in. "Did they really take all the cars?"

His eyes harden like flint. "I'll get your Nova back."

"What about *your* cars?"

"I'll get them back, too." His words are twice as firm and determined. I'm about to protest when my focus snags on the bruise beneath his eye, and my breath leaves me. "I'll never forgive myself—"

"If you don't get your cars back?"

"That they targeted you because of me," he says, then works the muscles of his jaw with a deep sigh.

"It's not your fault."

"They knew you're my weakness."

"I'm your weakness?" I echo. "Like kryptonite?"

"Like the girl I love."

Flutters ignite in my stomach instantaneously. The edges of my lips tilt up, and soft laughter tumbles out of me when he grins something so love-drunk in response. "I love you too."

His gaze gentles, and then he breaks into a devastating smile while I reach over and trace a heart over his chest. Slowly, he guides me back into his arms and pulls me close. It takes a few moments for the tension to leave my shoulders, but I melt completely into his embrace when he kisses my hairline.

"I love you so much," I mumble. "So, so much."

"Tell me something I don't know," he teases. "I know you're all in with me."

"I was so relieved when I realized it was you." My fingers bunch the material of his shirt. "When I realized you were rescuing me."

"I didn't do anything."

A protesting hum sounds from my throat, and I shake my head. He did so much for me. He called his dad for help. He called his dad *for me*. Someone he has a strained relationship with. Someone I know he doesn't want to interact with if given a choice.

"You got me out of there. *Alive.*" Hot tears spring into my eyes. "I was so scared. I thought I wasn't going to survive. All I could think about was that I was living on borrowed time since the night I nearly died on my bedroom floor."

"Oh, baby," he whispers, and his hand is slow as it goes up the line of my back. "That's not true."

"I thought I was going to die with my sister thinking I was mad at her." My rasp roughens my voice, and my vision blurs over with tears. "I thought I'd never see you again."

"Did they hurt you?" His tone is so gentle, but such a juxtaposition to the raw fury pouring off his body. There's tension in his every muscle despite him tenderly stroking the curve of my spine.

My head shakes. "Just my wrists and ankles. They might have been extra rough with me because I tried to pepper spray them." Without warning, my brain sprints back to that night—to the terrifying feeling of being grabbed from behind—and my lungs constrict.

With a rough swallow, I draw in a deep breath and try to anchor myself. *I'm in Dane's room. The door is locked. No one can get in. He will protect me.*

"You used mace on them?" His other hand gently circles my wrist, his thumb caressing the faint line marring the skin.

"It… didn't seem to work. It might have been expired or something. Lilian got it for me two years ago, so it probably did." Frustration and dread form a pit in my stomach, but Dane gives me a comforting squeeze before I can spiral. "I didn't realize the can could still feel full of liquid and no longer work. It was the only thing that made me feel safe, and they took it from me…"

"I'll get you a new one," he says. "And I'm going to hurt him for doing this to you."

"Dane."

"I will."

"I don't want you to get hurt," I say softly.

"I won't let him get away with it. I don't like people fucking with what's mine."

"*Dane*," I repeat, and he releases a gruff sigh. "Do you want to talk about your dad?" I simply don't want to hear him talk about fighting people anymore. "Or maybe your brothers?"

His stepmom showed me pictures of his half-brothers while she kept me company at the police station. Not only that, she had so many kind words to say about Dane. And countless photos of him saved on her phone.

She also gave me a card for the women's shelter she's on retainer for and told me about their trauma hotline, which was really nice of her. I'm pretty sure she's been dropping by every evening with homemade bread and soup, too.

"They play hockey," he mutters, snapping me out of my thoughts.

"Like you did?"

"Yeah, I guess." He falls silent for a couple of beats. "I love my mom."

"I know you do." My hand slips into his, and I offer him a reassuring smile.

He lets out a defeated sigh. "I don't want my memories of her to be tainted."

I shift closer, only to stifle my laughter when Onion Rings meows his grievances about the sudden movement. Finding Dane's gaze, I cup his face and run my thumb along the edge of a fading bruise. "You can love someone without putting them on a pedestal. I love my sister, but I also recognize all of her messy faults. She's loyal and fierce, but she's also pushy and hotheaded. She hurt me with what she did, but at the end of the day, I still love her and care about her."

His throat works as he peers steadily into my eyes. His thoughtful frown gives way to a clash of something vulnerable and guarded, and I can feel my heart fracturing into tiny pieces.

"They said a drunk driver was behind the accident, and I know the other guy was hammered that night, but I never realized my mom…" The despair in his voice is hard to miss. "My father never said anything. He just let me assume that someone else was the reason why she was gone."

"Maybe he was trying to protect you?" I suggest. "How old were you?"

"Nine." His Adam's apple bobs. "I just remember her being so happy and vibrant. It's my last memory of her. She was singing along to the radio—some Christmas song, I think. Then I woke up in a hospital, and they told me it was a T-bone collision, that my mom didn't make it, and that I was lucky to have gotten out of there alive with only my arm and leg broken."

With a sharp exhalation, I squeeze his fingers. "Was this why you stopped playing hockey?"

"Kind of." A bitter chuckle slides free. "After I got better, I was pissed that my father wanted to show up to my games for once. It was my thing with Mom. I didn't want him to replace her, so I quit. It's so fucking stupid, in hindsight. I always wanted him to show up to my games, and when he finally did?"

"You were just a kid," I murmur, and he scoffs and shakes his head.

Consternation steals across his expression, and his eyes become lost in thought. Every part of me wants to smooth away the small divot forming between his dark brows and take away his hurt. Do everything I can so he's able to smile widely again as if he doesn't carry the weight of the world on his shoulder.

"I felt so alone when my mom died. Like I was drowning. I was so lost. He married my stepmom a year after my mom passed away, and then they started having kids. It felt like he replaced me; it stung like hell to see him be a dad to them when he never once did any of that with me. It hurt to see him take time off of work to go to school events for them. Go camping with them. Do all this shit he never did with me."

"He never took you with them?"

"They always made me tag along. For every trip they planned. I always felt like an outsider. An interloper. The ugly reminder that he was married before."

"*Dane*—"

"Save your tears, Reese's Pieces," he mutters. "I don't want you to feel bad for me."

My heart clenches tight. "Do you want a relationship with him? You don't have to if you don't want to," I tack on quickly. I don't want him to feel pressured into doing something he doesn't want to do. I already know how *sucky* that is. "I'm never going to talk to my mom again, and that won't ever change. We're not obligated to maintain a relationship with someone just because we share DNA with them. Whatever you decide to do, I'll support you."

The corner of his mouth lifts. "Even if I decide to be an asshole?"

"Only you know what's best for yourself."

His features soften with this look of such sweet longing. "You know what's best for me right now?"

"Hmm?"

"You."

I snort. A tiny smile touches my lips when he wraps his arms around me and holds me close to his chest. Pressing my ear to his heart, I listen to the steady beat. My nerves subside as a wave of calm and security washes over me.

"If things go south—"

"You'll be my getaway car," I finish. "I think we've had this conversation before."

With a lopsided grin, he cranes his neck down and lifts a brow when I spare him a slightly impish beam in response. My feet remain flat on the ground, and within a pulse, a giggle bursts from me as he loops his arms around my waist and hoists me into the air.

The front door coasts open before I can kiss him, and I'm carefully set down the instant my gaze collides with my sister's. Her amber eyes glisten with tears, and mine prickle straight away.

Dane presses his lips to my hairline. "Text me if you need me."

I will, I mouth to him, biting back a smile when he traces a heart over his heart. Then I reluctantly wave goodbye before I enter the sorority house. Grabbing Lilian's wrist, I kick the door shut before my sister can continue glaring at my boyfriend with a look of contempt she doesn't bother hiding.

We're barely halfway across the living room when I'm tackled with a bear hug.

"I'm so glad you're okay," my sister sobs into my hair. "I'm so fucking glad."

"Can't. Breathe," I wheeze, gulping a lungful of air while she loosens her grasp. I peek up and nearly flinch when I see how bloodshot her eyes are and notice the prominent bags underneath.

"Please forgive me," she whispers. "We never should have paid Caleb to go out with you."

Heat blazes across my face. I don't think there'll ever be a moment where I'll *not* become embarrassed whenever the Caleb situation gets brought up.

"You shouldn't have," I agree. "That was a terrible thing to do."

"I know." Remorse flickers across her features. "We weren't doing it as a prank. We just wanted you to feel better about yourself."

"Yeah, that's what everybody said," I say, crossing my arms. "But I didn't feel better about myself at all when I found out the truth."

She winces. "I'm so sorry. For everything. We never wanted

you to get hurt—Swear to God. We even had a plan where Caleb would break up with you because he was too busy to date you just to soften the blow."

"That's how he was going to dump me?" I lift a brow. "*Wow*."

"It was a work in progress," she grumbles. "We just wanted to boost your confidence. Make you feel better about yourself. You were struggling after what happened—" Her eyes go round when her focus lands on my scar. "You're not… hiding it."

I glance down at my striped top, and a wry smile slowly stretches across my lips. "It's hot today. I didn't want to get sweaty." I pause. "We're in Southern California, not Vermont."

"We're not," she agrees, her voice rougher than usual.

I allow myself a quiet intake of breath, then bite my lip. "Did you truly believe I couldn't get a guy on my own? Or that I needed a guy to feel better about myself?"

"*No*," she gasps. "It was never like that. He was supposed to be a fun distraction. Someone to help you out of your shell. We thought it was a good idea at the time… but it clearly wasn't."

"It definitely wasn't."

"Don't blame Caleb for this," she continues. "He didn't want to be part of this—He was just a guy you liked—"

"Just because I liked him didn't mean you guys should go to extremes and force him to go out with me," I cut in. "I know you guys meant well, but I *didn't* need this at all. If I had known all along he wasn't into me, it would've saved Dane and me so much time and heartache wondering why nothing was happening with Caleb."

"Dane and you?" she repeats, arching a brow, and my cheeks scald with heat. I'm *not* going to tell her that my boyfriend tried to help me seduce a guy who was paid to go out with me. I don't think anyone in their right mind would *ever* utter a sentence like that out loud. Not even a CIA agent will get this confession out of me.

"I will leave if you insult my boyfriend," I warn her. "He literally—"

"Broke Travis' arm in self-defense."

"—saved me…" Shocked, my words taper off. "That's also true."

"Caleb told me earlier this week," she quietly admits. "Travis and his brothers found out who his mom was and about the money she left him."

My brow lifts. Caleb texted me a few days ago and told me how Travis had his friends rough him up a little, so it looked like Dane caused more damage during their fight, but I didn't realize he filled my sister in as well. Honestly, I was under the impression that Caleb still wasn't talking to her, given everything she put him through.

"I dumped him, by the way," she continues with a weary sigh. "I should have listened to you."

"You didn't, though." Emotions scathe my throat as I gawk at her. "You listened to Caleb, but not me? Seriously? He's just some guy. I'm your sister. I told you everything about Travis and what he did to Dane, and you never believed me once. But the second Caleb tells you the same thing, you just accepted it without a second thought?"

To her credit, she winces. "Reese, you tend to see the best in everybody. I know I haven't been Dane's biggest fan—"

I huff out a snort and fold my arms across my chest.

"But, Reese," she goes on, "he's always been such a massive asshole"—she holds up a finger when I glower—"and I was afraid you'd get hurt again because of him."

"He's not an asshole," I hiss. "And he'd never hurt me."

"You weren't there my freshman year," she reminds me. "He was always rude to everybody."

"He's—" I pause. She kind of has a point. I've seen him glare at people far too many times. "Okay, he's sweet once you get to know him. He's very sweet to me. I *know* he would never hurt me. I need you to trust me when I say that. I can't have you trying to control every aspect of my life."

"You don't understand how *terrified* I am of losing you," she rasps as tears start to shine in her eyes. "I don't want anything to happen to you. When I got the call from our neighbor that you were at the hospital? I was *petrified* you were going to die while I was stuck here, hundreds of miles away—"

"Lili." My word catches in my throat, and without a second thought, I pull her into my arms.

"I'm supposed to look out for you," she sobs into my hair. "And I couldn't—"

"It's not your responsibility to look out for me," I protest. "Lili, you're not my mom. You're my sister. You don't need to go overboard with it."

"I'll try, but I can't help it. Someone has to—" She breaks off as she clings to me. "I don't want anything to happen to you. I'm so afraid of losing you. When I found out you were snatched? Reese, it felt like my world ended."

My chest goes painfully tight. While we were still at the station, Dane's stepmom messaged her that I was okay on my behalf, which set off a flurry of panic texts from her.

I don't have my phone. They took it along with my can of mace and backpack. For the past two weeks, I've been texting her with Dane's cell to reassure her I'm all right until my replacement comes in the mail tomorrow.

"I'm sorry for scaring you like that."

"You have nothing to apologize for," she protests. "How are you so calm about it?"

"I'm not calm about it," I admit, swallowing past the lump forming in my throat. "This house is one of the few safe places left. I can't sleep without the light on. I need to triple-check the doors. I panic if anyone walks behind me." My voice fades. "Belford used to be one of my safe places, and now I'm *terrified* of going back to school... and having to walk by where it happened."

Lilian inhales sharply. "I can walk you to your classes if you need me to."

"We can, too." I jolt and peel away from my sister to spot the sorority girls crowding the stairs. I nearly squeak in horror as my shyness grips me.

"It's the least we could do," Peyton adds, and the other girls nod in agreement.

"If you give us your schedule," Jenna adds, "we can work something out, so one of us is available to walk you to all of your classes."

"And I know they offer self-defense classes at my gym," Karla states. "If it's something you want to consider. I'll go with you if you want."

"Me too!" Chrissy chimes in. "I've always wanted to take some courses."

"Or it can be something we can do together," Lilian suggests softly, and I'm so overwhelmed.

A whirlwind of emotions takes hold in my chest. I glance at them for a drawn-out beat, then reroute my attention to my sister.

Even though the whole Caleb ordeal is wrong, these girls have always been nice to me. They organized a bunch of fundraisers for me the moment they heard about my attack back home without Lilian ever asking them to. They have been super welcoming to me and would always leave nice and encouraging comments on photos I'd post online. They've never peer-pressured me into partying with them.

None of them are malicious types. I know that. Maybe that's why forgiving them for the whole *paying Caleb to go out with me* ordeal doesn't seem so hard to do.

Their intent was pure. Extremely misguided and so, so wrong, but pure.

So what if I'm too softhearted as my boyfriend and sister have always pointed out? I don't want to hold on to my anger any longer. Not when the whole *being abducted and thinking you're actually going to die this time* puts things into perspective. While their ill-conceived idea hurt me, it pales in comparison to everything else I've endured.

"Will you stay the night?" Lilian asks. "I miss you."

"Would you be okay with keeping the lights on?"

"Of course." She sniffles while she pulls away from me. "We can watch movies—" A frown crosses her face when I snicker. "What's so funny?"

"Dane and I have done nothing but watch a bunch of films," I admit, biting my bottom lip. "I'm honestly sick of them."

She lets out a theatrical gasp, and I wrinkle my nose.

"I don't mind just catching up with you," I continue, then pause, considering. "It's been a while since we've hung out."

"It has, hasn't it?" Her eyes glisten as they search my face, hesitating for a contemplative moment. "Are we good?"

Something reassuring and hopeful unfurls in my chest while I spare her a gentle smile. "We will be."

DANE

"Another dead end." The muscles in my jaw work as I climb back into Marco's car and slam the door shut. "The bastard's not there."

"Damn." He shakes his head and releases a low whistle. "I thought this was it."

"So did I." I glance sideways at the run-down house across from us. It's been two months since my garage was broken into. Two months since I rescued Reese from Wally and his friends.

Save for my Mustang, which I got back three weeks ago after the cops finally processed it, I've only found the Nova so far. Thanks to a tip from Shyla, I paid a visit to Wally's friend ten days ago, retrieved my girl's convertible, and left him with a busted face.

My two project cars are nowhere to be found. I'd write them off as losses if the fastback didn't cost me an arm and a leg. I don't know where Ol' Reliable is, either, which is a damn pity given the amount of time I've spent on it. A small part of me looks forward to tweaking the cambers on a replacement so it can drift just as well, but still. I can't seem to accept that it's gone.

"You think Sergei skipped town?" Marco guesses. "Or do you think he's lying low?"

"No idea." Huffing out an irritable sigh, I retrieve my phone from my pocket. There are a few unread texts from my girl that I answer while Marco starts his vehicle. "Thanks for coming."

He chuckles wryly. "Wasn't gonna let you fight Sergei alone."

"Don't think I can handle him?"

"I know you can't handle him," he retorts with a smirk.

"Thanks for the vote of confidence," I deadpan. "At least I can handle Sal. Been preparing the last few weeks for his ass to crawl out of his grave and tear me a new one."

"You think you could take him on?" His raspy laughter crinkles his dark eyes. "Get real, Kingsy."

I shake my head in amusement, then curve my lips at the picture I receive of Reese and her sister struggling to eat takeout sushi with the cat all over them. "Remember when he made us eat your aunt's cooking, so she wouldn't be offended?"

His mouth twists into a grimace. "I'm trying to forget one of the worst moments of my life."

I lean back and snicker, giving the passenger window a side-long glance. "You ever wondered what happened to it?"

"To what? Her cooking?"

"To Sal's shop," I clarify. "It's been a while, hasn't it? Let's go see what it's been turned into."

"I think it's still a mechanic's shop," he says dryly, and I snort.

"You think your sneakers are still hanging on the power line?" I lift a brow. "Come on, Divenanzio. I'll bet you five bucks they're no longer there."

"Prepare to lose five bucks," he mutters, and I chuckle while he takes a left at the next intersection. "Your girl has made you soft, Kingsy. Never took you as the sentimental type."

My grin widens as I peer out the window again. The city lights are starkly bright and neon against the dark, drizzling sky. Slick pavement and puddles reflect the blue under-glow kit of his vehicle. A sentimental streak flickers through my chest at all the familiar street signs we pass. "We used to race our cars here every night."

"Dude, are you dying or something?" he teases. "This is unlike you."

"After what happened to my girl?" I say with a shrug. "I've been more appreciative of everything I've got."

Glancing sideways at me, he bobs his head before he turns right onto another familiar and empty street. This one's always been a favorite of ours. Barely any red lights at this time of night. It's where we learned how to drift.

Before I can brace myself, he floors it, and the seatbelt locks against my chest. My head thumps into the headrest. My phone drops from my grasp and clatters against the floor as the car fish-tails across the wet pavement.

"Hey, slow down!" I shout and bend down to grab my cell as a bunch of crap from underneath my seat spills out from the sudden, sharp movement. "Don't want to hydroplane into that gas station."

"You've gone too soft." He eases off the gas right before the car splashes into a puddle, and I snort as I shove all the tubs of beach wax, hair gel, and body spray back so I don't step on them.

"Remember the crappy food we used to get there?" I snicker as my hand wraps tightly around another tube I come across while he abruptly swerves into the passing lane. Christ, I knew he treated the passenger side as an honorary junk drawer, but I didn't think he'd be this sloppy. "When we'd sneak out after midnight to take your dad's car for a joyride?"

He rasps out a chuckle. "I remember your ass puking in the bush."

Aiming a wry half-smile in his direction, I tip my head at the street corner the moment the car comes to a stop. Neither of us speaks as we stare at the spot where Sal's mechanic shop used to be.

It still looks the same for the most part. Just got a cosmetic change: a fresh coat of paint in what appears to be a different shade of blue and a new sign tacked at the top of the building.

"Will I be getting the five dollars in cash, Kingsy?"

"After you pull over."

"Right now?" My gaze cuts to him as he raises a brow and fixes me with an incredulous stare.

"My girl loves photography," I explain, and I don't fight my grin when I nod toward the shop again. "She just texted me and asked if we could do one of those recreated photos for her."

"What the fuck is a recreated photo?"

"We'll find out after you pull over," I say, and he shakes his head with a long-suffering groan.

"Man, you are fucking *whipped* for this girl." Thankfully, he obliges. I'm already out of the vehicle before he kills the engine, taking in the surrounding scenery and breathing in the crisp night air.

Nostalgia slams into me like a freight train while I pore over every little detail. There have been plenty of good times here. Lots of good memories over the years.

My attention slides to the sign where SAL'S MECHANIC used to be, replaced with some logo I don't recognize. Our spray-painted initials on the brick wall nearby have been painted over. The eucalyptus tree still has the rusty basketball hoop attached to it, though.

"All right." Marco rounds his car and treks over to me, snapping his fingers in my direction. "Let's make your girl happy. Hand me your phone so we can get out of here."

"You wanna bail already?"

"It's raining," he states the obvious.

"It's barely a drizzle," I respond as I pass him my cell. "Nothing we can't handle."

With a grin, I take a step back and watch him hold the device up to his face.

"What the fuck are we even recreating?" he mutters,

preparing to take a shot. "The time you puked in that bush? Or the time you tried to chug three cans of energy drink in a minute?"

"I have an idea in mind." My beam widens into something camera-ready and creases my eyes. "But I'll need your help."

"With what?" Cocking his head to the side, he gives me an inquisitive look, only to jerk back in surprise when he receives a fist to his jaw.

My phone clatters on the ground.

"What the fuck?" His brows barely knit together when my body slams into his and we go crashing into the concrete.

"Do you think I'm stupid, fucker?"

He sputters as his knee shoves against my thigh.

"Did you think I wouldn't find out?" I snarl while I smash the pink can of mace I grabbed earlier into his forehead. He bats it out of my hand, and the tube rolls out of my reach and into a nearby patch of weeds before I can cram it down his throat.

With a dark growl, he grapples me. I know his moves like he knows mine, that all strategies have been abandoned. We're just swinging blindly and throwing as many jabs and right hooks as we can with no coordination whatsoever.

Honest to God, whatever we're doing is just a step below wrestling.

"I know it was you! Not Sergei! *You! It was you who fucking betrayed me.*"

"You're picking"—he spits in my face—"some fucking bitch you don't know over me?"

"Look me in the eye and tell me it wasn't you who sent the goons after me!" I yank on the collar of his shirt and dig my fingertips into the base of his throat. "*Tell me it wasn't you!*"

With a hoarse wheeze, the flat of his hand smacks into my chest. I land another blow to his chin.

"Fuck you, asshole!" His other palm slaps the side of my face.

"Fuck me?" I slap him back. "No, fuck you—"

"Go to fucking hell—"

"Tell me you're not the reason why I almost fucking died in the alley that night!"

"I didn't know they were gonna do that," he rasps, then strikes me on the bridge of my nose. A sharp pain blossoms across my face as I return the favor, and he makes a gurgling sound. "I said you had my money—"

"You fucked me over 'cause you got in way over your fucking head again?" I sneer. "You fucking serious? I would have bailed you out. You know that! *I'd do anything for you!* I loved you like a brother—"

"Always the fucking hero!" he snaps. "Always easy to play the fucking hero when you've never had to worry about anything. Your dad will bail you out. Your money will bail you out. Nothing bad will ever happen to you. Your silver spoon ass gets everything handed to you on a silver platter. *Everything.*"

My disbelief overtakes the anger simmering in me, and I stare down at him. "Is this over the fucking car?"

"That car should have been mine!" he hisses. "You're not even part of the family—"

"*Sal* gave it to me. I didn't ask him for it—"

The air ceases in my windpipe when he socks me in the sternum. I sputter and deck him back twice as hard in the eye. His knee jolts up and hits me in the groin, and I double over. Blinding pain sharply spreads to my abdomen and shoots up to my chest, and my lungs forget how to breathe as my insides practically shrivel up. Just then, his fist pummels my jaw.

A sharp tang of copper floods my mouth while I roll out of the way before he can sneak another blow. With an agonizing breath, I push to my feet and almost stagger. My ribs ache in protest. My face stings like hell. My left eye is swelling shut on me. My gut still clenches and throbs from being kneed in the balls.

Cracking my knuckles, I spit out blood, then swivel toward him, and we stare each other down. Our fists are raised; our stances are squared and low. We're primed and ready as we'll ever be at this exact moment, but no one strikes first.

No one moves.

I can't bear to look at him—can't stomach it—much longer, but I stay stock-still as I take in the sight of him before me.

I see him, fourteen, grinning at me when he promised his uncle was not that much of a hardass.

I see him, sixteen, having my back and sneaking me out of my suffocating house after my father blew up on me again.

I see him, eighteen, telling me I was his brother while I picked his ass up after his old man knocked him around for the last fucking time.

I see him. Best friend. Brother. Backstabber. When I look at him, all I can sense is the blunt sting of his betrayal piercing me straight through the heart.

"You were a brother to me," I seethe through my gritted teeth. "I would have done anything for you. You could have asked me for the car—"

"I shouldn't have to!" he sneers. "It should have been mine!"

A ragged breath escapes me, and for a while, I can't think of what else to say. "What did you even do with it?"

He spits at the ground. "GC," comes his response, his voice low and devoid of any traces of warmth. "He'd settle my debt for me if I gave him the Pontiac."

Exhaling through the pain, I tear my gaze away and glance skyward. Everything fucking stings. "I would have helped you."

He's silent for a beat. "It was a lot of money."

"I would have helped you," I repeat, clenching my jaw as I consider my options. The pad of my thumb wipes away the trickle of blood at the corner of my mouth, and a harsh sound comes from the back of my throat. "You're fucking dead to me. You got that? *You're fucking dead to me.*"

Without waiting for his response, I snatch my phone from the ground and drag my aching, bruised body to the side of the building. The second I'm out of his eyeshot, I unceremoniously sink down against the wall and groan.

Pieces of fragmented glass from the shattered screen graze the flesh of my hands as I struggle to unlock the device.

Dane: come get me
Dane: and bring your first aid kit

***

"THIS IS GOING TO STING," REESE MURMURS, DISTRAUGHT. A whirlwind of emotions floods her wide brown eyes while she gently presses a wet cloth to my cheek.

"Think we've had this conversation before," I mutter and allow my eyes to fall shut. I inhale the familiar scent of coconuts wafting off her frame as she draws nearer, and my heart thrums a staccato beat in my ears.

Her touch remains gentle. "What happened?"

"Nothing to worry about," I say, because it'll devastate my girl to know the truth. My best friend betrayed me, and I've known for months now. I've always known he was involved.

Except for Sergei and Reese, he's the only other person who knows where my garage is.

Even if Wally discovered where it is, there's no way he would have figured out I've got kill switches installed on every vehicle of mine, let alone know where each one's located to take them all so easily within the hour I was gone.

None of the cars would start with the kill switches toggled on, even if hot wiring was attempted. I've *always* wired them in particular spots to keep them hidden, just as Sal had taught me. There's no way anyone would have been able to make it out of my garage with my cars so quickly without knowing about the switches in the first place.

The padlock left intact clued me in, too. Now I know where

the spare key went all those years ago. Now I truly regret not replacing the damn lock sooner.

Besides, Wally didn't even know about my girl. No one from that part of my life knew about her. The only person who's even aware of her is Marco.

Shyla asked around for me and found out it was all a ruse to keep me away from my garage. They took all of my cars in an attempt to throw me off. Wally wasn't the mastermind behind this, either, which is as obvious as one plus one equals two.

I've spent the last two months waiting for Marco to let his guard down. Waited weeks for him to believe I wasn't onto him. Watched him eagerly agree with me when I started floating the idea that Sergei—a fucking teddy bear who plays tea party with his grandkids and hates it when I show up for any exchange with a busted face—was behind it all. Besides Sal's glowing recommendation when I first started getting into fixing project cars, there's a reason why I only get my vehicles from Sergei.

Some part of me clung to the idea that Marco wasn't involved. That maybe I was wrong. I wanted to believe someone else was behind it—someone else *had* to be behind it. But then I found the can of mace shoved under the seat, and there was no going back from there.

"I *might* have to move." A sharp hiss tears loose from my lungs when the wet cloth prods an extremely tender spot near my temple.

"I think staying still is a better idea." Her brows knit in concentration. "I don't want to poke your eye out."

My raspy chuckle gives way to a dry cough, and I glance over her shoulder. Her sister's leaning against the convertible, watching us with this impassive expression. I don't think I'll be winning her over any time soon. Not for the next millennia, at least.

"Move from my apartment," I clarify, returning my gaze to Reese.

"Oh?"

My shoulder hitches, and *fuck*. I grit my teeth to stave off the groan as a throbbing ache works through my joints. "Thinking of moving somewhere closer to Belford."

"Why?" She leans in closer, her touch twice as gentle when she brushes my hair out of my eye. "You don't even go to your classes half of the time."

"Aw, baby, you're too polite. Let's be real here. It's *most* of the time." My chuckle lasts for a second before I groan. This time, from the sharp twinge in my ribs. "Might make the commute easier for us."

"For us?" The cloth almost slips from her hand while she gawks at me. "You want us to move in together?"

"Does the cat love to claw up that miserable futon?" The throb in my jaw overtakes the amused grin on my face, and I grate out a harsh breath. "Baby, you've been staying over every night."

"You don't think it's too soon?" she stammers.

"I think it'd be ridiculous to pay rent for an apartment you're not using."

Wearing a thoughtful frown, she squints her eyes at me, then gently pushes my hair out of my forehead. "I'll move in with you if you tell me what happened."

The few seconds that follow seem endlessly long. "I ran into one of the guys who grabbed you that night," I say carefully, and her chest hitches.

"You did?"

"He better think twice before he tries to put his hands on you again or else."

"No. No *or else*," she protests with pinched brows. "I don't want you to get into fights for me. I *hate* seeing you hurt."

"I promise to be very boring from here on out." I muster the most solemn expression possible. "Swear on my life, my bike, and my... car. I'll only listen to crappy music Blue Balls enjoys and talk about the weather with you."

She gently pokes my nose. It stings like fucking hell despite how light her touch is, but I power through so she doesn't freak out. "I'd rather you just stop getting into fights."

"Because you need to trick your sister into believing I'm not dangerous?" Despite the painful stretch to my split lip, I grin.

"You know why," she whispers, gently caressing the cut on my bottom lip.

I swallow hard as she holds my gaze, and warmth blooms anew in my chest. "Because you love me."

"Yeah," she whispers back. "Because I love you."

REESE

WE SIT THERE IN SILENCE, AS WE HAVE BEEN DOING FOR THE LAST fifteen minutes, and I pretend to text my sister while I wait for him to say something. After several moments, Dane finally heaves out a long-suffering sigh, then groans at the ceiling.

"I look like a fucking tool." My gaze flits to him as he tugs at a button, and his mouth settles into a firm line. "I look like a major prick."

"You look nice," I assure him, and his grimace deepens.

"I look like I'm about to ask if you'd like to sign up for an extended warranty," he grumbles before he glances sideways. "Have you heard about our extended warranty?"

Reaching over, I gently pry his fingers away from his button-up shirt. "You look nice," I reiterate and bite my bottom lip to suppress my amusement when he levels me with a grumpy expression.

I'll have to admit, it is jarring to see him dressed up for once. It didn't occur to me he possessed any clothes that weren't threadbare or covered in grease.

"Do I... look nice enough to get some last-minute action with my hot girlfriend?"

My brow arches. "What do you think, Daniel?"

A mischievous grin breaks across his face before he blinks innocently at me. "Yes?"

"No." My dry, blank stare only has him grinning harder. "Come on. We shouldn't keep them waiting."

"Goody two-shoes," he teases.

"*And* your getaway car," I tack on with a dorky little smile. Amusement crinkles at the corners of his eyes as he holds my gaze. "I'll get us out of here if things go south."

The corner of his mouth tips up even higher. His lopsided grin doesn't last long, though. Something hesitant clouds his features, and he lets out a rough sigh. "Let's get this over with."

"Everything will be fine," I reassure him, then press a quick kiss to his cheek before I climb out of the convertible.

The house looks like something I've always dreamed about growing up, but twice as picturesque and gorgeous. A white picket fence surrounds a big and luscious green yard. Neatly trimmed cypress trees line the front porch of a blue clapboard house. Potted flowers in vibrant shades of white, pink, and purple hang tastefully from the porch roof.

"Take a picture. It'll last longer," Dane teases, drawing my attention from the bay windows. He doesn't even make it halfway up the steps when the front door flings open.

"*Daniel!*"

He barely spares me a grumpy look when a boy half our age rushes outside and barrels straight into him. My beam widens when he mouths *save me* before his brother drags him inside.

I follow them into the house, where Dane's stepmom, Aisha, greets me with the warmest smile I've ever seen.

"Alex," she calls out. "Where are your manners? Say hello to Reese. You too, James."

Alex blurts something over his shoulder before steering Dane down the hallway and leaving me in the foyer with his mom and James, who awkwardly rocks on his feet.

He looks a lot like Alex, with his light brown skin, wide brown eyes, and dark curly hair. I would have assumed they were identical if Dane had never told me Alex is nine and James is turning eight next month.

"Hi." I offer him a friendly wave, and James freezes, ducks his head, and presses his chin into his neck.

He mumbles the word back, his voice barely a scratch below a whisper, and his face turns beet red. Hastily shoving his hands into his pockets, he feigns interest in the floorboards. I fight the twitch to my lips. God, it's uncanny how much he reminds me of Dane.

Without subtlety, he sneaks a peek at me, turns impossibly redder, and sighs in relief when Alex hollers for him. Hunching his shoulders, he stiffly shuffles toward the hallway and breaks off into a sprint.

"He's shy," Aisha explains the moment he's out of earshot.

"Yeah," I say. "Me too." With a tentative smile, I follow her into the living room, where a pitcher of lemonade and plates of cookies await us.

The interior is just as lovely as the exterior. Tasteful furniture and decorations in subtle shades of blue create a subtle seascape ambiance. A piano hangs in one corner, and dozens of framed photos are scattered across the mantle of an ornate fireplace.

"Your home is beautiful," I breathe, and a part of my heart melts at the shot of a younger Dane grudgingly trying not to smile for the camera while carrying one of his brothers on his back.

"This one's my favorite." Aisha passes me a candid picture of Dane showing his younger brothers the engine of the black sports car I spotted in the driveway.

"I can see why," I say softly. His grumpy glower is a common denominator in so many of them that this one is the odd man out. In the shot, he's slightly grinning while one of his brothers hangs on his back and he holds the other in his arms so they can look under the hood.

Only one other photograph captures his rare smile while he proudly shows off his hockey uniform, with his mom squatting beside him. He looks so much younger here, and he has her eyes. Her cheekbones. Her smile. Although, he was missing a tooth when the image was taken.

Slowly, my attention snares on a different picture—taken during high school graduation, based on the cap and robe he's wearing. Dane is wedged between Marco and a graying, potbellied man. Sal, I'm presuming, looks at him with so much pride despite the scowl Dane aims at the camera.

"How have you been doing?" Aisha's warm voice jolts me back to the present.

"I've been… okay," I admit sheepishly, then awkwardly chuckle when she gives me a concerned frown. "I've been taking self-defense classes with my sister now that I'm unemployed."

"Oh, I'm sorry—"

"No, don't be." My features slip into a reassuring smile. "It's for the best. I didn't want to stick around campus."

Since I don't want to bore her with the details about going to therapy, I take the opportunity to ask her questions about her job as a domestic violence attorney. While she gives me a quick rundown, I check out her wedding photos. I won't point it out to my boyfriend any time soon, but he looks a lot like his dad.

My gaze drifts to his high school diploma and lingers. "Daniel Ellis Kingsley the second."

"Ellis is—"

"His mother's name. I mean family name. *Maiden*—" My words break off with an awkward chuckle, and I'm more than grateful when she kindly offers me a glass of lemonade. I don't know if it's impolite to mention I'm a fan of her husband's first wife's movies, and I don't want to risk it.

For the next half-hour, we go through numerous albums and pore over countless pictures. She provides me with random tidbits here and there, which is much appreciated. But it's also somewhat heartbreaking to piece together what went down between him and his dad. It's tragic to hear how much his dad tried to be there for him and how painfully obvious it was that

Dane wanted the same thing, but they simply were never on the same wavelength.

"It's great to have Dane come see us," Aisha admits. "The boys missed him dearly."

"They haven't seen him in a while?" I make the obvious guess.

A weary sigh escapes her. "It's been a few years."

"Oh." My heart gives a soft pang. I still remember how much I missed my sister when she left for college. "That must have been hard for them."

Aisha nods and stirs her drink, then takes on a sad smile. "It was hard for Alex and James. Especially Alex. He blames himself for what happened between Dan and Dane."

"What happened between them?" I ask. "I'm not familiar with the details."

She drops her voice to a conspiratorial note. "A few years ago, when Dane was still in high school, he disappeared. Nobody knew where he was. It was just shortly after his birthday, and Dan was worried he ran away."

With a deep groan, I almost shut my eyes as I suddenly recall every detail about his beloved Mustang provided to me. "Let me guess. He hitchhiked—"

"To Arizona," she confirms. "Alex woke us up when he heard him come home in his new car... and Dan blew up on him. You have to understand—emotions were high. Dan was just worried sick and upset that he gave us such a fright." Something rueful takes hold of her features. "Dane left that night and stayed with Sal and his family for the rest of his senior year of high school. We never heard from him again until we got a call that he was in the hospital."

My heart drops like a lead weight. "The night he was attacked? At Belford?"

Her eyes become misty as she peers intently at her lap. "Yes."

"That must have been terrifying," I admit, and Lilian comes to mind. My chest constricts at the thought of her receiving a call from our old neighbor about me being admitted to the county hospital.

"It was," she whispers. "We were terrified that he might not make it." Abruptly, she sits up and blinks away her tears before her husband pokes his head into the living room.

"Grill's almost done," he announces, and I'm not kidding about how much Dane looks like his dad. They have the same dark hair. The same build. "Where's Daniel?"

"With the boys." Aisha gives me a sideways glance while she rises to her feet. "Would you mind—"

"I'll get them." Setting my drink down, I smooth the material of my dress as I head toward the boys' room. Mr. Kingsley gives me a polite smile as he introduces himself to me, but it doesn't quite mask the hint of nervousness in his eyes. I offer him a reassuring grin, then duck into the hallway.

I don't have to play a guessing game to figure out where I need to go. The door on my right doesn't conceal the chorus of bright and rowdy laughter coming from inside. I take a peek and almost snort. Dane took his dress shirt off.

As it is, none of them notices me. They're all too busy playing an imaginary hockey game. At least, I think they are. It honestly looks like they're just trying to hit each other's shins with their sticks.

Regardless, it's a sweet moment. Especially when Dane lets them gang up on him and pretends to lose. Retrieving my phone from my purse, I barely hold it up when Dane flashes me the softest smile I've ever seen, eyes crinkled and all.

Beaming back at him, I snap a picture of them right before James startles when he spots me standing in the doorway and accidentally jerks his hockey stick into Dane's ribs.

***

James still won't make eye contact with me. He mumbles *goodbye* to the ground while Alex reminds Dane nonstop that they're home from school at three-thirty, we *have* to be here at three-thirty, and we're supposed to pick them up on Friday at three-thirty.

My heart breaks again for the nth time today when Alex asks about Dane's motorcycle before he can take another step out onto the porch. Diverting my attention elsewhere, my gaze lands on James, only to see his cheeks become scarlet as his eyes dart to his sneakers.

"I'll show you my bike next week," Dane offers.

"Why not now?" Alex asks, and he gives Dane a pleading stare. "You can show us your motorcycle right now."

"Alex," their dad chimes in. "They have to go home before it gets too late."

"But… this is home," Alex mumbles, and my heart squeezes tight. "You just came back."

"Alex," their dad repeats, his voice rougher this time, but Dane cuts him short.

"Tell you what," Dane says, his throat working with a hoarse swallow. "After go-karts, we'll take you and James back to my place so you can see my bike. You guys can sleep over. I'll even order a birthday cake." He pauses, then looks over Alex's shoulder. "If that's okay with you."

With an audible exhalation, their dad nods. "Of course."

"If it's no trouble with you," Aisha quickly chimes in. "You could always celebrate your birthday here, Dane."

"No!" Alex protests. "I want to go to Daniel's." He immediately elbows James, who shoves him back. "We both do."

"Okay then," Dane says. "That settles it. After go-karts, we'll go back to my place."

It takes ten minutes before Alex grudgingly lets us leave, but only after he reminds us again to pick them up for go-karts at three-thirty. James burns the darkest shade of red when Dane loudly suggests to his youngest brother to hug me goodbye in a thinly veiled attempt to break the tension.

The instant we're inside the convertible, I reach for the pack of tissues in the glove compartment.

"You're really that upset about spending more time with my brothers, huh?" he deadpans, and I sniffle in response.

"They just seem so happy to spend time with you on your birthday."

"Yeah." Behind the bravado, there's a roughness to his word. "They do." He casts a sidelong glance at me, and I flash him a watery smile in return. "Any chance you know where I can get a cake on short notice?"

"My sister and I bake each other birthday cakes with box mixes we get from grocery stores," I suggest. "The fun part was always making it and adding extra sprinkles. It could be something you guys can do together."

He stares at me head-on. "Reese, they will eat all the batter before it even goes in the oven."

A peal of laughter slips free. "I'll bake one before they come over, so you guys don't get sick eating raw batter."

With that, we wave goodbye to his family once more before I throw the Nova in reverse. Pensively, Dane peers into the side-view mirror while I drive. I peel out of the cul-de-sac and take a turn, then cut the engine the moment we're a block away.

Without saying a word, I unclip my seatbelt, lean over the center console, and throw my arms around him. He immediately slumps into my embrace as a shuddering breath works through his chest, dropping his head on my shoulder. Short puffs of air hit my neck. His fingers clutch the back of my dress and bunch up the material in his fists. His frame trembles the second I stroke his back.

For several long minutes, it's all we do.

"You were right," he says finally. "It wasn't so bad."

I gently kiss his temple. "What made you decide to reach out to him?"

"I've already lost enough people in my life." His voice chokes off. "Figured I should appreciate the ones I have."

Squeezing him tighter, I bite my bottom lip and hesitate. "Is this about Marco?"

His body goes rigid, and at last, I have my answer. I'm not the smartest person on the planet, but I'd have to be extremely clueless not to notice that the locks have been replaced at his apartment, which seems pointless to do when we're moving to a place closer to campus next month.

"I'm sorry for what he did to you," he says, angling his head back to meet my gaze. "He knew how much you meant to me, which was why he targeted you."

My brow shifts into an imperceptible frown.

"Don't defend him, Snack Mix," he grumbles.

"I wasn't going to," I swear. "I didn't realize he was there when I was leaving my class that night." I pause, my thoughts heavy. "Was that why he was at the treatment plant?"

"Think so." A subtle tensing in his jaw snags my focus. "He probably thought he could pull one over me." With a weary sigh, he scrubs his hand down his face. "I never realized he took my spare key in the first place. I thought I misplaced it. It never even occurred to me he'd do that to me. Did he always plan on fucking me over? Did he ever care—"

"Don't go down that hill," I whisper, and anguish lines his features. The raw hurt gleaming in his eyes causes my heart to sink, and I reach over and twine my fingers with his. "Cherish the good times you had with him."

He lets out a harsh exhale, and I give his hand a gentle squeeze. "I don't know if I'll ever be able to cherish any memory I had with him. Everything's been tainted."

"He was your friend. He just wasn't a good one," I reply softly. "But you loved him for a reason. You clearly cared about him," I insist when he opens his mouth to object. "It doesn't say much about his character, but it speaks volumes about yours."

For a moment, he's lost in thought, his brows drawn together in concentration. After a long, *long* beat, he gives me a sideways glance and softens his gaze. "You're too good for me, you know that? I don't know how I've managed to land a girl as kind-hearted as you, but know that I'll never take it for granted. Any of it."

"I know that. I'm all in with you for a reason," I tease, rolling my eyes good-naturedly, and he husks out an amused chuckle. "Just don't break my heart and we should be good."

"*Never*." His response is immediate. "Wouldn't dream of it, Reese's Pieces."

With one final squeeze, I slip my hand out of his and start the car. "Ready to get out of here?"

In response, his eyes crinkle at the corners while his lips curve into his familiar, crooked grin. "Let's fiesta."

EPILOGUE

DANE

FOUR YEARS LATER

THE HOUSE IS CRAWLING WITH PEOPLE, AND WHAT SHOULD BE A TEN-second walk to the kitchen turns into a five-minute journey. I don't think I've ever seen this many sorority girls under one roof before. *Former* sorority girls, most of whom are here tonight to celebrate my girl getting her B.S. in civil engineering *and* her B.A. in art with a distinction in photography.

Reese didn't want to walk for either of her degrees, since she's still the shy girl I met all those years ago. My stepmom insisted on hosting something at their house instead to celebrate her accomplishments. Just graduating is already impressive, but engineering is no fucking joke.

I should know. I'm regrettably stuck at Belford for another year or two while I prepare for my senior thesis project for my mechanical engineering major. Reese has plans to get her master's, so there'll still be one face I want to see on campus sticking around.

Seriously, the amount of effort she's poured into her two majors deserves to be celebrated. I'm genuinely glad my stepmom scrounged a party together at the last minute or else

I would've taken her out to dinner like I had originally planned.

Once again, I catch a glimpse of Alex preening under the attention he's receiving from the girls while I pass by them. Unlike James, who's been a blustery mess since Karla called him a cutie, Alex is relishing every second of it as he brags about a game-winning goal he scored last season.

Just then, I'm stopped by my dad, who greets me with an arched brow. "Have you—"

"Not yet," I answer, and a cocky half-smile tugs at my lips. "Maybe tomorrow. Or later tonight, when it's just us. She's not a fan of big audiences."

He chuckles. "Let us know how it goes. Aisha will want all the details."

"I will not provide any," I reply dryly, and laughter lines crinkle the corners of his eyes. "Thanks again, though, for finding it for me."

"Of course." Sincerity fills his voice while he holds my gaze. "I'm glad we were able to. I thought we lost it in the move."

Our relationship isn't as volatile as it was back then, which I appreciate tremendously. I don't see him every day, but we make it a point to get together on Sundays for breakfast—just us two— before Reese and I come over later that evening for family dinner.

Things between us have been good. Not only did he help me track down Ol' Reliable and get it back for me after I wrote it off as a loss, but he went scorched earth on Walker and his frat brothers.

He got the best lawyers he knew to take on my case before the statute of limitations kicked in, and he made sure Belford expelled Walker's ass as they should have done from the very beginning.

Caleb testified. I never would have ever imagined I'd find myself in a position where I'm grateful for Blue Balls, yet here I am. I'm genuinely thankful for everything he's done.

Walker was supposed to get four years for felony assault, but he apparently got out early on good behavior. Last I heard, he moved to the East Coast. Good fucking riddance.

"Don't lose it," Dad says, and I huff out an amused scoff.

"Wouldn't dream of it." Mom's ring feels heavier in my pocket, even more so when he clasps his hand on my shoulder and fixes me with a warm gaze. "Don't get sappy on me now, old man."

"I'm happy for you," he says. "I truly am."

"Tonight's supposed to be about Reese," I remind him, my tone heavy with a tease. "Not me."

"Your mother would be so proud of you," he continues, and an influx of emotions rises in my throat. "Of what a great man you've become."

"You're getting a bit too mushy for me in your old age." My voice is a bit rougher. "But thanks."

Before I can say more, we overhear Alex bragging loudly about the time he rode a motorcycle for his thirteenth birthday. Dad slowly aims a frown in my direction.

"Don't you mean nearly pissing yourself while you sat on a bike for a second?" I holler, and Alex levels me with the biggest scowl I've ever seen.

Good Lord, one can only hope he won't turn into a broody little shit. I've got a new sense of appreciation for my dad and stepmom just for being able to handle my moody ass at that age. I know I was a fucking handful.

Feigning confusion at my dad, I slip away before he finds out James also got to take my bike for a spin. I manage to duck into the kitchen before I'm intercepted once more. Unfortunately, Reese is not here.

Her sister is, and she's giggling while she feeds Caleb a piece of cake off the tines of her fork.

To this very day, I still don't know how or when, what, where, and why on God's green earth these two are together. I don't think I actually want to know. It can remain one of the world's greatest mysteries for all I care. I'd rather listen to avant-garde experimental screaming than ask for details.

"As much as I hate to interrupt," I deadpan, and they glance my way. "Have you guys seen Reese?"

"What do you mean?" Lilian straightens. "Isn't she with you?"

Something like terror trickles into my chest and seizes my lungs when Caleb shakes his head.

"She's with your brother," he says. "Saw him whisper something in her ear before they went upstairs."

Well, damn. I hike my chin and am about to turn around when Lilian speaks.

"Did you—"

"Maybe after grad school," I cut her short. "Or when she finally gets a hang of parallel parking. I'm in no rush."

In response, Lilian simply lifts a brow, and Caleb mirrors her expression. I hold back my snort. They're not wrong. Knowing my ass, it's happening tonight. Luckily, Reese's sister doesn't seem against the idea.

She's warmed up to me... somewhat. We'll never become best friends. Hell, we're not even friends. We don't get along most days, but at least Lili hasn't tried to warn her sister to stay away from me anymore. As long as she leaves Reese be, I'm perfectly content.

With a nod, I head for the stairs, only to halt mid-stride at the sound of the doorbell ringing. Since my dad and stepmom are nowhere around, I reluctantly answer the door and find nobody there.

My stance grows tense, and I roll the sleeves of my button-up shirt up to my elbows and step outside.

Besides the numerous amount of cars parked on the curb, nothing looks out of the ordinary. In the distance, the sun sinks into the horizon and paints the sky in streaks of pink and purple. At the end of the driveway, dozens of star-shaped mylar balloons are tied to the mailbox.

My attention cuts to my left when I notice a stray blue one tied to the porch. I'm not sure what it's doing there. Before I even head back inside, something glints and captures my focus. My phone buzzes just then.

Taking a quick peek at the screen, I ignore the coded text and peer intently at the number I haven't seen in years. As always, my chest gives a slight pang whenever he comes to mind. I don't think it'll ever go away.

With a furtive glance around, I move to the side and untie the balloon, barely working on the last knot, when I hear, "There you are."

Quickly pocketing the Pontiac key, I shoot a grin over my shoulder and take a good look at her now that we're finally alone for the first time today. Her long hair hangs in beachy waves, and she's wearing a stunning blue dress that's no match for the prettiest smile I've ever witnessed in my entire life. I'd give up all of my cars just for more of these smiles.

"I've been looking for you," she continues.

"Funny," I respond. "I've been looking for you."

"Well, I wasn't out here," she teases, beaming brightly as she slips her arms around my waist. "What was that?"

"Nothing," I say smoothly, but that look on her face tells me she knows I'm lying. "Someone dropped something off."

It's as far as I'll go regarding the truth. I don't want to be the dumbass who ruins things when she's made so much progress these last few years. She's doing better. She doesn't freak out around people as often, and she's finally regained a semblance of security. After everything she's been through, I will *not* fuck that up for her.

She peers at me, her expression nonplussed. "For... your family?"

"Nah. For me," I clarify, then draw in a deep breath. "An old friend came by. Someone I haven't seen in a while."

Years, actually. I haven't seen Marco in years since our brawl. I haven't heard from him, either. I only hear his name in passing when I check in with Shyla, who keeps me in the loop about the people from my old life. Best to always be alert, just in case GC becomes a problem in my life again. Or Wally. But the last I heard, he's serving some time for several charges that'll take forever to list.

I'm not sure what Marco's been up to. I never asked Shyla for the details, but deep down, I know Sal wouldn't be happy to hear that his nephew had dropped out and been doing God knows what these past four years.

"Oh. And you didn't want to invite them to stay?" Confusion passes over her face while she peeks at the driveway. Some tension eases from my shoulders when her expression doesn't let up. Marco's a subject I try to avoid—especially tonight. I don't need her fretting over me.

Ignoring the dull sting in my chest, I shrug. "Nah. Tonight's your night." An easygoing grin snaps back in place as I wink. "Now, come on. Let's go back inside."

"I kind of want a breather," she admits, pulling her bottom lip between her teeth. "I just graduated today—"

"Fuck yeah, you did!" I cut in, and her sharp burst of laughter slides free.

"While I appreciate everyone just for showing up," she continues, "I want to relax after how hard my last final was. I don't want to deal with the questions all night long."

"Questions?" I repeat and groan when something bashful, yet knowing gleams in her eyes. "Don't tell me they—"

"James," she whispers. "When he was asking for my advice on girl problems."

"He's about to have brother problems," I grumble.

"Don't blame him," she says. "I, um, figured it out when he told me he can't wait to have a sister. I'm sorry I ruined the surprise—"

"Don't be," I cut in. "It's not happening here."

"It's not?"

"I know my girl. When I propose to you later tonight, Iris

Mae Vann," I whisper, placing my hands on the small of her back, "it'll be back at our apartment."

"Really?" Amusement sparkles in her eyes.

"Well, the cat will be there, too," I say dryly, and she snorts. "But it'll just be us two."

With a soft intake of breath, she traces a heart over my chest. "I can't wait."

"Me neither." My eyes crinkle, and I'm defenseless against my stupid grin when she enthusiastically cups my face and draws me in for a kiss. It's the sweetest one I've ever received and a reminder of how lucky I am to have a girl like her love me irrevocably with that big heart of hers.

Thank God I crashed into her life. I'm so grateful to have met her, and my life has been set on the right course since then. I wouldn't trade it—any of it—for the world.

The End

ACKNOWLEDGMENTS

If you made it this far, thank you for reading *The Crash Course* and taking a chance on a new writer. I never thought this book would see the light of day. The first draft was created in November 2015, and I abandoned it many times in the years since because I kept getting stuck on where I wanted this story to go for Dane and his Reese's Pieces.

That said, I want to dedicate this to my husband, even though he started cracking up when I asked him if someone could race in a sixties muscle car and *win*. Thanks for answering all of my questions about cars and the car scene. I truly appreciate everything.

A special shout out to my husband's pesky carburetor, which has been worked on so many times that I subconsciously had Dane working on *his* carburetors at least twenty times before I caught on.

And finally, I'd also like to thank in no particular order: Kat, Noori, Ash, Keri, Mei, and Ana. You girls helped me whip my debut into the best possible shape, and I'm forever grateful.

ABOUT THE AUTHOR

Born in the late 1900s, Elvie Everly has spent her entire life reading books in sunny Southern California and continues to do so with her husband and their two cats.

If she's not writing about sweet, swoon-worthy, and smutty romance heroes, she's most likely to be found hanging out with her husband, rooting for her favorite sports teams, or brainstorming about her next book to write.

This is her debut book.

elvieeverly.com
authorelvieeverly@gmail.com